All in Jest

Renowned Neurosurgeon in the Fight of Her Life

A Novel by Carl Douglass

Neurosurgeon Turned Author Writes with Gripping Realism

PO Box 221974 Anchorage, Alaska 99522-1974
books@publicationconsultants.com—www.publicationconsultants.com

ISBN 978-1-59433-330-9
Library of Congress Catalog Card Number: 2012950897

This is a work of fiction with every character, place, and event
being a product of the author's imagination. Any resemblance
to actual plain- tiffs, defendants, court personnel, lawyers, witnesses, medical malpractice court proceedings, or other persons,
places, events, is completely coincidental and unintentional.

Manufactured in the United States of America.

This book is dedicated to all of those competent, professional, and caring physicians who contribute to the welfare of the citizens of the world. Too frequently, patient encounters include the grim specter of a malpractice lawsuit hanging over the physicians' heads like the proverbial sword of Damocles. It is also dedicated to the defense attorneys who make it possible for the system to keep functioning despite disputes. Obversely, it is also dedicated to the plaintiff's attorneys who provide redress for grievances of trusting patients who suffer from the inadvertencies of their medical care and who would likely suffer from the injustices of a defense system that militates against them. The book is written in the hope that a better no-fault system will be implemented to obviate the entire malpractice process that is so inimitable to the needs of the people of medicine and their patients.

CHAPTER ONE

The plaintiff's attorney paused mid-tirade to take a sip of water. The brief interval of quiet that followed was grudgingly appreciated and respected by the parties to the suit and the large gallery of spectators. Everyone waited impatiently for the next salvo in the acrimonious conflict between the most successful American trial lawyer and the nation's best known and respected woman neurosurgeon.

"Isn't it true, Dr. de Montesquiou?" the attorney asked, pausing again for effect, "isn't it the simple truth that Dr. Norcroft fabricated a case for surgery from flimsy evidence?"

"I am afraid that is the conclusion that I would have to reach," Pierre de Montesquiou replied, looking directly at the jury and smiling slightly. "Much as I hate to speak or even think ill of a colleague."

Dr. Norcroft, sitting beside her attorney at the defendant's table, looked down so that the jury would not see her eyes rolled back in disgust.

"Could you review for us the elements of that medical evidence and why you think it should be faulted, why you think it is inadequate?" Paul Bel Geddes, attorney for the plaintiff, did a dramatic slow three quarter turn towards the jury, briefly flashed his copyrighted knowing grin and paused once again. Then, in a stentorian voice, he finished his question, "And why you think it led to this fine young man's untimely and unnecessary death?"

"It is really quite simple," the renowned French Canadian expert on pituitary surgery began his answer.

Neurosurgeon defendant Dr. Sybil Norcroft steeled herself to hear the description that could possibly spell the end of her rising career. Even a glance at the imperturbable face of her defense attorney failed to convey any calm to the roiling tempest in the surgeon's brain.

Sybil Norcroft, M.D., PhD, F.A.C.S., first saw Brendan McNeely as a patient on the third of January five years previously. The earnest young man's face and the events of the operation she performed on him had been indelibly imprinted on the surgeon's memories by the events themselves and by the conflict-laden aftermath. Brendan was her first and only operative disaster in ten years of neurosurgery practice up to that time, and the catastrophe had haunted her in a variety of anticipated and unexpected ways. On the third day of testimony in the malpractice trial against her, Sybil once again mulled over Brendan in her mind, unable to shake the memories long enough to concentrate on the testimony of the hired gun—Pierre de Montesquiou—brought in by the plaintiff's attorney, Paul Bel Geddes.

It was the first of July, the day she first met Brendan, five years before he became her patient. It was odd, even considering the lawsuit and the deluge of accompanying publicity, that she remembered the young man with such precision. Brendan had just finished nursing school and was full of enthusiasm in refreshing contradistinction to the world-weary, becoming-burned-out older nurses in the intensive care unit. Sybil recalled the contrast.

It had been something of a memorable day for Sybil herself, because it was the grand opening of the separate neurology-neurosurgery section of the emergency, post-op recovery, and intensive care complex of Joseph Noble Memorial Hospital. The facility was the latest in a series of major successes for Sybil Norcroft. She was five years out of her neurosurgery residency at the University of Texas and had worked feverishly to develop her practice. Sybil had achieved almost every goal of her life in that brief span of half a decade. She no longer had to listen to the condescension of her fellow physicians for her lonely role as one of the few female neurosurgeons in the United States. She was no longer hailed by the local feminist factions by the unimportant but often repeated paean that she was the youngest woman—youngest person—to complete a fully accredited neurosurgery residency. Sybil Norcroft had arrived. Even her detractors and enemies, of which there were now a few—neurosurgeons from the old SOB school of neurosurgery—to underscore that she was a mover and a shaker, had to admit that Dr. Norcroft was a force to be reckoned with. She had become the most significant money earner for the hospital, and there was nothing that the administrators of Joseph Noble Memorial Hospital would not do for their rising star. The Neuro ICU was their greatest concession yet.

The administrator, Michael Strong, cut the ceremonial ribbon and said simply, "This is another dream come true for Joseph Noble, making us the biggest and the best. Our tradition of service to the people of this city has always demanded that we give our best. This ultramodern facility is another milestone in our ongoing demand for the finest care for our patients."

He stepped aside and gestured magnanimously at the senior ICU nurses with whom he maintained a cordial mutual disdain.

"Speech! Speech!" one of the orderlies shouted.

A forest of thumbs-up signaled to whom the chanter directed his request, and all eyes turned to Sybil Norcroft, known to have been the real force behind the extravagant new treatment complex.

Heather Larkin, RN, head nurse of the unit, gave Sybil a solid elbow to the side and propelled her towards the cut ends of the ceremonial ribbon. Sybil was striking, a slim, Patrician Nordic with movie-star natural blond hair coifed by Hollywood's best. She wore a designer dress unapologetically and spike heels which accentuated her curvaceous and muscular calves. Sybil trotted athletically to the front and flashed a victory grin at the assembled nurses, administrators, and doctors.

"I can't take credit for this place, but I'm thrilled it's finally here. We can do for our patients in this suburb every bit as much as can be done at the Mayo Brothers or Mass General with this cutting edge equipment. Our annual budget allows for covering every need of the people in these beds that can be addressed at this point in medical history."

She looked over the beaming faces. It was her day.

"So let's get to work!"

"Let's have doughnuts! Forget about the work. We can work anytime!" said Jasper Heaton, the orderly who had insisted on having Dr. Norcroft speak.

He was Sybil Norcroft's greatest fan.

"She's something, isn't she?" asked the new nurse on the ward, Brendan McNeely.

"She's all of that and then some," said Jasper, who had edged his way close to an attractive young woman as he replied to the male nurse.

His contact with the attractive secretary seemed entirely unintentional since his attention was directed to the new male nurse. Jasper had his reputation as the hospital's chief swordsman to uphold and never let an opportunity pass.

"We're lucky to have her here. I heard that the university has offered her the moon to woo her away from JNMH," Brendan said, echoing the widely circulated scuttle-butt he had picked up from the admiring crowd.

"Yeah, she livens up the place. You'd be surprised what she's done to this place since she got here five years ago. Made it the best hospital in the state, at least neurowise. She made a ton of money, too. I don't begrudge her a penny of it. She is the worst workaholic I ever saw. Many's the morning I've had to wake her where she went to sleep on a gurney. And she's eye-candy big-time."

"I'd like to take on that job," murmured Brendan under his breath and with a smile.

"No, no, no. Banish those naughty thoughts, new nursie. Big Dr. Sybil Norcroft is not only rich, famous, and talented, but she is very married and to society as you might have guessed. The husband's family owns half the hospital, and all of Main Street. They breathe special air. You can count the pretty doctor among the untouchables. We are part of the crowd who doesn't call her "Sybil". Just admire from afar like the rest of us humble mortals."

Brendan gave a slight theatrical sigh. "So I guess it's off to work."

He made a smart about face and walked away.

"Watch it!" called Jasper.

Brendan turned to acknowledge the orderly's parting comment and walked straight into Sybil Norcroft, knocking the breath out of both of them. Brendan apologized profusely and excessively. Dr. Norcroft smiled indulgently at the overheated efforts of the young man, until his protestations began to interfere with her progress.

"Just try and be a little more careful. We all have things to do, and we have to look out for one another as we hurry. Now, if you'll excuse me."

She was gone before Brendan could apologize again.

"Nice start," said Heather Larkin, ICU head nurse, "you seem to have made a nice impression on the Snow Queen your first day."

Heather was smiling.

"Oh, man," Brendan groaned. "My goal since I started nursing school was to work in the Neuro ICU. I heard Dr. Norcroft talk about head trauma in one of the clinical lecture series. It's where I wanted to be, and now on day one, I just screwed my career."

"Don't get melodramatic on me. Sybil Norcroft doesn't know you exist. She's married to God and his family, does nothing but spectacular operations all day, and in her rare off hours, she is the twenty-first century's version of God's gift to women."

"I'm not sure that makes me feel any better. Anyway, what'd you mean by God's gift to women?"

"Oh, just that she is in big demand on the circuit."

Brendan had an uncomprehending look.

"The new softer, gentler feminist lecture tour. She is a member of a very exclusive organization of ultra-successful, ultra-high profile women who go around to colleges, companies, and the like giving the new PC line, sort of a *Jungfraus Uber Alles,* and isn't it nice that we treat you men so well anyway kind of group."

"Oh," Brendan said. "I'm too new here even to ask, but maybe I detect a little negativity towards...what did you call her—the ice queen? I take it you don't subscribe to all of the famous neurosurgeon's gender-based opinions?"

"You are too new, and it's the Snow Queen which could just mean that she is prematurely gray. And I guess I would be considered an old-fashioned sort of girl on the latest trend in feminism."

Brendan fixed Heather's face with rapt attention.

"And if you repeat one word of this conversation, I'll cut your throat, *capiche?*" she managed to smile toothsomely and malevolently at the same time.

Brendan did not get his throat cut and became an accepted part of the NICU social world in a short but grueling two weeks. He was as too-tired, as red-eyed, as profane, and as flippant as anyone on any of the three shifts by that time. If Brendan had thought that he would have a grace period to grow into the job, or to grow-up, which was more like it, he was decidedly wrong. At least he was wrong about the time-frame. He thought he would ease into the job and be comfortable with it inside a year. He never became comfortable despite his rapid passage through that educational crucible and his wonder at his own growing experience and expertise. At the end of the second week, Brendan was a very capable neuro intensive care nurse, and he and everyone else had forgotten just how short a time it had been since he had been newbie.

Some of the sets of toes Sybil Norcroft had stepped on in her ascent to the pinnacle level of the hospital elite belonged to every member of the Ear, Nose, and Throat department. On the third day after she obtained full operating privileges at Joseph Noble Memorial Hospital, Dr. Norcroft had admitted a woman with a prolactin secreting pituitary tumor. She scheduled a transsphenoidal pituitary tumor excision and did the entire operation with the help of an OR tech, thereby injuring every ENT surgeon in the house. To a man, every ENT surgeon deemed it his bailiwick to do the approach up the nose to the base of the skull with the neurosurgeon opening the floor of the sphenoid sinus and sella turcica and taking out the pituitary tumor lying above. Also to a man, every neurosurgeon on the staff who did the exacting lower approach to the pituitary was glad to have the ENT man do the approach, collect the cosurgeon's fee, and provide valuable backup and help in the primary part of the operation. Dr. Sybil Norcroft violated them all, particularly since she did the procedure in half the time and for the same fee that the two surgeons usually collected.

When she became aware that she was the object of a negative covert whispering campaign, Sybil ignored the patriarchy of the two surgical services.

When they became overt and challenged her openly for her solo practice of a series of thirty-one flawlessly done pituitary tumors done from below, she forever disingratiated herself by smiling and replying sweetly, "I just don't think nose-pickers should be involved in pituitary surgery, gentlemen. Have a nice day."

Sybil cemented relations with the ENT department by insisting on doing all of her own tracheostomies, heretofore an operation considered to be the sole province of the otorhinolaryngologists. When challenged, Sybil showed her critic what a fine job she had done on her most recent trach procedure and earned eternal enmity by letting slip the incidental fact that the patient was not her private patient, but in fact, she had been consulted by the pulmonologists for the sole purpose of providing a surgical airway.

Brendan McNeely began to develop a conversational relationship with the eminent neurosurgeon by assisting on a series of four tracheostomies in one marathon day of admitting head injuries. It never could be said that the two became friends—Dr. Norcroft did not become friends with the staff—but she did develop a certain rapport with the earnest young nurse.

"Passed your qualifying licensure test I hear from Heather," Dr. Norcroft said as her hands flew through the almost rote movements of the tracheostomy.

Brendan had to hurry to keep up.

"Yes, Ma'am," he said and quickly reached to place the hooked trach retractor into Dr. Norcroft's waiting hand.

"Today, Mr. McNeely, I need it today."

"Yes, Ma'am."

There was nothing to be gained by arguing. Dr. Norcroft meant nothing by her little jibes. In fact, Brendan was coming to see that the small digs were a sign of attention, bordering on acceptance.

"Not bad for the new kid on the block," she said when they finished.

That was the highest compliment the reserved neurosurgeon had ever paid him. It was the first and only one to date. Brendan felt as if he had arrived.

By the end of the fourth tracheostomy of that long difficult day of head injuries, Dr. Norcroft was conversing with Brendan; at least, she spoke to him regularly.

He interjected "Yes, Ma'ams," "No, Ma'ams," and "Thank you, Ma'ams" at strategic intervals.

"Nose pickers don't know when to do a trach. They make such a big production out of a little trach that I get embarrassed for them. They take every one to the OR, am I right, McNeely?"

"Yes, Ma'am."

"No excuse for not just doing them here in the ICU, don't you think, McNeely?"

"Seems like the place to do them to me. We did a passel of them today... saved the OR fees. I'd say that was a good day's work, Dr. Norcroft."

"Mind cleaning up, McNeely? I have to dictate these big cases of ours. Anyway, what's your first name? Do they give new nurses first names?"

"Yes, Ma'am. It's Brendan."

"Mind if I call you Brendan?"

"Nope. Of course not."

"Then, Brendan it is. And, at the risk of sounding like a bull dyke feminist, would you mind stopping calling me Ma'am. It's not strictly PC, you know, and for whatever reason, the term just grates on my nerves."

"Yes...Dr. Norcroft."

They both smiled at Brendan's obvious effort.

At the end of the third month of Brendan's career on the NICU at Joseph Noble Memorial Hospital, he was made charge nurse for the graveyard shift, and in a year he was assistant head nurse. His rapid rise was due, in no small part, to his having found favor with Dr. Sybil Norcroft, the undisputed queen of the neuro ICU. The degree of that favor was only partly due to the quality of the young man's work. The major part of the approval and support from Dr. Norcroft came after she met Brendan at a Rankin County Tennis Club cultural exchange with the sister city of Yogyakarta, Indonesia. Brendan had been keeping a secret. His family on his mother's side, the Mintons, were old friends and social equals of the Daniels, Dr. Norcroft's husband's family. Sybil's husband, Charles Daniels, and Brendan's father had been classmates at Groton. Furthering Brendan's career had followed the most natural progression after that. Consciously, or unconsciously, Sybil viewed Brendan as "one of our kind" and dropped the right word in the right ears at the right time.

Brendan was suctioning the tracheostomy on Juan Dominguez, one of Dr. Norcroft's weekend murdercycle admits. She had done an emergency midnight craniotomy to remove a subdural blood clot that was crushing the life out of the young gang-banger's brainstem. His prognosis was poor.

"How's our model citizen this morning, Brendan?" Dr. Norcroft asked breezily.

She always looked fresh and icy calm, even when she should have been exhausted. It was a matter of self-discipline. Her favorite T-shirt had a red circle with a line through it that canceled out the word "Whiners". Brendan could not recall a time when the well-known neurosurgeon had looked done in or disheveled even after an all-nighter in the OR. Even in a joke T-shirt, the woman was a svelte socialite with perfect makeup, not that she needed any.

"Still on the respirator, still decerebrate, still has dilated pupils, still incontinent," Brendan reported.

"Other than that, he's doing okay, I take it," Dr. Norcroft responded cheerfully.

Neurosurgery is not for the faint of heart or for those easily discouraged by failures beyond their control. Brendan laughed and stood up from his flexed position. He stretched out the kinks, drawing his scrub shirt tight across his thin chest.

"Brendan," Dr. Norcroft looked at him seriously.

"What?" he asked. *What had I done now?* he thought.

"What is that on the front of your shirt?"

Brendan self-consciously folded his arms across his chest and blushed. He avoided her eyes.

"Brendan," she urged.

"It's nothing, Dr. Norcroft. Some silly hormonal thing, I guess. I'm embarrassed. It just started happening a few weeks ago."

He was looking down, uncomfortable with her scrutiny and questions.

"Let me look. Please."

Brendan slowly dropped his arms. On the front of his shirt, immediately over his nipples, were two small, but unmistakable patches of sticky wetness. Sybil Norcroft observed the twin wet spots then reached out and rubbed one of the areas of wet cloth in her fingers.

"Milk," she said laconically. "May I examine your chest, Brendan?"

Her voice was gentle and persuasive.

"Sure. I guess. It's kind of public here, though."

"I start my office patient schedule at nine this morning. Come on over to the medical office plaza at quarter to, and I'll see you before I begin seeing the usual crocks."

"I'll be your first crock of the day then, Doc," he said jokingly.

"Brendan, I don't want to alarm you, but I don't at all think you are a crock. I really think this is something a bit more serious," she said kindly but decisively.

He shivered a little.

"What do you think it is?"

"Like you said, 'This is kind of public', let's look into this and talk about it in the privacy of my professional office."

Dr. Norcroft wore her determined look. Brendan knew better than to argue further. Her concern worried him. She did not express uneasiness frequently. Her reputation as the Snow Queen came from her icy calm in the face of trouble and her seeming indifference to other peoples' distress. If Dr. Norcroft was concerned, Brendan McNeely was worried.

"I'll be there. I want the straight skinny, Doc. Okay?"

"That's all I deal in, Brendan, you know that."

She gave Brendan a slight dismissive wave and turned to leave the cubicle to complete her rounds. It was six am.

"Eight forty-five sharp," she called over her shoulder.

"Yes, Ma'am," he said, emphasizing the 'Ma'am'.

She gave him a parting grimace.

At nine o'clock the next morning, the simple physical examination was completed.

"What do you think, Dr. Norcroft?" Brendan asked, patient up until then.

She had taken a thorough history from him while doing a thorough close off whole body examination with special emphasis on Brendan's leaking nipples, eye, and neurological systems. Most of her attention had focused on his chest and on his visual field examination.

"I can't be sure, but you have some increase in the size of your breasts, and as you saw, I could express a drop or two of milky stuff from your nipples."

"Not all that manly, right, Doc?"

"Manly has nothing to do with it. I'd bet a whole bunch that you have a prolactin secreting pituitary tumor as the source of this milk. There are other things, like adrenal problems, or some sort of weird breast disease that I don't know about, in the differential diagnosis, but when you hear hoof beats, you ought to think of horses first, not zebras."

"But pituitary tumors that cause milk production in men are pretty much 'zebras'. I mean, who ever heard of a man having milk from his breasts. Jeez!"

"I have," she said and looked at him levelly.

He glanced about as if seeking a place to retreat. He saw her diplomas, a tennis trophy on her bookshelf, her state medical license. On her desk was a bronze name plate on which was engraved, "GOD". He looked from it to her and shrugged to show his resignation.

"This is what we have to do," she said and proceeded to outline a thorough workup plan. "Is your health insurance any good?" she asked.

"It's with the Blues through the hospital. I presume they'll cover all this. We don't have to start the HMO and its third world level of coverage until next January."

"Then let's get started today. I'll have Rachel, my secretary, schedule the CT. I would prefer an MRI, but the insurance company wouldn't hear of it. We would be a month haggling over the question that is not terribly important. Anyway, you might be able to get the CT today since it's early in the week. You can get the blood and urine tests done at the lab without an appointment."

Brendan returned to Dr. Norcroft's suite of offices four days later. He did not have to wait. Dr. Norcroft took great pride in the punctuality with which she saw her patients. He was ushered into her private office half a minute before the time of the appointment.

"Have a seat. I have the results of the tests. We can look at them together," she said.

Sybil Norcroft, like most of her neurosurgical colleagues, was nothing if not direct. Apparently, small talk, or some said, bedside manner, was not part of the neurosurgical training curriculum.

"First, the hormonal workup. Adrenals and thyroid are okay. You're a little low on TSH, but that's probably still in the low normal range. What is significant is the prolactin level of 75. That's high, not off the chart, but high. Should be about 5. In my experience, lactation usually doesn't occur with levels under a 100 or even more, but, given the fact that you are a male, or maybe just something about your physiology makes you susceptible. Anyhow, the abnormality fits the clinical presentation, even if it is not statistically the most common. So let's look at the films."

She led him into the hallway where a bank of x-ray view boxes was stationed. The CT scan was already in place on the lighted boxes.

"The rest of the brain looks all right. No tumors, ventricular indentations, no anomalies. Bones of the skull look fine. I kind of wonder about this little thinning in the floor of the sella turcica...."

"I'm sorry, Dr. Norcroft, I forgot what the sella turcica is," Brendan said, a bit ashamed, knowing that he should have remembered from his anatomy classes in nurses school or from his work in the NICU.

He guessed that he was a little excited under the circumstances.

"Tsk, tsk," Dr. Norcroft said with mock sternness. "Means Turkish saddle. It is the fossa in the floor of the skull that houses the pituitary gland."

Brendan shook his head, vexed with himself.

"Maybe I just have milk producing Alzheimer's," he said in self-deprecation.

"Relax, Brendan. This isn't a test. I know this is stressful. Let's follow the evidence through to the end. I don't think too much about the thinning in the sellar floor, as I said. But I do think this little round lucent area in the middle of the fossa in the middle of the gland may be our culprit. There's no evidence of any tumor in the parasellar area or of any large pituitary tumor. Prolactin secreting tumors are usually very small. It's not a great picture, but I think it is highly suggestive of an intrapituitary adenoma."

"What's that on top of the sella?"

Brendan had straightened out a paper clip to use as a pointer. He indicated a rounded structure just in front of and above the bony concavity that held the body's master gland.

"That's the optic chiasm," she replied. "And that small lump above the gland...right there...is an artery, probably the basilar. Nothing to worry about. If you wanted to be completely thorough, we could do a cerebral angiogram and take a look at the vessels."

"No thanks, not if it's not absolutely necessary. Angios are punitive in my book."

Brendan had taken care of a host of patients after the procedure that required a needle puncture in the artery of the groin and passage of an injection tube up the artery where it was used as a conduit to instill contrast material into the vessels for outlining the vascular system. Nearly every patient complained that it was a miserable experience.

"We could miss an aneurysm, but that really is a zebra," said Dr. Norcroft. "I think we are pretty firm in our diagnosis without it, with the CT scan. Look right here," she indicated.

There were strand-like structures that Brendan presumed were vessels caught passing vertically and circular structures that he presumed were vessels seen end-on. The optic chiasm was almost as evident as a line drawing in his anatomy textbook. In the middle of the pituitary was a slightly irregular and indistinct ovoid area that was a few measures brighter than the surrounding pituitary tissue.

"Is that a tumor?" he asked.

"I'm pretty sure it is, Brendan," Dr. Norcroft answered.

"'Pretty sure'?"

"This is still medicine—biology, if you please. We can't be certain without a biopsy."

The sound of the word made the young man wince.

"As in surgery?" he asked, knowing the answer before he voiced the question.

"Only way, Brendan. And it is the definitive treatment."

"Transsphenoidal hypophysectomy?" he asked, taking care not to stumble over the mouthful of syllables.

"To be technical about it, not a hypophysectomy. It would be a transsphenoidal selective excision of a pituitary adenoma. The difference is a lot more than just semantic. We—I mean I—should be able to take out the little mass and leave the pituitary functional. You would probably not have to take pituitary replacement meds except during the post-op period, maybe a couple of months."

"Isn't there another way. Pills or something?"

"Yes, but they don't cure the tumor or do anything except hold down the growth. You keep the little time bomb ticking in your sella. If you stop the drug, bromocriptine, the tumor is likely to grow rapidly. The drug is not a cure. You know my bias, Brendan. I'm a surgeon. I believe in surgery. It is the only way to effect a cure. You want a cure."

"How safe is the surgery? I mean, I see all of your patients coming back to the NICU doing just fine. I don't think I have seen any complications. Am I right?"

"Pretty much. There is always the possibility of having a complication. Even in the best of hands. You need an experienced surgeon, a surgeon who has done a lot of these. False modesty is silly. I've done a lot, and I could count my complications on one thumb. For the record, I'll list the possibilities."

"That's not necessary, Doc, I trust you completely."

"I'll do it anyway. You need to be able to give informed consent, even if you are a nurse. There is about a one percent total possibility of one of these complications happening."

Dr. Norcroft spent the next three minutes listing a dizzying array of potential hazards—bleeding, infection, cerebrospinal fluid leaks, pituitary failure, death from the anesthetic, brainstem or blood vessel injuries, drug interactions, and allergies.

When she finished and looked at the patient for any questions he may have had, Brendan added, "Or the nurse drops the patient on his head in the ICU."

"And that's probably the most likely scenario for trouble of them all. Nogoodnik nurses!"

They both smiled.

"Any questions?"

He shook his head.

"Want to have a second opinion? By the way, does your insurance require a second opinion?"

"I don't want anyone else's opinion. I trust you all the way, Dr. Norcroft. In my book, you're the best. The hospital's health coverage doesn't require a second opinion so long as the doctor of choice is on the staff of JNMH. I'm satisfied."

"Want to do it tomorrow? I know that might come as a kind of a shock. It's a bit abrupt, but I have an empty OR slot tomorrow at about ten. I might not be able to get you in for another couple of weeks."

"Whew! That's a reality check! I guess I should. Nothing to be gained by waiting, I suppose. All right, what do I have to do?"

She gave the young man his instructions and a prescription for oral cortisone to protect his pituitary from the shock of surgery.

"See you in the morning. Don't be late," she said.

The following morning, Sybil stood at the scrub sinks cleaning her nails. She kept them as short as a man's to prevent the accumulation of any dirt and microbes. Her fingers were those of a pianist—long and very strong. Her hands were too muscular to be attractive, too hard and dexterous to be considered pretty. She was looking through the observation windows at Brendan who was in position for the transsphenoidal pituitary operation. Sybil ran through her mental pre-op checklist as she surveyed the room. Satisfied, she reached for a packaged disposable scrub brush.

"Hello, sweet thing," came a voice from around the corner, mildly startling her.

She recognized the voice of Darryl Hankin, chief of ENT.

"You're about to perform the miracle of one woman, or should I say, super woman, surgery on the scion of one our most prominent families, I hear."

"That's right, except for the part about sweet thing. Do you feel it necessary to act the part of a chauvinistic throwback all the time, Darryl?"

"Excuu-uuse me for being friendly, my dear. Do all the ladies at your Dyke Club carry such big chips around on their shoulders all the time?"

"I wouldn't know. And Darryl, how is it that you always seem to choose a time when there are no witnesses to spout your anti-women nonsense?"

She made her eyes wide with questioning above the surgical mask. She scrubbed her hands assiduously as if he were not there.

"Why not try a little sugar, Sugar?" Darryl persisted.

His voice was soft and sincere now. He moved close to her.

"I don't mean you any harm. Quite the contrary."

He moved a little closer.

"That's nice perfume. Chanel Number 5?"

"Alfred Sung, and please don't crowd me. I don't want to be contaminated... in any sense of the term."

"Ooh, feeling feisty today, are we? I like your spirit. I just wish we could get along. I'm not such a bad guy. I could show you my better side. We could do a lot working together instead of at cross purposes, you know."

He placed an affectionate hand on the back of her neck.

She stiffened immediately, almost reflexively.

"I consider that an assault, sexual harassment, Dr. Hankin. Do not even think of doing it again."

He withdrew his hand as if he had been burned. He glowered at her.

"You come by your title of Snow Queen rightly. You ought to hope that you never need a friend, sweetheart, because there will be precious few of them available. Have a nice cold day."

He abruptly walked off. Down the hall, she could hear him laughing as he met another of the surgeons about to start his day of operations.

Sybil's hands fairly flew through the preliminary approach to the floor of the sella turcica. In part, she knew that her movements were more rapid and intense because of her smoldering anger at her sexist colleague. She took a deep breath and told herself to calm down. No social dinosaur was worth a minute of her disgruntlement. He was beneath her disdain; in fact, she was more angry at herself than at him for letting him get under her skin.

The bone of the sphenoid sinus at the base of the skull drilled off easily, and the clean, glistening mucous membrane came out almost in one smooth sheet. The operation was proceeding better and more quickly than usual. Maybe it did her good to have a little righteous wrath.

She checked the small bone chisel to be certain it was sharp. Again, she went through her mental checklist at this critical juncture in the operation. She stepped back.

"Let's change gloves. Everybody. And wash off the powder. I don't want to get any powder granulomas inside the skull."

Regloved, she painstakingly chiseled out a small square of bone and gingerly lifted it away from the underlying dura of the pituitary fossa. The piece of bone was stuck by strands of connective tissue, and Sybil had to tease it away with a fine probe. She used the probe to undermine the rest of the bone of the floor of the sella turcica and ronguered out enough bone to give her a good view and an ample area to work in under the microscope. She noticed that her attention to the details of the surgery had calmed her, and she no longer thought about the boorish Dr. Hankin.

"Mary Ellen, please set up the video now. I want to record the rest of the procedure for the AANS meetings in Chicago. I have to give a paper on microadenomas, and this one should be ideal. It's a good teaching tool for the staff, too. Why don't you take some footage of the operative set up while you're at it, okay?"

"No problem, Dr. Norcroft. Watch your eyes while I snap the camcorder into place on the microscope strut."

The video picture was fuzzy and greenish.

"You can do better than that, Mary Ellen. It looks like we're working in a fungus," Sybil commented when she looked at the TV screen image of the operative site."

"Patience is a virtue, Dr. Norcroft," chided Mary Ellen, the circulating nurse.

She deftly twiddled the two adjustment knobs, and the image came into focus.

"How's that?" she asked.

"Much better. A little too red. Tone it down a bit."

Mary Ellen shook her head, "Nattering Nabob of Negativity. No offense meant," she muttered good naturedly and made the final adjustment.

"All right. I want everyone's attention. No talking. I'm going to open the dura," Sybil said.

Mary Ellen rolled her eyes at Tanya Jenkins, the scrub tech. Tanya did a small surreptitious and silent drum roll with her fingers. She took pains not to let Dr. Norcroft see the small gesture of disrespect. The doctor had a reputation for getting nasty over little slights. Tanya had been the object of her wrath more than once and did not feel like having a problem today. Tanya had been the one who coined the term Snow Queen in the first place. That was a fact she kept a strict secret.

"Camera on?" Dr. Norcroft asked.

"Yes, Doctor," answered Mary Ellen.

"Eleven blade knife on a long handle."

The scalpel was pressed firmly into Sybil's hand. She made a cruciate incision in the tough covering, making several gentle passes until she broke through. Dural venous bleeders oozed into the field, briefly obscuring visibility.

"Bipolar coag," Sybil ordered.

She buzzed the tiny bleeders and sucked out the small amount of accumulated blood.

"The opening's too small. Curved micro scissors, please."

"Sharp or blunt tips?"

"Sharp."

The delicate long-shafted scissors passed between the self-retaining retractors, keeping the tubular tunnel up the nose open. Sybil began to make little nibbling cuts in the limb of the cross on the patient's right side.

"Thick dura, tough," Sybil said, thinking out loud.

There was a little bleeding. Bright red.

"Coag," Sybil ordered.

She electrocoagulated the bleeder.

"Okay, I buzzed that one. Scissors again."

Sybil gently insinuated one of the points beneath the dural opening a distance of about three millimeters and mentally calculated the necessary further opening to give her access to the pituitary.

"That ought to be about right," she said to no one in particular.

She could feel beads of sweat forming on her forehead.

"Wipe, Mary Ellen."

"Yes, Ma'am," Mary Ellen said innocently and immediately regretted her choice of titles. She knew that Dr. Norcroft did not like being ma'amed.

"Mary Ellen," Sybil scolded mildly.

"Sorry, it just slipped out."

Very carefully and slowly, Sybil approximated the edges of the blades of the scissors and began the fastidious slicing through of the remaining dural impediment.

"Just about there, Doc," said Mary Ellen, watching on the video monitor.

Sybil ignored the nurse's small breach of her order for quiet. Her attention was riveted on that tiny spot between the blades of the scissors.

She advanced the cut the final two millimeters. There was a nanosecond of time when a small stream of bright red blood started out of the last opening in the dura. Then the microscopic stream changed into a Vesuvial eruption. A miniature fire hose force jet of arterial blood blasted out of the opening and obscured everything in sight with an opaque sea of blood. The actual outpouring was only ten or fifteen ccs of blood a second, but, under the microscope, it looked as if the gates of Boulder Dam had suddenly been opened and released a Lake Mead of blood.

Sybil Norcroft forced her attention to return to the witness in the courtroom.

Dr. de Montesquiou was declaiming, "To make a long story short, the pre-operative evaluation was altogether too brief and hasty, especially in one particular, and that led to a flawed diagnosis and to an inappropriate operation, and eventually to this fine young man's death."

"Objection. Witness is giving the summation. His response is not an answer, it is a speech," spoke up Carter Tarkington, Dr. Norcroft's attorney, from his seat at the defense table.

"Sustained," said the judge. "Jury will disregard that reply. Please keep your answer to the pertinent facts within your knowledge or based on your expertise. Let's have the question reread, please."

Dr. de Montesquiou waited until the question was repeated.

"Dr. Norcroft ordered a very short form of the pituitary workup. She should have done provocative tests to ascertain the function of the gland, to see if it was truly the source of this young man's very limited symptoms. She should have tested the secretions, and we have only her statement that there were in fact secretions, for the presence of fat, to be sure that the fluid was in fact milk. She should have ordered an arteriogram. Had she done so, she would, no doubt, have discovered the cerebral aneurysm that she perforated and caused the fatal hemorrhage. Finally, she should have repeated the serum prolactin levels. I am quite sure that a second value would have been normal or nearly so."

"Let's take your answer in parts, Doctor. Are there tests to determine the presence of milk in secretions from the breast?"

"Certainly."

"Are they expensive, difficult to obtain, available only in a few isolated laboratories?"

"Not at all. Any hospital could have an answer in a matter of hours, probably in minutes."

"What is an arteriogram, Doctor?"

"The doctor punctures a groin artery, places a slender tube into the artery through the needle, and passes that tube up to the vessels going to the head. He squirts contrast, a sort of x-ray dye, into the tube and takes a series of timed x-rays that show up the vessels."

"Is that an expensive, dangerous, or difficult to obtain test, Doctor? Are there only a few centers that can do that sort of sophisticated test?"

"Objection, compound question," Mr. Tarkington said.

There was no real enthusiasm in his objection.

"Denied. Witness may answer."

"The test has a cost, of course, since it entails a well-trained doctor to do the procedure, technicians to provide the needed help, and sophisticated equipment, but the patient in this case had insurance that would pay for the test. As to the danger, in good hands, there is less than one in a hundred chance of any kind of complication, and probably more like one in ten thousand or maybe even fifty thousand of a serious or crippling complication. Any full service hospital has the wherewithal to do angiography and thousands of them are done every day across North America. I am informed that the Joseph Noble Memorial Hospital has full facilities to do the test."

"Are you aware of whether such facilities were present five years ago when Mr. McNeely fell into the hands of Dr. Norcroft?"

"Objection! Objection! That is entirely uncalled for. Move to strike!" Tarkington was on his feet.

"Sustained. Mr. Bel Geddes, will I have to remind you to take care to watch your characterizations in the future?"

"No, your honor."

"I hope not. The jury will disregard that last question by plaintiff's counsel. Rephrase your question, Mr. Bel Geddes."

"Are you aware of whether facilities for cerebral angiography were available at Joseph Noble Memorial Hospital at the time Mr. McNeely was being evaluated five years ago?"

"Yes, Sir. I asked at the hospital."

"Objection, hearsay."

"Sustained. Strike the response. Rephrase your question, Counsel."

"Only answer of your own knowledge, Dr. de Montesquiou. Were facilities to perform angiography readily available in North America five years ago?"

"Readily."

"Was it common for hospitals such as Joseph Noble Memorial Hospital to have angiographic suites five years ago?"

"Objection, calls for a conclusion based on hearsay."

"Overruled. Witness may answer. It is within his field of expertise."

"Yes, it was common, really the rule for medium and large sized hospitals to have such capability. I am sure that the hospital in question considered itself a full service hospital and had angiography in order to qualify for that ranking in state and national accreditation."

Tarkington started to object but thought better of it.

"And what could have been, should have been, learned by an arteriogram?"

"Whether or not there was an aneurysm on an artery in Mr. McNeely's head. In my opinion there was, and that is the crux of the problem here."

"Objection. Answer exceeds the scope of the question and is not responsive. It is another concluding summary remark."

"Sustained. Jury will disregard. Strike the answer. Try again, Mr. Bel Geddes.

If Bel Geddes was getting frustrated, he did not show it.

"Of what benefit to the evaluation of Mr. McNeely would an arteriogram have been, Dr. de Montesquiou? In your medical opinion?"

"It could have ruled in or out the presence of a cerebral aneurysm, a crucial bit of evidence," de Montesquiou replied.

He turned to look thoughtfully at the jury as he did.

He's good, thought Sybil and her lawyer on the same telepathic link.

"And what is the significance of a cerebral aneurysm in this case, Dr.? In fact, perhaps you could enlighten the ladies and gentlemen of the jury about aneurysms."

"Indeed, I can," he said.

Sybil raged silently at the sheer arrogance of the pompous little Frenchman on the witness stand. "*Indeed, I can*," she mocked to herself, taking care to keep her face benign and expressionless lest the jury take offense.

"Aneurysms are small blisters, weak spots on vessels. They are weak enough to break and to cause bleeding. In the brain, such hemorrhage can destroy or compress vital centers. I have seen them many times. Very nasty."

"How much manipulation can you perform on aneurysms, Doctor?"

"Almost none. They are extremely fragile, sometimes only one cell layer thick."

"Could you...say, touch an aneurysm with the point of a knife, say, an eleven or stab blade knife with any degree of safety?"

"Objection, calls for a conclusion regarding facts not in evidence."

"Sustained. Rephrase your question, Counselor."

"Dr. de Montesquiou, I would like to ask you a hypothetical question. If a person had a cerebral aneurysm, and a surgeon made a three-millimeter long and two-millimeter deep cut with a sharp knife or the sharp points of a pair of scissors, what would be the likely result?"

"Severe hemorrhage."

"Possibly life-threatening bleeding?"

"Definitely."

"How could one know if a patient had such an aneurysm?"

"By doing an arteriogram."

"Was an arteriogram done in the case before this court?"

"No, Sir, it was not."

"Object to this entire line of questions. Assumes facts not in evidence."

"I'll allow some latitude here. How much further do you intend to pursue this line of interrogation, Mr. Bel Geddes?"

"I have finished. With the court's permission, I would like to obtain the doctor's opinion in another area."

"Proceed."

"Now, Doctor, let me ask you about the serum prolactin level in this case. Do you have a copy of the report in front of you?"

"Someplace. I can't put my finger on it just now."

"Perhaps I can help. Look at plaintiff's exhibit A, the office chart of the defendant. I believe we are looking for page eleven."

"I have it."

"Now, Doctor, could you describe that report?"

"It is a report from the Energetics Specialties Lab, New York, dated 5/9/01."

"Excuse me for interrupting, Doctor. In the United States, we usually present dates with the month first, then the day, then the year. Could you give us the date of that report in words so there will be no confusion?"

"The fifth day of September, two thousand one."

"Thank you. Please go on with your discussion of the report."

"In the mid portion of the report, under *Results*, the report reads: 'Serum Prolactin - 75'."

"What, if anything, is significant about that value, Dr. de Montesquiou?"

"Not much. That's the point. While normal values are in the range of less than five, in certain circumstances, it may be normal to have a value of fifteen. It is generally held throughout the medical literature that a value of 100 or more is clearly abnormal, and absent any other obvious cause, is indicative of a prolactin secreting pituitary tumor. Values less than that can be but are less reliable for the presence of tumor. There can be other causes of such modest elevations of the prolactin level."

"Doctor, could you tell us, please, what other causes there might be for a level of 75?"

"Breast fondling and sucking as in sexual activity. I believe the practice would have to be quite frequent. Most people would say excessive, even obsessive."

"Objection, vague."

"I'll allow it. But, Counselor, I am only going to allow so much latitude. I hope this is leading somewhere."

"I believe I can demonstrate a definite purpose to the line of questioning, if the court will indulge me for a few more questions."

"Proceed."

"In your long experience as an expert in transsphenoidal surgery and in treating pituitary problems, have you seen such a cause for an elevated level of prolactin?"

"Yes, a few."

"In what group of people did you find this elevation resulting from nipple manipulation, Doctor?"

Sybil quickly scrawled a note and slid it to Tarkington: "I am suspicious that this is leading somewhere dangerous."

Tarkington glanced at the note and acknowledged only with a scarcely perceptible tightening of his lip muscles.

"It was exclusively in young women. I am not aware of such practices in men, but then I do not see the number of, shall we say, the third sex, that are seen in the United States. Nevertheless, I don't think it happens with any frequency in men."

"For that matter, how common are prolactin secreting tumors causing lactation in men, Dr. de Montesquiou?"

"Rare as hen's teeth."

Sybil looked expectantly at Carter Tarkington to make an objection, but he only looked as if he were intently listening.

"Hmm, then Doctor, what possible explanation could there be for a prolactin level of 75 in this otherwise healthy young man? You don't have any evidence that he was a homosexual, a member of the third sex as you put it, do you?"

"No indication that he was bent that way, Mr. Bel Geddes, but there is another stronger likelihood."

Tarkington was afraid there might be. He passed a note to Sybil Norcroft: "?"

Sybil scribbled a reply.

"*Drugs.*"

De Montesquiou appeared almost apologetic as he turned slowly to the jury. "I have no such knowledge about Mr. McNeely. I mean about the...the deviation. But a more likely possibility, actually, a probability, is that the pituitary was stimulated by one of a group of drugs called the phenothiazines."

"What sort of drugs does that class include?"

"Major tranquilizers—drugs like Mellaril, Prolixin, and Thorazine."

Tarkington turned slightly towards Sybil and raised one eyebrow in a question mark. She shrugged to indicate ignorance by way of reply.

"Was Mr. McNeely on a phenothiazine, Dr. de Montesquiou?"

"That can be the only explanation," the witness responded with a look of minor triumph on his face.

"Objection, your honor. My client objects to this entire line of questioning as being irrelevant and entirely lacking in foundation or evidence."

"Gentlemen, approach the bench, please," asked the judge.

At the side bar, Judge Kendricks was barely audible in her effort to prevent the jury from hearing.

"Mr. Bel Geddes, is this speculation, or are you going to produce a witness or are you going to surprise us all with a heretofore unknown tidbit of information from the medical chart?"

Bel Geddes's voice was several decibels louder than Judge Kendricks's. Carter Tarkington rolled his eyes at the blatant effort to communicate with the jury sotto voce.

"Nothing in the chart, your honor, for this witness to testify to, but I am laying foundation for future evidence. I don't believe I am obligated to share plaintiff strategy with defense."

"But you are obligated to share your list of witnesses. The rules of evidence do not permit last minute introduction of witnesses who could have been made available to the opposing side for deposition by a reasonable and prudent effort on the part of the attorney making the introduction of the new witness," Tarkington said acerbically.

"Mr. Bel Geddes?" Judge Kendricks queried quietly.

"I will have such evidence against Dr. Norcroft, your honor. It will be brought out forcefully during the plaintiff's case."

He might as well have stood on the judge's desk and shouted it; his whisper was so stagey and carrying.

Kendricks shook her head, Tarkington started to object, the jury hushed, and their twenty-four eyes were fixed on the sidebar.

Bel Geddes asked sweetly and very quietly this time, "Was there anything else, your honor?"

Kendricks shook her head again.

"I just have a few more questions of you, Dr. de Montesquiou. I know you are tired. It has been a long day. Thank you for your patience."

"Glad to be of service, Counselor."

Sybil gave a groan. Tarkington put a quick finger to his lips.

"If Mr. McNeely did not have a pituitary tumor, then what did he have that caused his elevated prolactin?"

"I believe he must have been taking Thorazine or Mellaril, some phenothiazine."

"And what happened in the operating room to cause the terrible bleeding?"

"In my studied opinion, after operating on over 8000 of these cases, the lady doctor, there," the witness paused to point at the defendant, "put a knife into a cerebral aneurysm that was sticking down into the pituitary fossa. That aneurysm could have been detected by an angiogram, and this whole sorry catastrophe could have been prevented. The operation should never have been done. When it was done, it was performed with negligent and careless haste. This was a case of medical malpractice pure and simple. Maybe not so simple. I think it was criminal."

There was an audible chorus of inhalations from the spectators that was loud enough for the judge to rap her desk once with her gavel.

"Thank you, Doctor. I have no further questions."

Three reporters quietly walked out through the tall doors of the courtroom, pulling cellular phones from the jacket pockets of their blue blazers.

The initial shock of seeing that column of bright red blood erupting from the tiny operative site was enough to make Sybil Norcroft feel as if she would faint. It was the nearest she had ever come to fainting, and in all of her thirty-eight years of life, it was the worst she had ever felt. For the rest of her life, Sybil would never quite be able to exorcise that image. The worst thing about the feeling at the time was the sense of paralysis. The shock, dread, indecision, fear, anger, and visualization of the worst-case scenario passed through the neurosurgeon's nimble mind like a slow motion tape with time to examine and to suffer from each surging emotion. In fact, the time that elapsed from observation to action was well under a second.

"Large bore sucker," Sybil ordered.

She placed the large suction apparatus as near the site of bleeding as she dared.

"Get me the muscle fragment I took out of his leg at the start. Wrap it in gel foam soaked in thrombin. When you have it in a pair of pickups, hand it to me."

Sybil held out her right hand in a position of readiness. She continued to evacuate blood with the other hand.

"Howard, T and C ten units of blood and ten units of fresh frozen plasma," she said to Howard Derriel, the anesthesiologist.

"Way ahead of you, Sybil. I'll take care of my end. Mary Ellen, set up a strict blood loss regimen. Sybil, I know how you feel about this kind of case, but do you think maybe you need some help? You don't have enough hands for this."

"You're right, Howard. First things first. Tanya, what's taking you so long? I need that muscle plug ASAP, now, even today. You can take your siesta later."

"It's right here, Doctor. You were talking."

"This is not the time to argue, Tanya. Understand?"

"I understand, Doctor."

Despite the urgency of the situation, there was a note of hurt in Tanya's voice. "*It's not my fault that things are going badly,*" she said to herself.

"Get me a neurosurgeon, stat! I need help. Mary Ellen, just call the desk and find out who's on call and get him here!

The muscle plug washed out of the operative site like a twig in Niagara Falls.

"Get me a cotton ball soaked in hydrogen peroxide."

The video ground on showing minute after minute of torrential bleeding. When the foaming cotton ball was pushed up against the bleeding site, the video showed nothing but a cloud of whiteness. Without anyone paying the filming any attention, the videotape recorded 72 minutes of redness, attempts at tamponade, desperate conversations.

"I think I have it stopped for a minute. This'll never hold, though. How're you coming on getting me some help?"

"Not great, Dr. Norcroft. This is Saturday, everybody's gone somewhere. Dr. Nielson is on call, and he is up to his knees in alligators in OR 4. They've got a GSW to the head, and the patient chose this particular minute to bleed out and to have his brain swell out of his head. Nielson says he'll be at least another hour and to find someone else."

"And?"

"And, so far, nada, zip. Nobody is in the valley. It seems to be neurosurgery sluff day. They have not been able to rustle up a single head cutter."

The video image began to change from stark white to pink and then to deep maroon red and then to the earlier bright red swirling arterial column. The cotton ball splashed out of the speculum retractor in a gesture of futility.

"Okay to use uncrossed blood, Sybil? BP is starting to go down, and I have given all the D5RL and plasma that could possibly do any good. His blood is starting to look like cherry soda."

"Go ahead. Do anything you have to do. Just don't let this boy die, all right?!" Sybil's voice was stressed and pleading.

Howard listened for any note indicative of loss of control and decided that there was none.

"GET ME SOME HELP! GET ENT IF YOU HAVE TO!" Sybil shouted.

Nothing was stopping the bleeding now. She knew that this could not go on much longer.

"Take it easy, Sybil. That won't help," Howard soothed.

"Don't patronize me, Doctor. If I were a man, you would just swear and try to help. Don't treat me like some helpless out-of-control girl, thank you very much!"

Howard gritted his teeth and held his tongue.

"Here's another cotton ball, Doctor," said Tanya calmly.

Sybil sucked out as much of the blood as she could and inserted the ball onto the bleeding site. She pressed as hard as she dared, knowing that directly above the site of bleeding lay the optic chiasm and the brainstem. It was becoming a case of damned if you do and damned if you don't.

"How can I help, Dr. Norcroft?"

Sybil did not have to look up to know that the voice belonged to Darryl Hankin. Worst fears realized.

Sybil swallowed all of her pride and mastered her tongue with a ferocious effort.

"Thanks for coming, Darryl. I have a bleeder that won't quit. I think I'm in the carotid artery, some sort of anomalous branch. I need you to cut a big piece of muscle out of the leg. I already have an incision. Just reopen it."

"No sooner asked than done. Your wish is my command, my dear."

Dr. Hankin rushed out to do an emergency scrub. He was back in two minutes and flew into the proffered sterile operative gown. He produced a four by four centimeter block of still quivering muscle and waved it near Sybil's peripheral vision.

"That big enough, hon?" Darryl asked with too much cheerfulness for the situation.

"Great. Cut it in fourths, wrap them in Surgicil or Gelfoam and soak the pieces in thrombin. Tanya can hand them to me as I need them. Next, arrange to open his neck. I'm afraid that I am going to have to clamp off his carotid, maybe even both of them."

Howard Derriel's gloved fingers were already pressing on the neck trying to compress the carotids but without apparent success.

Sybil got a muscle ball up into the operative area, but it was too large and blocked vision and got stuck. She wasted several precious seconds getting it out.

"Half that size, Darryl."

She put the next ball of muscle and coagulative materials into place and managed to get the torrent to slow to a gentler stream.

"I'm pushing as hard as I dare, Darryl. Much as I hate to do it, I guess we have to go after the carotids in the neck."

"My head and neck training is going to finally pay off. I'll have you a carotid exposed in a jif, hon, don't fret your pretty little head."

Sybil bit down hard on her tongue to keep from screaming at the silly chauvinist. But she knew she needed him. The bleeding started up again.

"Sybil, I've given him ten units, four of them were uncrossed. We're losing ground. If you can't get control of that hemorrhage in ten or fifteen minutes, we're gonna lose this boy," Howard said dispassionately.

It was just a matter of fact, and everyone in the room knew it.

"Darryl, put a clamp on both common carotids. It's our only chance."

Sybil put more pressure on the bleeding site with a little success. The bleeding decreased about twenty percent.

"I've lassooed one, sweetheart. You sure you want it cinched?" Darryl asked, making it altogether clear who was in charge of this train wreck.

"Do it," snapped Sybil.

"Done. Any luck?"

"No visible decrease. Do the other side. This is a real Hobson's Choice—a live gork or a death in the OR. It's the only thing I know to do."

Sybil was at her wit's end but was fighting not to let that MCP Darryl Hankin see her cry or break down or give up.

"Got it!" Darryl exulted.

It was the world's most awkward position for operating. Darryl was working in a convoluted stance. He deserved a couple of 'attaboys' he thought to himself.

The blood abruptly slowed to a slow pulsatile stream.

"All right, good work, Darryl, Howard. We are getting into the manageable range. I think I can get it to stop if you make sure he has enough FFP to provide some clotting factors."

"He's had ten units of fresh frozen plasma to date. I have ten more coming. They have to come in from the County Hospital. We're all out here. Do what you have to do now while there's still some capacity to coagulate left," Howard urged.

"Let's pack all these open wounds," said Dr. Hankin. It was ENT to the rescue, but even the iron men of ENT know their limits. "I can't get at those wounds now. I'll hang in here 'till you're done, little lady. Glad I could be of help."

The man was positively gloating. Sybil never thought she could hate any person so much. But she needed him. She would have to be civil.

"*I will not react*," she said over and over to herself. "*I will get through this... and without barfing or screaming*."

She placed the last of the muscle packs that Darryl had made. It fit perfectly. The bleeding finally stopped.

CHAPTER TWO

The courtroom was stuffy—hot and full of the smell of tension. Sybil Norcroft felt the worst she could remember, second only to that awful day five years ago that had brought her to this untenable position. She was sure that she did not have a chance after the devastating direct examination of Pierre de Montesquiou. It had been a stroke of the greatest genius and the best of luck imaginable for Paul Bel Geddes to have gotten the world's acknowledged number one expert to testify for the plaintiff's side. The famous French Canadian had certainly skewered her defense. He had not missed a single turn of the screw.

"*The prostitute*," Sybil groused to herself.

Carter Tarkington stood and walked calmly over to the witness stand. He kept back a distance of about four feet to be sure that he did not violate Judge Hendricks's rule against approaching too close to any witness.

"Good morning, Mr. de Montesquiou. Is that the proper form of address in your country, or are surgeons called doctor in your country?"

"I prefer the title I have earned of doctor, thank you. The same as in your country."

"Perhaps I'm getting your country mixed up with Great Britain. They refer to surgeons as mister there, don't they?"

"They do. But I'm Canadian. French Canadian. That is quite different, young man."

"Yes, quite different. Let me ask you then, Dr. de Montesquiou, do you practice in the United States?"

"I am called upon to lecture all around the country, young man. I teach neurosurgeons from all over the world, your country included."

"My country...yes. Perhaps I wasn't clear in phrasing my question. I'll rephrase. Dr. de Montesquiou: Are you licensed to practice in the state of Massachusetts?"

"No."

"In New York?"

"No, I am not."

"In New Hampshire, then?"

"No." De Montesquiou glared at Tarkington, who maintained a completely bland, almost avuncular, expression despite the incongruity in their ages.

"How about—"

"Objection. Counsel is badgering the witness."

"Sustained. I suggest you come to the end of this line of inquiry promptly. Make your point, Mr. Tarkington."

"Mr...I'm sorry, *Dr.* de Montesquiou, are you, in fact, licensed to practice in any of the fifty states of the United States of America?"

"No, but—"

"Thank you, you've answered my question."

"—but."

"Thank you, Doctor. Have you ever been licensed to practice in the United States?"

"No."

De Montesquiou glared daggers at Tarkington, aggravated by the defense attorney's imperturbable, almost cherubic expression.

"Have you ever performed an operation in Massachusetts?"

"No."

"In New Hampshire?"

"No."

"Anywhere in this country?"

"No."

"Have you ever practiced medicine, and by that I mean under the definition of the law, taken medical histories, performed physical examinations, made diagnoses, and prescribed therapy or performed procedures in the United States?"

"No."

"Never?"

"No."

"Not anywhere in our country?"

"No."

"Has your actual practice of medicine, of neurosurgery been entirely limited to Eastern Canada, to the province of Quebec, to be precise?"

"It has, but—"

"Thank you, Doctor. And was the entirety of your formal training obtained in your home province as well?"

"Yes, I mean, that is, I have been to all of the major clinics in the world." De Montesquiou glared defiantly and arrogantly at his antagonist.

"Sir, my question was about your formal training. Do you mean for us to understand that you were trained, that you were a resident, a certified trainee in, and I quote, 'all of the major clinics in the world'?"

"That's ridiculous. Of course not. I never—"

"Thank you, Doctor. Please, once more for the record, tell us where you received your training in neurosurgery."

"Well, if you must have such a narrow definition of training, then I have to say Quebec. With one significant exception, that is."

His eyes twinkled at a minor bit of one-upmanship in the offing.

"And would you tell us, please, what was that exception?"

The arrogance in de Montesquiou's face had subtly changed to one of thoughtfulness. He was wondering why the attorney was pressing this small exception.

"I trained in the performance of transsphenoidal surgery under the hands of the foremost professor in the world, Professor Gerard Montaigne, in Paris."

He looked smug once again.

"Not in the United States."

"No."

"Were the training centers in the United States inadequate in some way?"

"Yes, indeed they were. They did not nearly measure up to the French standards. Montaigne was the pioneer."

The looks on the jurors' faces were hard, almost angry. De Montesquiou could have bitten his tongue. He felt tricked into voicing his latent Gallic anti-American bias in front of a group of concrete bread and potatoes, red, white, and blue conservative American New Englanders. Mr. Bel Geddes closed his eyes briefly in exasperation.

"Then, with this extensive experience outside the United States and this great paucity of experience in our country, how is it that you can be such an expert on American medical standards, on the definitions of malpractice unique to our system, both in its medical and legal intricacies?"

"Well, young man. I mean to say that I am not an American lawyer."

He had not meant to do so but the words 'American lawyer' came out with a distinct note of Frankish disdain.

The jurors frowned once more.

"But," he hastened to regain the high ground. "I am aware of the world wide accepted standards of neurosurgery, and most certainly, of the practice of pituitary surgery, especially via the transsphenoidal route."

"And this level of expertise is present despite a near complete lack of experience in this country, isn't that right, Dr. de Montesquiou?"

Tarkington deliberately emphasized the foreignness of the physician's name.

"If you wish, yes."

"Objection."

"I'll withdraw the question. Let's go on to another area. I have heard the complaint registered against doctors that they protect their own, that they enter into a tacit conspiracy of silence when it comes to criticizing their colleagues. How is it then that you are here testifying against one of your own, a fellow neurosurgeon, if I might use the term loosely?"

The entire courtroom chuckled briefly at the difficulty with the term "fellow".

"I would agree that doctors are sometimes accused of not policing their own. That seems to be predominately a complaint heard in the U.S., incidentally. In my country, there seems to be an open exchange, even of criticisms. At any rate, I am here to answer a higher calling, to render my judgment above such petty considerations. I believe that I am acting in the manifest best good of neurosurgery, and more importantly, in the interests of the well-being of our sacred patients," de Montesquiou announced grandiloquently.

He was positively beaming.

"That is certainly a lofty reason, Dr. de Montesquiou. Would that more witnesses acted out of such high principles. And not out of petty considerations, I believe you put it. In that vein, Doctor, what would you consider a petty consideration?—desire to injure the reputation of a competitor, perhaps?"

"Yes, that would certainly rate as petty, and does not apply to the present case since no stretch of definition could suggest that Dr. Norcroft and I are competitors."

"Or perhaps for purposes of male chauvinism—to put down an uppity woman?"

"That is mean and petty and beneath my dignity. I am insulted by your insinuation, Sir."

He looked indignant.

"Forgive me, Doctor, it was not my intention to imply such a base motive on your part, but rather to get a better feel for the level of incentive that would bring such an eminent physician as yourself to this obscure community to right a perceived wrong. Then let us consider a final incentive," Tarkington paused a moment, long enough to elicit a perplexed look on de Montesquiou's imperial face, "that of money, filthy lucre. How much filthy lucre," his tongue caressed the words, "were you paid...exactly?"

"I am unsure, young man. I believe it was something on the order of $300 an hour. Something on that order."

"Would that be U.S. dollars or Canadian?"

"U.S."

"And how many hours have you donated to this mission to set the world right, Doctor?"

"Objection!"

"Sustained. Confine yourself to the evidence and forego the sarcasm if you please, Counselor."

"Sorry, your honor, in the heat of battle, I forgot myself."

"Proceed."

"Doctor, exactly how many hours are you being paid for? To the nearest dollar or so, how much does that amount to in total U.S. dollars?" Tarkington's tone dripped sarcasm, even if the words coming out of the court stenographer's machine would appear untainted.

"I can't say exactly, but I think I have contributed about ten hours, including the deposition, viewing the radiology studies and the video of the operation. That amounts to, let's see—"

"Mathematics not your forte, Doctor? Would the amount be around $3000 USD, give or take?"

"That's about right."

"And that is all duly recorded with your bank, Sir?"

"Well, if it is any of your business, yes, I have deposited the checks with my bank in Montreal"

"All of them?"

"Sir?"

A faint hint of alarm passed over de Montesquiou's face. He daintily daubed a few beads of sweat off his upper lip with a Parisian monogrammed handkerchief.

"Have you deposited all of your checks with the same bank, Dr. de Montesquiou?"

"Yes."

"And that represents the entire payment made by Mr. Bel Geddes, the plaintiff's attorney to you?"

"Objection."

"Overruled."

"What bank was that, Doctor?"

"The Bank of Montreal."

"I have here a copy of the bank statement for your account. We subpoenaed those records. Let this sheet be entered as Defense Number 1. Counselor, here is a copy for you."

Tarkington handed Bel Geddes a sheet without looking at him.

"Just one thing, Doctor, would you read the amounts of the checks deposited to your account from Mr. Bel Geddes?"

The witness read of a series of checks and did the arithmetic for Mr. Tarkington.

"A total of $3300," he announced, unable to keep the note of small triumph out of his voice. "I misjudged by $300, forgive me."

"No problem with that, Doctor. It seems that you were perfectly accurate. So at least we know that while your reasons for testifying were not altogether altruistic, neither were they in any way exorbitant, would that be a fair conclusion?"

"I suppose so. I am well aware that many expert witnesses charge a good deal more."

De Montesquiou's face had regained its former arrogance and defiance.

"Indeed, I would have to agree with you there. Now, it happens that I have a second bank document, also obtained by subpoena. This one is from the Royal Bank of Canada in Ottawa. Counselor, here is your copy. I believe that should be Defense Number Two."

"Enter it," ordered Judge Hendricks.

"Objection to this whole line of questioning as irrelevant. The witness has already testified that he was compensated and at a reasonable rate by our own state standards. This amounts to badgering, your honor." Paul Bel Geddes was on his feet.

"Overruled. I'll allow it. But, Mr. Tarkington, get to the point promptly, will you. We are approaching the noon hour. Will you have much more for this witness?"

"Only a couple of more questions before noon, your honor, then another hour or so this afternoon."

"All right, get on with it."

"Do you recognize this document, Dr. de Montesquiou?"

"Of course, what of it?" he snapped.

"Could you tell us the nature of this bank account, Doctor?"

"It is my university research account. It has nothing to do with this case. Nothing at all."

De Montesquiou was glaring daggers at Tarkington. Intermittently, his eyes flicked briefly towards Paul Bel Geddes who never made eye contact with his witness.

"Would you be kind enough to read aloud for the jurors the entries indicating checks from Mr. Bel Geddes's law firm. I have taken the liberty of highlighting them for you. And further, I have included those additional entries from Mr. Bel Geddes's two partners, lest we leave anything out."

Tarkington's delivery was syrupy polite.

The witness read off a series of large checks, this time omitting the sum.

"My addition brings that to a total of $30,000. Correct me if I'm wrong," said Mr. Tarkington acidly.

"That seems about right," the witness said quietly as if it were a matter of monumental indifference.

"And would you, please Sir, tell the court and these jurors the reason you received $30,000 from the law firm of Stewart, Bel Geddes, and Loughlin?"

"They were contributions to the university research," de Montesquiou responded promptly and with assurance.

"Let's be precise, Doctor. The contributions were to your personal research, isn't that right?"

"I suppose that's right."

"Let's don't suppose. Were the contributions made to your personal research fund, yes or no?"

"Yes," he responded abruptly. "That's right, what of it?"

"Yes," Mr. Tarkington said as if he were musing.

Now he was standing next to the jury box and looking directly at the jurors.

"What of it? Perhaps we can get at the answer this way. Who controls the purse strings of that account?"

"I do."

"You determine where the money goes, no questions asked? At least none by the university?"

"I guess you could put it that way."

"A simple yes or no, please."

"Yes."

"And the plaintiff's attorneys just up and decided to make a very generous contribution to the research efforts of Pierre de Montesquiou, Canadian surgeon and professor, out of the goodness of their hearts, out of the clear blue sky, to coin a phrase? Is that what you would have us believe here?"

"Believe what you like. It is true. My research is among the most important in the world. They seem to have recognized its value and wished to contribute. What is wrong with that?"

"My, yes, what could be wrong with that? I have only one further question, Dr. de Montesquiou. Have all of these monies from Mr. Bel Geddes been reported to the Canadian tax authorities?"

"I...."

"Objection, irrelevant."

"Sustained. Strike the question and the response. About done, Mr. Tarkington?"

"Very nearly, your honor. I have a brief series which should not take more than ten minutes."

"I hope not, Mr. Tarkington. The jury deserves a punctual noon break."

The jury looked towards the judge with relief and appreciation. She had won them over.

"Proceed."

"Dr. de Montesquiou, in the lengthy description of your qualifications as was brought out in your early testimony, I believe you told the jury that you were the author of one of the foremost books on the subject of transsphenoidal surgery, am I correct, Sir?"

"That is correct. It would not be immodest to describe my book as the authority on the subject. In all modesty, I am only the senior editor."

He looked down, being appropriately modest.

"Ah, Dr. de Montesquiou, that *is* modest of you. I understand that you wrote six or eight of the most significant chapters yourself, isn't that right?"

"That's right."

He allowed himself a small smile that was not as modest as his early expression. He glanced at the jury for their admiring gazes.

"In fact, wouldn't it be correct to refer to your work as the 'Bible' on the subject, as is the common approbation given such a definitive book by the medical community?"

Tarkington was solicitous and warm.

Bel Geddes and de Montesquiou wondered where this was going. Tarkington was establishing his opposing witness's bona fides beyond the level that even the plaintiff's attorney had thought would be taken as overkill when he had puffed the doctor's standing in the medical community to the jury in his early questions of the French Canadian. The last thing in the world Bel Geddes wanted to do was to interfere with the golden flow of communication between his star witness and the jury with an ill-timed objection.

De Montesquiou surveyed the jury. Rural bumpkins, the lot of them, including the country lawyer facing him. He decided to give them a little leavening education.

"It is perhaps an overstatement to think of my book as the 'Bible', Counselor. I heard it described once in a way that seems more accurate and to the point, medically speaking. It was compared to the works of Galen, and all books afterwards should be known as 'Galenic Operas'. That was not my description, but perhaps it fits."

"Forgive my ignorance regarding classical matters, Doctor. I got my undergraduate education at CUNY, night school, actually. Perhaps some of the jury could use a refresher about Galen and whatever a Galenic Opera is."

"Happy to oblige," de Montesquiou condescended.

His quick glance assured him that the jury was suitably impressed with his erudition.

"The point of reference comparison between my book and the works of Galen is that Galen's works were considered so authoritative and timeless that they were memorized. Even further, they were rendered into verse, so the common students and physicians could better learn them. Finally, over the nearly 400 years of their primacy, Galen's utterances were put to music and presented as operas to preserve their wisdom and to encourage their promulgation throughout the civilized world."

And, thought Sybil, listening to the man's flagrant self-aggrandizement, *Galen's original works, and especially the Galenic Operas, were the very antithesis of science, the triumph of uninformed authoritarianism and consensus over the experimental method.*

She longed to launch a debate, but knew she simply had to sit and listen to the Frenchman's drivel. What Carter's reason for pursuing this line of questioning was, she could not fathom.

"Thank you, Dr. de Montesquiou. I think I truly see the level at which your book should be accepted. I am sure the jury has a firm concept and will bear the importance of your book in mind as they deliberate.

"I have no further questions, your honor."

"Mr. Bel Geddes?"

"None, your honor."

Who was he to detract from that soaring paean?

"We are ready for lunch if your honor deems it an appropriate cutoff point," volunteered Carter Tarkington.

"Until two o'clock," Judge Hendricks ordered.

True to his word, Darryl Hankin waited patiently until the patient could be repositioned for the closure. His prepaid tee time at the Westhaven Country Club had come and gone, but he did not complain. Sybil Norcroft surveyed the damaged body of Brendan McNeely. Her eyes took in a large gaping leg wound and two irregular, asymmetrical neck wounds, far larger than a proper carotid surgery would have required. The scars would be dreadful, if the handsome young man lived long enough to have scars. She Betadine swabbed all of the wounds herself and redraped them so that the fields again took on the semblance of a surgical operation instead of looking like a battle-field casualty. Sybil relaxed enough to emit a heavy sigh.

"My sentiments as well," said Dr. Hankin in all sobriety.

Sybil was angry. She inwardly cursed herself. The disreputable quality of the incisions was the last straw. She had no one to blame but herself. Dr. Hankin had been working under abominable conditions when he did the neck and leg procedures. It was a wonder that the openings were as neat as they were. She wanted to rage at him, at the anesthesiologist, at the patient, even. But she directed her wrath at the one responsible, the captain of the ship. She silently ran down her entire rather extensive list of expletives, applying all of them to herself.

"3-0 chromic catgut," she requested and held out her hand to receive the needle holder.

Sybil closed the right side neck wound while Dr. Hankin closed the leg wound. They worked together to close the left side of the neck.

When the last 5-0 monofilament nylon skin suture was in place, Sybil looked over the anesthesia screen at Howard Derriel who was busily adjusting a clogged IV line.

"Howard," she said, "you can shut off the gas now, we're done up here."

"I hate to say it, but I haven't been giving him any anesthetic for the last hour, Sybil."

The anesthesiologist's flatly delivered statement was like a stinging back-hand facial slap to the exhausted and tense woman neurosurgeon. She could not escape the import of that observation. If luck were on her side, Brendan would be awake by now. *It is better to be lucky than good,* Sybil thought, but right now she felt neither lucky nor like a good surgeon. She sagged a little.

"Let's get him straight to the NICU, no need to stopover in the PAR. Okay with you, Dr. Norcroft?" asked Howard.

"Whatever," Sybil replied listlessly.

She felt thoroughly defeated. The worst was yet to come. She had to face the family. How she wished for that particular cup to be taken from her.

The cortege of grim-faced doctors and nurses wheeled the gurney with its inert occupant down the hall to the NICU. Brendan's family was waiting in front of the intensive unit door, having been directed there by the risk control officer of the hospital, but having been given no insight into their son, grandson, and brother's condition.

"Dr. Norcroft," cried Brendan's distraught mother, "what's going on? How's my boy?"

"Let me get him settled in his ICU bed, and I'll be right back out to answer your questions and tell you all about it," Dr. Norcroft said gently but firmly and edged the gurney past the anxiously onlooking family.

"Don't envy you this one, Sybil. I wouldn't be a neurosurgeon for all the tea in China. ENT's the thing for me. Nobody ever dies. I can't remember the last disaster I even heard of. I hear this is the crème de la crème of the valley out there. Good luck," Dr. Hankin said.

He gave a little wave as he turned and headed for the rear entrance of the NICU.

"Thanks. Thanks for all of the help, Darryl. You were great. I owe you," Sybil called after him.

The confrontation with the family was as grim as Sybil might have expected it to be. Although medical laymen, they were neither unsophisticated nor naive. Only fools would have missed the fact that the situation was grave, and these people were no fools. If it ever occurred to Sybil Norcroft to be less than candid, she knew that now was not the time nor was this the place.

"Hello," she said as soon as she entered the conference room where the risk officer had assembled the family. "For those of you who don't know me, I am Dr. Norcroft, Sybil Norcroft."

"What's going on, Doctor?" asked Carl McNeely, Brendan's father, and the tacitly acknowledged family spokesman.

He was the well known chairman of the board of Computer Exporters International. Brendan's mother sat white faced and white knuckled in a corner easy chair.

"The direct answer to that question, Mr. McNeely, is that I'm not altogether sure, and it will take time, maybe even a day or two to be sure. Let me tell you about today's happenings, starting from the beginning and bring you up to speed about where we are right now."

"Happenings?" whispered several of the family members in the background.

Sybil started from the very beginning, about finding the galactorrhea and how embarrassed Brendan had been about his milk production, about the laboratory findings, and then she launched into a detailed description of the course of the operation not sparing herself, even the smallest jot or tittle. She praised Dr. Hankin's role for coming in to assist in the emergency situation, explained the decision not to take the gravely ill young man to the post anesthetic recovery room, and his current status in the NICU.

When she finished her narrative, she asked, "Any questions?"

"A bundle," said Carl McNeely. His face was a mix of determined anger and fear. "I'll settle for one right now. Is my son going to live, Dr. Norcroft?"

"I honestly don't know, Mr. McNeely. He has failed to wake up, and usually people do by this time after an operation of this kind and the type of anesthetic he received. He could die. It is premature to speculate at this point. I can be definitive in forty-eight hours."

"Then I have a second question. Maybe it, too, is premature. But here goes. If Brendan pulls through, will he have his faculties? Do you expect him to function normally?"

"That's another fundamentally good question, and unfortunately, I still can't give you a real answer yet. Let's plan to meet each morning somewhere between six thirty and seven when I make my rounds. I will give you the latest then. I'm sorry about this turn of events. I would give anything if this problem had not occurred, but it did, and now we have to deal with the situation as it is. I'll be with him as much as it will help," Sybil concluded with a note of earnestness that expressed human concern, admitted responsibility, but did not suggest fault.

"I am going to ask another neurosurgeon to consult, Doctor."

It was expressed with such matter of fact resolve that Sybil knew that her problems had just begun.

Brendan McNeely did not awaken by rounds on the second day post-op. In the interim, he had demonstrated reactivity to noxious stimuli only on his left side and over the course of twelve hours had become progressively less reactive, decorticate, decerebrate, and finally was responsive only to respiratory system stimuli. When Sybil left his bedside the previous night, his EEG had erratic slow giant waves, and his pupils were fixed and dilated. His only response had been a slight cough when the endotracheal tube was moved. On morning rounds, a repeat EEG was a flat line, more sophisticated brainstem electrical tests were similarly unresponsive; and Brendan did not respond to either cold or hot water placed in his ears. There were no brainstem reflexes, and he did not flinch in the slightest at even deep, painful stimuli.

Sybil had been dreading this moment. She knew she had to face the family, but would have given anything just to have been swallowed up by the earth at that moment. Before going out to the quiet conference room, Sybil wrote her concluding progress note and last set of orders.

She called to the charge nurse, "Angie, can you get the medical examiner's office for me. Brendan is gone. I need to report it."

Silent tears were streaming down Angie's face as she handed Dr. Norcroft the telephone. Angie and Brendan had been friends, had even dated a few times. There was not a person in the NICU who did not know and like him, and there was not a dry eye anywhere. Some of the eyes quietly shone recriminations at the neurosurgeon.

"Hello," Sybil said into the receiver, "this is Dr. Sybil Norcroft at Joseph Noble Memorial Hospital. May I ask with whom I am speaking?"

She wrote in the progress note, "Douglas Stringham, ME aide."

"Mr. Stringham, we have just had a death here in the neuro intensive care unit. The deceased's name is Brendan McNeely, middle name Alfred. Yes, Sir, that's B-r-e-n-d-a-n A-l-f-r-e-d M-c-N-e-e-l-y," she spelled for the aide, then gave Brendan's vital statistics, age, date of birth, diagnosis, and cause of death—exsanguination during surgery.

"Is it standard to do an autopsy, Mr. Stringham, in cases like this?"

Sybil listened to the answer, as did Angie on the other line. Half a dozen NICU workers had gathered around to listen to Sybil's end of the telephone conversation. Among them were the orderly, Jasper Heaton, who looked at the pale neurosurgeon's face with unfeigned sympathy, and Heather Larkin, RN, CNRN who was less kindly disposed. She was inclined to think that the arrogant Dr. Norcroft might just have gotten herself into trouble by not using an ENT assistant like everyone else, and the cost was a dead boy, not just any dead boy, but one of their own. Her teeth were grimly set on edge.

"I see," Sybil responded. "I'm sure you are terribly busy there, and I sympathize with your department, but it's still your job to do autopsies; and I want an autopsy on this patient. I want to know why he bled to death."

Dr. Norcroft listened with mounting anger showing in her face. She was becoming flushed.

"I really don't care what you want, Mr… I demand an autopsy. If that is a problem, you have the medical examiner himself give me a call. I'm in the book. There will be hell to pay if you don't do a postmortem. I expect special attention to the pituitary fossa and the carotids. Do I make myself clear, Mister?!"

Sybil listened for a moment longer, shook her head in disgruntlement at whatever was being said, and concluded with a terse, "Good day to you, as well, Sir. I will be expecting a phone call in the next twenty-four hours." She put down the receiver and muttered, "Pipsqueak."

The confrontation with Brendan's family was less emotional than Sybil had anticipated. The McNeely's were made of stern stuff and had watched Brendan's steady deterioration over the past two days. The formal declaration of death came neither as a surprise nor a shock. They listened with patient resignation as Dr. Norcroft gave them the unembroidered details of the findings.

"He is brain dead, by every criterion. There is absolutely no hope of recovery. His heart keeps beating, and his lungs keep inflating and deflating only because of life support machines. When I turn them off, all of that will stop in a matter of minutes. I am dreadfully sorry about this turn of events. I cared for Brendan personally and feel some of your loss. We did everything we could, but medical science is just not up to the problem or combination of problems we encountered with your son. He will be taken to the medical examiner's office where they will do an autopsy. Then your designated funeral home will receive him. Can I answer any questions?"

Brendan's mother, her face swollen and puffy from crying, looked bewildered and seemed to be struggling to understand as if she had been spoken to in Chinese.

"I can't understand this, Doctor. He was so young and healthy. What happened? Why is my boy, my only son, dead? I want to know that. This was supposed to be a safe operation. You are supposed to be the best. How can this be?"

The questions were emotionally cathartic, rhetorical. The distraught woman did not expect answers. She knew in her heart that there were none. Or, at least, that none would be forthcoming right then.

Sybil reached out and rested her hand on the forlorn woman's shoulder. Mrs. McNeely recoiled from Sybil's touch, almost as if she had been injured. A look of the purest hate gleamed out of her reddened eyes. Sybil took an involuntary step back towards the door.

"Doctor," said Carl McNeely in a hoarse magisterial voice, "you have not heard the last of this. Not by a long shot."

His look of hatred was mingled with a clenching of his jaw muscles that bespoke austere determination.

The family's consulting neurosurgeon, Blackman Schwartz, agreed with Dr. Norcroft's diagnosis and found no fault with her NICU treatment. Together, they started to remove the life supports, a silent, businesslike, and sad set of tasks. As the two neurosurgeons moved the patient's body in the course of their ministrations, one of Brendan's great toes moved upward in a spastic dorsiflexion and his leg stiffened slightly and momentarily at the knee.

"Peripheral reflex, doesn't change the diagnosis," observed Dr. Schwartz and deflated the balloon of the endotracheal tube.

"Stop!" cried the voice of Heather Larkin.

The certified neurosurgical registered nurse put her hand on Dr. Schwartz's forearm to prevent him from extracting the breathing tube.

"He moved, he isn't dead! Not quite anyway. It's too soon. He isn't dead!"

She was angry. She looked at Sybil Norcroft with undisguised hostility.

Sybil ignored the provocation and maintained a civil tone and a calm expression.

"Yes he is, Heather. That was a transient peripheral reflex. You know that his brainstem reflexes are gone, and his EEG is isotonic, completely flat. We ran a strip for five minutes without a spike. Take it easy, Heather, it's hard on all of us."

"It's Mrs. Larkin, *Doctor*. And you don't need to patronize me. I can see. This man's not dead. You can't wait to put him in the ground so your precious reputation will be saved. There's no hurry. We can repeat the EEG. If you go ahead and undo the rest of his supports, I am going straight to Michael Strong, the administrator. Don't think I won't."

Now, Sybil was provoked. She could not afford to have her judgment nor her authority challenged in her own NICU. Her voice was quiet, cold, and hard.

"Take your hand off, Dr. Schwartz. Let's get one thing straight here and now and for henceforth. I am the doctor, the expert. You are the nurse, and for all your extra training to get the neurosurgical certification, you are still the nurse. Our roles are established by laws. Now, I am going to do my work, and you are not going to interfere, or *I* am going to Michael Strong. Understand? Now go out and get me someone who can maintain his or her objectivity—a professional."

Sybil had not intended to be insulting, just to let Heather know where the bear slept. Heather, already angry and emotionally at the end of her tether, clenched her fists, held her tongue, and did a smart about face and left. She went directly to the administrator's office.

Mr. Strong listened to the excited senior nurse at first with a patronizing indifference, then upon learning who the patient and his family were in the community, grew deeply concerned. He put aside his papers for the third time that day, and followed the nurse down the two flights of stairs to the NICU. They were too late to change anything. The tubes and lines were separated from their lifeline machinery. An EEG and an electrocardiogram were running, and both were dead flat. It was over.

Michael Strong shrugged his shoulders without saying anything. He was loathe to get involved in medical matters unless they bubbled up to the administrative surface. So far as he could see, the matter was closed and could not be changed.

Not so with Heather Larkin. She was incensed. Her pleas, her professional opinion, her demands, had gone entirely unheeded.

"You think you're God, Dr. Norcroft. I've seen that sign on your desk. *GOD*. But even you can't get away with just taking away the life supports of someone who isn't already dead. Only God can make that kind of a decision. You are not above God, and you are not above the law. I am going to report you!"

Her voice had become shrewish and shrill.

She heeled about and left hurriedly before she said anything more. Angie took over her duties when Heather left the NICU early.

Shortly, Sybil Norcroft was left alone with the body of her patient, Brendan McNeely. When she was sure that no one would come in, Sybil allowed tears to cascade down her cheeks, rivulets of hot brine that scalded and angered her. Sybil had endured the insults of her medical school classmates, the demands of unreasonable taskmasters during her residency, the unfair competition in practice that had made her work twice as hard as any man to gain her position, the neurological injuries and deaths to patients that accompanied her chosen field of endeavor, and she had never shed a tear. She had never folded and acted like a silly, petulant, emotional woman. She had lost patients before and handled the anguish with stoicism. Now, she was personally involved, threatened, and a young man about whom she cared, more than she had realized, was dead. His light had prematurely been snuffed out. It was not fair. Life was not fair. And no one cared a whit about how she felt, she who always had to be so tough, the Snow Queen. She knew they called her that, and she resented it deeply. And now the irrepressible tears would not stop coming, no matter how hard Sybil fought them. A great barrier had burst open.

At two o'clock on the dot, Judge Kendricks rapped her bench with her gavel. "Everyone here and in his or her place, bailiff?"

"Yes, your honor."

"Let us proceed, Mr. Tarkington. I'm counting on you to finish the cross on this witness this afternoon."

'Thank you, your honor. I believe we can finish before five. Dr. de Montesquiou, I'd like first to ask you if you have seen the videotape of this case?"

"Yes."

"Just briefly, what did you see? Let's cut to the chase and consider the point of bleeding. No use boring the jury with the preliminaries."

"I saw an eleven blade knife, and incidentally, I never use a sharp pointed knife for that opening cut into the dura."

"Was that incision pretty much in the midline, not out lateral in the area of the carotid artery?"

"That's right. The incision was too deep. It cut into an aneurysm, and then there was the most terrible hemorrhage."

"You saw the aneurysm, Sir?"

"Not directly. It had to be there under the dura waiting for the disaster of an ill-placed incision."

"Let me be clear on this, Sir. Did you or did you not see the aneurysm itself?"

"No. I did not, but—"

"Thank you, Dr. de Montesquiou. One last question about the video, just a technicality, really. You said that you spent a lot of time reviewing the videotape, even charged for it, is that right?"

"Indeed. I was very thorough."

The arrogance of the man was never more evident. His plump patrician face with its pampered Van Dyke beard reflected his superiority.

"My question, just for the record, as I said, just a technicality, how long was the tape, the tape you looked at. That was a copy of the original, right? Sent to you by Mr. Bel Geddes?"

"I reviewed the tape of this operation. It was provided to me by Mr. Bel Geddes, or someone in his office, I can't say that exactly. It was precisely 39 minutes long."

He smiled.

"I thought you might ask for such a detail; so, I made a note of it."

He looked pleased with himself, like the young cat who has just caught his first mouse. In the intellectual game being played out in that courtroom, he had just scored a small bit of one-upmanship. The attorney had not been able to trap him into any kind of admission of doing a shoddy or incomplete job. De Montesquiou gave a look of satisfaction with his performance at this juncture to the intently observant jury.

Carter Tarkington paused briefly to make a quick note on the yellow pad lying on the attorney's podium.

"Now, I'd like to explore the opinions you expressed about the diagnosis and surgery of Mr. McNeely. Is it not a reasonable assumption that a person, no, that the deceased in this case, had a prolactin secreting tumor if he had galactorrhea, an elevated serum prolactin level, a thinned sellar floor, and CT evidence of a pituitary tumor?"

Dr. de Montesquiou turned to face the jurors, to talk to them.

"Stated that way, that would be a reasonable conclusion, but...."

"Thank you, Doctor. Now..."

"I have not finished the answer to your question, and the impression...."

"Yes, you have, Doctor. The answer was quite adequate."

"Objection. Your honor, the doctor needs to be able to answer the question and not to be cut off when Mr. Tarkington has what he wants. The witness is an expert, and as such, should be given the courtesy of allowing him to explain."

"I agree. Objection sustained. You may answer the question, Dr. de Montesquiou. Take your time."

"Thank you, your honor. As I was trying to say, phrased as the defense counsel put it, the diagnosis would be fairly clear cut. A layman would be able to glean the diagnosis out of a medical cook book. But professionals need to proceed with more care. First of all, in this case, no one but Dr. Norcroft ever saw the milk production that she characterized as galactorrhea. We have only her word that it was ever present. Secondly, the prolactin blood level of 75 was too low to be sure that it was a tumor, and it was more likely from ingestion of drugs. Lastly, I am not at all sure that what we are looking at on the CT is a tumor, that the sellar floor is actually and focally thinned. And, in addition, I believe there is an aneurysm demonstrated on the CT. To my way of thinking, the diagnostic workup was flawed, the decision to operate was precipitous, and the operation was performed well below the standard of care for neurosurgeons. The worldwide standards were all violated."

"And are you free of bias, Dr. de Montesquiou, you with your $300 an hour salary and your $30,000 neatly tucked away in a research account controlled solely by yourself?"

"I believe that I am."

"Then with that admirable objectivity of yours, Sir, can you not consider that a reasonable professional would conclude differently from your own judgment that the elevated prolactin, the history and the finding of galactorrhea on her own examination, and the suggestive imaging evidence that there was a surgically removable tumor?"

"No, Sir. I am the world's premier transsphenoidal surgeon. I can say that in all modesty and without fear of contradiction. I say there was no tumor. The operation should not have been done and was done badly. And that is all there is to it!"

"And 'thus spake Ozymandius, king of kings, look on my works ye mighty and despair!'" said the defense attorney with a theatrical flourish.

"Objection! Your honor, I protest!" Bel Geddes was shouting.

"No need to raise your voice, Counsel. And you, Mr. Tarkington, shame on you. You know better than that. The jurors will ignore that last remark, and it will be stricken from the record. Don't let it happen again, Mr. Tarkington."

"I stand chastened, your honor."

He did not look chastened. The judge leveled a look at the defense attorney but forbore to say more.

"Dr. de Montesquiou, what was the cause of this hemorrhagic accident in surgery, then?"

"The simplest response to that question is that Dr. Norcroft cut an aneurysm. That's the long and short of it. Here, let me show you on the CT scan."

"Be my guest."

The doctor found the film he wanted and put it on the courtroom view box. He pointed to a thickening above the sella. He smiled indulgently at the jury.

"No possibility that the carotid artery was located anomalously, or that there was a major arterial branch crossing the floor of the sella where it should not have been, or even that Dr. Norcroft extended her incision too far laterally?"

"We never say never or impossible in medicine, Counselor, but the first 999 possibilities are that Dr. Norcroft missed an aneurysm and the one out of a million is any of the other causes," de Montesquiou pontificated. "I might add that I have never seen nor heard of such a case in all my years of a so-called anomalous carotid; that's the excuse of the careless surgeon."

"I'm not sure that the numbering system adds up, but I think I understand your message. What about the possibility of Dr. Norcroft having cut too far out and nicking the carotid, Doctor? Would that be in the one-in-a-million category?"

Sybil Norcroft winced slightly wondering where this line of questioning was leading since it did not tend to put her in the best light. She kept a poker face.

"I hate to admit this, but I think that's correct. I am certain beyond any reasonable doubt—way beyond, in fact—that Dr. Norcroft never got a chance to make her incision too far lateral. She ran into the aneurysm and broke a hole in the dike. Even if it would put Dr. Norcroft in a better light than she deserves, I'd have to say that the chances are less than one in a million that she did anything other than cut into an aneurysm as the cause of the bleeding and death of this unfortunate young gentleman."

The eminent doctor-professor had a look of supreme confidence tinged with sadness at having to criticize a colleague.

"You mention that it is better than she deserves to make a harsh criticism of her. I take it that you are aware of some long dismal history of improper conduct on Dr. Norcroft's part, or you know some egregious bit of conduct in this case that you have not yet shared with us about her that would make Dr. Norcroft unworthy of even the consideration of anything but a litany of evils, of which you have *reluctantly* selected the worst as the only plausible consideration. Since you are, by your own statement, objective, and not testifying for filthy lucre, we can assume that you are nothing of an advocate for the plaintiff's side in so saying, can we not?"

"I, ...well, I should say, I suppose that I may have overstated myself a fraction."

"Ah, down to cases. Dr. de Montesquiou, do you know of anything negative concerning Dr. Norcroft's record?"

"Well, no."

"Do you know anything about her beyond the case before this court?"

"Well, yes, I know that Dr. Norcroft is very well thought of in neurosurgery circles for her work in pituitary tumors with lateral extensions and other skull base neoplasms. She is probably the foremost woman neurosurgeon in the world, despite her relative youth."

The answer was delivered with a Gallic flourish bordering on the romantic. He intended his praise to offset any personal animus or lack of deference to the fair sex of which he may have been suspected.

"I don't know how they do it in the courts where you come from, Doctor, but I'll ask you. Do you think Dr. Norcroft is deserving of a trial? Of a fair trial? Or should we just say 'off with her head' after we hear what you think about the situation? You being so objective and all."

"Objection! I object. This is entirely uncalled for. This is an eminent physician deserving of respect here. I object to this whole line of questioning!" shouted Paul Bel Geddes.

He was not participating in theatrics. He was genuinely angry. His face was livid.

"Don't object anymore, Counselor. And do not ever again raise your voice in my courtroom. Do we have an understanding?"

Judge Hendricks spoke quietly and civilly to Mr. Bel Geddes, but she was looking intently at Carter Tarkington.

"Yes, your honor," responded Bel Geddes.

Tarkington and Dr. Norcroft knew that the defense attorney's turn was close at hand.

"I am out of patience with you, Mr. Tarkington. First of all, we will strike your last question and the witness's response. I admonish the jury to ignore that question and answer as well as not being either proper or relevant. Ordinarily, I would call a sidebar discussion or a meeting in chambers, but I believe the jury should hear this. Mr. Tarkington, if I hear another such breach of courtroom etiquette, I will hold you in contempt. Do you have any questions, Sir?"

"No, your honor."

Tarkington was stone-faced.

"Then proceed with caution," the judge ordered.

"I have no more questions for this witness, your honor," Tarkington said unrepentantly.

"Call your next witness, Mr. Bel Geddes."

"The plaintiff calls Douglas Stringham."

The witness was sworn.

"State your occupation, Mr. Stringham."

"I am an aide for the Caldwell County Medical Examiner's office."

"And were you serving in that capacity on the morning of September 8, 2001?

"Yes, Sir."

Stringham was nervous. He looked about frequently, shifting his eyes from the plaintiff's table, to that of the defense, and to the judge's bench on the dais. He did not establish or maintain eye contact with the jurors. Between answers, he chewed his nails.

"Did the name of the deceased, Brendan McNeely, come to your attention on that day, Mr. Stringham?"

"Yeah, it did. It sure did."

"Please describe for the court what impressed you to remember the name."

"Okay. Well, see, like I got this call. It was early, I remember that. A lady doctor, some kinda surgeon, called the office. She like reported that there had been a death. This guy, this McNeely guy, had died that morning. She said that he had had like a bleeding spell in the OR. That's why he died, she said. Wasn't no big deal, she said. Just like happened, you know, like that kinda sh—, uh, stuff happens in surgery. Who was I to know? Like who was I to question a brain surgeon?"

"What did you say? Do you remember?"

"Youbetcha. I went right by the book. I go, 'do you want a autopsy, Doctor?' She goes, 'No, this is like just a routine thing, you know, part of the deceased's disease, kinda thing we expect'. That sorta explanation. I remember goin', 'But don't you think like we oughta find out why there was bleedin'? She goes, 'It's just routine. Besides, the family don't want no autopsy. Some kinda like religious thing,' I think she mentioned."

"Then what did you do?"

"I took her word. She's a big doctor an all, you know. I just logged in the case and like asked to talk to the nurse. But the doc had already hung up. I hadda call back, like I wasn't busy nor nothin'. Doc was snotty about it, real curt. Like you know?"

"I understand. Thank you. I have no further questions.

Sybil passed a note to Tarkington that read, "Complete fabrication. Opposite is true. He made all of that up out of whole cloth."

Tarkington glanced at the note but made no acknowledgment that he had seen it.

"Good morning, Mr. Stringham," he said affably.

"Mornin'," the witness responded warily.

"It is 'Mr.' isn't it? I mean, you're not one of the doctors, are you?"

"No, I ain't."

"Are you responsible for making the decisions at the medical examiner's office?"

"No."

"Who makes the decision about whether or not an autopsy is done by the medical examiner?"

"One of the doctors."

"Then they review each of the cases called in?"

"Sorta."

"What does 'sorta' mean?"

"Well, it's purty busy in that place. Like, usually what happens is that the aides give a list of cases for the docs to decide on. Then one of the docs will go, 'Yeah, do it or no, don't do it.'"

"And did you put Mr. McNeely's name on that list?"

"I can't remember that. Maybe yes, maybe no. Like, man, that was like five years ago, you know."

"Yes, now that you mention it, it does seem like a long time ago. Do you have a pretty good memory, Mr. Stringham? Would you say it was better than average?"

"I like to think so. Yeah."

He grinned. His teeth were in need of straightening. A front incisor and a molar from each side were missing.

Sybil was feeling hostility. It was too bad that the inventor of the toothbrush had not called it the 'teethbrush'. *Maybe Mr. Stringham's smile would have fared better*, she thought.

"It seems to me pretty remarkable that you can remember this one case from out of the past, from five years in the past. I guess you don't have that many cases, is that right? Or maybe there was something special about this case that made it stand out in your mind, in your memory?"

"There was something special. It involved a swell, one of the RBs from out in the valley."

"'RB'? I'm not familiar with the term. Please enlighten the court."

"You know."

"No, Mr. Stringham, I really don't."

Stringham was squirming, looking nervously at the judge and over at the jury box. He sought but did not find help from the defense table.

"Uh, it means rich, 'R' for rich. You know."

"I thought it was 'RB'?"

Stringham was obviously uncomfortable. He was blushing. "Rich...Bad guys, somethin' like that. Just a expression, Jeez."

"We'll let it drop. I forgot now, how many people did you deal with in a day? Give us an estimate of how many calls, how many autopsies, how many visits to the office you handle?"

"I can't remember 'zactly."

"Just an estimate, Mr. Stringham. Your best try, please."

"Must be like fifty a day, somewheres near there."

"We've done a little investigating on our own. Would it surprise you to learn that your office averages 250 calls, just the telephone calls, every day, six days a week, twelve months a year?

"If you say so."

"Not me. Your office says so. Now, by my calculations, that is roughly 7500 calls a month, give or take, or about 90,000 a year. That seem right to you?"

"Yeah, maybe. We're pretty busy, all right. Like, I work real hard, I tell you."

"How long did you work at the ME's office before September 8, 2001, Mr. Stringham?

"Objection, irrelevant."

"I was wondering myself, Mr. Tarkington. Is this leading somewhere?"

"Indeed, your honor. Just a few more questions, and I will make that amply clear."

"Proceed, but don't try my patience."

"Did you understand the question?"

"I don't remember what you said."

"Would the court recorder please read back the question?"

He did.

"I hired on…let's see, I was eighteen. That's—let's see—five years, yeah, like five years."

The witness smiled at his feat of memory and turned so that the jury could witness his accomplishment.

"How long have you worked with the ME's office since?"

"Seven years and three months."

This time his answer was prompt and crisp. He was very pleased with himself.

"How many of those 250 calls a day that come into the office do you handle by yourself?"

"There's four of us aides, about half enough, I say. So I handle, let's see…."

It was a tough math problem. Doug Stringham had never been that good at story problems.

"About 62 or 63 calls, 63 cases a day if you do your share."

"I do more'n my share," Stringham blurted, asserting his industriousness of which he was justifiably proud.

"So of the 90,000 calls a year that came into the office for the five years you worked at the ME's office before the day Dr. Norcroft called you, something on the order of half a million calls total, allowing for slack days and vacations, and the like, you handled upwards of 112,000? To be conservative, let's say more than 110,000?"

Tarkington enunciated the large number with stark clarity.

"Seem's right." Stringham had no idea where this was heading, but he thought that he was looking better all the time.

"Yeah, I been workin' my buns off, like for years."

"And of the 700 plus thousand calls fielded by your office since that day back in 2001, you had to have dealt with some 170,000 to 180,000, give or take a few?"

"Um-hmm," Stringham muttered.

It was hard to keep his attention on the boring numbers.

"Please answer yes or no, so the stenographer can record your answer."

"Yeah."

"That's a lot of calls. Keeps you very busy, I presume. Am I right, Mr. Stringham?"

Mr. Tarkington seemed real friendly.

"Yeah. I'm a hardworker. Like you got that right."

"How is it, then, Sir, that out of nearly 250,000 to 300,000 calls that you yourself handled in those thirteen years of service, you remember that one lone call from Dr. Sybil Norcroft way back on September 8, 2001?"

Mr. Tarkington's expression had turned hard, distinctly unfriendly now.

Stringham was beginning to feel like he had been had.

"I dunno, I just do. That's the long and the short of it."

"Do you know Dr. Norcroft? Were you familiar with Brendan McNeely or any of his family? Was there anything, anything at all, special about that call?"

"I dint know none of them people. Like they're all too high and mighty for the likes of me. I guess I remember how bitchy the lady doctor was. Thought she was like such hot stuff. That's probably it, now that I think about it."

"Was this the only bitchy doctor you ever dealt with, to use your phrase, Mr. Stringham, in all those thirteen years and 250,000 or 300,000 phone calls?"

"Naw, they all think their's don't stink. Sorry, your honor. They're about all real snotty. I just remember that one for some reason."

"Maybe I could help you come up with that reason, Mr. Stringham. Tell us, please, how many times did you meet with Mr. Bel Geddes, that's the man over there at the defense table, the one with the handsome beard?"

The light bulb over Stringham's head was beginning to turn on.

"Uh, well, maybe like about three times. I guess."

"It was exactly three times, wasn't it, Sir?"

"Yeah."

"When was the last time?"

"'Bout a month ago, best I recollect."

"It was exactly nine days ago, isn't that right?"

"If you say so."

"What did you talk about in those meetings? I see from Mr. Bel Geddes's records that you spent about forty-five minutes each time. I guess you had a lot to discuss."

"We talked about me rememberin' about the doctor's call to the ME's office, stuff like that."

"Did the name of Brendan McNeely come up?"

"Yeah."

"More than once?"

"Yeah."

"How about the name of the defendant, Dr. Sybil Norcroft, the lady brain surgeon? Did it come up?"

"Yeah."

"More than once?"

"Yeah."

"In fact, didn't both of those names come up many times in those three forty-five minute meetings? Didn't you, in fact, spend considerable time talking about them?"

"Yeah."

"Did you contact Mr. Bel Geddes because you were a good citizen, and you remembered about that call, and thought that you had something to offer in the interests of justice?" Tarkington asked, his voice friendly again.

"Uh, well, no, like it wasn't 'zactly like that."

"Exactly how was it?"

"He, uh...well, he sorta called me, called me first, near as I recollect."

"And was it him, and by 'him' I mean the plaintiff's attorney, that brought up the names, and not you?"

"Yeah."

"One last question, and then you may step down, Mr. Stringham. Are you being paid by Mr. Bel Geddes for being a witness? Are you being paid more than you make at the ME's office in a day?"

"Yeah."

The next witness called by the plaintiff was the distinguished head of Ear, Nose, and Throat Surgery at Joseph Noble Memorial Hospital, Darryl James Hankin, M.D., F.A.C.S. In direct testimony, he recounted the events surrounding the ill-fated transsphenoidal operation on Brendan McNeely. His delivery was articulate, professional, and unemotional. Sybil's mind wandered back in time to the actual events being scrutinized by the lawyers, the judge, and the jury on this uncomfortable day.

The surgery committee meeting following the unfortunate medical mishap and death of Brendan McNeely, RN, four days previously, was an unmitigated nightmare for Sybil Norcroft. She had a pristine record, even her medical records were regularly kept up to date unlike 90 percent of her medical staff colleagues. She had never been sued, never been the subject of a hospital, licensing board, or insurance disciplinary action in her five years of practice, and that made her a decided exception among her peers with five or more years in practice, especially her real peers, the neurosurgeons. Scrutiny on doctors had become onerous from back as far as the Clinton presidential administration and seemed to worsen every year. Sybil considered herself lucky to have escaped the spotlight until that night.

She remembered debating beforehand whether or not to go to the meeting. She only had to attend fifty percent of the meetings to remain in good standing, and they were always deadly dull. Her husband, Charles, had a meeting of his own; so, out of boredom, as much as anything else, she decided to attend.

The chart review and discussion of the financing of the new wing of surgical beds went by pro forma. It looked as if it would be a short meeting, an idea that appealed to everyone present.

"Any further business?" Abdullah Sa'id, chairman of the surgery committee, asked.

"I do have one thing, Dr. Chairman, if I may? Although the chart won't appear for review until next month, I think this is something that should come to the committee's attention tonight."

It was Darryl Hankin from ENT speaking. He had been standing inconspicuously in the back.

"Go ahead, Darryl. No need to be so formal."

"Thanks, Abdullah. We get criticized for not policing ourselves, you all know. I think I have a matter that needs some policing. I want to get your slant on it. It kind of embarrasses me to talk about this because the surgeon involved is here in the room, a committee member. I'm sorry, Dr. Norcroft, but I think this should be brought out into the open."

Sybil shot a glance at Dr. Hankin's malevolently innocent face, handsome and tanned. There flashed through her mind that this was payback time for her having supported his nurse in a sexual discrimination case she brought against her boss. It had been a fiasco. The good old boys of the patriarchy had marshaled their forces behind Hankin and had soundly whipped the nurse by producing half a score of women from his own office who denied that any such event ever took place. Sybil had ended up looking like something of a fool to the rest of the medical community, even though she had earned her measure of accolades from the feminist community. She knew that she had earned Hankin's enmity for her part in the situation, but that had been three years ago, and she had figured that bygones were bygones. Evidently, she was wrong about that, her flash thought signaled.

"You have the floor and our full attention, Darryl, go ahead," said Dr. Sa'id.

"Last Wednesday," he began, and then recounted in exquisite detail all of the events of the case.

Sybil could not fault him for lack of objectivity or for incompleteness.

"I find fault, and I've brought this up before, with the fact that Dr. Norcroft refuses to have a competent, and by that I mean, an M.D., assistant in her transsphenoidal cases. She has always made it abundantly clear, including in public forum, that she considers the surgeons of my specialty to be nose pickers and that our services are superfluous. Thus far, she has been lucky. Until last Wednesday. This case is the classical horrible example that proves the rule. What concerns me is the arrogance of the *woman*. She seems to consider herself above the conventions, above cooperation, above the common sense measures that all of us have to employ to protect our patients. Much as I hate to do it, I am calling for a formal censure. I am asking that Dr. Norcroft's transsphenoidal privileges be suspended until her practices can be investigated. If she is allowed to return to doing those delicate, and I tell you here, largely ENT, operations, then, I demand that she have an M.D., and preferably an ENT, specialist with her on every case. I think the approach up the nose should be limited to ENTs. That's what I think."

A burst of adrenaline swept through the collective veins of the surgery committee members. It was unusual for a doctor to be criticized in public and so directly, and it was unheard of for a committee member to be humiliated right in front of the whole group. Michael Strong, attending as the representative from administration, wrung his hands, fearing a potential lawsuit by Dr. Norcroft for defamation of character. Abdullah Sa'id, the most polite and careful man in the western hemisphere, fretted over the blatant breach of decorum. The rest of the members of the committee were roused to a height of interest that none of them could recall having experienced in their three year terms of office.

"Dr. Sa'id, fellow surgeons, I feel that I have been blind-sided by this. I had no warning and have not made the slightest effort to defend myself nor my practice. I won't take up your time tonight, but I will prepare a written account and defense. I'll say this one thing tonight about the self-serving conclusion by the head of ENT. I have to deal with the HMOs just like you do. They control the expenses and the allotment of patients. If I have an ENT assistant every time, I will quickly become too expensive for those bloodsucker accountants in all of the HMOs. I won't be allowed to do the cases, this hospital will lose the business, and no one will be better off. Except possibly a few hungry ENT docs who get in on the few transsphenoidal cases before my practice and the hospital's pituitary surgery business dies. Think about that. In my own defense, and from a pure medical standpoint, I am perfectly capable of doing the cases without an assistant and a scrub tech is more than enough. They are very good, in case you haven't noticed. I'd match up Tanya Jenkins against any other assistant. I think there are a number among you who would agree."

"Until last Wednesday," piped in Dr. Hankin, unwilling to be cheated out of the last word.

The meeting adjourned on that sour note. Sybil submitted her defense, a document that became the property of the surgical committee and the hospital and never saw the light of day outside the institution, since internal investigatory documentation of hospitals is sacrosanct from outside exposure by statute. While the document itself was carefully and self-servingly crafted and reworked until it portrayed Dr. Norcroft as a superbly qualified and capable surgeon victimized by the happenstance of a vascular anomaly, it was the nonstop political pressure that she brought to bear that saved her in the end. It was a close thing. The final vote for censure and for suspension of privileges was six for, eight against, one abstention—Dr. Sa'id—and two excused absences with three no-shows out of a twenty-member committee. The charges, the debate, and the committee's action never saw light in the public. The only casualties were Sybil Norcroft's stomach lining, and any pretense of comity or civility between her and Darryl Hankin. Thereafter, the two surgeons would just as soon spit in the other's eye as speak to one another.

"I have no further questions for this witness," said Paul Bel Geddes, indicating the end of his direct examination of Darryl Hankin.

"Dr. Hankin, would it be safe to say that you and Dr. Norcroft over there are on unfriendly terms?"

"I couldn't argue with that characterization, Counselor," Hankin replied to Tarkington's first question.

There were no preliminaries, no adjustment towards the hard questions to come.

"Wouldn't it be more accurate that you hold each other in an attitude of mutual animosity?"

"That might be a little strong, but it's not far off the mark."

Hankin's handsome tanned face darkened as he looked over at Sybil Norcroft sitting expressionless at the defense table.

"Could that personal animus influence your testimony here today, Sir?"

"Not at all. I am reporting only the facts."

"No bias?"

"None."

"Have you ever become aware, of your own personal observation, of any other doctor or surgeon who has made a mistake or caused harm to a patient, or fell below the standard of practice for the community? In all your twenty-one years of practice, Sir?"

"I might have. I suppose I have. Nobody's perfect."

"Not even doctors?"

"Not even lawyers."

"*Touché.*" Tarkington smiled.

Hankin relaxed a little and allowed himself a wan smile.

"Did you ever report any other doctor, any surgeon, any medical practitioner or provider of any kind or description to any official body for censure?"

"You mean other than Dr. Norcroft?"

"Other than *her.*"

"No. Not that I can think of."

"Ever criticize another doctor in a deposition?"

"No."

"Ever testify publicly in court against another doctor?"

"Never. Never had cause before."

"I see. And it's just coincidence that you are testifying against the defendant here today, and that you bear her ill will?"

"You could say that."

Tarkington shook his head. He was looking at the jurors at the time.

"Objection. Counsel is conveying an opinion to the jury by his actions."

"Mr. Tarkington, please stand away from the jury box. Confine your activities to the question and answer format. That's how we do it in court. Save the rest for the theater."

"Yes, your honor," Tarkington said.

He did not look as sheepish as his voice would have indicated.

"Dr. Hankin, were you in the operating room throughout the entire procedure performed on Mr. Brendan McNeely?"

"No, I wasn't."

"At what point did you enter the case?"

"When it was going to hell in a hand basket."

"By that colorful turn of phrase, do you mean after the onset of difficulties?"

"Yes."

"So you did not see the opening of the case?"

"No."

"Nor the approach to the floor of the sella turcica?"

"No."

"Nor the removal of the sphenoid sinus bone, mucosa, or the bone of the sella?"

"No."

"Did you, then, see the incision in the dura so that you could say exactly where that incision was made and whether or not it was done carefully and properly?"

"Well, not exactly."

"We're being exact here, Dr. Hankin. This is a case about exactness. So am I correct in assuming that all you really saw of the pituitary operative site was a lot of blood issuing forth from the nasal opening?"

"Yes, but...."

"Yes, or no, Sir?"

"Yes."

"And nevertheless, you consider yourself in a position to criticize the performance of that portion of the operation that you did not even see?"

"I know that transsphenoidal surgeries are not supposed to result in exsanguination of the patient. Any fool knows that."

Hankin's eyes glinted. He seemed to be enjoying the game of confrontation, although he had to admit to himself that, thus far, he was faring only middling well.

"Are there any possibilities as causes of the bleeding of which you can conceive other than those that mean malpractice on the part of the surgeon?"

"Well, I guess I could think of some."

"But you have not mentioned any of those possibilities to this court, nor in deposition, have you?"

"No."

"Would that seem to you to be the fair and objective evaluation of an impartial professional physician with no ax to grind?"

"Well, maybe not exactly. I mean, I wasn't there to talk about all of the other possibilities. I mean, it was about malpractice, wasn't it? I don't recall ever being asked, now that I think about it."

"I have only one more question, Dr. Hankin. Actually, it's a repeat of a previous question. I ask you once again, Sir, does bias and prejudice against this woman," Tarkington drawled out and drew attention to the characterization of Sybil's gender, "prompt you to give your critical testimony in the matter before this court? Can you in all good conscience tell us that you are not influenced by your bad feelings towards her?"

"Yes. I mean, no," Hankin stuttered, trying to unravel the pair of questions that hung over him like the proverbial, 'have you stopped beating your wife?'

"Objection, compound question."

"Sustained."

"No further questions of this witness, your honor."

"All right, strike that last question and answer. The jury will disregard the interchange. You may step down, Dr. Hankin. Call your next witness, Mr. Bel Geddes.

"Heather Larkin, RN, CNRN," the bailiff called out.

She entered through the main doors and strode purposefully to the witness stand.

Mrs. Larkin was sworn, her qualifications as a nurse and NICU administrator were presented ad nauseam, and the meaning of the initials after her name was elucidated with great amplification. She testified for thirty-five minutes about two salient points: The first was that Dr. Norcroft had cut off the lifelines of the deceased prematurely, and in effect, murdered him. The second was that Dr. Norcroft had insisted on calling the county medical examiner herself in order to obviate the performance of a postmortem examination to prevent the possibility of a gross surgical error being revealed. She was a good witness—unemotional, but not uncaring. She was convincing.

Sybil glanced at the spectators whenever she could without drawing attention to herself. Brendan's family stared fixedly at Heather as she testified, looks of anguish on their faces. The jurors were poor poker players as well. Most of them had looks that bordered on anger. Sybil began to worry.

"Your witness, Counselor," said Paul Bel Geddes.

"Thank you, Counselor. I have just a few questions, Mrs. Larkin. You prefer Mrs. Larkin, don't you?"

"I do."

"You don't fancy yourself much of a feminist, I take it. You're not a Ms., are you?"

"I'm not much impressed with that sort of thing, no, Sir."

"You're aware that the defendant, Dr. Norcroft, is something of a minor celebrity among people of the woman's movement, are you not?"

"That's an understatement. She's well known."

"You don't care for her or her feminist views, is that a fair statement?"

"That's fair. So what? It has nothing to do with the facts of this case."

"Um-hmm," Tarkington mused. "Let's get to the heart of the matter, 'the facts of this case', as you so adroitly put it. You told this court that the defendant...excuse me, I'd like to be exact in quoting you."

He made a small show of rifling through his notes.

"Ah, yes, you said, 'She,' meaning the defendant, 'might as well have put a pillow on his face.' Do you recall making that statement?"

"Yes, and I meant every word of it."

"Indeed. Are you familiar with the procedures employed to establish the diagnosis of brain death, in contradistinction to death of the organism?"

"Yes, it's part of my training and work. I see it and assist regularly. I am familiar, all right."

There was a glint of antagonism in Heather's cold grey eyes.

"Did Dr. Norcroft's notes indicate a significant deviation from the practice involved in making the diagnosis of brain death?"

"Not her notes."

"Did her notes reflect falsely, that is, did she do one thing and record another?"

"No, not exactly, but…."

"Did she do multiple neurological examination physical tests over an extended period of time?"

"She did."

"An EEG? A repeat EEG?"

"She did all of that."

"Was her procedure in this case substantially at variance with that done by other qualified doctors who work in the NICU?"

"No, except...."

"Different than her own usual standards of practice?"

"Not exactly, but...."

"What was it that led you to make such a serious charge, in effect accusing this doctor of committing murder, Mrs. Larkin?"

"Thank you for finally letting me answer," Heather said testily.

Tarkington nodded infuriatingly.

"The doctor was in such an all-fired rush to get rid of Brendan so that everyone would not have to come by and bear witness to her colossal mistake, that she ignored signs of life. She pronounced him dead and removed his life supports when he was still alive."

There was a chilly stillness in the air-conditioned courtroom, much as there had been when Mrs. Larkin conveyed her inflammatory testimony during direct examination by Paul Bel Geddes. There was not a sound in the courtroom. It was as if they were collectively holding their breath.

"Yes, that sign of life. I believe Dr. Norcroft made note of that in her last progress note...no, the next to the last, where she describes the final brain death examination. She describes some motor movement that she says is 'primitive,' a 'primitive, peripheral reflex.' I take it you don't hold with the notion that there can be movement below the neck in a patient that is brain dead. Is that a fair statement, Mrs. Larkin?"

"Sometimes a little old-fashioned horse sense needs to be used, Mr. Tarkington. It isn't all gadgets and technology or cookbook, even in the twenty-first century. Brendan moved right before the end, even without being stimulated. He was alive."

She glared her defiance at the attorney.

"But the two doctors, two, mind you, both neurosurgeons, disagreed with you, didn't they?"

"Yes."

"They overruled you because they said that in their experience, the peripheral reflex activity was not consequential. The reflex movement notwithstanding, Mr. McNeely was brain dead—the same as dead. Isn't that what took place?"

"Yes. They were being the all-knowing, all-powerful doctors. They made a decision that should be left to God. They played God. That one keeps a sign on her desk that says she *is* GOD."

"But they played by the rules of medicine as they are known, is that not a fact, Mrs. Larkin?"

"Oh, I guess so. But I will always know that they should have waited."

"Let's go on to your second charge. You testified that you overheard Dr. Norcroft speaking on the telephone with the aide at the county medical examiner's office. Correct?"

"Yes, I did."

"What was it you heard? Before you answer, let me caution you. You are under oath not to commit perjury. Are you fully aware of the penalties for perjury?"

"Yes."

"All right, tell the court what you heard on the telephone that day five years ago."

"Yes, Sir. There was not much to hear. Dr. Norcroft, the defendant, sitting right over there, said, 'No autopsy. This was just a routine case. Death wasn't much of a surprise, actually.' I remember how she said, 'actually,' and looked over at me, like I was going to give her support."

"That about the total of the conversation, the gist of it at least, Mrs. Larkin?"

"That's right. I think she said something to the effect that they could send the body to the mortuary. No problem with doing that right away."

"Thank you, Mrs. Larkin. That's all the questions I have for now. Subject to recall your honor."

"You are still under oath Mrs. Larkin. You are not to discuss this case with anyone. You may now step down, but you may be called back. Please make yourself available," the judge instructed.

CHAPTER THREE

As soon as Sybil put down the receiver after her conversation with the aide at the medical examiner's office, she turned to Angie Church and asked, "Get that?"

"Yes, Doctor. I guess we have the path lab arrange for Brendan to be transferred to the MEs, right?"

"Um-hmm. Will you take care of it? I am feeling so terrible that I think I'll cancel my schedule and go home, assume the fetal position, and turn the electric blanket up to nine."

"We all feel the same way, Doc. Hang in there. It's not your fault. You did everything you could. There'll be better days," Angie comforted.

On an ordinary day, Sybil would have responded brusquely to Angie for patronizing her, and on an ordinary day, she would have shrugged off the death with a philosophical small raise of her shoulders and toss of her head and would have gone back to work like the Snow Queen she was supposed to be. But this was not an ordinary day. Sybil Norcroft felt wounded to the quick and unable to face any more that day.

Sybil quickly wiped away the tear that had formed disobediently in the corner of her eye. She used the sleeve of her lab coat and made it seem like an unconscious gesture. Heather Larkin, the head nurse, saw the gesture and sneered.

Sybil could not escape seeing Heather's disdainful expression.

"I hope our professional disagreement won't tarnish our working relationship, Heather."

"It's Mrs. Larkin, *Sybil*." There was an unmistakable undercurrent of challenge in the use of the doctor's first name. It was rare for nurses or ancillary personnel to address doctors without the title of respect. Around JNMH, Sybil Norcroft, was known by most as 'we don't call her Sybil, the Snow Queen'.

Sybil ignored the discourtesy with difficulty.

"Sorry, Mrs. Larkin. Still, I would hope that this unfortunate case can be put behind us. I did do the best I could for Brendan. If you think about it for a minute away from the emotional charge of the moment, I think you'll come to that conclusion as well."

Sybil extended her hand to shake Heather's. The head nurse acted as if she had not seen Dr. Norcroft's gesture of conciliation. Sybil persisted for a moment or two longer while Mrs. Larkin acted as if Sybil had spit on her hand before tendering it for shaking then let her hand drop. She flushed with embarrassment.

"Now, if it's all right, Dr. Norcroft, I have work to do."

Mrs. Larkin turned rudely away.

"I'd like for us to get together and talk about this another day, Mrs. Larkin: I really would, for all our good," Sybil said, making a final effort at appeasement.

It was as if she had not spoken.

Angie Church looked darkly at her head nurse as Heather hurried by on her way to take care of the urgent need to suction the Tucker boy's trach, a task handled by nurse's aides, customarily.

Just as she turned to enter the Tucker boy's room, Heather looked back and said, loud enough for Sybil to hear, "I don't know about any personal meeting with you, but you can rest assured that you have not heard the last of this from me, not on your sweet patootie."

"Call your next witness, Mr. Tarkington," Judge Hendricks ordered.

The plaintiff had rested and now the defense case was underway. Hendricks was under pressure to get this trial over with as soon as possible. The court dockets were swollen to overflowing with civil cases that had been in the mill for eight or nine years, many were approaching the time statute of limitations.

"The defense calls Angie Church, RN."

Angie swore to tell the truth, the whole truth, and nothing but the truth. She gave her name and professional qualifications—head nurse in the emergency room at Joseph Noble Memorial Hospital.

"I know that you are very busy, Ms. Church. Thank you for coming, today," began Mr. Tarkington. "I have very few questions for you in the matter before this court. First, how is it that you became acquainted with the deceased, Brendan McNeely?"

"He was a coworker, a nurse on the NICU, while I was working on the unit."

"And Dr. Sybil Norcroft?"

"She was one of the neurosurgeons at the hospital. She spent a lot of time on the unit. I got to know her there."

"Would you describe your relationship with either of these people as friends as opposed to a friendly professional relationship?"

"Our relationships were mutually friendly, but only on a professional basis. We didn't party together or anything."

"Do you feel any special fondness for Dr. Norcroft, a fondness that might lead you to give biased evidence in her favor?"

"No. Dr. Norcroft was not the friendship generating type. I respected her, thought she was okay personally, but I can't say that I really like her."

"So you consider yourself neutral, objective in regards to Dr. Norcroft's actions, particularly on the day of Brendan McNeely's death?"

"Completely."

Angie came across as a professional, a completely self-assured and comfortable young woman.

Sybil was grateful for that. It was too much to expect that the former NICU nurse liked her, Sybil did not really even want that from those who worked beneath her in the pecking order.

"Describe, please, in as objective terms as you can, and to the best of your recollection, the telephone conversation Dr. Norcroft had with the ME's office on that day."

"There is very little to say. I heard both ends of the conversation. Dr. Norcroft informed the ME's aide, a Mr. Stringham, about Mr. McNeely's death. She asked him to see to it that an autopsy was done, it was very important, she said. She was a little put out that the aide would not commit to getting an autopsy done, but by the end of the conversation, both Dr. Norcroft and I were of the same mind that an autopsy was going to be performed."

"What occurred then?"

"First, Dr. Norcroft asked me to arrange transfer to the Medical Examiner's lab down town, then she and Heather Larkin, the head nurse at the time, had a little run-in. I thought she was being unreasonable to the doctor."

"Describe the run-in."

"It was nothing much. Heather was mad at Dr. Norcroft. She hinted that the doctor hadn't done everything right in the surgery, that she had turned off the machines too early the day Brendan was declared brain dead for some evil reason. Dr. Norcroft looked hurt but didn't say anything more than that she wanted to get together with Heather when things cooled down."

"What did Heather say to that?"

"Something to the effect that she, Dr. Norcroft, had not heard the last of this. She implied that she, I mean, Heather, was going to do something more, I guess make trouble for the doctor."

"Thank you. I have no further questions."

Paul Bel Geddes approached Angie.

"Good morning, Ms. Church."

"Good morning, Sir."

"Not much fun being a witness, is it?"

"Makes me nervous, but it's a duty. I don't mind."

"Good. I don't have many questions. How can you be sure of the telephone conversation between the defendant and the ME's office? After all it was five years ago, and you must have had hundreds, probably even thousands of telephone conversations in the meantime."

"First of all, I have had no more than a handful of calls to the ME's office about deaths, and Brendan McNeely's was the only death of a fresh surgical patient I have handled personally, thank God. Also I remember the day as being terribly tense. We all cared for Brendan. He was the only coworker I have had who died. Most of us are healthy and don't have much trouble. Finally, I remember the tension between Heather and the doctor. It was uncalled for. Heather was wrong to do that, entirely unprofessional. It stuck in my mind."

The plaintiff's attorney hesitated for a moment, obviously trying to decide on whether to ask an additional question. Evidently he thought better of the idea and decided to cut his losses.

"Thank you, Ms. Church. No further questions."

"The defense now calls Dr. Myron Short."

Dr. Short was the defense's neuroradiology expert called to counteract the testimony given in the plaintiff's case in chief that there should have been an angiogram done.

Not to have done so was a breach of the standards of care, the plaintiff's witness had asserted emphatically. Dr. Papanickolas, the plaintiff's neuroradiologist, had been unbending on that point but had conceded on another telling point that he saw no evidence of an aneurysm on the CT, the eminent neurosurgeon from Canada's opinion notwithstanding. Papanickolas had been less helpful to the defense under cross-examination on the subject of whether there was a tumor present. He had left it at, 'I cannot be certain'.

Dr. Short was sworn, his impressive list of qualifications were delineated. He and Dr. Papanickolas matched degree for degree and honor for honor.

"Doctor," asked Tarkington. "Let's get right to the heart of the matter and examine the CT scan. If you would, Sir."

The computerized scan was put up on the view box again.

"This is the pituitary, this is the optic chiasm. Here we see the basilar artery and one posterior cerebral."

He pointed out the structures with an opened up paper clip.

"This irregular little area inside the pituitary, the light area, is a microadenoma."

Dr. Short was not one to equivocate.

"No doubt about the presence of the tumor?"

"None."

"Dr. de Montesquiou from Canada pointed to this structure," Tarkington took his time and led the witness's and the jury's eyes to the nubbin of gray that de Montesquiou had singled out, "and said it was an aneurysm. He used the statistical observation that there was only one chance in a million that it was anything else. Is that an aneurysm, Dr. Short?"

"No."

"Thank you. I am finished with the witness, your honor."

"Mr. Bel Geddes?"

"How can you be so sure that is not an aneurysm, Dr. Short?"

"Wrong location, wrong shape. That is a portion of the basilar artery."

"But you can't be certain without an angiogram, isn't that true, Doctor?"

"That would be the capper. But I'm sure."

Dr. Short was not shakable. Bel Geddes knew better than to press his luck much further.

"Is it not the standard of medical care to do an angiogram on every case of suspected pituitary tumor?"

"Certainly not, Sir. There are risks to angiography that rival those of trans-sphenoidal surgery. You should have a good reason to do an invasive arterial study. In my professional opinion, there was no indication here. It would have been meddlesome and carried risk."

"Dr. Papanickolas thought it was necessary, Sir"

"Reasonable men differ. I think he is mistaken," Dr. Short said without arrogance or rancor.

"What about an MRI or MRA? Would those studies not have given more convincing evidence, especially of the status of the blood vessels?"

Expensive Magnetic Resonance Arteriograms had almost replaced old-style even more expensive catheter angiography by 2009.

"I doubt it, but I would not argue the value of that test. I would have liked to have seen a Gadolinium enhanced MRI scan. But we have to realize the practical world conditions under which these physicians were working and under which most physicians are forced to work nowadays. HMOs control 90 percent of the medical population, and hardnosed insurance companies control the rest of the paying market. I still find it hard to call patients a market. They simply will not allow or pay for expensive tests such as MRI scans or PET scans. The choices of the doctors are very limited. The purse string holders call the shots. I am as sure as I sit here that Dr. Norcroft was *only* able to obtain a CT. The CT was enough to make the diagnosis even if it did not give the full measure of comfort Dr. Norcroft or I would have liked."

Feeling that he was not really getting anywhere, Mr. Bel Geddes wrinkled his brow, gave his head a little shake to signal disbelief, and said, "That's all I have."

"It's getting late in the day, ladies and gentlemen. We'll adjourn until tomorrow," said the judge and rapped the wood cylinder on her desk with her gavel.

She repeated her admonitions to the jury, and the tired and hot jurors and the rest of the participants wearily headed out of the courtroom.

A frigid but polite and correct relationship settled between Heather Larkin, RN, CNRN, and Sybil Norcroft, M.D., PhD, F.A.C.S. after that initial confrontation in Brendan's room and later at the telephone. Sybil was aware that her every action, spoken and written word, was under the microscopic scrutiny of Heather's uncompromising fault-finding eye. Sybil was called to task for her failures to write full progress notes, to come promptly for NICU calls, for bloody seepage on her patients' dressings, for ordering nonstandard doses of drugs. The criticisms were all exactly correct to the letter of the law and were all written in the nurse's incident reports and in memos to the chart review nurse in charge of surgery committee charts. It was onerous for Sybil, but she elected to remain silent and not to complain. She also elected, with difficulty, not to respond in kind. Every human being makes mistakes, and no one could withstand the scrutiny Sybil underwent. She could have found similar fault with Heather's work, but intuitively, she recognized that it would not benefit her or her work; so, she kept quiet.

Angie Church, on the other hand, grew angry and resentful upon receiving a similar carping treatment and shortly after Brendan McNeely's death, transferred to the ER where she blossomed. Three years later, she was the head nurse of the emergency room section, one of the three most important positions among the nonadministrative nurses in the hospital.

Sybil was noticed, that is, she received notification of the intent to sue, the infamous ninety day letter, by Brendan's parents eleven months after his death. That notice was couched in the chilly language of an official courtroom subpoena. Sybil informed her malpractice insurance company, DIPC—Doctor's Indemnity Protection Cooperative—of the intent letter, and she was assigned to the law firm of Schmid, Principle, Tarkington, and Henley. The named partner, Carter Tarkington, took the case himself owing to the prominence of both the defendant and the deceased young man's family. The letter from Paul Bel Geddes to Mr. Tarkington was substantially less formal and correct. Bel Geddes had a reputation for flamboyance, both in his courtroom and deposition comportment, and in his written communications. His letter read:

Dear Carter,

It is our fate to joust once more. I represent the bereaved parents of one Brendan McNeely, Carl and Priscilla. Your client, one Sybil Norcroft, did, with malice aforethought, set out to butcher and maim unto death this young man for the purpose of extracting money. Dr. Norcroft, and I shudder to grant her that title, wantonly, and with total disregard for McNeely's life or limb, made a spurious and woefully improper diagnosis, performed an unnecessary operation, botched the technical procedure with near criminal incompetence, and committed fraud by subterfuge— she obtained consent from the unfortunate young man based on a tapestry of lies.

I am inclined to press for criminal charges, but will grant you the opportunity to communicate with me before I take that serious step. This is a *res ipsa loquitur* case, Carter. Perhaps the best thing for you to do is to assent to a reasonable settlement, say, ten million dollars ($10,000,000). I believe there is a possibility that the parents would see their way clear to avoid the criminal prosecution if a reasonable disposition of the case were to be made with dispatch. They are upstanding members of the community who do not wish to injure the errant doctor, only to see justice done for their fine boy. After all, Dr. Norcroft comes from the same set of notables. I am sure even she would wish to set things right.

I look upon this case, not as a routine piece of my every day work, nor do I find incentive in any fee that might eventuate to me. This is a case that cries out for recompense, the doctor, and indeed, the medical profession at large, needs to be brought up short and to learn their duty. They will not police their own, therefore, I, and the other members of the American Trial Lawyers Association, must stand up for the unfortunates who cannot defend themselves against the monolithic structure of American Medicine. This is a crusade, a *jihad*. I trust that you will do the right thing and convince your client to settle. It is the right thing, the just thing and "let justice be done, though the heavens fall".

I remain,
Respectfully your colleague in the opposition,
Paul Devon Bel Geddes, Esq.

When Carter showed the turgid letter to Sybil at their first attorney-client meeting, the two of them had had one of the few laughs they would share during the course of the arduous pretrial preparation and on into the trial itself. Sybil felt threatened by the suit, her first.

"I receive all these big bucks; so, you can take it easy, Dr. Norcroft. Relax. This is a long drawn out process. I would not be the least bit surprised if this business lasted five or even six or seven years. You can't keep yourself tense all of the time. I'll let you know when to tense up. Otherwise, just go about your work as always. Don't let this injustice shake your confidence. You are a fine surgeon, a credit to your profession, and perform essential services for your patients. Now, let's get down to work.

"When was the first time you met Mr. McNeely? Don't leave out a thing," Tarkington said.

Sybil was sure that the suave, tanned, and relaxed attorney schmoozed all of his clients the same way, but it was comforting, and he was right, she had to take it easy or she would wind up her spring so tight it would snap, if she did not work on stress control.

It was four years later when Carter told Sybil, in effect, that it was now time to tense-up. He announced that, at long last, Paul Bel Geddes had subpoenaed her for a deposition. Tarkington, the trial attorney, and two of his firm's associate litigators drilled and prepared Dr. Norcroft for her deposition over a two-day period. They went over her understanding of the facts of the case, of the literature, of the patient himself, and of the law. They fired hard questions, harangued her, toughened her. Sybil Norcroft was a novice when they started, but a confident professional witness when they finished. She thought she was ready to face Paul Bel Geddes. With careful forethought, Sybil was wearing her best power outfit, a dark grey silk suit with a strong pink blouse and a string of pearls. She complimented her outfit with black spike heel Gucci shoes.

Sybil met Carter and his chief associate, Hyrum Willis, in the lobby of Bel Geddes's office building ten minutes before the scheduled deposition.

"Ready, Dr. Norcroft?" Hyrum asked.

"As much as I'll ever be, I suppose," she replied, nervousness showing in her face and voice.

"You'll do fine, Doctor," soothed Carter Tarkington, patting her arm reassuringly. "Just remember to think of Bel Geddes with no clothes on." Sybil smiled at his effort to calm her.

"And remember the most important dictum in the law," Hyrum Willis added, "*Illegitimi non carborundum.*"

"Give me credit. I don't wear down all that easily," Sybil told the two men.

"I am sure of that. Shall we?" asked Mr. Tarkington, pressing the elevator button.

The offices of Stewart, Bel Geddes, and Loughlin occupied the entirety of the eighth floor of the new City Panorama building. The building itself was ostentatious, all art deco and marble, color and flourish. The firm's suite of offices was a veritable study in grandeur—overcrowded with original objects d'art and oversized solid imported hardwood furniture. The rugs were deep, a flamboyant peach color, that did not match the pastel avocado green silk papered walls. The deposition-conference room was gaudy with Picassoesque modern paintings of disembodied women, melting suns, and a motif of eyes and ears that Sybil supposed had to have some sort of meaning. The tackiness of the room brought the second smile of the day to her furrowed face. The members of the defense team sat at the twenty-foot long Philippine mahogany table on uncomfortable unpadded chairs. The secretary departed, leaving them alone.

"I—actually, we—have had considerable experience with Paul Bel Geddes, Dr. Norcroft," said Carter Tarkington once the three of them were more or less comfortably seated. "My bet is that he will be thirty minutes late."

"I'll take you up on that," said Hyrum Willis. "I'll bet it'll be more like forty-five or an hour. How much do you want to go?"

Carter laughed.

"I hate losing, so I won't bet. You are too close to the truth for comfort. I was just trying to keep Dr. Norcroft's hopes up."

Sybil smiled again, a more worried smile than before. In ten minutes, the court reporter arrived, and the four of them settled in for a long, quiet wait. There was very little conversation, and all of that was meaningless, careful, urbane chitchat.

It was two minutes short of an hour beyond the scheduled time for the deposition when the large conference room doors swung open. A strikingly beautiful secretary, one whose typing ability was no doubt secondary, held the door so the firm's partner could effect a grand entrance. The two attorneys rose, almost reflexively to shake their opponent's hand. Sybil started to rise, but some streak of anger made her resume her seat.

Bel Geddes beamed his copyrighted good-natured hail-fellow-well-met smile displaying expensively capped, overlarge, and overly white teeth. Everything about the man was overdone. His suit was impeccable white linen, and his shirt of Sea Island cotton, white on white, all but glowed. He wore a tie that was not so much bright or loud as it was luminescent, so much so that Sybil thought it would probably glow in the dark. It looked like one of the paintings in his office but one done in florid colors with fluorescent paint. The tie demanded that attention be focused on it and its wearer. He was preceded by an aromatic cloud of blue smoke from his Hoyo de Monterrey cigar.

"Hello, Carter, how nice to see you! I haven't forgotten our last encounter, you old rascal. Gained a little weight since then, haven't you?"

Bel Geddes scrutinized Tarkington as if it really mattered.

"Gotten over the worry of the Sonel v. Saint Mary's Hospital, I take it," he laughed.

It was evidently a private joke appreciated solely by himself. Seeing that none of the others were laughing made Bel Geddes guffaw.

"I have not had the pleasure," Bel Geddes said, now focusing the sunny beam of his smile on Hyrum Willis, having participated in a contest of hand strength with Carter Tarkington that the plaintiff's attorney won with ease.

"Hyrum Willis," the associate said. "We met during the Sonel v. Saint Mary's case—Dr. Blanchard's and Theresa Ogilbie's depositions."

Bel Geddes towered over the diminutive Hyrum. He extended his large, hirsute hand and crushed the smaller man's, laughing with pleasure when Hyrum grimaced slightly. Hyrum hurriedly decided to say no more, hoping that Bel Geddes would lavish his attentions on someone else.

"And who might this lovely young thing be?" Mr. Bel Geddes said, approaching the court reporter who was as plain as a Kansas prairie and all business.

She did not exchange smiles.

"Barbara Lithgow, Mr. Bel Geddes, I'm the court reporter. Before we start, I wish you would speak to your receptionist about the check. She said that I would have to bring it up to you. You agreed with our office to have one ready upon my arrival."

Paul Bel Geddes did not look at all crestfallen. Sybil thought she was reading too much between the lines when she presumed that the attorney was a deadbeat when it came to honoring his bills and commitments.

"Let's get started, then we can take care of the check, all right, dear?" Bel Geddes said and started to turn away from Ms. Lithgow.

"I am afraid that I have my instructions, Mr. Bel Geddes. I will need to have the check before I can turn out any work. The office insists."

She smiled sweetly, but Sybil was sure that she was not about to back down, and that she probably had good reasons for her insistence on being paid upfront.

"And my name is Lithgow, not dear. I like professional decorum...old fashioned, I guess."

She was no longer making a pretense of smiling.

Bel Geddes maintained his sparkling toothy smile, but his faded hazel eyes became icy.

"Well, dear, if you insist. I could choose to be insulted, but it is too nice a day."

He pressed a button, and, shortly, the starlet temporarily working as a law secretary hurried in manifesting the excessive mobility of her parts in her rush. The attorney spoke briefly to his secretary who rushed out promptly.

In the interim, Mr. Bel Geddes discovered the deponent, who had remained sitting.

"Ah, the eminent Dr. Norcroft. I'm Paul, okay if I call you Sybil?"

He extended his hand, but Sybil ignored it. She did not rise, and she did not extend her hand.

"No," she said. "I am Dr. Norcroft, Mr. Bel Geddes. Good morning."

"Happy to have you here, little lady."

Sybil's face involuntarily squeezed in an abbreviated wince. She chastised herself silently and quickly for having allowed the boor to elicit a rise out of her.

"It's a lovely day," he said. "I think we can have some fun here. Might's well enjoy our work. Life's too short to take it all too seriously."

He was effusive in his pleasure at the day and with Sybil's company as if they were old and bosom friends. Sybil began to feel a small rise of bile in her throat. They were looking eye to eye, neither willing to be the first one to blink, when the vividly underdressed secretary burst through the conference door again. She handed Bel Geddes a pale green check, and he turned it over to Barbara Lithgow without comment.

Bel Geddes sat down, and, without preamble, went through the formalities of the deposition for the record. He asked Sybil for her name and occupation, where she went to medical school, and where she had done her residency, but ignored all else about her celebrated career to date.

"I trust you brought a *curriculum vitae* with you, Doctor. We can dispense with a recitation of all the honors and degrees you doctors insist on padding your depositions and CVs with if you did."

Sybil produced a copy of her CV and passed it across the table to the plaintiff's attorney. He marked it as "Plaintiff's No. 1."

Bel Geddes rambled through a series of questions, many of them repetitive, many of them seeming well away from the subject of the case of Brendan McNeely. He often paused to ask altogether irrelevant questions.

"I love your perfume, Doctor. What is that?"

When Sybil appeared reluctant to answer, he smiled disarmingly, and repeated, "Really, I'd like to know. I think my significant other should smell as good as you."

"Charley," responded Sybil.

"Ah, yes, love Charley. Expensive stuff, no?"

"I suppose it is."

Later, after a particularly nasty but astute set of questions on the performance of the surgery, Bel Geddes suddenly stopped, almost mid-sentence, and asked, "Are those earrings real silver? They look like Mexican silver, Taxco, right?"

It was slightly disorienting to Sybil. She supposed that that was Bel Geddes's intention.

"Right," she said noncommittally.

In fact they were cheap costume jewelry given to her by her ten-year-old nephew. She had worn them purposely as a small insult to Bel Geddes and towards the entire proceedings as if they were not worth getting fixed up for.

Bel Geddes then rattled off a rapid-fire series of questions about the diagnosis, what did Sybil think was the minimal prolactin level to warrant pituitary surgery, why had she not done an arteriogram, why was there no MRI, and why had she so blatantly lied to her innocent patient. Sybil fielded all of the questions with aplomb since she was well within her area of expertise. The very staccato character of the question and answer series was becoming a contest of wits and wills between the incisive attorney and the keen witness. Tarkington appeared ready to object several times but thought better of challenging the flow. He thought it would be good for Bel Geddes to see what he was up against. Most doctors, as medical witnesses, came across as hostile, weak, ill-informed in their own specialties, emotional, and slow witted—no match for the prepared biting hostility of the interaction of the deposition. Sybil Norcroft was acquitting herself very well, and Paul Bel Geddes could not help but recognize that he had come up against a superior intellect and a worthy opponent.

Suddenly, Bel Geddes halted his stream of questions. He leaned back on the hind legs of his conference chair and locked his fingers behind his neck. He gave an exaggerated stretch. As he put his chair back down on its four legs, he glanced at his watch and reached over in an apparently absent-minded gesture, and pushed the unseen button.

"I'm famished. How about you, little lady?" he asked, giving a look at Sybil.

She interpreted the look as an examination of her face as to whether she was reacting to his stupid MCP characterizations. Usually, she was prompt to set Male Chauvinist Pigs right, but it was clear that he was looking for her to react, and she strove to make her face inexpressive.

It was unnecessary for Sybil or anyone else to answer. As if on cue, the conference doors swung open, and two starlets—secretaries in their day jobs—marched in bearing platters of steaming bagels, crockery tubs of specialty butters, assorted jams, and cream cheese. The two young women bustled to the center of the room and leaned over to set their platters down, one in front of the plaintiff's attorney, and one in front of Sybil. The two defense attorneys made a conspicuous effort not to look as far down the secretaries' dress fronts as the young women's attire permitted. Sybil avoided reacting to the generous display. Bel Geddes could not resist a smile, and he allowed himself a surreptitious little bottom pat as the woman on his side of the table turned to leave.

"Have some, they're great," he enthused.

"No, thanks," said Tarkington and Willis.

The court stenographer simply shook her head.

"Just for the sake of politeness, Dr. Norcroft. This is just professional, nothing personal going on here. No need for us to be unfriendly, eh?" Bel

Geddes said to Sybil as he smeared a generous dollop of cream cheese on a savory multi-grain bagel half and passed it over to Sybil.

"Here you go, that's a good girl."

He piled Kiwi jam on a wheat raisin bagel of his own and began munching on it.

Sybil was hungry and growing tired. She thought she could use a little jump start from the aromatic bagel. It was coming out of Bel Geddes's pocket, why not?

She took a generous bite and nodded in minor acknowledgment to the attorney. As soon as her mouth was thoroughly full and salivating, Bel Geddes set his own bagel aside and launched into another sequence of difficult and unfriendly questions, this time about the informed consent discussion she had had, or as he suggested, had not had, with Brendan McNeely. He caught her with her mouth full, and in her haste to respond to his insulting questions, she choked a little. She put her hand to her mouth and coughed up a sodden chunk. To her embarrassment, it fell onto the front of her immaculate dress, making an obvious mark. When she looked up at her questioner, she realized that he was wearing a self-satisfied 'gotcha' expression.

Sybil gave herself a swift mental kick and vowed never to let the man do anything like that again. The questions shot at her like a machine gun. Bel Geddes was brilliant. He never looked at a note, and he always seemed to be able to put a negative spin on the direction of his questions that Sybil felt compelled to respond to in her own defense. She was now on the defensive, getting a little rattled. Some of her answers were not as crisp or as demonstrative of her confidence or knowledgability as before.

"Objection," Carter Tarkington finally said. "Counsel is not letting the witness answer, she is two questions behind. Dr. Norcroft, would you like to have the last two questions and answers read back to you?"

Sybil recognized the reprieve and respite her advocate was offering.

"Yes," she said. "Please."

The court reporter worked back on her paper tape then repeated the questions and answers while Sybil regained her breath and her composure. She now responded carefully and thoughtfully.

Bel Geddes had a habit of interrupting or of suggesting his own ending to a slowly developing sentence on the part of the witness. Tarkington now objected frequently, giving Sybil a chance to complete her answers her own way.

During the break for lunch, he cornered with Sybil and worked to get her back on the winning end of the contest between her and Bel Geddes.

"Look," Tarkington said, "he's famous for these silly diversionary tactics. Don't let him get to you. We have all the time in the world. As long as he sees that he can rattle you, he will keep it up. He wants to get you to make some sort of self-incriminating admission inadvertently or as a Freudian slip. Don't think for a second that he is just crazy. There is a method to every bit of his madness. Hang in there. You are smarter than he is, and you know a whale of a lot more about medicine. He is just more cunning than you, and he uses that attribute as a substitute for intelligence or knowledge of the law. Keep your cool and he won't be able to get at you. You have to keep very well in mind and all of the time that you did not commit malpractice. There is an explanation, a good medical reason for every criticism he levels. Keep thinking, don't let him divert you or surprise you, and you will come out of this looking great. I have complete confidence in you."

The afternoon session was serious, all business, from Mr. Bel Geddes. The change in his demeanor and delivery was perceptible to every person in the room. Now, he consulted notes, phrased his questions very exactly, appearing to repeat questions, but with minor nuances of difference each time. He was clearly concentrating on avoiding any omission of any area of the case. The questions were detailed, calling for Sybil to search the chart, or to pause to remember, or to think. She had never considered some of the subjects the attorney introduced, had not read the nurses notes, she had to admit, to her chagrin. It was a thorough see-saw, sometimes he was up, sometimes she was. It was tiring, and the grilling was beginning to take its toll.

At four o'clock, Bel Geddes made another of his acute and abrupt diversions. He listened to the answer Sybil tendered to his question about why she had not responded to Heather Larkin's demand that she do more testing because Heather, in her official nurse's note, and in a formal incident report, insisted that the patient was not dead when the life support machinery was discontinued.

As Sybil's answer entered the last few measures, Bel Geddes disappeared under the table. The attorneys, Barbara Lithgow, the stenographer, and Sybil all looked at each other in mild consternation. They were aware that Paul Bel Geddes was crawling around beneath the long conference table. After a long, awkward silence, and some teeth gritting by Sybil and her attorneys, Paul Bel Geddes's disembodied voice came up through the table top.

"Dr. Norcroft?"

Sybil felt a little silly in responding to the table top. She waited.

"Dr. Norcroft?"

His voice was now more insistent.

Sybil looked at Hyrum Willis and Carter Tarkington who both shrugged, smiles beginning to curl at the corners of their mouths indicating that they were used to Paul Bel Geddes's shenanigans. Sybil did not respond. She determined not to be goaded into this latest bizarre silliness.

She felt a tapping on her shoe and moved her foot self-consciously.

"Dr. Norcroft, are these Guccis?" Bel Geddes asked.

Before Sybil could answer, he had gently placed his warm, pudgy hand around her ankle. She could feel his pinky ring. She jumped involuntarily. He laughed with glee, obviously tickled at the success of his prank.

Sybil primly moved her legs back out of his way and fought back a wave of frustrated anger. She knew she would sound adolescent if she made a fuss about the unwonted contact. The portly attorney backpedaled out from under the table, holding his pen in his right hand.

"There you are, you little rascal," he said, as if that fooled anyone.

"A final question, Dr. Norcroft," he said with disarming affability.

Despite her every effort, Sybil was pale, and felt shaken. That made her angry with herself.

"Didn't you just drop the ball with this patient? You were so busy with all your committees, your speeches to feminist groups, your lucrative and overwhelming surgery schedule, your responsibilities to the social register of Westminster County. Weren't you just the least bit distracted, presuming that this was a ho-hum case, one you could just notch up on your gun butt, and you didn't think about him or his findings all that much? Didn't you just drop the ball, as rattled as you were by all that outside responsibility? Maybe you get rattled sometimes, what do you say?"

Sybil would have given almost anything to let the cup of gall that was giving testimony in open court pass from her lips. The day had come. She had waited more than five years to tell her side of the case, to defend herself, and to retrieve the self respect she felt that she had lost in the deposition with the devilishly unorthodox Paul Bel Geddes three years previously. She had never been able to forget entirely the last set of questions the plaintiff's attorney had fired at her nor to shake the self-doubt that he had engendered in her by them. She knew that that had been the man's intention, but it was as if the ideas had been implanted in her psyche under hypnosis, and they could not easily be dislodged.

She was pondering her own reactions when she was surprised to hear her name called.

"Next witness."

The judge was speaking, but she seemed far away, as if she were in a distant room.

Sybil worked to get herself back into the courtroom present and to the deadly serious drama that threatened her career.

"The defense calls Dr. Sybil Norcroft."

Sybil forced herself to stand, made sure that she did not get light headed or to sway, and strode resolutely to the witness chair on its raised dais next to the judge's bench. She remembered and obeyed her attorney's instructions and looked at the jury, determined to direct her answers to them. She concentrated on her face, made the muscles give an expression of concern, but of confidence. She hoped that she looked professional and objective, and above all, innocent. Unlike her little calculated snit in the deposition, Sybil had taken the utmost care with her dress, her jewelry, and her face that day. She wore an attractive business suit, professional but feminine. She combed her hair out so she could take advantage of its length and luster. She did not want to come across in the least way as a tough, uncaring, ballbreaker, nor did she want to appear weak or uninformed—anything less than her long struggle to be a successful neurosurgeon entitled her to be. Neither arrogant nor fearful, just competent, believably competent, that was the demeanor Sybil worked to project. It took real concentration.

"State and spell your full name," the bailiff requested.

Sybil did so. She began to calm her nerves. It was better now that it had begun. She was grateful that she would be questioned by her own attorney first.

"Do you swear to tell the truth, the whole truth, and nothing but the truth, so help you God?" the bailiff asked, checking to see that her hand was on the Bible and the other was at the square.

Sybil responded in the affirmative. It was her every intention to do so and her fervent hope that the jury would believe her over Pierre de Montesquiou, Heather Larkin, Douglas Stringham, or Darryl Hankin, who had preceded her.

Her defense attorney, Carter Tarkington, put Sybil completely at her ease with a litany of questions designed to bring out her many accomplishments. She allowed herself to talk to the jury, not just to answer the questions, when she told of being her college valedictorian, first in her medical school class, of having to work and to compete in the unfairly patriarchal world of organized medicine. She did not dwell on the subject of the bias she had experienced, knowing that many of the spectators and the jurors were sick of hearing about anything to do with political correctness and did not really believe that sexist discrimination still went on. It was the twenty-first century, after all. She could tell, however, that she had struck a responsive chord by the small changes of expression in the faces of a couple of the women jurors.

Tarkington took his time, better than an hour to get to the heart of the matter before the jury.

He asked her to "tell us, in your own words, what transpired between you and Brendan McNeely during the conversation wherein you sought to obtain fully informed consent for surgery, Dr. Norcroft."

Sybil responded at length in a conversational tone and in minute detail, giving both her explanations and his questions. The jury was fully awake and interested.

"Did you cheat this young man? Tell him lies? Trick him into having an operation just so you could make some money or add to your impressive list of patients to increase your standing with your colleagues? The jury would like to know your motives."

Sybil responded almost angrily, defending against any impugning of her motives.

In conclusion, she said, "I do not need any money from surgery. My husband is wealthy enough that I would not have to work a day to enjoy a life of comfort and plenty. I operate because I am well trained and competent. It seems old fashioned even to admit to an idealism, but I work because I truly think I can help people. To come to the point of your question, I thought I could help Brendan McNeely by removing his pituitary tumor."

To defuse the sting of the cross examination they both knew was coming, Tarkington led Dr. Norcroft laboriously through all of the tough questions about the preoperative workup, the decision to operate, and the decision not to use an M.D. or and ENT specialist as an assistant.

He came to the seminal event.

"Dr. Norcroft, I believe we can best learn about the problem in surgery by looking at it, by reviewing the videotape you caused to be taken and made sure was saved, fortunately for this jury. We can all see what happened. I will ask you to narrate and to tell us what happened."

The video was of high quality. Tarkington made a show of fast forwarding to the moment of the dural incision, and then put the picture on pause just as the knife blade was poised to make the now infamous lateral cut.

"Before you describe what we are about to see, Dr. Norcroft, could you help us with some of the technicalities of the tape?"

"I'll do my best."

"I was wondering...exactly how long was it, I mean, the whole tape?"

"72 minutes, to be exact."

"Pardon me, Doctor. Did I hear you correctly? Did you mean to say, 72 minutes? Or did you misspeak?"

"I am correct, I checked on that; 72 minutes is the length of the videotape."

"That seems odd. I recall testimony given in this courtroom that the tape was much shorter."

He made a short display of riffling through his notes.

"Yes," he said, "here it is. I thought so. Could we have the court recorder read back the testimony of Pierre de Montesquiou, the man from Canada, who came down here to accuse you of such terrible things, who told us how carefully he studied this case before coming all the way down here to testify for Mr. Bel Geddes."

Tarkington read off the exact day and time of the testimony.

The court recorder was able to find it with only the slightest of delays owing to Mr. Tarkington's assiduous accuracy.

She read in a monotone voice, "Question: 'My question, just for the record, as I said, just a technicality, how long was the tape, the tape you looked at. That was a copy of the original, right? Sent to you by Mr. Bel Geddes?'

"Answer: 'I reviewed the tape of this operation. It was provided to me by Mr. Bel Geddes, or someone in his office, I can't say that exactly. It was precisely 39 minutes long. I thought you might ask such a detail; so, I made a note of it.' I believe that is all there is in the record about the length of the tape, Mr. Tarkington," the stenographer said in her completely nonjudgmental voice.

"How would you explain that discrepancy, Dr. Norcroft?"

"Either the Canadian witness," Tarkington had instructed her to hammer home the foreignness of Dr. de Montesquiou, "made a gross error of, let's see...31 minutes, or he looked at a shortened version."

"You mean a doctored copy?"

"Objection! Relates to facts not in evidence. I object!" called out Paul Bel Geddes from his chair beside Brendan McNeely's parents at the plaintiff's table.

"I'll allow it," decided the judge after a moment's pause.

"I would have to say so. Yes, a doctored copy, one with parts left out."

"Would that shortened version have shown all of the pertinent data, the entirety of the case, even the hemorrhage, the excitement, your unguarded moments during that drama?"

"Obviously not."

"Can we be sure that Dr. de Montesquiou, the expert from Canada, had a chance to see the incision you made? It is right there on the tape for all in this courtroom to see today, is it not, Dr. Norcroft? Could he have been able to render a proper judgment without that?"

"Objection."

It was half-hearted. Bel Geddes knew he did not have a chance. He also knew that his star witness, the eminent Canadian transsphenoidal surgery specialist had already returned to Montreal and would not be back to refute this testimony. He groaned inwardly and waited for the judge's ruling.

"Overruled. You may answer the question, Doctor."

"The tape is crucial. Whatever any of us may say in this courtroom, those pictures stand on their own. They demonstrate what went on. It appears that the Canadian witness did not get to see a full half an hour of the tapes, and I can only conclude that he based his judgment on an altered tape. Perhaps he cannot be faulted in his objectivity, but rather, he just did not have the true evidence before him," Sybil said to the jury.

She spoke to each one of them earnestly, conveying her objectivity, her minor dismay that the former witness had been less so. She thought that she did it rather well, too.

"Well, let's go on and look at this tape. Feel free to stop whenever you wish, Doctor. You have a clicker, I think."

"I do."

The picture began to move again, and every eye in the courtroom was riveted on the sharp pointed knife as it descended into the dural covering beneath it. The knife made an unwavering, shallow vertical cut. The edges parted cleanly, exposing the gray-tan glandular tissue below. The videotape was moving in slow motion, just as the incision had seemed to Sybil when it was being done. She recalled every excruciating nanosecond of that incision.

"Now, the vertical incision is done. Note that the dura is opened, and the gland can be seen peeking through. See."

She stopped the tape and identified the areas with her laser pointer. She was surprised at the steadiness of her hand. The tape started again, moving inexorably towards the fateful lateral cut.

"Now, watch," Sybil was no longer the defendant in a courtroom, she was a lecturer, helping her students to understand. "The point of the blade is scratching the dura, slowly passing through the first leaf. The dura has several layers, incidentally. Now, look, the incision is beginning to open up, there by the vertical limb," Sybil pointed as the action continued. "Notice how close we are to the midline, barely a couple of millimeters lateral. The carotid artery should be nearly a centimeter out of our way. Still no bleeding, no problem."

There was not a sound in the courtroom. The expectation of the long anticipation of the erupting hemorrhage was electric.

Sybil knew that the moment of truth was very close. She stopped the tape, let the jurors see how small the incision was.

"That's magnified six times, so figure how really small that incision is, how close to the midline."

She started the tape again. The point of the knife moved again. Now there was a short, brisk emission of blood from the corner of the incision.

Several of the jurors moved back, almost as if they had were about to get splashed, the video's quality was near perfect.

"Now, here I put a pledget of cotton to staunch that little bleeding."

The tape was speeded up, but for five minutes there was nothing but the boring view of white cotton over the incision.

"Here, I'm removing the pressure," Sybil said.

She could feel her heart quicken, her breath come in shorter and shallower gasps, just as it had on that awful day. She felt a tinge of the faintness and nausea she had felt back then. She fought to keep her voice steady.

"There it's dry," she said.

Strictly speaking, there was a small trickle still oozing out, but everyone was reassured. The doctor had said that it was nothing.

"Now, we're ready to go a bit further."

It was as if the incision involved everyone, the use of the group pronoun 'we' seemed timely and appropriate.

Scissors tips moved into the opening. The hand holding the instrument was steady and sure. The extremely keen steel edges bit into the dura opening what seemed like one cell at a time. The jurors, judge, and attorneys breathed a small sigh of relief, or at least of release of tension. The scissors advanced a hair's distance further.

"Now," Sybil said, like the voice of some prophetess of imminent doom.

Her comment was timed perfectly.

The blades of the scissors moved ever so slightly, and a brilliant red geyser of blood exploded into the picture obscuring everything else. There was an audible gasp from one of the jurors. Sybil and her lawyers did not dare look in the direction of the jury box at that moment.

"Let's go back a little, Dr. Norcroft, if you would?" Carter Tarkington asked.

Sybil backed up to the point just preceding the massive hemorrhage. "How far lateral is that, Doctor?"

"From the midline, I'd estimate no more than three millimeters."

"And from your studies in medical school anatomy and pathology classes, and from your extensive surgical experience in this area, how far out would you expect the carotid artery to be if it were located in its normal position?"

"A good centimeter, sometimes a centimeter and a half—more than triple the length of the incision we're seeing in the video."

"That doesn't seem that far to me?"

"In neurosurgery, that is interplanetary. Under the microscope, it is well out of the field. By neurosurgical standards, I never came close to it."

"Then you did not cut into the carotid artery in its normal position?"

"Definitely not. I'll show you."

Sybil ran the tape again and pointed out again how close she was to the midline and, parenthetically, how far she was from the expected position of the carotid. The jurors had now seen that portion of the tape enough times to imprint the slow motion images indelibly in their memories.

"You did not cut into the carotid artery over in its rightful position. Then we are left with the conclusion that the Canadian doctor, the one who came down here for $35,000 to accuse you and to testify against you was right. We have to conclude that you cut into an aneurysm. Is that about it, Doctor?"

"Not at all, counselor. Let's run the film one more time. I hope the ladies and gentlemen of the jury are not getting tired of this."

They did not look tired, or bored, or that their attentions were flagging. The now familiar scene was played back again.

"Look under the dura, here," Sybil said.

She pointed out the grey-tan of the gland showing beneath the opening.

"Aneurysms are blood red tense sacs. Nothing like that here."

She advanced the tape.

"Now, right up to the time of the hemorrhage, no aneurysm."

She used her laser pointer. A wider expanse of glandular tissue revealed itself under the dura. Then the hemorrhage started, and Sybil backed the tape a fraction.

"Notice where the incision is being made...right now."

The point of the blade was nibbling in the dura, above the level of the gland, not inside the dura at all. The hemorrhage erupted again, and Sybil backed up, paused the tape with the points of the scissors in the middle of the dura. The jurors had that picture to ponder as Sybil concluded.

"No, the cut that caused the bleeding was in the folds of the dura, not beneath it where an aneurysm might have been. There was no aneurysm, none at all. You have seen that for yourselves, ladies and gentlemen."

For another hour, Tarkington took Sybil through the videotape, pausing at intervals to have her show the heroics of her attempts to staunch the overwhelming bleeding. At times, her voice broke with frustration, then with grief, an emotion that was not lost on the jury.

When the defense attorney was sure that he had made his point with the tape, and before he lost the jurors' attention, he switched subjects.

"Doctor, I saw on that tape that you used a pointed knife to start the incision, is that right?"

"Yes, an eleven blade. That is pretty standard."

"That's not what the man from Canada said. He told us that it was unthinkable, or words to that effect, to use an eleven blade knife for this incision. Do you recall that?"

"Yes."

"He has even written a book on the subject of transsphenoidal surgery, has he not? I seem to recall some testimony that indicated that that book was so authoritative that it is respectfully known as 'the Bible' of transsphenoidal surgery."

He mused for a moment, then riffled through his notes. "I remember, now. Dr. de Montesquiou, the man from Canada, in all modesty, suggested that his book could best be described as a 'Galenic Opera,' referring to the great physician born in AD 129, whose words were literally sung as gospel for more than 1200 years. Who are you, a private practitioner here in the States, to refute such an authority?"

"I don't need to."

"I beg your pardon, Doctor?"

There was shuffling of feet, a few throats were cleared. The jurors, indeed everyone in the courtroom, was once again in full attention on the conversation at the witness stand.

"He impeaches himself, the doctor from up there in Canada. He did write a textbook. It is considered the Bible on the subject by many. I used it to learn about the surgery, and I used it to prepare for my defense in this case."

"I have a copy of Dr. de Montesquiou's book. Would you identify it for us?"

Sybil read the title and the fly leaf. It was Dr. de Montesquiou's book.

"Please mark this as Defense exhibit number 4." Tarkington said, addressing the bailiff.

"I believe it's number 3, Sir," the bailiff corrected humbly.

"I'm sure you're right," Tarkington responded gracefully.

The exhibit was marked into evidence, and Tarkington showed the opposing attorneys and the judge the copy of the book.

"Would you explain the discrepancy you alluded to a moment ago, Doctor. I'm sure the jury would be interested."

"I can show you two important ones."

She flipped the pages. It was not difficult since they were plainly marked by yellow sticky labels. It looked more impressive for her to search a little.

"Here. First of all, on page 403, let me call your attention to the diagram. It shows a cruciate incision being made in the dura."

"Would you read the caption under the diagram, Doctor?" Tarkington asked helpfully as if wild horses could drag Sybil away from doing so.

"I will. 'Standard dural incision being made with an 11 Bard-Parker blade'."

"So in Dr. de Montesquiou's own book, he describes the use of an 11 blade as being 'standard,' isn't that right, Dr. Norcroft?"

"That's right."

"That is not what he said in this courtroom when he came down from Canada for $35,000 to accuse you is it, Doctor?"

"No, Sir. It most definitely is not."

"You mentioned a second significant discrepancy. Would you point that out for us?"

"It's on page 56, in the section on anatomy and pathology."

She took a moment to find the exact page and paragraph.

"I'll quote the Canadian author, de Montesquiou: 'I have seen four and am aware of six more instances in which one or the other or both carotid arteries were in the dangerous position of curving towards the midline. In some instances, the two carotids actually met in the middle—exactly at the point where the incision and principle activity of surgery takes place in trans-sphenoidal pituitary operations. This represents a profound danger to the patient and to the doctor of major hemorrhage. Fortunately, the majority of the carotids lie beneath the dura and will be seen and protected after the dural incision is made. The truly troublesome cases are those in which the major vessels lie completely within the leaves of the dura.' A little further on Dr. de Montesquiou says, 'The danger of encountering the anomalously placed carotid would be obviated by doing routine preoperative arteriography. However, that is impractical and not recommended since the risks of arteriography, although low, would nearly equal that of the surgery, and would exceed that of encountering the anomalous artery, given the rarity of such anatomical variations.' Many of the chapters in the book were written by other authors, with de Montesquiou acting as editor, but this particular one was written by de Montesquiou himself, the man who testified in this courtroom."

It was quiet for a few moments. There was no underestimating the seriousness of this revelation.

Tarkington capitalized on it with a laconic question, "Dr. Norcroft, what do you conclude from the discrepancy between the Canadian witness's $35,000 testimony here and the statements in his own book?"

"He lied. To have made a mistake or to have forgotten one thing such as the anomalous arteries could perhaps be considered within ordinary human memory frailty, but to have missed both such significant factors coincidentally demands a suspension of healthy suspiciousness that is beyond the generosity of any but the most naive," Sybil responded.

"Objection, your honor. This is grossly improper and counsel knows it. Dr. de Montesquiou has left the country. He cannot be here to defend himself and to answer to these scurrilous charges," Bel Geddes argued.

"Of course he can, Counselor," said Judge Hendricks in her most reasonable voice. "We will be happy to hear his rebuttal testimony any time during the course of this trial. Let us know, please."

Bel Geddes knew. His star witness would not be coming back. He had bigger fish to fry and was already in Jakarta to be the featured speaker in the Pan-Asian Medical Association meetings. Besides he already had his money, and any inducement to return would be weak. Bel Geddes sat down trying not to look as forlorn as he felt.

"No further questions, your honor. Your witness, Mr. Bel Geddes," said Carter Tarkington, no hint of gloating in his expression.

CHAPTER FOUR

After the deposition, Sybil felt depressed. Her attorney, her friends, and her family all reassured her, told her not to be overly concerned. They might have been telling her to grow tall or to develop fins. She knew that what they were saying was logical, objective, and right. It was her attorney's job to suffer the slings and arrows of outrageous procedural attacks. Her friends buoyed her up with the wholly sanguine observations that Bel Geddes was just a sexist of the worst order, that he was just trying to get her nanny, and that she could rid herself of that particular demon of the patriarchy by throwing herself into her work and into the cause. Her family importuned her for more of her time, more of her enthusiasm, more of her old self. They meant entirely well, and for her benefit, and Sybil knew that she had in the past neglected and was now neglecting the people who mattered most in favor of the jealous mistress, neurosurgery.

To avoid ruminating about the death of Brendan McNeely, about the lawsuit and the inexorably approaching trial, and about the attack on her character—the offensive against her medical soul—that the malpractice suit represented, Sybil forced herself to see more and more patients, to do more frequent and more difficult operations, and to advance her standing in the professional organizations—the American Association of Neurological Surgeons, and the Congress of Neurological Surgeons. She was indefatigable, driving herself every day until she fell in bed exhausted, too tired to think or dream. To all outside appearances, Sybil Norcroft was the quintessence of the driven professional in full command of her mind, her life, and her career.

To herself, her family, and her close friends, she was troubled and depressed, merely avoiding the thoughts of the malpractice trial, not coping.

Sybil rubbed her sleep-deprived eyes. They felt as if emery powder had been poured in them after a marathon day of seeing the 'crocks', as she described them, in her office clinic. Thirty-one patients had come through. Twelve were follow-ups after surgery and took about five minutes each. The rest were the walking wounded of the world—the workman's comp victims, the blaring hypochondriacs, the lonely old women with an assortment of rheumatic aches and pains, and the oddballs with pains, twitches, and perversions of sensation that defied the logic of the neurological examination and of all medical knowledge and experience. It was seven p.m. She saw the last patient out the door and wearily typed in the meager office progress note on her PC. She gave her tired eyes a good rub before she forced herself to go see the stack of hospital consults that had accumulated during the day.

The first hospital consultation patient of that marathon day had been Renee Thollier, a middle aged African American woman. Sybil was asked to see her about her terrible leg pain. The history gave Sybil almost everything she needed to know. The woman had thrombophlebitis, and the calf of her leg was swollen to the point that the skin was stretched taut and shiny. The woman's calf muscles were exquisitely tender, and she had a flagrant Homan's sign. Even though Sybil tested for the sign very carefully and gently by slowly bending her foot towards the swollen shin, the poor woman shrieked in unexaggerated agony. What Sybil could not be certain about, and the technical reason that she was consulted by the woman's family physician, was that the pain extended all the way up her thigh, even though the thigh did not participate in the phlebitic swelling and tenderness. The neurological exam was unhelpful because the woman was in so much pain that she could not cooperate. Repeated sensory testings gave differing results; nothing was definite. Sybil longed for a straight forward, simple ruptured disc patient that she could operate upon and cure and be looked upon as the heroine. She sighed and wrote her note.

Sybil told the referring physician that she would have to return the following day and reexamine Mrs. Thollier. She did not feel that neurosurgical imaging tests were indicated that night, and agreed with the ongoing anticoagulation treatment. At any rate, an operation was out of the question at the moment because of the danger of subjecting to surgery a patient who could not clot her blood and who had the imminent danger of sloughing off a blood clot from her leg to her lungs.

It was late afternoon the next day before Sybil was back on Mrs. Thollier's ward. She picked up the woman's chart and headed directly to her two-bed room. Mrs. Thollier's roommate, a massively obese, Henna-dyed hair septuagenarian lay whimpering in her bed. Mrs. Thollier's bed was empty.

"What happened, Mrs. Poletti?" Sybil asked, worried at the old woman's obvious distress.

"Died," she snuffled. "Whole night long. They was in here hurtin' her chest, putting things in her. I could tell they wasn't goin' to do no good. She was blue when they got here. I rang the bell half a dozen times. Took their sweet time gettin' in here, too."

Sybil made an acute about face and walked swiftly to the nurses' desk. "What happened in 302?" she asked.

"You mean the thrombophlebitis?" the weary LPN asked by way of response. Sybil nodded.

"She threw an embolus. Everybody got there right away, but there wasn't a thing they could do. Happened right at the end of shift, maybe two hours ago. Took 'till half an hour ago to clean up, big mess...everybody had to stay overtime."

She went back to her task based charting.

Sybil was sorry for the patient and for her doctors. She thanked her lucky stars that she had not tried to operate on the patient, or the pulmonary embolism and the death would have happened on her watch. She forgot about Mrs. Thollier.

On the weekend, Sybil indulged herself in a rare luxury and slept in. Her husband, Charles Daniels, leaned on his elbow and looked down at his wife's serene face. She felt his eyes on her and partially waked up, prepared to be a shrew.

"What?" she asked when she saw his impish smile. "What's so funny in the middle of the night?"

"First of all, it's nine o'clock on a Saturday," he grinned at his witty allusion to the song from the last century that was still popular. "And second of all, in case you hadn't remembered, I did. Happy birthday!"

Sybil looked puzzled, like she was forcing her sleep drugged mind to do arithmetic.

"That's right," she said sheepishly. "I entirely forgot. I knew there must have been some reason for me to sleep in. Now leave me alone. I don't have to be at the hospital until noon, and I don't plan to waste a minute of the time between now and then being awake."

She made as if to turn on her side.

"You'll miss your great present, then," Charles said enticingly.

He knew she would not be able to resist his blandishments. For all her acquisitions, feminism, professional objectivism, and protestations that she was beyond all that, Sybil Norcroft, M.D., PhD, F.A.C.S. loved surprises and presents.

"Tell me, then I can get back to sleep," she ordered in her drill sergeant's voice, the one she used when she was trying to get something from the lab or a floor nurse when they were too busy.

"Nope," Charles whispered in her ear, "this is a sight thing. You have to come with me."

"Where to?" Sybil asked.

She had one eye open now.

"You have to come with me, or you can't see it and can't know how great it is," Charles wheedled.

He laughed when he saw the struggle going on in her mind as mirrored in her expressive face.

She opened both eyes now and worked up a scowl.

"Might as well, can't get any rest anyway."

An affectionate smile broke through her attempted glower.

"Put on old stuff, cowboy shirt, Levis, and kickers. Let's get a move on!"

Sybil hated natural early risers. Although she got up early every morning, it was drudgery for her.

She felt like one of her old drunk patients whom she remembered saying, "Can't see how anybody anyplace can get up before ten. Myself, I don't stop throwin' up until noon."

They drove out into the country, about five miles out of town on the farm road system. Sybil had forgotten how much she liked doing this, being free of the office and the hospital, being with her husband, just feeling happy. She was afraid it would weaken her.

They pulled into a rutted dirt roadway that led down a tree-lined drive towards a decrepit old Dutch Colonial house that had once been quite lovely, Sybil imagined. On either side of the drive were fallow fields with remnants of fences. There were no animals, old machinery, or sounds that hinted of the life that must once have thrived there. Charles wheeled around a circular driveway in front of the house. The drive had been neglected for so long that weeds were growing in its center. A mildewed fountain statue of a nymph stood as a forlorn sentinel in front of the house. Sybil raised a quizzical eyebrow at her husband.

A broad grin spread across his face involving his lips, teeth, cheeks, and eyes. Sybil remembered that she loved Charles' face. It was middle-aged and etched with smile lines, hinting of laughter and jokes just beneath the surface. She knew that she had been neglecting that face, and had a twinge of repentance.

"Well, do you like it?" he asked.

He beamed.

"Like what?" she asked dully.

Was the man telling her that he had bought her this decaying old barn of a house?

"This." Charles swept his hand in an expansive 360 degree arc.

Sybil took the time to survey 'this'. At first she saw the weeds and decaying boards, the dead limbs of the trees, and the cratered road. Then, giving in to his enthusiasm, she let herself see the road as a straight beige ribbon, neat and smooth passing under a canopy of arching green trees, the house gleaming white with a blue grey roof and shutters.

"Tell me about it, Charles. What is this? What am I supposed to think about all this?"

He grew serious for a moment.

"Sybil, I feel like I've lost you. I used to be jealous of medicine and all it entailed, but it never worried me. Since that SOB lawyer launched that suit, you have moved away from me, somewhere inside of you where I am not allowed to follow. I want you back. Someday you'll beat that conniving little rat, and your career will get back to its proper perspective. I don't want to wait that long. I want you now, or as near to now as possible. This present, given with the greatest of thought and my true love, is for the healing of your soul. You'll never go to a shrink about your depression and your agitated response to it. So how about a consuming project, a hobby, if you will? This was once a fine horse ranch. It can be again. It's yours to build. I'll just kibitz from the sidelines."

Sybil could see the mended fences, gleaming white in the noonday sun, the rye grass fields nourishing thoroughbreds. She suspended her doubting pragmatic nature and let herself feel it.

"It is wonderful, Charles, I...I don't know how to thank you. I cannot imagine how I will be able to do any of it, but it is good therapy just to contemplate it."

"I know a way," Charles ventured, the merriment back in his voice and on his face.

"Way to do what?" she asked, being purposefully slow-witted.

He ignored her bit of theatrical obtuseness.

"The way to thank me," he said.

She turned coquettish.

"The usual old way?" she queried with a mischievous smile of her own.

"Um-hmm," he hummed and laughed richly. "It's only ten. We can make it if we really try before I lose you to your patients for the rest of the day."

They jumped in the car, Charles drove, risking a speeding ticket at every speed trap along the county road system. The two of them raced each other up the stairs of their Georgian house, leaving a trail of odds and ends of clothing that any Boy Scout could follow.

It was the best day Sybil had had since Bel Geddes had sent her the intent to sue letter three years ago. She threw herself into the job of planning a grandiose horse farm and began to heal. She began to have more 'best days' with Charles. A month later, she took her husband to the ranch with a set of landscape architectural plans in hand, and they sat on the decrepit verandah of the old house until the sun set, dappling its light through the trees along the approach road. Life began to look good to Sybil again.

The following morning, Carter Tarkington received a 'Dear Colleague' letter and Sybil received a ninety-day intent to file suit letter from their mutual nemesis, Paul Bel Geddes, alleging severe negligence in the care of Renee Thollier.

Dear Colleague in the Opposition:

It is with deep regret that I inform you that yet another unfortunate who suffered "care" at the hands of neurosurgeon, Sybil Norcroft, has found her way to my office seeking rightful redress. Specifically, the family of one Renee Thollier, deceased, has come to me to begin an entirely meritorious action against your client. Dr. Norcroft neglected Ms Thollier to death, a death that was foreseeable and entirely preventable. I ask you, Carter, when will the members of the medical profession begin to police themselves? Until then, it will be up to attorneys such as you and me.

At any rate, I have sent a ninety-day letter to the nefarious doctor. I expect you will be receiving a telephone call from her or from DIPC any moment. Perhaps, in the interest of collegiality, we can have an early settlement conference between the two of us and save everyone a great deal of trouble. It is a simple *res ipsa loquitur* case, a fact that I am sure will be evident to you as soon as you review the record.

I await your call. Until then,

I remain, your fellow advocate,

Paul Bel Geddes, Esq.

Dear Dr. Norcroft:

Please be informed that my clients, Alphonse and Sophronia Thollier, aunt and uncle of Renee Thollier, deceased, intend to commence a legal action from wrongful death against you related to your care, or more specifically, your neglect of Ms. Thollier while she was under your responsibility.

In short, Dr. Norcroft, in ninety days you will be sued for egregious failure to provide a proper diagnosis or appropriate or timely care for this woman who depended on you. You would be well advised to inform your insurance company and your attorney of this official intent to sue letter.

Sincerely yours,

Paul Bel Geddes, Esq.

Attorney at Law

Sybil called Carter Tarkington while she still held the ninety-day letter in her hand.

The smug joviality of Bel Geddes's facial expression started up Sybil's poorly damped down hostilities, even before he asked his first question in the court-room cross examination in the McNeely case.

"Dr. Norcroft, how large was your surgical fee for the treatment of Brendan McNeely?"

She consulted her notes.

"Including pre and post-operative care, my office billed a total of $22,000."

"Is that with a professional discount?"

"Yes. Ten percent."

"And how long did you spend in the care of this young man all told—office time, in hospital care, and the operation?"

Sybil flipped through the computer printouts from her office. Tarkington had warned her to expect detailed questions about her fees.

"Twenty-one hours and thirty minutes."

"Or about a thousand dollars an hour. Isn't that about right?"

"Approximately."

"Not bad pay. Lucky for you the fee wasn't based on outcome," Bel Geddes added malevolently.

"Objection!" called out Carter Tarkington.

Bel Geddes had paused in his delivery of questions, knowing that the objection would be automatic.

"Sustained," said Judge Kendricks, looking down from her raised bench.

"Withdrawn," said Bel Geddes perfunctorily, but he gave the jury a slow meaningful look. "I understand that you are a pretty hardworker, Dr. Norcroft. Would that be a fair statement?"

"Yes, depending on your definitions."

"Let's flesh in the definition with a few details, since you brought it up, Doctor. You testified here that you are on committees of the Congress of Neurological Surgeons, the American Association of Neurosurgeons, the Woman's Caucus of Neurosurgery, and the AMA Working Committee for Change for Women in Medicine. I presume that each of these organizations require some of your time?"

"Yes."

"You see roughly 100 patients in a three-day office week?"

"I think that's about right."

"And operate three days a week?"

"Yes, on average."

"That occupies some eight to ten hours on each of those operating days?"

"About that."

"And see consultations in the hospital every day?"

"Just about."

"And take call three nights a week?"

"Yes."

"And give lectures all around the country for the Professional Women's Feminist League and the Group for Rational Change in the Feminist Approach at least twice a month?"

"Yes."

"Let me see, Dr. Norcroft, did I read somewhere that you have a husband?"

"Yes."

"So I guess you have to tear yourself away from your important activities and throw him a crumb now and again?"

"I have a family life, yes, Sir."

"Oh, do you have children, Dr. Norcroft?"

"No."

"I should think not," Bel Geddes said with a cruel twist to his smile.

"Objection. Uncalled for."

"I agree. Sustained."

"Withdrawn. So you make a lot of money practicing a lot of medicine, make yourself important in professional committees, and make yourself famous on the feminist lecture circuit. Do you make yourself pretty tired with all of that making, Dr. Norcroft?"

"Like everyone else."

"Hardly. It makes me tired just hearing the description of your schedule."

Sybil waited and watched Bel Geddes's face, unwilling to look away and give him the satisfaction of scoring even a little point.

"Objection. Counsel is editorializing. I don't recall hearing a question."

"Sustained. Let's get on with it, Counselor."

"You were called into the hospital to see three consults after nine o'clock on the evening before you operated on Brendan McNeely. That was after a twelve-hour long operating day. Somehow, you were able to make two runs to your office to see patients that your office girls wedged in. Tell me, Dr. Norcroft, how tired were you when you started that operation on Brendan McNeely?"

Finally, the punch line.

"No more than usual. I work hard most of the time. I am acclimated to it."

"No foggy mind from lack of sleep, no shaky hand from overtiredness, no diverted attention from all of those things you do to make money, to develop your standing in the organized neurosurgical community, to make your name into a household word by your public persona as a feminist?"

"No."

Sybil turned to the jury to give an answer. On their expressionless faces she read doubt and incredulity. She knew she was just being paranoid. She hoped so, anyway.

"Let's turn to another area," Bel Geddes announced before Sybil could come back from the previous series of questions fully.

She was off-balance and knew that was exactly Bel Geddes's plan. She fought to regain her internal gyroscope.

"Dr. Norcroft, is it true that you have a nameplate on your desk that reads, 'GOD'?"

"Yes. My office staff gave it to me as a little joke."

"Um-hmm. What was it about you that made that an appropriate little joke?"

"I can be something of a hard taskmistress at times, I suppose."

"And a little inclined to arrogance?" he asked it so innocently.

"Well, I suppose all professional people are perceived that way at times."

"I see. Could it be some of that arrogance that prevented you from using ENT specialists to open the surgical field in transsphenoidal cases or even to be included as assistants? I understand that is a common practice, perhaps so common as to be considered the rule."

"I do not need an M.D. assistant."

Sybil could have kicked herself for her answer. She sought wildly for a cushioning parenthetical addition.

"Thank you."

"I have found the nurses to be excellent and very experienced assistants, and it is far less expensive for the patient to use them."

"We are well aware of your magnanimity for the patients—a thousand dollars a minute wasn't it?" the plaintiffs' attorney asked sarcastically, taking full advantage of her discomfiture.

"It would have been worse if an M.D. had been the assistant," Sybil responded lamely.

She should have said "more costly." She would have to watch herself.

"You had a great deal of difficulty during the operation, did you not?"

"Yes."

"You needed an ENT specialist's help, did you not?"

"I wanted a neurosurgeon. I finally had Dr. Hankin from ENT come in and assist."

"Too proud to ask for what the patient needed, too proud to admit that you were in that kind and level of trouble, isn't that so, Dr. Norcroft?"

His face was a mask of hate. It was personal, and his expression exceeded even the bounds of his overtly hostile questions.

"Not at all. I asked for the most competent help I could get as early in the problem as my judgment indicated the need."

"A need that would not have arisen had you had a physician as an assistant on a routine basis. Is that not the sum and substance of that operative disaster and the cause of this unfortunate boy's death? Your huge ego got in the way of good judgment, and this boy paid the ultimate price?"

The courtroom had grown quiet as the spectators looked on fascinated at the deadly verbal joust. Now there was silence. Sybil's worst personal fears lay in that question. Had she failed Brendan? For the wrong reasons?

"An assistant would have made no difference. There was an anomalous artery in the dura. It would have been cut, no matter who did the operation and no matter who might have been helping. The only way Brendan could have been saved was to have the magic viewpoint of being able to see into the future and to have canceled the operation before it was started. I am only a mortal, and not a clairvoyant one at that. I do not possess such vision."

"Not God?"

"Certainly not."

Court adjourned for the noon break. Tarkington made sure that they sat alone in an obscure cafe a few blocks from the row of restaurants frequented by court people.

"You are doing fine. All of this is old hat. We have laid the groundwork of defense against all of his attacks. Don't worry. The jury is not being sucked into his innuendoes, and his evidence is weak. Hang in there."

"Have you noticed that this has turned into a kind of personal crusade on Bel Geddes's part? He seems to be insulting and attacking for no other purpose than to express his dislike for me. It's almost scary. I'm glad all the trappings of the courtroom are there to buffer against his personal animosity," Sybil observed, still smarting from her morning on the witness stand.

"Don't let him wear you down. It's just tactics. Once this is over, he will be his usual jolly and affable self, a complete phony."

The afternoon continued in the same caustic vein. Sybil's intentions were all twisted towards Bel Geddes's cynical spin on them—the inconclusive lab data, the hackneyed rehash of the arteriogram issue, the suggestion that she was too tired, too preoccupied with her own career, and too arrogant to give Brendan a fair and full and careful effort during the operation.

They adjourned at six o'clock that evening because the judge was becoming concerned at the duration of the trial. She wanted to convey a message to the opposing attorneys to move along more briskly or face long days in court, a specter that was not part of lawyers' congenital makeup.

Sybil's old ennui had returned when she finally dropped into bed that night. She was unable to see any brightness on the horizon. Charles was disturbed by the change in his wife wrought by her day in court facing the weasly creep of an attorney. She seemed to have lost the spark that had been lit by her enthusiasm for the horse ranch, El Caballo Suave Ranchero, he had given her almost three years ago. Charles fretted as his wife slept fitfully.

The first question in the courtroom the following morning was fired on the dot of nine o'clock.

"Did you declare Brendan McNeely dead prematurely so you could get the evidence of your spectacular failure out of public scrutiny, Dr. Norcroft?"

"No, Sir. I most certainly did not."

She was indignant, her face in high color. She glared at Bel Geddes.

"The head nurse of the Neurosurgical Intensive Care Unit, a very highly trained and experienced professional, says you did. How do you respond to her accusation?"

"Heather Larkin disliked me then, and for some reason that is unclear to me, now hates me and treats me as a personal enemy. That clouded her judgment and resulted in her efforts over the years to discredit me. This case is only one example. The examination I performed, along with Dr. Blackman Schwartz, was standard, thorough, and complete in every regard. I might add that Dr. Schwartz was the neurosurgeon selected by Mr. McNeely's family to monitor my treatment of their son. Brendan McNeely was dead, brain dead, which is the same thing. Heather Larkin was just upset about losing a nice young man who worked with her, and she could not handle it. She sought someone to blame and fixated on me."

"Why did you try to cover up your mistake, to bury the evidence, as it were, by asking the Medical Examiner's office to refrain from doing their routine autopsy? You recall that Douglas Stringham, the ME Aide testified as much in this very courtroom, do you not, Doctor?"

Sybil's hackles were up, and her teeth were bared.

"Oh, you bet I do remember that testimony. It was a fabric of lies from beginning to end. Angie Church, the floor nurse, witnessed the entire conversation and confirmed that it was a pack of lies. I asked...I begged for an autopsy. It was in the interest of good medicine, and it was in my own best interests to demonstrate what had happened. I am sure that we would have found an anomalous artery that could not have been avoided and would have exonerated me had we done a post on him. When I hung up the phone, I was of the understanding that an autopsy was going to be done. I was disturbed to learn later when it was too late that one had not been done. Even at this moment, I would be willing to let my fate in this case depend on an autopsy done on his body. He could be exhumed and examined, if the court wanted to pursue this question that far."

"You will have to admit, though, Doctor, that it all worked out pretty conveniently. The evidence got buried...."

"Objection! Objection!"

For the first time in the trial, Tarkington was on his feet.

"Sustained. The jury will disregard and the statement by the plaintiff's attorney will be stricken. I don't want to have any more of this, understood, gentlemen? Keep it civil and within the etiquette of the courtroom or face contempt charges. Any clarification required?"

The judge's nerves were becoming as frayed as everyone else's.

The opposing attorneys each replied, "No, Ma'am."

"Proceed," Judge Hendricks directed.

"The plaintiff has no further questions for this witness, your honor."

Tarkington stood and announced, "The defense rests."

Carter Tarkington requested, for the sake of continuity, and in the spirit of the contest, that he be assigned to handle Dr. Norcroft's second malpractice action, the Renee Thollier case, as well as the first. DIPC was entirely amenable; they liked ongoing physician-client relationships. They knew that malpractice suits were part and parcel of the modern practice of medicine, and physicians performed better in the legal arena when they were represented by someone with whom they had established a bond of trust, at least as much of a bond as was possible between physicians and attorneys, as precarious a union as that between lamb and wolf. Sybil agreed readily since the pretrial phase of the McNeely case seemed to be progressing as well as could be expected, and she had no reason to complain about Tarkington's work thus far. She had studiously avoided knowing attorneys as a matter of principle; consequently, she had no particular reason to consider another choice.

They met over lunch in the Walter Raleigh Hotel, and Carter gave Sybil two reassurances.

"Dr. Norcroft, I know this is a huge hassle, being sued. But believe me, it comes as part of the turf. Neurosurgeons get sued all of the time—more than any other specialty. I am here to take the heat as much as possible. Don't take this too personally. Try to think of it as part of business, distasteful, but necessary."

"Easy for you to say," she countered. "It's nothing personal to you lawyers, just business. Where would you be if there were no disputes or suits? I think Paul Bel Geddes views it as a game, and gets his kicks out of making doctors squirm and worry. I remember Aristotle's quote: 'Little boys throw rocks at frogs in jest, but frogs die in earnest.' It is not quite as easy for me as it is for you given the difference in our perspectives."

Tarkington reached for the ketchup for his French fries.

"Great invention," he mused. "Best thing ever happened to food." He laughed. "Permit me to give you a couple of practical reassurances."

"I'd like that," she said and put down her Rueben sandwich to give him her whole attention. "It would be refreshing to think that there was anything reassuring about being sued by this Renee Thollier with whom I scarcely had any interaction, and against whom I did no wrong."

"The first thing is that I really think this thing will go away by itself. Paul is just being Paul, just testing the waters to see if he can get a fish to bite. My bet is that he won't think it's worth the cost to pursue you once he is certain that the company is not going to throw him a few thousand just to keep him off their backs. Be patient."

"And the second reassurance?"

"The McNeely case won't come to trial in anything less than two years. You have given your deposition. There is nothing more for you to do until the time of trial. A lot of water can pass under the bridge between now and then. Who knows what will happen? My advice, and I know that I am becoming repetitious, is for you to relax. I have broad shoulders, let me carry it until trial, then, you can reengage. How about it?"

"I'll do my best. I'll tell you, though, this second malpractice suit makes me mad. I look like some sort of quack. My reputation is going to suffer; the fact that I have done nothing improper is a matter of indifference to my critics and to the community. No one will bother to look at facts. If there's smoke, there must be fire will be the prevailing sentiment, I reckon."

The conversation spoiled her appetite, Tarkington's reassurances notwithstanding.

Despite their considerable assets, Sybil Norcroft and her husband, Charles Daniels, delayed the major building on the ranch until she could find people who would do the construction for something less than a fortune. After more than a year, she had not been able to do so. Often, in the evening, she sat on the dilapidated porch steps and looked longingly in the direction of neighboring vegetable farms and fruit orchards with their gangs of immigrant planters and pickers toiling away in the neat rows that bespoke long and careful cultivation. The fences and buildings on those farms were well maintained, even attractive, and the farmers who owned the properties were hard pragmatists, good agribusiness people. Sybil knew they could compete in a fine margin industry, and they were nothing of gentry farmers like her. All she wanted was not to squander away the family fortune on her hobby. Her husband had given her a loving gift and had attached no strings. But Sybil felt a dogged determination that she could not let his gift become a drain on them.

As she enjoyed the glow of the late afternoon sun and the peacefulness of her musing, she saw, in the distance, a small group of people—men, women, and children—clamber over the fences that separated her place from the adjoining huge peach and pear orchards. At that distance, they all appeared about half an inch tall. She was curious, not enough to rouse herself to get up, but interested.

When the troupe became an inch high, Sybil turned to watch their progress. They were heading directly towards her, evidently working their way across her ragged pastures in the direction of her road. When they were two inches high, by squinting, she could tell that they were Hispanics, presumably Mexicans. Their clothing had that look. The three men wore gaudily colored and patterned serapes that stood out in the last rays of the dying sun. The three women were clothed in long pastel dresses that rippled and flowed in the changeable light breezes of the afternoon and swayed with the movements of their supple hips. Five or six scampering children ran alongside and around their elders, evoking an occasional gesticulation from one or another of the adults.

By the time the Mexicans were six inches high, Sybil could see the deep bronze of their skin, the good, albeit rough, quality of their clothing, and the wide brimmed straw sombreros that spoke of their relative prosperity and of their origins. She could also hear the shrill noises made by the children, and in the background, what sounded like the crying of one or more of the women.

She was right. When the small band of Mexicans, obviously three small families, drew abreast of her position on the porch, it was evident that the women were crying. When they saw her, the three women turned their faces and wiped away tears, pretending that they were merely removing the accumulation of perspiration from their stroll.

"*Buenas tardes, Señora,*" called out the eldest of the three men.

"*Buenas tardes, amigos,*" Sybil replied, demonstrating the full extent of her Spanish. "Do you speak English?"

The families stopped, glad for a respite from the sun. Sybil got up and walked towards them, and they all backed into the shade of the tall oak that stood majestically in Sybil's side yard.

"*Asi, asi...*some," said the spokesman.

"You look thirsty and tired. Would you like to rest? I have some Cokes."

For some reason, Sybil had brought a large cooler of soft drinks out. They kept cool for days in the efficient cooler.

"No, *gracias*," said the spokesman, acting shy. "We are fine. Thank you for your kindness."

"Please. I have plenty. You don't need to feel shy. It looks like we're neighbors."

The Mexicans looked at Sybil with curiosity to see if she was sincere or taunting. Deciding that it was the former, they looked questioningly at each other.

"*Tal vez*, we share a bottle, if that would not be too much," the woman with the self-appointed spokesman said. "Thank you, lady."

Sybil passed out sugary Coca Colas to each of the adults and seeing their ill-concealed delight and the yearning in the faces of the children, she said," Would it be all right for the little ones to have a can or two to share. I don't have any cups or anything."

"Yes, *mil gracias, Doña*," said the mother of four of the smallest children.

She was obviously unused to generous treatment, and was curious more than anything to see what this was about.

The adults sat together on the unsafe and creaking porch drinking their sodas as the sun sank behind the horizon. Sybil could detect a tension developing among the Mexicans. They held short conversations in Spanish. She knew that the men were urging the women that it was time to go. The women looked profoundly dispirited, and when they looked back in the direction of the adjacent ranch or spoke with head nods in that direction, the men appeared angry and agitated.

They began to get up.

"We must go, now. Thank you for your kindness, lady. We have not seen much of that today," the spokesman announced.

"Pardon me, but I do not know your names. Mine is Sybil. Sybil Norcroft."

She enunciated and emphasized the unfamiliar sounds to the Mexicans.

"*Perdón, Doña*, I am Pancho Rodriquez, and this is my wife Carlita. These are my friends Jose and Maria Innocenta Pomposo-Alvarez, and Marcos and Viviana Hernandez."

Each of the men and women gave a small bow as his or her name was introduced.

Sybil studied their faces for a moment, then repeated the names: "Pancho and Carlita Rodriquez, Jose and Maria Innocenta Pomposo-Juarez, and Marcos and Viviana Hernandez."

They looked pleased and impressed.

"Escuse me, *Doña*, I am Maria Innocenta Pomposo-*Alvarez*."

She looked down shyly, embarrassed at having the temerity to correct the *Doña*.

Her brown face was laid open for a rebuke. Sybil was sure the young woman had heard many such in her short life.

"Thank you. I think I have your names now. Please forgive me, *amigos*, but I could not help but see that you looked sad, maybe angry when you arrived. It is not my business, but is there anything I could do to help?" Sybil asked.

Now it was her turn to look down with shyness. She was afraid that she had overstepped and was intruding.

The Mexicans looked hurriedly at one another. They were reluctant to comment, but the women were expressing their needs. The word *niños* came up repeatedly. After a minute-long pause, Pancho Rodriquez shrugged his shoulders, and Carlita timidly spoke, evidently expressing the thoughts and wishes of the group.

"*Perdón Doña,* we are sorry to say it, *pero* we have no place to stay this night. We have no money."

"Could you stay here? This house is old and in bad condition, but it is cover."

"That would be most kind, *Doña,* for the one night. *Gracias.*"

"I am afraid that the little ones will get cold. I have blankets at my own house. Would one of you come with me? We can get some... Please, it's all right," Sybil said.

Carlita walked back to talk to the rest of the Mexicans who had now distanced themselves a dozen feet from Sybil.

There was a brief discussion. Carlita returned and said, "*Si, y muchas gracias por todo*"

In her nervousness she forgot to use English.

"Will you come with me?"

"I will," Carlita said.

They drove out along the approach drive and onto the county highway. The closeness of the two women opened a floodgate of emotion in the stoical Mexicana. She began to cry softly.

"What's wrong, Carlita? Have I done something to offend you?" asked Sybil.

"No, no, *Doña, nunca.* I am embarrass. We are like beggars, like gypsies. We are not like that. All of us are hardworkers. It is not our fault. We work for what we have. We are embarrass because now we cannot. It is a bad thing to have to depend on the kindness of strangers. Can you understand?"

"Of course, please...tell me about it."

"The *patrón, Señor* Mac Donal, he did not pay us. We work for two *meses,* all of us work. He laugh at us, say we lazy, and he no pay us. That is not the *veras, Doña,* we are hardworkers. Not like the *Norteamericanos.*"

Sybil hoped that she was regarded as the exception.

"Now, we have to go. Find another place to work. I worry. The *niños.*"

"He can't just not pay you, Carlita. There are laws."

"Not for us. He say he send for the *migros,* the immigrations. You *entiendes?*"

Sybil was not sure of the word, but the meaning was clear. She understood. These people had been cheated, treated like slaves, threatened and turned out. It made her furious. Carlita filled Sybil in on the details as they drove. Sybil collected bedding and stopped by a fried chicken fast food restaurant and bought enough food for two meals for the families.

"What if I go to McDonald and talk to him about getting you your money?" she asked Carlita.

"Don't do that, *Doña, por favor.* We do not have green cards. We will have to go back. It is very hard for us there. And the immigrations will put us in jail. There is a new law now for ten years. They don' just send us back. We will be separate from the *niños. Por favor.*"

Sybil recognized the realities. The mood in the country was to turn the illegals in to the law and to prosecute them. Relations with Mexico had deteriorated to the level of diplomatic formality over the question. Since the death of NAFTA during the Preston administration that had seen the reversal of almost all of the socialistic and liberal policies of the Clinton and the Gore administrations, the Mexicans had publicly and loudly proclaimed that the *Norteamericanos* had betrayed them once again. The borders were much more effectively sealed, and the steam escape valve that the border had once provided the pressure cooker of poverty and corruption to the south was no longer efficacious. Things were indeed very hard down there. Sybil was sympathetic and assured Carlita that she would not interfere. The two women drove the rest of the way back to Sybil's ranch in silence. Sybil was germinating a thought.

After the food was distributed and the blankets laid for the meager night's rest they would afford, Sybil approached Carlita and Pancho with her idea.

"I have a business proposition to make to you, to all of you."

The couple put down their food so as to avoid the discourtesy of talking with food in their mouths.

"*Si?*" asked Pancho. "We are listening, please."

"My ranch is falling apart, and not much work has been done on it for many years as you can see."

They nodded.

"I thought you could come and work with me, work for me, and we could build a good place together. I will pay you honest pay for honest work. I will not cheat you or report you. I ask you only to work well for me. What do you think?" she asked them in a business voice.

She was not offering charity, and wanted that to be clear. It was the dignity of work and business.

They were taken aback. It was too much good fortune in one day for them not to be suspicious. They were used to being cheated by the farmers and ranchers who employed them, and had to wonder whether this time would be any different.

"We must talk about this," responded Pancho.

There followed a lengthy conversation, sometimes with raised voices and shaking heads.

"We will start out with honesty, *Doña*. We have no place else to go. It would hurt us bad for you to cheat us. We ask that you think of us as people, like yourself. Please do well by us, and we will work most hardly for you. We agree to work. Please not to let immigrations know," Pancho said.

He was a man of dignity, and it pained him deeply to seem to be begging.

"I give you my promise, Pancho. I will come back tomorrow, and you can help me with what we need to do to get started. The first thing I can see is the need to get you all into decent places to stay."

The arrangement worked nearly perfectly. The Mexicans were grateful and demonstrated their appreciation by working as only Hispanics and Chinese can do. The first weeks were spent in building simple cottages for the workers. The Mexicans marveled that they were being paid to build their own habitations. And Sybil was as good as her word. She paid each adult a regular biweekly wage in cash. In a few months, painted white fences grew, the old house was torn down, and the approach road became smooth. Sybil began to feel that she was getting the best of the bargain.

Carter Tarkington was accurate in his prediction. Paul Bel Geddes made an offer to settle the Thollier case for $40,000, about his costs to date. When Tarkington sent a terse negative reply, Bel Geddes wrote:

Dear Carter,
   You win. I lose. Send the dismissal and waiver papers for the Thollier case. I'll get you next time; the McNeely case is mine!
As always,
PBG

Sybil was at once pleased at the result and annoyed at the effrontery of the trial attorney. It was apparent that it was all a game to him, something about winning and losing. Sybil took it personally; the latest installment merely increased her growing odium for the man.

Two years later, as the McNeely trial loomed with reality on the horizon, the patience of the judge for Bel Geddes's continuations nearly exhausted, Sybil began to study the case from every aspect with the zeal of a missionary. The approaching trial made her nervous and irritable. Her husband, Charles, and El Caballo Suave Ranchero provided the only effective solace for her. Charles was a rock, a listener, a friend. The ranch now had a row of attractive cottages, the framework of a rambler house, and her two Tennessee Walking Horses, the first breeding stock.

The day of the trial itself was a melancholy one, a rift in the fabric of Sybil's life that had otherwise become so harmonious and satisfying. She dreaded the trial, but most of all, she had to steel herself for that eventual day when the findings of the jury would either absolve her or condemn her.

Judge Kendricks let the jury go early after Tarkington rested the defense case and the two attorneys had presented their summations. Kendricks wanted them to be morning fresh to be able to concentrate on his delivery. She took her instructions very seriously and expected everyone else to do so.

Her parting words to the attorneys were, "Meet me in chambers in an hour. We will hammer out the jury instructions if it takes all night. I want to give them the instructions bright and early tomorrow and have them in deliberation no later than ten."

For all the work that had gone into the instructions, they seemed obvious, simple, and concrete to Sybil. She was not sure what all of the fuss had been about. Her main, in fact, her only concern, was getting the jury out to their deliberations and their returning with a verdict.

When she finished, Judge Kendricks thanked the jury for their efforts, for doing their collective duty thus far, and sent them to the jury room. Sybil had never been a religious person. It was hard for neurosurgeons to believe in powers greater than themselves both from the standpoint of arrogating good results to their own efforts and of consigning their bad results to the agency of outside malign forces, and to their near universal faith in learnable science. At the moment the jury left to deliberate, however, Sybil Norcroft knew why the old expression, 'There are no atheists in foxholes,' had such enduring currency. She gave an awkward little prayer for herself, unsure whether to address Father or Mother in Heaven.

CHAPTER FIVE

Pancho had become the *de facto* foreman of Sybil's ranch, in part because he was the eldest and most experienced of the *Mexicanos*, and in part because he was a natural with horses. He had spent a lifetime caring for horses. The place of his birth and youth was that segment of northern Mexico and southern Texas, Arizona, New Mexico, and California that should be its own country by virtue of shared language, customs, and interests. The land and the people were dry and hard, spoke Spanish at least as commonly as English, on both sides of the arbitrary border the people worship Catholic Mary and an assortment of integrated aboriginal nonChristian saints, and abide by a code of laws more similar to that in the western United States during the century from 1810 to 1910 than to the present one. The code was a harsh cowboy era one—might prevails, the weak obey, no one sends for the law or entertains other esoteric notions of justice than primal self-defense. If you want to keep it, defend it. Families come first in that forbidding land, then trusted friends, then the church, then the community at large—the latter two groups representing a weak and attenuated interest. In Pancho's and in the other Mexican families' minds, Sybil Norcroft was more than the employer, the *Patrona*; she was a real friend—almost family.

Sybil drove out to the ranch to wait for the jury's verdict. She carried her Blackberry in her suit coat pocket, dreading, but hoping to hear its tinny ring. It gave her a measure of tranquility to see the new fences, the neat roadway, and burgeoning little community of ranch out-buildings, and the stud and mare that had cost her so dearly.

Pancho came out to greet his *Patrona*. "*Buenas*," he said. "I see that you are troubled, *Doña*. Is this the day of the jury?"

"*Sí*, Pancho. I am worried. This is very important to me. It would hurt me a lot to lose in the court today," Sybil said as she allowed Pancho to assist her from the car.

He was the only man she ever permitted to show her chivalrous courtesies, but with the stolid *Mexicano*, it seemed to fit. They had fallen into a communication habit of dropping a few words of Spanish and Spanglish into their majority English conversations.

"Would you like to talk about it, *Doña*?"

Pancho had a gentle way, and Sybil had found in him a natural wisdom and a placidity that were a comfort. But she preferred to be alone with her concerns that day.

"No, *gracias*. I would like to sit and think. I'll just watch you and the others work."

In the distance, she could see the other two men moving bales of hay into the new barn.

"*Entiendo, Doña*, my Carlita will bring to you some drink. We were just having our *loncha*."

"*Gracias, me gustaria*," Sybil replied absently, pleased that her Spanish was coming along, slowly, but easily.

Pancho left his *Patrona* to her own private thoughts.

Her horses gamboled about the paddock, full of vigor and enthusiasm. Sybil envied them their uncomplicated lives. She had purchased both the Tennessee Walker stallion and the mare from the horse farms of Ocala, Florida, during the only nonmedical meeting trip she and Charles had made that previous year. These prime breeders had cost her an even one million dollars for the stud and $350,000 for the mare. If beauty alone were the criterion for cost, the price was fair. The two plantation horses showed the richness of their American Standardbred, Thoroughbred, Morgan, and American Saddle Horse blood. The stud was 16 hands high and weighed slightly under 1400 pounds, the mare 15.5 hands and 1100 pounds. Both were bays, more muscular, heavier, and stouter than the popular quarter horse, less refined than the thoroughbred.

Both horses had been gently broken to the saddle, and with their calm, even temperaments were easy to approach and a pleasure to ride. The defining characteristic of the breed, and a quality that was present in near perfection in George and Dolly, was the natural smooth and fluid gait, the running walk. The horses were now walking one behind the other seemingly for Sybil's enjoyment, swiftly—six to seven miles per hour—and effortlessly, one front foot striking the thick grass of the paddock a fraction of a second before its diagonal hind foot. The hind foot overreached the forefoot print, giving each horse a reaching, slightly straining appearance. The lines of their backs moved in a sinuous straight motion free of any to-and-fro rocking or torsion. For Sybil, the powerful equines were beauty in motion. For a few moments, she forgot about the trial and the jury.

Carlita strode silently up to where Sybil stood at the paddock fence. She laid a small platter of *empañadas* and a glass of pulpy lemonade on the broad top of a fence upright. Sybil smiled her thanks.

Carlita quietly said, "*Disfrutas del momento, Doña mía, estos tiempos son transitorios, muy transitorios.*"

Almost absently, Sybil translated for herself—'enjoy the moment, my lady, such times are fleeting, very fleeting.' That was an apt description of her life of late. A wellspring of anger towards Paul Bel Geddes, the self-appointed nemesis of Sybil Norcroft, intruded. She charged him with the limitation of the *momentos alegrías* of her life. For the first time, she recognized a base emotion in herself that she had not previously detected—hatred. She hated Paul Bel Geddes. For a brief moment, that emotion swept subconscious feelings of attack and vengeance to the usually guarded surface of her psyche. She would have considered herself immune to the ignoble impulses to do anyone bodily harm before that moment, but now, in an unprotected contemplative interval, she saw herself striking out like a muscular Amazon or lithe Valkyrie choosing who—Bel Geddes—would die and be escorted to Valhalla.

She shook off the choleric thoughts and tried to regain the dreamy tranquility that she had been enjoying as she contemplated her horses. She could not bring back the *tiempo transitorio*, and blamed Bel Geddes. Her mobile rang.

She gave a start. She knew the jury was in. The moment of truth was upon her, and she felt as if she were not up to facing it. Like a child, she wanted it to be postponed.

"Hello, this is Dr. Norcroft," she said into the thin cellular receiver.

Her voice sounded more normal than she would have imagined. She was surprised at that.

"Dr. Norcroft, this is Angie Church in the ER. We have a train wreck here."

"I'm not on call," Sybil pointed out, annoyance surfacing in her voice.

"I know. Everyone else is up to their lower lips in alligator water. It's been one of those days. We need you."

Angie never exaggerated, and it went without further explanation that she had exhausted other avenues.

"I'll be there," Sybil said.

She hoped it had not sounded like a groan.

She ran back to her car. The sudden exercise felt good. Her mind cleared away the obscuring mist that had been accumulating during her reverie of animosity against Bel Geddes. She forgot the weasel as she sped into the hospital. Along the way, she telephoned the highway patrol to let them know that she would be breaking every speed law in order to get to the emergency room. She could not help but savor a tiny one-upmanship over the cops. She could speed with impunity.

The ER looked like a war zone front line army surgical center during an attack. Sybil hurried up to a pair of patient gurneys standing in tandem in the hallway. She lifted the sheets on each of the stretchers and immediately wished that she had not. There were two dead children, both badly mangled.

"Car crash?" she asked Angie as she marched into the ER surgery suite.

"Yes. Worst MVA this year. Two kids down; mother and father in the suites with multiple injuries. A bunch of gang-bangers from the other car are in number three. First thing we need you for is the father. Decreased LOC, says he can't move his legs. You'll have to find a place in line. He's got a bad flail chest, bleeding out. Have a nice time."

Angie's attention was back on the artificial blood bag she was setting up.

Sybil wedged herself in between the general surgeon on call and the ER doc.

"Okay if I poke around?"

"Dr. Norcroft? Glad you're here. Feel free. Kind of cramped quarters. I've been as busy as the proverbial one armed paperhanger in a hurricane, so my neurological left something to be desired. Give us the word about the head and the cord. We've got to get this guy to the OR unless you say that you have to crack his head or back and that takes precedence. I think he'll die from his chest wound if that's the case," assessed the ER doc, who was nominally in charge.

The general surgeon was the one actually calling the shots in the rapidly deteriorating situation.

"He awake?" Sybil asked.

"Yeah, kind of fadey, but we can talk to him."

"What's his name?"

"Turner. Jason Turner."

"Jason!" Sybil called over the din.

"Yeah?" the patient moaned.

"I'm Dr. Norcroft, the neurosurgeon. Can you hear me? Do you under-stand me?"

"Yeah, I'm kinna foggy."

"The doctors need to work on you. Listen to me. Answer my questions, and I won't ask any more for a minute, okay?"

"Okay." Jason's voice was trailing off.

The ER team was fighting to put in a second chest tube and one set of nurses was trying to restart an antecubital IV line in collapsed veins.

"Tell me your name, your age, and what day it is!" Sybil shouted to be heard over the ambient noise and to penetrate the accumulating fog in the man's brain. His blood pressure was 50/40.

"Huh?" Jason responded.

Sybil had to prod him to get that.

"C'mon, Jason. Try," Sybil pleaded with him.

No one else paid her any mind. They continued with their work with des-perate but controlled haste, jostling the dress suit-clad neurosurgeon who was out of place among the horde of green scrub suits.

"Okay, Doc, I'll try."

He summoned up some reserve from somewhere down in his blood and oxygen-starved brain.

"Name's Jason Turmel...Turner...Turner. What was the other thing? Ah, Jeez, that hurts."

Another IV was placed in a neck vein.

"Your age, and what day it is."

"Oh, yeah. Jason Turner. Ouch! Man that's killin' me!"

The second chest tube was sewed into place. Jason tried again.

"Jason. I'm 38...no, I'm not. I'm...I think it's 39. Ouch! What else? Oh, yeah, it's Wednesday. My little girl's birthday. The 16th. How is she? How's my little girl?"

"Can't tell you right now, Jason. Hang in there. Can you feel this?"

She jabbed his left leg with a pin.

"Ouch! Jeez, I'll say," the beleaguered man yelped.

There were too many hurts coming too fast.

"This?" Sybil asked.

This time, she stuck the right leg, but less vigorously.

"Pin. Yeah, pin," he said, his voice slurring. "Jason Turner. 38."

"One last thing, Jason. Wiggle your toes and fingers."

Nothing happened.

"Jason!" Sybil snapped. "Wake up. Just one more thing."

"Yeah, Jason."

"Wiggle your toes and fingers."

He did, a few feeble movements, but enough to convince Sybil that he was getting motor messages down his cord.

She tapped the ER doc on the shoulder.

"I'll butt out. He seems okay neurologically. Hard to tell for sure. I think we're just seeing hypoxia and hypotension. He needs to get some blood up to his squash, I think. You guys go ahead. I'll help where I can and just observe him."

"Great, thanks, Dr. Norcroft. I feel a lot better," the general surgeon, Peter Midgel, said without looking in her direction. "We've got to get this poor train wreck stabilized and into the OR PDQ, or we're going to lose him."

"I'd love to have a CT or MRI, but we'll have to compromise. Do what you have to do."

No one responded. Sybil did a cut-down on Jason's ankle and put in a large line. The team was now running blood and blood substitute through four separate ports. The monitor showed the BP starting to edge upward.

Angie shouted into the ER surgical suite, "Doctor, one of the gang bangers is crashing. Nothing neuro, but could you lend a hand? I think he needs a trach!"

Sybil looked down at the smart and expensive gray silk suit she had worn to court that morning. It was spattered with blood and vomitus. It would probably have to be thrown away, she mused idly.

"Be right there. Set up the trach tray. If you think of it, it probably needs to be done," she said.

"Way ahead of you, Doc," Angie assured her.

Angie had both good judgment and courage. Sybil admired and appreciated that in her.

"You assist?" Sybil asked.

"Can't," replied Angie, moving out of the room, "got to get the other three homeys over to x-ray and to the ortho suite. Dickie Thompson's good. He'll help."

"Okay."

Sybil swiftly moved into number two, the auxiliary ER surgical room. The young patient was writhing on the table, his skin color turning blue and advancing to purple. No air was coming through. His face was smashed. His nose was flattened beyond recognition, and the nostrils were full of hard clotted blood. The boy's mouth was occluded with a blackened, grotesquely swollen tongue.

"Give me some gloves, Dickie. Quick!"

Her hands were covered with Jason Turner's blood. She had not had time to don latex gloves on the way into Jason's room. It was a serious oversight, but could not be helped now. Sybil was glad that is was the family man's blood and not that of one of the gang members. She thought her chances might be better. She, like all of her colleagues, was now, by reflex, exquisitely careful of blood. She was fastidiously careful to avoid touching needles or blood for fear of getting hepatitis C or HIV. The most recent HIV strain—number VII— was the deadliest and most rapidly fatal mutation yet. Researchers at the NIH were beginning to see disturbing small similarities to Ebola Zaire, a suggestion that they were of a common origin from somewhere in rain forest Africa.

While Sybil performed the tracheostomy on the boy gangster—he could not have been more than eleven years old—she saw that Jason had been rapidly wheeled out, presumably to the OR.

"Get an HIV and a HepC on him for me, Daniel," she called to the hurrying group.

Dr. Krempen shouted, "I will!" as he and Peter Midgel and the pulmonary technologist rushed by, pushing the gurney as fast as they could.

The gangster's respiratory tract was restored. He pinked up and waked up. He snarled at Sybil and mouthed an obscenity at her.

"And thanks to you too, young man," she muttered wearily.

She had not expected anything more.

She took off her gloves and washed her hands. She realized that she had not thought about the McNeely trial in the past three hours. She thought she should be grateful for small favors. She found a pair of wrinkled, but apparently clean scrubs and slipped into a bathroom and changed out of her bespattered and ruined clothing.

She called upstairs to the OR. Jason was still alive, but barely.

The desk nurse in the OR told her, "We got a chest cutter working on him. Farouk Ibn al-Hebreaus. How'd I do on the pronunciation?"

She had struggled with it.

"No worse than I do," Sybil said.

Once again, she had cause to thank her lucky stars that she had been spared some misery. Ibn al-Hebreaus was an unapologetic sexist and anti-Semite who could not be convinced that his repulsive attitudes towards women and Jews might have some currency in his native Egypt, but they were regarded as Neanderthalic in twenty-first century United States. She despised him for his boorish comments and blatant discrimination against the women doctors and nurses. He held her in equal disdain for the mere fact that she was a woman who was not a shy retiring homemaker. He loved to taunt her with his suggestions as to where women belonged—none of the places included anywhere a physician might work. And she and Ibn al-Hebreaus had had a memorable run-in, one that became entrenched in hospital gossip and lore in perpetuity.

"He's a good chest man. Glad he's there," Sybil said to the desk nurse, biting her tongue to keep from saying more.

"Yeah, but between you, me, and the gate post, I don't let him anywhere near me," the desk nurse confided.

Sybil knew all about his quick skillful fingers, and his charmed life at avoiding detection when he groped an unsuspecting female doctor, nurse, or ancillary person.

"Play heads up ball. See you," Sybil said. "Give me a call when you know something, okay?"

"Will do, Dr. Norcroft. I take it he doesn't have anything neurological."

"I don't think so, but I want to examine him again when he wakes up."

"If he gets off the table. I wouldn't give better than 100 to 1 odds against on that right now from what they're saying."

"Thanks, bye."

"Bye, Doc. Hey, we're all pulling for you in your malpractice case. That about done with?"

"Yes. "

"Good luck, bye."

Sybil and the desk nurse put down their receivers at the same time. It was good to know that she still had some supporters.

She called Carter Tarkington's office.

He was there.

"Any news?" she asked without preamble.

They were about as familiar with each other's telephone voices as they were with those of their respective spouses at this point.

"There is. Bailiff called over to tell us that the jury said they had one more question and were ready to wrap it up otherwise. I was about to call you. We're going to head back to the courthouse. I think you might want to come along. I don't think this is a false alarm, but you never know."

It was four-thirty. Sybil was dog-tired and filthy. She hurried into the OR dressing room shower. It was known colloquially as the Sybil Norcroft Memorial Shower. She considered that bit of community sophomoric lore to be one of her small successes, despite the rancor that lay behind it.

The first day she had entered the Operating Room at Joseph Noble Memorial Hospital, she had caused a stir, a ripple on the tranquil surface of one of the last bastions of the hospital's patriarchy. She inquired about where she should change her clothes. The orderly told her that the nurses' dressing room was the third door on the left in the first hallway.

"I am not a nurse," she had announced feistily. "I am a surgeon. Where is the doctor's dressing room?"

She remembered the young man's grin of participatory devilment. He loved feminists, they caused so much trouble.

"First door on the left, second hallway. Have a nice day."

He watched her all the way to the bend in the corridor.

Sybil steeled herself and opened the door. To her relief, there was no one in the entire dressing room and lounge area. She found a green sheet and walled off a bank of lockers near the doorway to the shower room. She laid out her scrubs and hung her street clothes in a locker. For good measure, she took a shower. As she slipped on her scrub shirt to become fully covered, Dr. Ibn al-Hebreaus pushed aside the curtaining sheet and stood before her naked and dumbfounded.

"Lady," he shouted. "This is the doctor's lounge! You have no business here. I am dressing."

"I'm Dr. Norcroft, Doctor. We haven't met."

She eyed the angry Egyptian naughtily.

He acted as if she had not spoken.

"You go to the nurses' dressing room."

It was a flat statement and an order. Ibn al-Hebreaus was used to having his orders obeyed, especially by women. This one just stood there...like she belonged. He got angry.

"Perhaps you didn't hear me, Doctor," Sybil said. "This is the doctor's dressing room. I am a doctor. Ergo, I am dressing here. Nurses dress in their place. We doctors will dress here."

He was at a loss for words. The orderly who had directed Sybil to the doctors' dressing room had slipped unobtrusively into the locker room and stood quiet as a mouse and listened.

"You had a shower? In the men's shower?!" Ibn al-Hebreaus shouted.

He was furious at her effrontery.

"Right then it was my shower," Sybil retorted with the hint of pride of ownership that netted her the reputation as a serious ball breaker and resulted in the captioning of the shower as being Sybil Norcroft's.

One piece of fallout from the confrontation was the undying enmity of Farouk Ibn al-Hebreaus for the newest neurosurgeon on the staff.

That was the past, and now, Sybil returned her mind to the problem at hand, the denouement of the McNeely trial. She did not dare to take the time to drive all the way home to get proper clothes. She wore fresh scrubs and put on a lab coat she found hanging in the doctor's lounge. Carter Tarkington and Hyrum Willis were waiting at the defense table when she hurried in. The plaintiffs and their attorney were at their table as well. It was evident without discussion that the jury had said that they were ready.

"All rise," commanded the bailiff.

Judge Kendricks swept in and took her place.

"Bring in the jury," she ordered.

Sybil strained to get a hint of their verdict, but the jurors wore expressionless faces. Sybil wished that she was half the poker player they all were. They sat in their assigned seats.

"Ladies and gentlemen of the jury, have you reached your verdict?"

"We have."

The forelady handed a sealed verdict envelope to the bailiff who took it to the judge. Judge Kendricks opened the envelope, read the verdict, and wiped her face of all expression. She looked at the jury and never glanced at either the plaintiffs' or the defense's tables.

Sybil wrung her hands. She was sure her face betrayed her soaring anxiety. Her face was wan, weary, and grey.

"Madam Foreperson, what say you in the matter of McNeely versus Norcroft?"

"In the matter of McNeely versus Norcroft, Superior Court Case Number 5/28/2009-82901—the case numbers reflecting the date of commencement of the trial—we, the jury, find in favor of…"

Sybil felt heart palpitations. She was sure the forelady was pausing.

"…the defendant, Sybil Norcroft."

Sybil sat like a statue, afraid that she would break the spell and wake up to find that she had heard wrong.

Carter moved first.

"Congratulations, Dr. Norcroft. I never doubted for a moment that you would be exonerated. Congratulations!"

Sybil roused.

"Thanks. Thanks to you, Carter…and to you Hyrum. You did a great job. I owe you a lot. I want to treat you to the best dinner they can cook at The Chez Saint Jacques."

The haute cuisine restaurant was famous in the region, apparently a copy of an exclusive club in old Saigon during and even before the Vietnam War mid last century.

"You're on. Mind if I have a hug?" Carter asked in his ebullience.

"Take two," Sybil said, and matched her words with two exuberant squeezes. She kissed Hyrum's cheek, which made him blush.

Judge Kendricks called down from her bench, "Ladies and gentlemen, if we could please restore order."

Her reference was directed largely at the throng of spectators who were leaving the courtroom, led by a cadre of media reporters. Sybil could see the television cameras and crews just outside the doors waiting to pounce when she left. She shivered. No television had been permitted in courtrooms since the O.J. Simpson murder trial in Los Angeles back in the nineties.

"Would you like to have the jury polled, counselors?" Judge Kendricks inquired once order was restored.

"Yes, your honor, the plaintiff certainly does," demanded Paul Bel Geddes.

He appeared shocked, in a state of acute discombobulation. It was obvious that he had not dreamt that the verdict could go against him. He had a deeply hurt expression on his face.

Sybil loved it. Carter winked at her and nodded in Bel Geddes's direction. They shared a warm grin.

"The defense would also like to hear a polling of the jury, your honor."

The judge queried each juror in his or her turn. The verdict was rendered 11 to 1.

Agnes Harley, a retired bookkeeper, put it for the majority, "That Canadian doctor came down here and lied. Didn't look at the right video, out and out lied about how the operation is done. Even his own radiologist said he was wrong about that aneurysm thing. He got $35,000 to lie, enough to move a saint."

The lone dissenter said, "I thought that Dr. Norcroft was an arrogant and uppity feminist, just trying to prove that she's as good as any man. She wouldn't get help, and she wasn't paying attention. That's what I thought. I don't care what the others think. I'd vote thissa way again."

She was a frumpy little woman with defiance in her gaze.

"We will appeal, your honor," Bel Geddes stated anticlimactically, his face drained of color and bravado.

"Forget it, Dr. Norcroft, it's over," said Carter. "Go home and eat raw meat."

CHAPTER SIX

Blackman Schwartz met Sybil in the hospital cafeteria a week after the verdict in the Brendan McNeely case was delivered. There had been an initial buzz around JNMH about the case, like the small town community that it was. By the time Dr. Schwartz asked if he could share the table with her, the suit and the verdict were history.

"Congrats, Sybil. I knew you would beat Barratry Paul, but I have to confess, I had a moment of pause when de Montesquiou from Quebec came down here to testify. I was surprised to learn that he had joined the world's oldest profession. You'd think it was beneath him."

"Thanks, Blackman. I had some very anxious moments during that trial. It took something out of me. As for de Montesquiou, I guess you can never overestimate the power of greed. It pains me, in retrospect, that a man of his international stature stooped to that level. I would love to be able to get the RCMP or the Canadian Tax Service to investigate his finances. I hardly think this was de Montesquiou's first time to play fast and loose with the tax laws. Wouldn't it be interesting to see a record of the number of times he has sold a neurosurgeon colleague down the malpractice river?"

"Keep on the high road, Sybil. You'll never regret it. My clinical practice is about finished, and I can give that advice from the standpoint of seeing a lot who didn't. When I saw the announcement of the verdict in the paper, it brought to mind something that the rest of the neurosurgery department has been thinking about for some time."

"And that is?"

"We have never had one of our people in the surgery chairmanship in the history of the hospital. It's about time. It's past time that we did. At the last neurosurgery division meeting, while you were unavoidably detained by Barratry Paul, we hashed the idea around, and there was unanimous agreement that we ought to push for it. We were also unanimous about pushing you, Sybil. You should be the next chief of surgery. What do you say?"

"Sounds like a French election, Blackman. I was the only one absent; so, I got elected."

"Not hardly. We looked at every neurosurgeon. You were the unanimous choice, like I said. Don't you feminist types say that 'most of the time the best man for the job is a woman'?"

Dr. Schwartz had a gentle sense of humor.

She knew that he was, for the most part, in sympathy with the gender issues that had dominated American thought for more than three score years.

"I'm not political, Blackman, you know that."

"Baloney."

"They've never had, and they will never have a woman chief. It goes against the grain of every one of those old boys in the network."

"Double baloney."

Sybil laughed.

"You're not going to let me have a gracious way out of this, are you? I'm beginning to think you're serious."

"It's good to see that you can be right about one thing, at least. The whole committee is serious, and we have done a little canvassing. I think there is a real possibility here. It would be a feather in your cap, and it would be good for the hospital. It's time to shake the place up a little. I put a little bug in Michael Strong's ear. He would love to break the stranglehold that Darryl Hankin, the nose picker, and old Tom Petler, the perennial incumbent, have on the surgical service. He has to be discreet, but he'll pull a few strings for you."

Blackman *was* serious. She was complimented, and figured that the timing was not an accident. If she had not gotten a favorable verdict, her outlook would have been a good deal less rosy. She was inclined to be coy about it, but that would just be a waste of time, something the old boys might expect that a dithering female would pull. She decided not to dither.

"I'll do it, Blackman. I have a few scores to settle, as you may know. I would love to get that job and change the power structure as much as anything I have ever wanted. It might be great fun," she said.

No one ever campaigns for hospital office. It is not done. The potential candidates are put forward in the rumor mill, with innuendoes, possibilities, and what-ifs. On their parts, the potential candidates are the most self-effacing people who ever lived—shy, reticent, humble—never deigning to do anything but to protest how much of an imposition and a bore it would be and how much better one of the other surgeons would be. Still, there was just a hint in the voice, an idle comment about changes that needed to be made, a look of determination when issues of hospital politics arose. Sybil did them all.

Her candidacy was formally put forward by Blackman Schwartz in the June general medical staff meeting. Sybil was appropriately reserved and not self-aggrandizing, but she did not refuse. Darryl Hankin and Tom Petler, along with another of Sybil's perpetual detractors, Farouk Ibn al-Hebreaus, publicly poo-pooed the possibility of Sybil Norcroft being the chief. After all, hadn't she just come through a messy malpractice trial that had hardly brought kudos to JNMH? They worked too hard at it. The other surgeons remembered all too well that Dr. Hankin had testified against one of their own in a malpractice case. That was a violation of the code in most of their minds, a whoredom they would not soon forget. Instead of regarding Sybil as having been besmirched by the accusations leveled against her, the other surgeons took the attitude that there but for the Grace of God go I. They rallied around her, and in August elected her chief of surgery by a three-quarter's majority.

For three months, Sybil found her duties as chief of surgery to be mundane, largely a rubber stamp for the work of the professional quality assessment nurses who did the trench work of reviewing surgical charts and fielding and investigating charges and complaints against members of the surgical staff. Then she learned about the trap Tom Petler had set for her when he left the chief post.

Dr. Petler had been fending off queries and complaints about one of the long time anesthesiologists, Fritz Kellogg, for nearly four years. The two men were old golfing buddies and invested together in apartment complexes. Tom Petler, as chief of surgery, also controlled the anesthesiology section, and in his position of power, had saved Kellogg from serious action from the staff or the hospital.

By July, a month before the new elections, Petler had been pressed seriously by the JNMH administrators and by a determined group of surgeons to do something about his old friend, Fritz. The would-be anesthesiologist had been taking liberties with sleeping patients, falling asleep during operations and neglecting his patients, and was too deaf to hear the surgeons and doctors. He had not kept up with or did not know about the recent improvements in his specialty, and, according to the quality assurance nurses, had an abysmal record of anesthetic complications. Petler had twisted, turned, obfuscated, cajoled, and evaded Fritz's critics, but the effort was beginning to tell. In July, a determined group of young surgeons, angry that their legitimate complaints had been summarily shunted aside for years, filed suit against the surgical committee and its chairman for dereliction of duty.

Petler had never been sued before, and disdained those unfortunates on the medical staff whose medical practice was so egregious as to warrant such a public condemnation. It came as a shock to him when he was sued. Friendship was one thing, and blood was another. He thought that the plaintiffs and their attorneys were out after his blood. Petler made a visit to the office of the hospital's attorney's office. After a brief chat, the two of them had lunch with the attorneys for the plaintiffs arrayed against him as chief of surgery and against the hospital. By the time they finished dessert, Petler had agreed to step aside and to allow the problem to fall on his successor in return for having the suit against him dropped. He convinced the attorneys that the next chief would, in all likelihood, be a woman who did not know nor care about Fritz Kellogg, and would not hesitate to throw the old anesthesiologist to the wolves. Furthermore, he stressed, she was an iron ovaried feminist who, besides being a man hater, had an overriding ambition. She would not hesitate to get rid of Dr. Kellogg to enhance her standing with the upcoming crop of surgeons. That would allow Petler to exit the problem of dealing with the improprieties of his old friend gracefully. The suit was dropped before the second cup of coffee arrived.

Tom Petler had been true to his word to the lawyers. In the critical last month before the elections, he quietly contacted his old and long time supporters and told them of his decision to quit, leaving out the role the Fritz Kellogg matter played in the decision. He called upon the old boy network to support the woman, Sybil Norcroft, whom he now wanted to see elected for his own reasons. He assured his old friends that the reason would be evident in a short time if they would only grant him this favor and remain patient. Sybil was surprised to be elected by a 75 percent majority.

She learned of Tom Petler's dark legacy when Katrine Letz, the head quality assurance nurse, brought her a formal letter from Steven Kirkpatrick, a thoracic surgeon, who demanded an investigation of Dr. Kellogg's performance in one of his cases, and announced a boycott of the Joseph Noble OR by his entire HMO group until the matter was resolved. He stated baldly that

Kellogg was a menace to the hospital's patients and he, Dr. Kirkpatrick, was sick and tired of being ignored.

"This is all news to me, Katrine. It sounds like I've been guilty of some kind of cover-up, but I haven't heard a thing about this before. How about bringing me up to snuff," Dr. Norcroft asked the nurse once she had digested the contents and the underlying wrath of the letter.

"I shouldn't be saying this, Dr. Norcroft, but you got dumped on. Tom Petler has been sitting on the Kellogg complaints for months, years. I have a stack of them. I kept a listing of all of the charts involved in case one day they became necessary. Maybe you ought to go over them. You didn't hear about it, but there was nearly a suit about it this summer. Some of the surgeons are up in arms over old Kellogg's behavior and want action. Now. Didn't it seem a little odd to you that Petler slipped away into the night without a fight? He just wanted to let some other sucker deal with this problem, and you were elected."

Sybil thought that she was savvy to the world of medical politics, but she recognized immediately that she had been living like a hot house plant until now. This was her introduction to the real world, it seemed.

"Let's get the anesthesiology subcommittee together to review the charts before we do anything else," she requested of Katrine.

"Won't do any good, Dr. Norcroft. Kellogg is the head of the section. He reviews all of the charts and decides which ones need attention. His never do. You won't be able to meet the anesthesiologists without him being present. He knows where all of the skeletons are hidden, and none of the gas passers will say anything against Kellogg publicly."

Sybil screwed up her face, working over her options.

"I'll go over them myself. If they look bad, then we will deal with them and with Dr. Kellogg in the full surgical committee meeting. Can you get the charts and any pertinent complaint letters to my office by tomorrow afternoon?"

"This afternoon if you want. It would do my old heart good to know that something was finally going to be done."

"Tomorrow's soon enough. Meantime, I'm going to give Fritz a call."

Sybil waited until after the surgery schedule was done for the day. Then she called Dr. Kellogg through his answering service.

"Fritz? This is Sybil Norcroft."

"Glad to hear from you. By the way, congratulations on winning the election. It will be real interesting having a woman run the show. What can I do for you?"

"I think we need to have a sit-down talk, Fritz. You know that I have to sift through the complaints that come in for the surgical service."

"And that's a shame. I've been saying for years that the anesthesiology department should be made free standing to streamline the service and to relieve the surgery department of the burden of dealing with anesthesiology concerns. Poor Tom Petler about went crazy having to make some sort of comment on all of those idiotic complaints."

"That will have to be a subject for another day, Fritz. The matter at hand is some long unanswered complaints about some of your cases. The lot has been dumped on my head. I need to go over your charts with you. Get these things out of the way. Could you meet me on Friday after the schedule?"

"Ah, sorry, Dr. Norcroft, I'm leaving town, going to Vail to sun and hike. Been waiting for this for a year. Maybe when I get back?"

"I'll call you then, Fritz. We can't procrastinate this anymore. There are serious matters brewing over your cases. I need to resolve them."

"No problem, glad to accommodate. I'll be expecting your call."

Sybil could never corner Fritz Kellogg. He was either busy with a case, hurrying off to an investment meeting, having lunch with his broker or his lawyer, leaving town, or could not be reached by his answering service. Sybil was pressed by the young surgeons and by the hospital administration to do something definitive. She became frustrated, then angry. It was clear that Fritz was avoiding her, and he was a master at evasion. When the original suit that had been held over Tom Petler's head was threatened against Sybil, she decided to do something effective.

She rearranged the agenda of the surgery committee meeting for the upcoming month and placed the evaluation of Fritz Kellogg's practice as the sole agenda item. He was specifically invited, although an invitation was not necessary. As head of the anesthesiology section, Kellogg was obligated to be present and had maintained a nearly perfect attendance record in the past. On the night of the committee meeting, Fritz did not show up. A letter from his attorney came in his stead.

Dr. Norcroft:

Be advised that my client, Frederick "Fritz" Kellogg, considers any public discussion of his practice of medicine to be a libelous invasion of his privacy and a defamation of his personal and professional character. Be on notice that should you or your committee publish in any form, verbal or written, any excerpt from his cases, testimony regarding his level of care, or a reprimand however benign, he will launch an action

against you. Dr. Kellogg does not regard your committee, one made up of his professional competitors, to have a valid jurisdiction. If his practice methods are to be scrutinized, they must be done in his presence and with his attorney in attendance. They may only be investigated by his peers, the anesthesiologists of Joseph Noble Memorial Hospital, and only under the direct auspices of the hospital's governing board.
Submitted to the board, this day, 18 October, 2009.
Signed: Oliver C. Webster, Esq.

Sybil read the letter to the members of the surgical committee. They voted unanimously to review Kellogg's charts then and there. Michael Strong, the administrator, who did not have a vote on the committee, protested to no avail. When the committee finished at one o'clock in the morning, they voted to have Dr. Kellogg appear before the principle committee of the hospital, the Central Medical Committee, to defend himself against charges of incompetence, negligent malpractice, and inadequate training. It had been discovered during the course of the evening that Dr. Kellogg had never had any formal anesthesiology training. Instead, he had essentially apprenticed with one of the well known old anesthesiologists thirty-five years ago and had never been to a refresher course or obtained Continuing Medical Education credits since. CME was required of all members of the hospital staff to keep up their privileges. With Tom Petler's assistance, Kellogg had slipped through the cracks.

Fritz Kellogg received a hand-delivered letter the following day requesting his presence at the Central Committee's upcoming meeting. The same day, he fired back virulent letters to Sybil Norcroft, to the president of the hospital staff, and to the hospital administrator to the effect that it would be a cold day before he would ever submit to any such public humiliation. The following day Sybil, every member of the surgery committee, every administrative officer of the hospital, and the hospital's board as a unit, received letters of intent from Oliver Webster. In Sybil's case, she was threatened that a $20,000,000 lawsuit would be formally filed in 90 days.

The letter was brought to Sybil as she sat in her office between patients on an especially busy day.

"Dr. Norcroft, sorry to do this to you," her secretary had said apologetically. "The marshal just brought this in, and we signed for it."

She had dropped the envelope on Sybil's desk as if it were a hot object or a repellent thing she could no longer bear to touch.

Sybil opened it, shook her head, and groaned a little.

"What more can happen?"

She had had her fill with the legal system. There would certainly be no reasoning with Fritz Kellogg from here on in.

The *more* Sybil dreaded happened mid-afternoon the same day. The same shy secretary sheepishly knocked on Sybil's office door.

"Come in," Sybil called.

She was hurriedly trying to get through the dictation of the admission history and physical examinations for the three patients that she had found in the office who needed and had agreed to surgery. With three more clinic patients and four hospital consultations yet to see, she was feeling pushed for time and did not welcome the interruption. Her tone of voice was brusque.

The secretary stood quietly in front of Sybil's desk as the doctor finished her dictation. She looked down and would not meet Sybil's gaze.

"What is it? What now? I'm too busy for all of these interruptions."

"Gladys told me to bring this in now."

Gladys was the office manager.

"She said you always wanted to hear bad news as soon as it came."

The girl looked as if she might shed a tear.

Sybil's heart sank. She mollified the stridency of her voice.

"Take it easy. I never kill the bearer of bad news...I just want to most of the time."

She managed a wan smile.

The young secretary handed the envelope to Sybil and backed to the door to avoid risking further interchange with her boss. Sybil settled into a deep funk just by seeing the return address on the envelope: Stewart, Bel Geddes, and Loughlin, Attorneys at Law.

Dear Dr. Norcroft:

This will serve to inform you that you are being sued. Ninety days from the above date, my clients, the family of Jason Turner, deceased, will commence action in Superior Court to collect damages for the wrongful death of their family member. This letter satisfies the requirements of the law with regards the need to provide a timely communication of that intent.

My office expects the courtesy of a prompt reply from you or the attorney of your choice.

Paul Devon Bel Geddes, Esq, for the plaintiffs, Mary C. Turner, wife, and Tremaine and Jesse Turner, parents.

"Jason Turner?" she asked. "Who on earth is Jason Turner?"

The question was as much rhetorical as it was an inquiry, but the secretary produced Turner's chart. Presuming that she was no longer needed, and without looking back, the young woman departed. Sybil glared at the letter with an irrational hatred. She felt that she could feel the animosity from Paul Bel Geddes seeping from between the lines of prosaic legality.

Sybil quickly riffled the pages of the office chart—there were very few of them. She speed read the contents.

"He's the guy I saw in the ER for Daniel Krempen and Peter Midgel," she said aloud although she was alone in the room.

She read further.

"He did not have a thing neurological. He was fine. He crumped from bleeding in the chest."

She shook her head in bemusement and continued. The discharge—death—summary contained a notation that Jason Turner had entered the OR under Dr. Midgel's care. Midgel had called in a chest cutter, Farouk Ibn al-Hebreaus. Sybil had a brilliant and dreadful flash of intuition, as real as if it were a memory.

Her avowed enemy, al-Hebreaus, said to the family and to an attorney, "If only they had called me sooner...."

She shuddered with revulsion at the thought of the greasy little man. He had to be the reason why she was caught up in Bel Geddes's fishing expedition.

During the McNeely case, her lawyer, Carter Tarkington, had told her over and over not to be intimidated by the opposing attorneys, no matter what they said or did. Here she was trembling in her figurative boots, Gucci slip-ons, in fact, and she had only been threatened. To be technical about it, she had not even been formally sued yet.

"*I have to get a grip on,*" she admonished herself.

It was easier said than done. She found it hard to concentrate for the rest of the afternoon. She gave her clinic patients and the in-hospital consults short shrift of her personality, dealing with them in a flat, concrete manner, correct and polite but diffident. She had no patience that day for the three women she saw with their all-over and nowhere pains and the two men whose only real goal was to find a soft touch of a woman doctor who would see the need for them to receive regular narcotics prescriptions.

This time, when she reported to her malpractice insurance company that she was about to be sued again, the company assigned her to a junior member of the firm of Schmid, Principle, and Tarkington, judging that this was no more than a nuisance suit and did not warrant the services of one of the firm's named partners. Sybil did not know whether she should be relieved or angered.

Susan MacIntosh was a good lawyer and an especially good listener. Sybil warmed to the young attorney at once.

"So what am I up against?" she asked as soon as she had told Ms. MacIntosh everything she could remember about the Jason Turner case.

"If this were anybody except Paul Bel Geddes as the plaintiff's lawyer, I would presume that you would be dropped in the first round of discovery. But Bel Geddes has a mean streak. He loves to hold on to his victims until the bitter end, just for spite, it often seems to me. Maybe it's for money, maybe some of the defendants or their insurance companies cave in and fork over some extortion money just to get him off their backs, and that keeps him hopeful. But I still think it's just meanness. My advice is not to do that in this case, Dr. Norcroft. Unless there is something I don't understand here, he will have to dismiss you in the end. He'll never get an expert against you. Also, I get the idea from communicating with his office that Bel Geddes has some sort of little personal vendetta against you. Is there something to that?"

"There seems to be," agreed Sybil. "I presume that it has something to do with Carter Tarkington and me beating Bel Geddes and his French Canadian prostitute in a case a while back. I don't presume to understand the psyche or even the overt thinking of attorneys. No offense."

"None taken. I will be working with Hyrum Willis on this case. I think you've met him."

"He worked on the McNeely case."

"He's very thorough. A good lawyer."

"He seemed to be."

"Anyway, we'll get back to you. If Bel Geddes is true to form, there won't be any depositions or substantive work done for years. Don't get in a twist about this. Let us do the worrying, okay?"

"I'll try. But I have a sneaking suspicion that I will sleep uneasily until the deposition when I will stop sleeping at all. I try not to let this get under my skin, but there is something about Paul Bel Geddes and his crusader hypocrisy that rankles, despite everything I try to tell myself about going with the flow and that this is just the price of doing business."

"I think I understand, even though it is a whole lot easier being the attorney instead of the defendant, even in a nothing case like this one. It's easier to be a civil attorney than a civil client, I'll grant you. I'll be in touch. Don't fret too much, Dr. Norcroft. Like my old daddy used to say, 'This, too, shall pass away.'"

Sybil did maintain a low grade anxiety over the Jason Turner case, but, with the passage of two years, the threat and dread passed to the back of her mind. Her practice had now matured to the point that she could take off more time and could pursue her growing love of horses. She continued to breed soft stepping horses, adding several beautiful silver grey Paso Finos to her collection of fine Tennessee Walkers. The original stallions and mares were now producing a profitable tag of colts, and she was beginning to place in a few of the shows that she and her Mexican grooms and handlers worked on so hard. Pancho and Carlita Rodriguez, Jose and Maria Innocenta Pomposo-Alvarez, and Marcos and Viviana Hernandez had remained with her and accorded her near familial devotion after seven years of living on Sybil's ranch and working on the project of erecting the buildings, enclosing the paddocks, and preparing the horses for shows. In December, 2009, Sybil celebrated her first profitable year after seven years of gentlewomanly ranching. She was $143 in the black.

She was so pleased with herself and the ranch's profitable status at long last that Sybil decided to splurge and buy the magnificent Missouri Foxtrotter stallion she had been craving to have for years. Ring Pride, from Middleton Stables, Stratford, Missouri, exceeded her profit by $249,857. The beautiful animal had a shimmering bay color and white front stockings. His champion level gait, both instinctual, and the result of four years of the most careful training, was the smoothest Sybil had ever seen and was picture perfect on video, even at slow motion, whether the horse was walking at nine miles an hour or cantering at 13. Both speeds were considerably faster than the average Foxtrotter.

The Foxtrotter gait was unique in the horse kingdom: walking with the front feet and trotting with the rear. Ring Pride's rear feet overstepped his front in a sliding motion that almost placed his rear tracks atop the front ones (capping). Both front feet were on the ground at the same time. The right front and left rear feet were on the ground at the same time with the rear foot coming down slightly later than the front because of its overreach. Viewed from the side, the pommel did not rise or fall more than half an inch. The beautiful animal was a study in fluidity of motion, with or without a rider.

She threw a party for her family and for all of the people who worked on her ranch. Either by design or by happenstance, the party became, like all of the parties at the ranch, a fiesta with an unmistakable Mexican flavor.

Pancho took a seat at Charles Daniels's and Dr. Norcroft's table, uninvited. The relationship between Sybil and her husband and the original set of Mexican men and women had ripened to the point that such familiarity was the rule.

"Greetings *Patron* and *Patrona*," he said.

The titles were now more affectionate and familiar than they were formal and distancing.

"Good evening, Pancho. How is Carlita?" Charles asked.

"*Ella duele le cinturon*, but nothing important. We were able to dance tonight," he replied with the assurance that Charles' question was more than an idle greeting.

Carlita had had back troubles of one kind and site or another since she had come to the ranch. Sybil had treated her off and on, did an MRI that was negative, and Carlita had pursued traditional Mexican shaman medicine thereafter. It caused Pancho concern that his *Patrona* would be offended, but Carlita's adherence to her old ways merely amused Sybil.

"Horses look good, no?" Pancho observed.

"Especially good, Pancho, thanks to your work."

At first, Charles had cautioned his wife not to be too free with praise for fear that the Mexicans would take advantage of her. They, on the other hand, had become so confident in the honesty and directness of Dr. Norcroft that they thrived on her sparing accolades and responded affirmatively. Charles had learned not to give vent to any comments about stereotypical Latinos. These people were no more stereotypes than he was, and he had become comfortable with that salutary fact.

"Thank you, *Patrona*," Pancho responded and made a gesture with his head and hand that simulated the tipping of his *sombrero*.

"I am happy that you and the Rodriguezes and the Alvarezes have stayed at the ranch. I like the new boys you brought up from Sonora. They are good men. I trust them. That is also thanks to you."

Pancho looked down in shyness.

"And I want to ensure that you and your men and your wives want to stay here and do the same good work."

"We are satisfied, *Patrona*," Pancho said with some feeling.

"What would you think of sharing in the business and not just in the work, Pancho?"

"None of us has ever thought of your rancho as just work, *Patrona*. We look at it as our place."

"Good. I want it to be your place. Part your place, anyway. I want you to buy a share in the ranch and share in the expenses and the profits. You know we made a big profit this year."

Pancho laughed.

"I keep the books. I know about the $143. Now, if we can just get back the rest of the 200,000 to 300,000 you've sunk into the ranch, to say nothing of the three million in the stock and the millions in the *hacienda grande*."

She made a face at him.

"But now we are on the road to success, Pancho. I will sell you and the others 20 percent of the ranch if you want to buy it. You can work off the debt. You can become a grand *patron* yourself. What do you think?"

He looked stunned. He had not been sure what Dr. Norcroft had been talking about before. When it registered that she was serious, he found himself uncharacteristically at a loss for words.

"Pancho?"

She smiled indulgently.

Charles Daniels looked at his wife with genuine affection. For all her reputation as a professional with brass ovaries, she was a genuine soft woman—no fool, certainly she had no deficiencies when it came to judging character—just a woman with some saving graces after all.

"I would be honored, *Patrona*. I do not know what to say. This is the best thing that happened since we came here and since we got our green cards. Maybe this could help us become citizens. It is too much. I will have to talk to my Carlita and the others."

He seemed uncomfortable now, antsy. He obviously did not want to sit on this great news.

"Go talk then, Pancho. You are too nervous to sit with us," Sybil said with an indulgent grin.

Pancho looked grateful for her social grace, and bade them good evening.

Pancho had no difficulty in convincing his *paisanos* to commit themselves to the debt entailed in becoming part of the ranch's ownership. Sybil, with Charles's blessing, took the unprecedented step of loaning the Mexicans the money to buy into the smooth stepping horse breeding business. They had worked and scrimped to pay her, and when they achieved 20 percent ownership of the ranch and its stock two years later, they achieved freedom from formal economic indebtedness. They were in bondage for life by their own choice to the *Patrona* who had treated them as equals and had made them in legal fact her partners in the horse business.

The ranch had two years of genuine profit—well over $100,000 each year. She put the profits into a Paso Fino stallion with the full agreement of her new partners, and the profits began to accelerate in the third year of the partnership.

Sybil's practice of neurosurgery progressed to the point that her reputation afforded her the opportunity to confine her practice to brain surgery, a situation envied by the vast majority of her colleagues. There was the nagging annoyance of the Jason Turner case seething around out there in the void somewhere, but she did not accumulate any additional malpractice cases, and her insurance premiums were even decreased. She was at the pinnacle of her career.

Susan MacIntosh finally made the inevitable call.

"Deposition is set for the twenty-second of October. This time it's for sure. Judge Atkins told Bel Geddes that he won't let him fool around anymore scheduling and descheduling appearances and depos. So gird up your gussets, Gertie. It's the real thing this time."

"I knew I was having too much fun for it to last," Sybil said. "It's been so long that we need to get together and go over my testimony before the deposition."

"I'll give you a couple of days, more if you like."

"Have your administrative assistant call mine," Sybil requested.

The two women shared a small laugh. No one had secretaries any more. 'Secretary' was déclassé now—it bordered on an insult to demean anyone with the title of 'secretary'. Both women had bent with the wind and chalked it up as another little victory for the feminist cause.

"Okay, we'll make it the two days before the actual deposition," Ms. MacIntosh said.

The two women and Hyrum Willis labored twelve hours a day for two days over Sybil's testimony until none of them could stand to mention another word about the case. They covered every hostile possibility that Bel Geddes could throw at Dr. Norcroft during the questioning. At six o'clock on the second day of their efforts and 18 hours before the deposition was scheduled, Susan's administrative assistant called her in the conference room where they were wearily finishing sandwiches and their fourth round of coffee for the day. Susan listened for a few minutes, thanked her assistant, replaced the telephone receiver, and scowled.

"What?" asked Sybil.

"My administrative assistant informs me that somehow he has managed to do it again."

"*He*, meaning Bel Geddes, I presume?" Willis half stated and asked in the same sentence.

"Clairvoyant," said Susan humorlessly.

"Elementary, my dear MacIntosh," replied Hyrum with equal lack of mirth.

"Let me guess, too," put in Sybil. "*He* has succeeded in having the deposition continued still another time."

She had colored with anger.

"I'm afraid so, Dr. Norcroft. I'm so sorry."

Susan shrugged in futility.

"Aren't there any rules? I mean, don't attorneys have to obey contracts, court orders, judges' rulings, etcetera, like us lesser mortals? This is absurd, a travesty. And this is the most unfair arrangement I have ever seen. He gets to manipulate and harass me at will. I have to take it because I'm a doctor."

"A plaintiff," contributed Hyrum.

"And what is the excuse this time?" Sybil asked.

"The judge himself called the office and said that the continuation was granted because of an illness in Bel Geddes's family, his mother-in-law, I believe my administrative assistant said."

Sybil Norcroft snorted.

There were two more absolute deadlines for the deposition that came and went. Sybil learned to grind her teeth and to ignore the scheduled dates. She no longer told her administrative assistants to alter her schedule. Susan MacIntosh apologized each time, but told Sybil that the judges all bent over backward to make sure that defendants could not register any complaint of unfairness against the judge in their case. That was a cause for a turnover on appeal. The judges defended their system, stating that they did not really condone harassment of defendants, especially those with deep pockets, and particularly physicians, but, after all, how could poor people have access to the system if certain allowances were not made? It was a socialist definition of fair that politicians and jurists had embraced with activist fervor since the American Trial Lawyers Association had contributed so decisively to the two victories of Bill Clinton's presidential election efforts at the end of the twentieth century. Sybil Norcroft's inconvenience did not even rise to the level of an historical footnote against such lofty sentiments.

Fritz Kellogg found that he had made two incorrect assumptions. The first was that the court system in general would be interested in his cause—the little man oppressed by the monolithic hospital and medical establishment. The second was that having a woman as head of the surgery department meant that eventually she would crack and find it easier just to let the matter of Fritz Kellogg drop into obscurity or that she would punt and let there be created a department of anesthesiology at JNMH, a free-standing department that would be given jurisdiction in his case, and that his fellow anesthesiologists would see to it that the matter would drop.

Through his lawyer, Dr. Kellogg filed motions in the county court who said that they did not have jurisdiction. State courts ruled that it was a matter for the hospital to handle and would not admit his plea into the state court system. Frustrated at the local and state level, Fritz went so far as to file a federal action alleging restraint of trade. The reviewer asked only three questions: What were the requirements for practicing anesthesiology at Joseph Noble Memorial Hospital? Did all of the anesthesiologists on the staff have to measure up to the same set of standards? And did Dr. Kellogg meet those criteria? When even Dr. Kellogg's attorney had to admit that an "old boy" unwritten exception to the hospital's requirements was extant for Fritz, the federal courts summarily refused to go further with the action.

Fritz Kellogg retired embittered at Sybil Norcroft and JNMH and left behind a legacy of division on the staff. A minority of Fritz's old friends, including Darryl Hankin and Ibn al-Hebreaus, held her responsible and formed a nucleus of political antagonists that persisted all through her tenure in office as the Chief of Surgery. Sybil gained a rock solid reputation as a hard-nosed stickler for the rules and as a good friend and a bad enemy as a result of the Kellogg episode.

The third date for the Jason Turner deposition was in February, 2013. Susan told Sybil to show up for this one because Bel Geddes was running into trouble in his case, and he now needed some kind of additional boost that, for some reason, he thought could come from what Sybil would have to say. This tidbit had been casually dropped by Paul Bel Geddes in a bar association dinner a week ago, after the disinhibition of a few martinis. Sybil gave more credence to a drink occasioned slip by the plaintiff's attorney than she did to any volume of his sober utterances, and rearranged her schedule.

She met Susan MacIntosh and Hyrum Willis on the ground floor of Bel Geddes's tacky art deco building. Sybil had purposely come only five minutes early. The two attorneys did not seem at all anxious.

"Glad to see you, Dr. Norcroft," said Hyrum and extended his hand. "I see you decided to come only an hour early this time."

The three of them shared a short laugh.

"Let's go see what sort of sideshow Bel Geddes has cooked up this time," said Susan.

They went up the elevator and emerged into the lavishly redecorated offices; the entire floor was occupied by Stewart, Bel Geddes, and Loughlin. The last time Sybil had been there, it had been done in expensive crass—art deco à la early Halloween—like the outside of the building itself. Now the suite of offices was decorated in rich excessive 17th century French, as garish and tasteless as that period could produce, and as out of place in the law office as the previous almost comical art deco had been. The secretary had not changed. Her dress still looked as if it belonged to her younger, slimmer sister. She showed them to the conference room. The court recorder, a man, was already in place and waiting.

The attorneys and the court recorder exchanged cards.

"This is Dr. Sybil Norcroft, the deponent," Susan announced.

Sybil and the court recorder shook hands, and Sybil handed him a copy of her curriculum vitae.

Paul Bel Geddes was only thirty minutes late, something of a record for him. He appeared to be his usual overly busy self.

"Hello, hello," he boomed and flashed a telegenic grin all around, showing off his mouthful of new porcelain caps that were an opalescent white that drew immediate attention to his mouth.

He proceeded to shake hands with everyone in the room. Sybil left her hands in her lap under the edge of the conference table when it came her turn. There was a long awkward moment while Bel Geddes stood with his hand outstretched, looking Dr. Norcroft directly in her eyes. He finally dropped his hand and shrugged it off.

"Let's begin," he said. "No use wasting our valuable time."

Sybil groaned inwardly at his hypocrisy.

"Sybil? Do you mind if I call you Sybil?" he asked as his lead off.

"I do. It's Dr. Norcroft."

"I find titles stuffy, don't you? Wouldn't it be tedious if you had to address me as Attorney Bel Geddes or Mr. Bel Geddes, Esquire?'"

"You may be addressed however you wish, Mr. Bel Geddes. It is still Dr. Norcroft."

"Well then, *Dr.* Norcroft. I believe we can dispense with your credentials. I see that you have given the court reporter a copy of your CV. You are a doctor of medicine, am I right?"

"Yes, I am."

"Licensed to practice in this state currently?"

"Yes."

"We won't need any further information about your training or qualifications at present. I find the claims to training beyond medical school to be grossly inflated these days, anyway, don't you?"

The fact was that he was not too far wrong, Sybil thought. It had been one of her minor campaigns in the state medical association to get rid of the pseudo specialty societies and to disallow their nearly nonexistent training claims.

"No, Sir," she answered stubbornly, unwilling to concede on the slightest point. "Certainly not in my case. I will be happy to verify every item on my CV, if you wish. We can spend most of the morning doing that if it would please you."

"I'll stipulate," he said, and he flashed a smile with his new teeth that absolutely trumpeted his magnanimity.

Sybil renewed her determination not to let that baroque contemptible get under her protective shield.

"Why did you state that Jason Turner was neurologically intact, *Dr.* Norcroft, when in fact you knew that he was in extremis?"

Evidently, Bel Geddes had tired of his own irrelevancies.

"Because he was neurologically intact."

"His level of consciousness was fading, was it not?"

"Yes, due to blood loss. He was able to carry on a lucid conversation even in the midst of painful stimuli and despite his low blood pressure. I judged him to be suffering from blood loss, but to have no neurological injuries attendant upon his accident otherwise."

"He could have had a blood clot on or in his brain, could he not?"

"Not in my opinion."

"But you didn't check, did you?"

"I did a thorough neurosurgical emergency examination. I am an expert, and in my experience, the findings presented by Mr. Turner were not indicative of an intracranial mass."

"But you did not do a CT or an MRI, did you?"

"No."

"And you should have, isn't that right?"

"No."

"*No?*"

"No."

"Dr. Norcroft, isn't it below the standard of care to have failed to obtain one of those studies?"

"Not at all."

"Since I am not a doctor, perhaps you could explain that answer. I, for one, cannot comprehend how the negligence you showed could be excused."

"Objection. There is no evidence of any negligence." Susan stated calmly.

"I still want an answer to my question. This is my deposition, after all."

Bel Geddes looked petulant, theatrically so, like a little boy left out of the game of tag at recess.

"You may answer the question wherein an explanation of your decisions and actions was called for, Doctor."

Susan looked meaningfully at Sybil.

"I will be happy to. First of all, there is no such thing as a so-called standard of care. That is a myth created by attorneys so they will have something to say. Second of all, in the case of Jason Turner, it would have been manifestly dangerous, fatally so, to have wasted any time doing a test that I knew would be normal. It might have suited the desires of an attorney looking to prove a case, but I had to help in the care of a rapidly dying man. His problem was his chest injury, not his neurological system. He had no significant signs of a mass, no evidence of serious head or spine trauma, and emergency x-rays of his cervical and thoracic spines revealed no fractures or subluxations. In short, there were no indications to do a neurosurgical operation, and every indication that his chest injury needed immediate attention."

"I'm sorry, Doctor, but did you say that his thoracic spine x-rays were normal?"

"I said there were no fractures or subluxations, to be precise."

"But, Doctor, if memory serves me right, there were no thoracic spine x-rays done."

He dropped the fact like a bombshell. He looked at her as if she were the cat who had just been caught in the canary cage.

"That is incorrect."

"It is?"

He had a genuine moment of pause from her calm assurance. He knew for a fact that only emergency cervical spine films had been taken.

"Yes. As you said earlier, you are not a doctor, and you could not have been expected to know that the emergency chest radiographs, several of them, amply demonstrated the thoracic spine, both in the PA and lateral aspects. Almost all of the thoracic vertebrae could be accounted for in those films."

"Oh," he said.

"Yes," she said.

"This man bled to death. I have formal testimony from the chest surgeon who was eventually called in that Jason Turner's death was unnecessary, if only he, the chest surgeon, had been called in sooner. Dr. Norcroft, why didn't you call in the chest surgeon?"

"I was only a neurosurgical consultant. The ER physician and the general surgeon were in charge. It was not my place to make such a call. I am definitely not an expert in chest trauma or chest surgery."

"Isn't it more accurate to say that the reason that Dr. Ibn al-Hebreaus was not called in was because you and he are on bad terms, and he offends your feminist sensitivities?"

"That is patent nonsense."

"But the only plausible reason for you to order your colleagues not to call in Ibn al-Hebreaus who was the only thoracic surgeon on call is it not?"

There were two flagrant misconstructions of the facts in that question, and Sybil at first wanted to shout at her tormentor that there was no defense against his charges except that they were ridiculous. She forced herself not to respond in anger. She calmed herself.

"Dr. Norcroft? Did you hear my question? Shall I have it read back to you?"

"I heard you. I am considering my answer. There are two errors in your scurrilous presumptions. First of all, I was in no position to order any physician to do anything. I was not even in charge of the Jason Turner case...."

Bel Geddes interrupted when Dr. Norcroft took a breath.

"Are you or are you not the chief of surgery at Joseph Noble Memorial Hospital? Answer me that."

"Objection. Counsel is badgering the witness. She already has one question before her and is trying to answer. Counsel rudely interrupted and added another. Let her finish her answers," Susan MacIntosh called out.

"Thank you," said Sybil.

She quickly marshaled her thoughts.

"I'll finish my answer to the first set of questions. As I was saying, I have no authority to order any physician. In fact, in the situation, I was at the service of the other two physicians. Secondly, the decision to call in Ibn al-Hebreaus was made by Dr. Midgel and Dr. Krempen, based, I presume, on their assessment of the situation. They were rushing the patient to the operating room while I attended to another patient in the emergency room. As I recall, I was doing a tracheostomy when Mr. Turner was finally stabilized enough to take him up."

"But you are the head, chairman, or chairwoman, or chair*person* of the department of surgery, are you not?"

"Oh, yes, your second question. I am indeed the chief of surgery, the chairwoman of that department. And no, I do not wield from that position any dictatorial powers like some bygone divine right empress. Hospitals don't work that way. Doctors won't work that way. Even in HMOs, doctors maintain their autonomy and responsibility under the law. If I ordered a doctor around, he would just laugh at me. If I made it a practice, the staff would find a new chairperson."

Bel Geddes stared at Dr. Norcroft for several moments. She could not be sure whether or not he was trying to assess her answer, or framing his next question, or deciding his next tack. Then, disarmingly, he grinned at her as if they were old pals who had just been engaged in synthetic amicable verbal joust.

"I think it's time for a break. I need to visit the little boy's room and to stretch the legs. Consider that you have the run of the place. Say half an hour?"

He abruptly stood up and left the room.

Sybil looked at Susan who rolled her eyes.

"Typical Bel Geddesesque antics. Don't let him get to you. Let's walk around."

The two women and Hyrum Willis opened the double doors of the large conference room and stepped out into the carpeted hall. The carpet was thick and lush underfoot. They all noticed the richness of the floor covering.

"He does it to impress clients and to intimidate defense lawyers. It speaks of his success, his magical success," said Hyrum, making a small gesture to indicate the sumptuous walls and floors.

The three rounded a corner on their way to where they presumed the office's refreshment center was located. They met Paul Bel Geddes almost head-on.

"Oopsie!" he effused with a surfeit of ersatz smiling camaraderie.

"Excuse us, Paul," said Susan politely but without a trace of warmth.

"I've been thinking. Coffee helps me think," Bel Geddes said, his toothy smile still fixed in place.

Sybil was sure she could smell alcohol on his breath and presumed that the help for his thinking came from that two carbon chemical fragment rather than from the bitter alkaloid stimulants of coffee.

"Why don't we go have a little sit down in my office? I have something I think you'll like."

Susan looked at the man with unfeigned suspicion.

"Is this to do with the case, Paul? I really think we should get to the business at hand and get the deposition over with."

Sybil was curious.

"Patience is a cardinal virtue, Susan. All in due time. Is that Poison you're wearing. It's a lovely smell. I mean that."

Susan shook her head; she had heard it all before.

"Paul...."

"C'mon. A few minutes can't hurt. We can have a little tour of the office along the way."

He turned and started away. The other two lawyers and the defendant meekly followed.

"This is the refreshment center. All kinds of goodies in here. The main problem with this place is keeping the hired help out of it and slaving away at their computers."

They stopped at every doorway. He opened each door without knocking.

"This is Horace Stewart's digs."

He paused in thought.

"These are Horace Pilgrim Stewart's digs."

Horace did not seem to appreciate the interruption of the crucial interview with his skittish client.

At the door of the next office, Bel Geddes said, "This is Marty Loughlin's domain. He insisted on keeping the old decor, killjoy."

Loughlin was not in his office. The place was totally incongruous with the 17th century theme of the rest of the office complex. It was full of Depression Glass *objets d'art*, watercolors of pastel women in flapper dresses and hats, and disproportionate bulky overstuffed furniture.

"How passé," Bel Geddes muttered.

He took them into the bathrooms. There were no modern toilets. All of the usual porcelain fixtures had been replaced with 19th century water closet equipment that, although admittedly antique looking, was as out of place with the 17th century decor as was Martin Loughlin's art deco.

They were then led into a large room with a handsome mahogany writing table in its center and two matching rolltop pigeonhole desks in the far corners of the room. The table and the two desks each had a delicate, uncomfortable looking straight back chair facing it. The walls were lined with very modern looking floor to ceiling sliding file cabinets. Bel Geddes pushed a button and one of the cabinets slowly and silently moved forward along ceiling runners. A long set of hanging files appeared.

"This is the nerve center," Bel Geddes said with obvious enthusiasm. "My idea. Can't have everything old fashioned. These are the office files. This is where Jason Turner's folder—our next tidy little gold mine—sits."

He pointed to a small space between hanging files. The receptacle for the folder was there, empty, the name clearly printed on it.

"And look here," he exclaimed, showing too much enthusiasm for a mundane detail of office procedure.

He pushed a button to retract the first set of files and another button to bring out another stringer of files from the center of the wall

"Ah, here we are!"

He wiggled his index finger in a come-on gesture to Sybil. She felt a little foolish playing along with his boyish pranks, but she followed.

"And here we have our only failure!"

He laughed out loud at his joke. He was pointing at the Brendan McNeely folder.

Sybil smiled with saccharine sweetness. "And soon, you'll have another," she said.

"I don't think so" he said in a low conspiratorial voice. "Let's go to my office."

Paul Bel Geddes's office was unexpectedly neat. Sybil had presumed it would be as cluttered and incomprehensible as the man's mind seemed to be. He had a huge desk, a magnificent piece of English craftsmanship. The wood and brass fittings were polished to a fine luster. On one side of the large desk was an outsized waste basket, and on the other was a top of the line paper shredder. On the desk sat a large computer, scanner, printer, modem, and fax machine. Bel Geddes was not a computer expert, evidently, because a set of instructions, in Dick and Jane simplicity, obviously typed out by his secretary, had been inserted between the heavy plate glass cover and the table top. Bel Geddes's briefcase, bulging with papers, sat in a niche in the bookshelf behind his head.

An old English hunt table stood by the window that overlooked the city. On it stood a double magnum of Château Lafite 1945. Near its base, a price tag had accidentally been left in place - $7110, Herrod's. There were three issues of the ultra haute magazine, *Aria d'Italia*. There had been fewer than ten issues published, Bel Geddes was quick to inform Sybil and her attorneys. It was advertised as the "Cornerstone of Modern Graphic Design." There were five uncomfortable period chairs facing the desk. Bel Geddes took a seat at his desk and indicated to the others to sit as well.

"Perhaps you are wondering why I have called you here," he said and laughed hard at his own humor.

Sybil, Hyrum, and Susan winced at the corniness.

"I've been thinking," he said.

"I hope you didn't do yourself any harm," Sybil said.

He laughed uproariously at her sarcastic attempt at one-upmanship.

"Good one," he said. "Anyhow, I don't see why we necessarily have to be at odds here. Maybe we can do a little fence mending."

Susan's eyes narrowed in undisguised dubiety.

"What do you have in mind, Paul?" she queried.

"Well...perhaps with a modicum of cooperation between us, I could see my way clear to drop Dr. Norcroft from the case early on. That's not to say that I don't have a very strong case against her as part of a cabal to deprive poor Mr. Turner of his money and his life."

Susan sighed.

"Tell me, Paul. What sort of cooperation did you envision?"

"Always the lawyer. I like that about you, Susan. But you ought to loosen up, trust your fellowman a little. I have a straightforward completely legitimate proposition for the good doctor."

Sybil had never liked the appellation 'good doctor'—it always seemed to be condescending—and she was becoming annoyed at being referred to in the third person as if she were not present in the room.

"Stop fencing, Paul. What is your offer?"

"All right, to the point, then. Dr. Norcroft is the chief of surgery at Joseph Noble Memorial Hospital and was in that position when the Jason Turner incident occurred. She is an expert. If she were to give testimony for the plaintiffs in the Turner case, I would consider dropping her from the list of defendants."

Sybil's eyebrows shot up. Susan looked at Bel Geddes's face with serious concern. Hyrum shook his head vigorously.

"Well, what do you think? Fight me or join me?" Bel Geddes said and leaned back in his chair to await the decision.

"I would have to speak with my client alone, Paul. This is rather sudden, and I think I know her response, but I would have to confer with her."

"Sure. No problem. You stay here. I'll go putter around outside for ten minutes, then I'll come back for your answer. That fair?"

"Fine."

He got up and left. As he passed Sybil, he gave her shoulder an affectionate pat. She steeled herself not to shrink away.

"Can you believe the chutzpah of that guy?!" exclaimed Hyrum when the door closed.

"I know what you are going to say, Dr. Norcroft, but for pro forma, we at least have to go through the motions of having a privileged conversation about Paul's offer. It is offensive, but quintessential Paul. Just consider it another distasteful ploy in a series of obnoxious encounters with the man. Don't take any of his nonsense personally," Susan said.

Sybil was growing tired of attorneys presuming that they knew her mind, or that they could make her decisions for her. It rankled her a little that Susan and Hyrum underestimated her intellect and her ability to cope with the opposing attorney and that the two defense lawyers viewed her as a one dimensional character—stolidly ethical, medically idealistic and naive, and predictable. She steepled her fingers in front of her face and stared straight ahead while she studiously weighed her options and tried to envision the consequences of pursuing each of the several alternatives.

"How about just giving him the finger and putting the gloves back on and going in there and finishing the depo?" asked Hyrum in a pugnacious tone.

He had developed a deep and abiding disdain for Paul Bel Geddes from the first time he met him in one of the firm's cases three years before when he first joined Schmid, Principle, Tarkington, and Henley. Nothing in the interim had softened that antipathy.

"I'm in full agreement, Dr. Norcroft, at least about finishing the deposition. My colleague gets carried away in his enthusiasm. Turning down Paul's offer goes without saying. We might as well tell the man and get on with it. Okay, Dr. Norcroft?"

Sybil reacted as if she had just awakened.

"No, it's not okay. I'll take the deal."

Susan and Hyrum looked dumbstruck.

"I want out of this stupid case. I will dictate the terms to Bel Geddes. I want to talk to him alone."

"But, Sybil...Dr. Norcroft...you can't mean that...you can't want to—" Susan sputtered.

Hyrum looked angry, betrayed.

"It's like 'marrying the devil's daughter and inviting the old folks to dinner,' as someone once said. You can't get into bed with that guy and not come out...soiled."

He looked at Sybil with rapidly developing anger tinged with sadness. He had respected and admired the self-possessed woman until now.

"I don't plan to get into bed with that guy, Mr. Willis."

Her voice was icy calm.

"I plan to do business with him. It is presumptuous of you to think that you know me or my mind. I will deal with Paul Bel Geddes on the issue of testifying. I am requesting the two of you, as my attorneys, to address the necessary waivers and so forth to extricate me once and for all from this farcical suit."

Her eyes glittered with animosity.

Hyrum was not sure but that the anger was directed at him.

Susan seemed subdued. She gave a little defeated shrug of her shoulders and fought to keep her opinions out of her facial expressions.

"All right. We'll call him back. However, as your attorney, Doctor, I advise against any communication between you and Paul that excludes us."

Sybil regarded Susan's comment as little more than the disclaimer of an attorney working to deflect responsibility.

"Advice received and considered. I still want to talk to him alone."

Sybil's voice was now flinty hard, her mind set.

"As you wish. But please remember that I warned you against it in the strongest way," Susan said as a parting shot.

Sybil made a dismissive gesture with her hand.

Hyrum clenched and unclenched his fists. He almost jumped out of his chair and strode rapidly to the office door and flung it open. Paul was standing in the hallway laughing with one of the nontyping administrative assistants. He looked up as Hyrum stepped into the hallway.

"So soon, Hyrum?" Bel Geddes asked smugly.

"We are ready for you to return, Mr. Bel Geddes," Hyrum said with unnecessary formality.

He could not keep enmity out of his voice or off his face.

Bel Geddes appeared not to notice and followed the younger attorney back into his office and took his seat behind the great desk.

"I take it that you have reached a mutually agreeable decision regarding my offer?" he asked, taking pleasure at the obvious discomfiture of the three people facing him. "Would you like to share with me?"

"My client wishes, against my advice, I might add, to accede to your proposal," Susan said.

Her face was dark. She had striven to remove the telltale signs of anger from her visage but had only succeeded in achieving a look of resignation.

"Well, I salute her perceptiveness and her strong sense of medical ethics. Maybe there's hope for the medical establishment after all," Paul goaded.

Hyrum sat glumly aside, unwilling to participate further.

"Do you want to have the papers made up, or should I?" asked Susan.

"It just so happens that I have already taken the liberty of preparing the necessary documents," Bel Geddes said with a guileless expression.

"How convenient," said Susan.

"How predictable," said Bel Geddes.

He looked straight at Sybil as if the two of them had made a secret pact. He was now sure that he understood Dr. Norcroft. For all her hauteur, she was no different from any of the rest of the prostitutes in his string of physicians. It was only a question of the price.

"Pass it over, Paul," said Susan.

He slid the papers to the middle of the desk so that she would have to get up and retrieve them. She perused the documents quickly. The wording was simple. He dismissed the case against Sybil Norcroft, and she waived her right to sue for malicious prosecution. Susan passed the papers to Sybil who signed them with alacrity. Paul took pleasure in the doctor's evident complete and easily won capitulation.

Susan kept her copy and passed the other copy back to Paul, making sure that it did not go beyond the middle of the desktop, another little tit-for-tat gesture. Paul opened the Jason Turner file and placed the documents in it and set it aside.

"I presume that concludes our business," he said and stood as a dismissive signal.

Hyrum and Susan stood; Sybil walked behind them.

They left the room, and as they did, Sybil turned back to Bel Geddes and said, "You and I need to have a few minutes alone."

Bel Geddes leered as if he had just received an indecent proposal.

"But of course, my dear."

Susan turned and gave Sybil a brief parting glance; there was no masking her disappointment. Hyrum Willis hunched his shoulders and looked straight ahead.

"Please wait here a moment, Dr. Norcroft. I'll go excuse the court reporter."

She nodded and resumed her seat. He was gone less than three minutes.

Bel Geddes returned looking satisfied and at ease with the world.

Sybil spoke as soon as he sat down.

"Paul? Do you mind if I call you, Paul?"

"Not at all, Sybil. What do you have in mind?"

"A simple business deal, one that is committed to paper, say...one that is similar to the agreement between you and Dr. de Montesquiou from Canada."

"$300 an hour and expenses? That's standard."

"On paper, yes. And the rest that he was paid, more like 1000 dollars an hour."

"I take it this is a time for full candor. I want to know a few things up front. Like, are you wearing a wire?"

"A what?"

"A recording device."

"Good grief, how cloak and dagger. I wouldn't know the first thing about such things."

"Then you won't mind being searched."

"I would mind very much."

"I wasn't suggesting that I do the searching, although...."

"Maybe by one of the women in your office. Is that what you had in mind?"

"For now."

"All right, let's make it quick. I want to conclude our business and get back to my work."

"No sooner said than done."

He pushed a button on the console behind him. Shortly, one of the buxom secretaries entered.

"Nance," he said. "Search this sweet thing and see if she is carrying any weapons or if she is wired. Can you do that?"

"Sure."

It came out in a Bronx accent that made the word almost into two syllables.

Sybil followed the woman to one of the ladies rooms. She detached herself from what was being done to her, thinking all the while what an ugly world Paul Bel Geddes must inhabit. *Living and working with the bottom feeders must make you a lot like them*, she thought.

"I don't know if he wanted a body cavity search," said the secretary.

"Believe me, he doesn't," said Sybil emphatically.

Her tone and expression left nothing to speculation.

Once back in the office, Bel Geddes said, "Sorry, I can't be too cautious in my business. You never know."

"No problem," Sybil told him. "Let's get finished."

154

"You were talking about ten bills an hour. You are new to this professional witness business, Dr. Norcroft. I'll tell you where the bear sleeps. In all candor, your testimony is not worth that much. This is not the case for that kind of bread. The going rate is 300 an hour plus a tidy little bonus, say, a couple of thou if we win. The idea is that you become part of my team. I call on you for info, opinions, and, of course, for testimony in open court. This case is a slam dunk for me, but I need good people for the future. I will be open with you, Doc. You have no history of testifying. That, and your high standing in the profession, are your main marketable qualities. I'll have hot cases where you can help skewer one of your hapless colleagues. You'll have to make a few little compromises to get the big bucks. Think you're up to that?"

Sybil gritted her teeth and turned her mouth into a symbol of determination.

"You know, Paul, I have been on the wrong end of the stick for too long. This courtroom stuff doesn't look all that difficult, and I think I can go head to head with anyone that a defense can produce. I have developed some expensive tastes and need the extras you can provide. I hope we are understanding each other. I want in on the big cases. I want real money. Let's don't be coy about it."

"This change seems rather sudden, Sybil. How come?"

"It's not all that sudden. I've been thinking about it ever since Carter Tarkington exposed Pierre de Montesquiou's income just from you. I have always been the good girl. It hasn't been getting me anywhere. I want some of what de Montesquiou's been getting."

"Your surgeon friends won't like you."

"Big deal. They don't like me anyway. No loss. My social interests revolve around the horsey set; they only care if you have money, not how you got it."

She gave him a calculating look.

"And it's to be $450 an hour on this case or no deal. In the future I will have a thousand."

Bel Geddes was pensive for a minute or two.

Then he said, "All right, Sybil, we're a team on the Turner versus JNMH, Midgel, and Krempen, et. al. case. If that case works out, I'll get you into the big time. Consider Turner a probation. There are some instructions. Absolutely, under no circumstances, talk to any other lawyer, doctor, friend, or family member about the case, you are our ace-in-the-hole. I want the other side to keep guessing right up to the end. You take the high road in any conversations. No matter what, I don't want you to be deposed. You are so above reproach that I don't think they will even ask. Especially with the

155

stuff we got in the deposition today. I am not going to list you as an expert. You will come in as a percipient witness—testifying as to the facts. You will be established as the chief of surgery and a trauma expert. You can work your magic and prove yourself then. I'll pay you the tax free way."

She raised an eyebrow.

"Under the table. Do I have to spell everything out? You have to get to be more perceptive if you're going to be able to fly with the med-mal witness crowd."

"Sorry. I'm new. I'll get up to speed. You spoke of me being on probation. That changes the tenor of things a bit. Since we aren't going to be all chummy and trustful, I want to be paid up front on this first case. I guess that I'll be spending about 24 hours on the case what with preparation, travel, and actual in-court testimony. That comes to some $10,800."

"Dream on. I figure more like five hours—$2,250."

"Then I don't want to play. I lose that much out of my pockets when I sit down on a couch. I'll go as low as $8,000 and not a cent less."

"I do think you are catching on. I'll give you $6500 now, today, and if we win big, I'll kick in another two thou. That's the fair market value of your services. Ask around."

"All right. I'll go low-ball this go around, but, after that, I want in on the real money. I'll prove my worth. You don't have a thing to worry about on that score."

"I'm sure not. Here, my offering of good faith."

He opened a large corporate check and invoice book and wrote out a check for $6500.00. He made a note on the check and on the invoice, *For Witness Services*.

She picked up her coffee cup.

"Here's to a long and profitable relationship."

He lifted his, "Confusion to our enemies."

They made a salute out of taking a drink together. She allowed him to put his arm affectionately around her shoulder as he showed her to the door. When she got home, she took a long hot shower and washed her hands three times in very hot water.

CHAPTER SEVEN

2013 was a good year for Sybil Norcroft, M.D., PhD, F.A.C.S. George and Dolly's four year old filly, Moccasin Walker, sold for $28,000 and their young horse, three-year-old Walking Conquistador, sold for $74,500. Two foals from Ring Pride by Beautiful Girl, a Middleton Stables mare from Stratford, Missouri, netted $81,000 each and would have brought in more if Sybil and her Mexicans had been able to provide proper training. Sybil and her partners held on to the oldest and best of George and Dolly's progeny, the golden auburn five-year-old, Sun Walker, that won its fourth best in show championship trophies in 2013 and the deep reddish brown, Bai Walker. The two Tennessee Walker champions and Ring Pride were insured for a million dollars each. All of her Tennessee Walkers had luxuriant black manes and tails and one right foreleg that was a gleaming white stocking. They were, if nothing else, beautiful. The Mexicans trained them lovingly, and all of the horses were becoming champion smooth-gaited animals.

The contrasting silver grey Paso Finos were flourishing, still too young to be sold, but would be broken to the saddle this year and their gaits perfected in another year. Then they would become a mainstay of the ranch's income base. Like the Tennessee Walkers' training, the Mexicans were infinitely patient with the Paso Finos. The men used only Pelham polo bits and had advanced beyond the use of cavessons by the time the horses were three years old. They never used martingales or harsh bits. Whips were not permitted on the ranch. If a horse was so unruly or skittish that a whip was necessary, Sybil and the Mexicans sold it at a minimal profit and concentrated on the horses whose temperaments and fine training, along with their silken gaits made them of great value.

The ranch was now paying its way, and in another two years would be operating at a profit, having paid off its substantial start-up debts. The Mexicans were now serious and well informed business people. They had reinvested their profits, and Sybil had allowed them to buy a total of 30 percent of the ranch. The men, women, and children held their *Patrona* in veneration, and they were held in true affection by her. Whenever she came to the property, she was treated with the respect that had once been accorded the grandees of Spain by their forefathers.

Sybil invited Paul Bel Geddes and his fourth wife, Sophronia, an attractive, but abrasive African American woman, to her victory dinner celebration after Sun Walker won his championship.

"How nice of you to come," she cooed when Mrs. Bel Geddes entered Sybil and Charles's foyer.

The tawny skinned beauty had scarlet nails fully an inch long, wore five large diamond rings, and her neckline plunged below her umbilicus. She had a tattoo of a mythical African god-woman on her sternum with flares of a cloak wafting out onto the swells of her breasts.

"You look lovely," Sybil said.

Sybil personally showed the couple into the dining room. Bel Geddes's greedy eyes took in paintings by Monet, Matisse, Caillebotte, Casset, and original Georgia O'Keeffes. One wall held only a huge Shannon mirror with painted Églomisé decoration. In the corner of the room was a small, elegant Queen Anne table. A T'ang dynasty vase with fresh Sarah Bernhardt peonies, bearded iris, and Moonlight violas sat on top. An 18th century Glin Sideboard with a delicate open fretwork cornice displayed Dr. Norcroft's Dresden china. Paul's soft shoes slipped luxuriously over the 16th century Kashan Austrian Hunting carpet. The interwoven threads of silver and gold added highlights to the rich silk of the carpet. He took in the profusion of horsemen in pursuit of deer and the winged gods chasing lions and buffaloes done in exquisite miniature in the woven design. He felt at home or, at least, that this was what home should be like for him.

Bel Geddes was in his $1600 Giorgio Armani suit—by Paul's usual standard—a conservative light gold color. He wore three large diamond rings and a $100 silk Hermès tie. His shoes, Bally moccasins, were made of gorilla skin, a fact that he did not share with everyone. He was in good spirits having decided that an invitation into Sybil Norcroft's horsey circle was *de rigueur*. He had arrived.

Sybil placed Bel Geddes next to her at the immense Honduran mahogany Chippendale table during the service. The usual rule of boy-girl, boy-girl, and no one next to his or her spouse applied. It was the place of honor, and Bel Geddes basked in his newly won glory.

"How's the preparation for the trial going?" she asked as they ate their *Etuvee de Moules de Bouchot et Petits Coquillages au Curry et a L'Oignon Doux. et Choux de Bruxelles.*

They were served from a burnished silver chafing dish and ate with matching Primrose design silverware. He did not really like the slimy looking mussels, and he had always hated Brussels sprouts, but he would never have admitted it.

"Piece of cake, my dear. It's a shoo-in. I am loaded for bear. I wish it was tomorrow."

He enjoyed the onions encrusted in deep fried sesame seed flour. He picked at the mussels and hoped she would not notice.

"I see mega-bucks in our future, old Syb, mega-bucks."

'Syb' and 'old Syb' had become his favorite terms of endearment over the months he had been cultivating her. He felt that the diminutive of her name leveled her and made the famous doctor more approachable. She did not seem to make any protest.

"I'm a pragmatist, Paul. I'll believe all of that when the check is in my bank and approved."

The wine steward poured him a glass of Château Pétrus. Bel Geddes fancied himself to be an oenophile and recognized that he was being served the world's most expensive Bordeaux. He savored the soft richness of the merlot in the wine.

"Checks, my dear, *ma petit chou.*"

He looked to see if she flinched at being called a little cabbage, a term one of his fancier friends had told him was exactly the right thing to call a woman with whom you were intimate.

She did not emit the slightest flinch. She passed him the shaker of Guérande marsh salt. It was gray, not very appetizing to look at, but good to taste, he found. Gourmet fare was not all bad.

"Um-hmm," she mused in a world weary sigh.

He resolved to get her a juicy case to prove that he could deliver. She was an investment, a delicate flower to tend and cultivate, and one that would pay beautiful dividends in the years to come. He was sitting on the edge of the pot of gold. He was on his best behavior.

"I'm sorry, I never asked. Have you any children, Paul?"

The wine steward poured him another glass of Chaillot Bouchons. The strains of a Scarlotti sonata wafted over the unobtrusive sound system.

"I do. I thought I mentioned that. I have a sixteen-year-old daughter. She's in Switzerland, at finishing school."

He thought she would like that.

Sybil's face lit up.

"How wonderful! Does she ride?"

"The school teaches dressage, but apparently not on any kind of serious competitive level."

"I might be able to help if she is really interested."

The wine server brought Paul a crème de cassis.

"That would be wonderful, Sybil. How nice of you. Catherine is a fine young horsewoman, I think. At least, I believe she has real potential. She is the apple of my eye, so I could be the least bit biased."

"Please give me her address. I will tell my dear old friends Le Comte d'Odiel and la Parincesse de Bavière of Andalusia, Seville, to be exact. They have wonderful horse ranches and a riding school without peer. They would be happy to have your lovely daughter train with them."

It was a heady thing for a man whose early boyhood had been spent on the streets of Marseilles scrapping for a *sou* to be discussing the enrollment of his daughter with Spanish nobility in a riding school for the ultra rich and privileged. He wished that his papa had lived to see this day.

He had a second La Grande Dame champagne and accepted a large and exclusive Davidoff cigar when he left that evening. His wife, Sophronia, was as impressed and as happy as he was. She had been seated next to Charles Daniels and had been treated like visiting royalty. Like her attorney husband, she was entranced by the prospects of the developing relationship with the crème de la crème of the social register of Westminster County.

When the Bel Geddeses left at the end of the evening, Sybil presented the attorney with an illustrated copy of the Bocuse Cookbook. Inside the front cover, she had placed in her inimitable handwriting the inscription, "To Paul - may you have success in the pursuit of the right. Sybil Norcroft".

Sybil's practice was stable and profitable. She had joined the crusade against a national health service that had been successful in 2010. It appeared that the cyclic demand for socialized medicine reared its head about once a decade. Sybil had resisted joining any large marketing groups, HMOs, or accepting any payment plan that refused to pay her standard fees-for-service, and that included the federal and state Medicare and Medicaid programs. At first, she had found it difficult to get enough patients to have a really profitable practice, but her courage and perseverance paid off, and now, she was able to pick and choose her patients and to specialize her efforts. As a result, her practice had afforded a handsome, after taxes, seven-figure income. She was in considerable demand on the speaking circuit for medical associations and specialty organizations to detail how she avoided being swallowed up in or defeated by the huge capitation medical businesses. The mood of the country was beginning to swing away from corporate medicine. Americans were no longer willing to accept poor quality medicine, long waiting periods to receive care, being thwarted in their desires to have necessary tests, and to see their premiums going to make obscene profits for the stockholders of the insurance companies. Sybil was the right person at the right time, and she was at the pinnacle of her professional life. She had become easily the most famous neurosurgeon, and probably the most respected and best known physician in the United States. Her fame bordered on the movie star level.

Paul Bel Geddes was ecstatic over his new star witness's fame. The Jason Turner trial was only a month away, and with Dr. Norcroft as his star, he could not lose. He referred in private to her as his best secret prostie, and saw dollar signs every time he encountered the well known doctor. He was going to use her in trials for the next twenty years until her reputation, like the rest of the prosties on the circuit, would no longer support continued courtroom appearances. He would be retired by then anyway. Her professional standing at that point would be of no more than secondary consideration.

In public, he could not have been more effusive in his praise of Dr. Norcroft. She heard grumblings by Drs. Krempen and Midgel and the hospital administrators about Bel Geddes's favorable comments concerning her. She refused to comment or become defensive over the fact that she was one of the plaintiff's witnesses. Since she never commented or was seen to be a professional witness in any other case, the defense elected to leave her alone. The two defendant doctors assured their attorneys and the insurance company that

Dr. Norcroft was a real doctor first and foremost and would not sell them out. No one was all that confident, however.

The trial of Jason Turner, Dec. versus Drs. Krempen and Midgel, and the JNMH opened on March 17, 2013. The selection of the jury took eleven days, indicative of the rancorous climate of the case. No one intended to give the slightest millimeter of ground. Bel Geddes scheduled Sybil to testify on the fifth day, following Turner's wife, mother, father, eldest son, and Dr. Ibn al-Hebreaus.

Because she was a witness, Sybil could not observe the testimony by any of the other witnesses. On the eve of her testimony day, she and Bel Geddes met in his office. He served Brut champagne, already celebrating. The case was going so well that he expected a mid-trial settlement offer.

"I have to tell you about old Ibn al whatshisname," Paul said, a little giddy from his fourth snifter of bubbly. "He crucified them. He all but made them out to be deliberate murderers. 'If only they had gotten me in at the beginning, if only I had been able to get into that boy's chest sooner, none of this would have happened. I am so sad for the family. I could have saved their son, you know. I really could have'. His best line was, 'They kept me out because I'm Persian. For that bit of closet racism, a boy died. Will our country never be rid of the scourge of bigotry?' I taught him about 'scourge', and I made him change over to the racism phrase instead of the original idea that you and he were enemies. It packs more punch anyhow."

"Good strategy, Paul. It looks like it is in the bag. Maybe you don't even need me tomorrow."

"Oh, yes I do, my dear. Look, Syb, you are going to be the last nail in the coffin lid. With your status and presence, they are finished. I'll tell you the truth, I think they'll be after me for a settlement when you get done. It will be late Friday afternoon. Judge Martini will adjourn for the weekend with your testimony fresh in the jury's mind. I frankly don't think we will still be in trial come Monday."

"I'm happy for you, Paul. You've worked very hard, done everything an attorney could do. It's no wonder you're so successful. Here's to you."

She raised her glass, and he downed his fifth snifter, unembarrassed to toast himself.

At two thirty the following afternoon, the bailiff announced, "Plaintiff calls Sybil Norcroft."

Sybil was nervous, like a performer with the first night jitters. She took the witness seat and was sworn in.

Paul Bel Geddes approached Sybil and leaned his elbow familiarly on the railing in front of her, making sure that the jury could see her well. She was wearing a striking Fabrice original in swirling, almost party colors and a Baum and Mercier 22-karat gold bangle watch. The effect was well beyond the demure professional physician image that Bel Geddes would have preferred. He would have to educate her about dress; you had to think of everything for the doctor witnesses. They did not seem to catch on very quickly.

"Dr. Norcroft," he said, "I'd like to go through your qualifications for the jury. I have a copy of your curriculum vitae and will use it, but feel free to add whatever information you think is necessary, all right?"

"Yes, Sir."

She was beginning to settle down. Her heart rate had dropped ten points since she had sat down. She removed her index finger from her wrist pulse.

"Let's start with your high school career. You attended Cate School in California, where you graduated as the valedictorian. Tell us about that part of your education, please."

Sybil told of the prestige of the school, of her honors, and her activities. She had been a medalist in swimming. She disliked the blatant self-aggrandizement inherent in this part of her testimony, but it was quite evidently how the game was played.

"Objection," the defendants' attorneys both said. "What is the purpose of this line of questioning in this matter before the court?"

"Your honor, I seek to establish my client's bona fides as an expert and to do so, I have to verify her educational background."

"She is not listed as an expert, your honor."

"Please approach the bench."

The attorneys gathered at the side bar.

"Please let me know what you are doing with this line of questioning, Mr. Bel Geddes."

"I am establishing Dr. Norcroft's bona fides as a person competent to render a judgment in this case. In fact, she is in a unique position to do so. I need to lay the foundation by bringing out her pertinent background."

"But she is here as a percipient witness, not an expert, your honor."

"Her unique position in the hospital and in relation to the other doctors requires a certain expertise. That needs to be established for the jury."

The judge sat thoughtfully for a moment.

"I'll allow it, Mr. Bel Geddes. But, Mr. Drakeson, you may treat her as an expert, even as a hostile witness, if you so choose."

"You can count on it."

Drakeson glared at Bel Geddes. He was sure that Bel Geddes had sand-bagged him, and it would not be the first time.

Paul returned to his questioning.

"Thank you, Dr. Norcroft. That was an impressive start. Now, could you tell us about your undergraduate college years?"

Sybil went into detail about her National Merit Scholarship to Mills College, her college career replete with its awards and commendations, the bronze medal in the NCAA swimming competition her senior year, her senior paper on the *Periodic Decline and Cyclic Rise in the Career Status of American Medicine*, and her prize-winning valedictory address. She listed her clubs, participation in the school's symphony orchestra as its pianist, and her year abroad as an exchange student at Cambridge.

"I presume you had no time for a social life with that full schedule, Doctor," Bel Geddes said affably.

"Not much, I suppose. But I did meet my future husband while I was at Mills. The education wasn't a total waste."

She smiled.

The jurors laughed. She felt that they were with her.

"Then medical school. Yale University, again on a scholarship. Please elaborate, if you would, Doctor."

"There is not a lot to tell. I was a hardworking, rather penurious medical student like all the rest of my classmates. I took an interest in neurosurgery early on and that led to my taking time after graduation to get a PhD in medical science. My field of research was in the biochemical correlates of the pain of deafferentation."

"And, once again, you graduated magna cum laude."

"Yes."

"And I see here that your PhD degree came from Harvard?"

"That's right?"

"Any special honors there?"

"No, just the degree."

"And your doctoral dissertation was expanded into a book, I understand."

"Yes, Sir."

"How many books and papers have you written, Dr. Norcroft?"

"As author or co-author...forty-six."

"Were both the M.D. and PhD degrees required for acceptance into your neurological surgery training residency?"

"Yes, both."

"Most impressive. I am sure it was a highly sought after position to become a resident."

"There were only ten residency positions in the entire country available that year. I believe the number has climbed to thirteen this year."

"Then your residency in neurosurgery. UCLA, correct?"

"Yes. The residency was seven years long."

The jurors looked impressed, almost awed.

"I see that there were some honors involved."

"I received the Van Wagenen award as a resident researcher, the Robert Rand Memorial Teaching Prize for my work with junior residents and medical students, and finally, selection to be the chief resident of the UCLA Hospitals."

"And over and above all that, you found time to get married and to contribute significantly to the great women's rights cause that is so vital to the well-being of our great nation, isn't that right?"

"Objection, irrelevant."

"Sustained. Is this going to take much longer, Counsel?"

"Not at all, your honor. I expect to finish with this witness before adjournment today."

"That's the best news I've heard all day. Don't let me detain you."

"Now, Dr. Norcroft, did you have occasion to work with trauma patients during your training?"

"Extensively."

"Did you restrict your involvement to neurosurgical injuries?"

Sybil had coached Bel Geddes on this line of questioning.

"Not at all. Most the injuries we saw in training, and afterwards in practice, for that matter, were compound injuries. By that I mean multiple different injuries to multiple different areas of the body in the same patient. It was common to have to deal with patients who had neurological injuries or who required a neurosurgical evaluation during the course of their workup and treatment for their other injuries."

"Were any of the patients with whom you worked suffering from injuries to their chests?"

"Many."

"Serious, even life threatening chest injuries?"

"Yes."

"Injuries with severe bleeding, falling blood pressure, shock?"

"Yes to all of those conditions."

The defense attorney started to object, but thought he would be seen as being nitpicking, so he held his peace.

"Have you had experience with such injuries since you finished your residency and started your fine neurosurgical practice?"

"Many times."

"Dr. Norcroft, what is your current position at Joseph Noble Memorial Hospital?"

"I am the chief, the chairperson, of the department of surgery."

"Of surgery or just of neurosurgery?"

"The entire department, including all specialties."

"Emergency medicine and general surgery?"

"Both of those."

"Are Dr. Daniel Krempen from the emergency room and Dr. Peter Midgel from general surgery under your jurisdiction as the chief of surgery?"

"Yes, they are."

"So you are in charge of their work?"

"In a manner of speaking. I am directly responsible for quality assurance evaluation of their work, at least."

"Then, I take it you are in a position to evaluate, even to judge their work?"

"Yes, that is part of the mandate of my elected position."

"Even though you are neither an emergency room specialist nor a general surgeon?"

"Yes. As a result of my unique position in the hospital and based on my experience and training."

"Objection, no foundation!" Dr. Midgel's attorney insisted.

"I think the foundation has been laid. The jury can take the testimony into consideration. Overruled."

"Tell me, Doctor, did you have occasion to be involved in the treatment of Jason Turner, deceased?"

"Yes, I did."

"Can you describe your involvement?"

Sybil carefully recounted her call to the ER indicating the need to hurry to attend a patient in extremis, her neurosurgical examination in the hectic period of attempted stabilization of the badly injured man, and the frantic efforts of the nurses and doctors in the emergency room.

Bel Geddes thought she was making the physicians sound too caring and competent, but his main need was to establish the negligence in getting proper surgical specialty care in time.

"And when the patient left the emergency room to go to the operating room, was he still bleeding profusely?"

"He was."

"Did the doctors and nurses seem to be aware of the gravity of the situation? Were they hurrying, or were they acting in a routine fashion, taking their time, almost as if this were an elective case?"

Paul had coached Sybil for hours on this particular point. In their sessions, she had come to sound very convincing that the bumpkin doctors and lazy preoccupied nurses took their sweet time to get the victim stabilized and transported to the OR.

Sybil moved her gaze from the jury where she had been looking throughout her testimony, and turned towards Bel Geddes. She smiled.

He looked down, so no one else would be able to accuse him of coaching his witness during her testimony. It was critical that the response he wanted come voluntarily.

She drew in a slight breath and said, "They seemed to be deeply concerned. They had been working frantically and efficiently in the ER, and now they had to go to the OR even without full stabilization. They ran down the hallway to the OR elevator."

She said it with perfect aplomb and without taking her eyes from the attorney.

Bel Geddes started into the next question just as he had rehearsed it two dozen times with her and before his office mirror another several score times, "Then, Doctor, how would you characterize such wanton—"

He stopped mid-question as the impact of what Sybil had said sunk in. He coughed. She must have been nervous and fluffed her lines. It was a bad slip, and he would have to do damage control.

"I believe you meant to say that they seemed nervous and busy, but that they did not seem to comprehend the gravity of *this* patient's condition. Isn't that right?"

"No, Sir. To the best of my recollection, the two physicians and the nurses were moving full speed ahead. They had a plan and were working at it as fast as they possibly could."

"Well, Doctor, I would like to ask you if an attempt, any attempt, any effort at all was put forth by these doctors to get a chest surgeon involved in this tragic situation?"

Bel Geddes had recovered. He knew he had a willful witness on his hands, a woman who always thought she knew the best thing to do or say and had to be in control. She had suddenly decided to alter his scenario a little with an extemporaneous improvisation. She did not want to appear to be his stooge. That was it. As he reflected on what she had said, he thought it was not such a bad idea, made her look more objective.

"Absolutely. I personally heard Dr. Midgel order Lillian Hemmet, RN, to call the chest surgeon on call. At one point, she came up to Dr. Midgel and quietly told him that she had put in calls to several thoracic surgeons as well as the doctor on call and could not get any of them to respond."

"Who on earth is Lillian Hemmet?"

Bel Geddes's pique was roused, and he could not prevent himself from asking the obvious question, even though he did not know the answer to the question he was posing, a cardinal risk in witness examination.

"One of the ER nurses. I believe she has since left the hospital...moved to Australia, if memory serves me right."

"I saw no records of the calls to the chest surgeons in the nurse's notes. How do you explain that, Doctor?"

He was angry, wondering what Dr. Norcroft thought she was doing.

"She did not write the notes. Mary Anders did. She was the designated scribe for the case. Apparently, she did not know about the calls. It was very hectic. Writing down such details had to take a backseat to more pressing problems. It's a wonder that there were any coherent notes at all. I applaud the nurses for their efficiency."

"*You could have waited the rest of both of our lives and not said that,*" thought Bel Geddes bitterly. "*What is this woman up to?*"

He said, "It's pretty difficult to ascertain the truth or lack of it regarding the contention that calls were made, since this Hemmet person is on the other side of the planet."

"Not at all. I have communicated with her myself. I have a letter from her, with her notarized signature. She responded to my questions. I have my letter to her as well. Here, you might like to see the letters...in the interest of justice."

She produced a folder with the letters neatly encased in plastic binders inside.

"Objection!" Bel Geddes shouted.

"Objection? Your honor, can an attorney object to his own witness? I've never heard of such a thing," responded Krempen's attorney.

Bel Geddes looked humiliated. He had lost control of the situation, of his witness and, apparently, of himself. He fought to regain control.

"I'll overrule the objection. Counsel may continue to question his witness, and the witness may continue to respond."

Bel Geddes was furious. It would have been the better part of valor to say, "No more questions," but he wanted to force her into giving him what he wanted, he had to wring some concession out of her. She had betrayed him, and now he was twisting on the gibbet. He had to try.

"But if this mythical Ms. Hemmet tried so hard to get a chest surgeon, how is it that she so remarkably seemed to overlook Dr. al-Hebreaus? He has testified in this courtroom that he never received a call until the two unqualified physicians were in the operating room and had opened the poor victim's chest. How do you explain *that*, Doctor?"

The acerbic edge to his voice served to confuse the jury. They looked at him as if he were intentionally alienating them.

He was feeling desperate.

She smiled at him then turned to the jury, "I myself called Dr. al-Hebreaus. I got the same answer from his answering service and from his home that the nurses did. He was busy, couldn't be disturbed until after his tennis."

The courtroom had become quiet.

"You don't care for Dr. al-Hebreaus, do you, Dr. Norcroft?"

"Not especially. I think he is a flagrant male chauvinist and an egoist in general who allows his prejudices to get in the way of his professional work. But he is not so terribly unusual in that regard. As a surgeon, I find him arrogant and abrasive but competent. Our relationship is strictly professional."

He thought she was perhaps throwing him a straw.

"Is it your opinion that Dr. al-Hebreaus is fully capable of dealing with a complicated and difficult surgical problem such as was presented by Jason Turner?"

"I consider him to be professionally capable, a good technical surgeon."

Bel Geddes continued to seethe inside, but he had calmed himself enough to realize that he would be doing his client no further good by continuing to question this terrible woman. He decided to quit while he was on a positive note, albeit a thin one.

"No further questions, your honor."

He was soaked in sweat. He guessed his systolic blood pressure to be a 1000.

"Your witness, Counsel," said the judge. "I think there's time left in the afternoon. Perhaps we can finish with her testimony altogether and be ahead of the game. Wouldn't that be an exceptional treat?"

"Thank you, your honor. I have very few questions."

Drakeson did not dare delve too deep. He could not believe his good fortune. One of Bel Geddes's witnesses, essentially one of his famous surprise experts, had just given him the shaft, and there was danger of undoing what she had created with her testimony.

"Dr. Norcroft, thank you for your patience. It has been a long afternoon for you. I will try and be brief."

"Thank you."

"Let's see if I understand your testimony correctly. You have stated that Drs. Krempen and Midgel worked hard and efficiently, and apparently competently to try and save Mr. Turner, that every effort was expended to get a chest surgeon to help, that it was difficult to get the other surgeon in promptly, and our two physicians went ahead with dispatch to do the necessary operation. Is that about the gist of your testimony so far?"

"Objection, leading the witness. Those were not her exact words."

"Would you like to have Dr. Norcroft's testimony read back, Mr. Bel Geddes?" asked the judge.

Paul thought he saw a wicked twinkle in the eye of the court. Bel Geddes knew that it would not help his case to repeat and entrench in the minds of the jury the exact words of his Benedict Arnold of a witness. He ground his teeth.

"No, your honor. Let's move on. I withdraw my objection."

"You occupy the surgical chair for the hospital, is that not what you testified?"

"Yes."

"In that capacity, did you have occasion to perform a critical review of Jason Turner's chart?"

"I did."

"Did you find evidence of malpractice?"

"No."

"Did you find that the hospital, or Dr. Krempen, or Dr. Midgel had performed below the standard of care for such a case?"

"No."

"Did you then or do you now hold the opinion that either Dr. Krempen or Dr. Midgel committed malpractice, or did anything deleterious to the health of Mr. Turner, or made any harmful wrong decisions in his case?"

"No."

The attorney knew he was on a roll. He decided to pursue his line of questioning one more step and then to quit. Barring the unforeseen negative answer from Dr. Norcroft at this juncture, she had all but made his case for him. It was a defense attorney's dream come true.

"If Dr. al-Hebreaus had been available earlier and had been involved in the care, and especially in the early portion of the operation, would the outcome have been different? Would Jason Turner be alive today?"

"No."

"How would you characterize the care provided by the hospital, by Dr. Krempen, and by Dr. Midgel for Jason Turner?"

"Even though the outcome was bad, the care was good. Not just good, excellent. Mr. Turner and his family were fortunate to have Dr. Krempen and Dr. Midgel as their doctors."

It came out so flat and emphatic that Bel Geddes knew he would have to throw in the towel.

"I have no further questions, your honor," said the defense attorney.

"You may step down, Doctor. Do you have any further witnesses, Mr. Bel Geddes?"

The judge's voice had softened noticeably to a nearly sympathetic tone. Bel Geddes wanted to scream. He was now the object of pity!

"No your honor. The plaintiff rests."

Sybil Norcroft was not in the courtroom when Bel Geddes was able to break free. He called her office, then her home. He was angry and abusive with the office receptionist who told him that Dr. Norcroft was not taking any calls that afternoon and would be gone for the weekend. He was infuriated when he tried her home phone and found that it was no longer an active number. She had had her telephone number changed that very morning. When he was finally alone, he roared his impotent fury at a hapless toilet in a roadside men's room. She had planned the whole thing, it was a cold blooded, calculated trap, and he had dropped into it all the way.

On Monday morning, Sybil's operating morning, Bel Geddes asked the judge for a two-hour recess. He used the time to go to the hospital and to wangle his way into the inner sanctum of the operating room. He dressed in scrubs and waited until Dr. Norcroft came out of her operation, dictating into her handheld Dictaphone.

"Dr. Norcroft, how nice to see you."

"And you, Paul. What brings you into the hospital?"

As if she did not know. He had made a vow not just to try and get even but to get revenge a thousand times over. He would not let her force him to an unseeming tirade.

"I came to get my money back, Syb, old girl."

"It's Dr. Norcroft to you, Paul. Only my friends call me by my first name. Incidentally, it is Sybil, never 'Syb'."

He did not want to appear petty by jibing at her over her precious name.

"Whatever," he said with exaggerated indifference.

She infuriated him by bestowing a winning smile on him.

"I want my money back. You stabbed me in the back. The money was for value given. I got less than no value. You owe me."

He had a hard bellicose look.

"If I recall correctly, the check memo read: *For witness services.* You got witness services. I received only fair compensation—your words—you can check the standard with the courts if you like—also your words."

He choked on his words.

"This is not over, dearie. You will rue the day you crossed me, you cocky...woman."

It was the worst thing he could think to say about anyone on the spur of that moment. It even sounded silly to him. He always seemed to come up with the short end of the stick with her. Bel Geddes looked at Sybil with unnerving menace. His pride, his manhood had been hurt.

"Don't be mad, Paul. There will be other clients to fleece, other juries to flimflam. I'm sure you'll find a way to be as rich as you want. Just not from me and certainly not *with* me."

"I don't get mad, sweetheart. I get even. You had better give thought to getting a food taster."

He could not wait to get out of her domain. Besides, he had work to do. He had to go see a couple of attorneys about a mid-trial settlement.

CHAPTER EIGHT

Gerrit van der Hoef's grandfather had worked in the Westminster County boat yards making tug boats. Gerrit's father had worked in the boat yards on sailing ketches, and now Gerrit worked there on navy contract boats—mostly variations of PT boats. He had worked there for 17 years, and as near as he could recall, he had hated every second of every day that he had worked in the shipyard. The work was monotonous and back breaking. He had to bend to rivet and glue, sometimes twisting and stretching to reach a corner or up inside a built-in boat locker. He had lost his first wife because of the boat yard; the place made him so jumpy and angry all the time that she had finally left him, ran away with a shoe salesman. He did not blame her or the shoe man, just the boat yard.

His back hurt all of the time, had for years. He could not remember for sure when he had not had back pain. Although he did not like the pain anymore than any other sane man would, he had reached a sort of steady state with his discomfort. It was always there like an old scold of a wife who never shut up. He could put up with it most times, but he did not have to like it. The worst thing about it was that he still had to work.

Gerrit had seen the company doctors a dozen times or more for his back pain. Most of the time, they told him to "suck it up" or to "get more exercise"; some of the time they put him to bed rest for two days, never more than that, or a couple of weeks of physical therapy that got him off work for a couple of hours three times a week for those two weeks if the doctor was young or new on the job.

They all gave him the same answer to the same question that he asked each of them every time he saw them in clinic, "No, you are not eligible for permanent medical disability for this little back pain."

Worse, none of them would give him a prescription for oxycontin.

He saw an orthopedic surgeon once who agreed with the company doctor's advice and suggested further, that if he wanted to get off work permanently, he had to stick a pin in his eye, or accidentally on purpose, cut off a thumb. That choice seemed a little worse—not much—than having to work in such awful pain; so, he always went back, grousing and ill-willed.

Then his symptoms changed rather markedly. One day on the job—the injuries that took him to the doctors always happened on the job—he lifted a box of rivets and twisted to set the box inside the hull of the punt he was building. The box was not even heavy. He developed a sharp increase in his background back pain. That did not trouble him overmuch, it happened frequently. This time, however, he also developed pain that started in his right buttocks and radiated all the way down his leg to the toes, and it was far worse than his back pain had ever been.

Evangelina Santa Maria Juarez was a tired woman. She was tired of working all the time as a motel maid for a tyrannical Korean boss and a shiftless husband who drank up all of Evangelina's overtime. She was tired of dragging her two sons away from the Diablos, young Pachucos, who thought they were the Messiahs for the downtrodden Hispano-Americans eking out meager livings in the barrios of the Southwestern United States. The Diablos were nothing but gang punks with no future, and Evangelina hoped for better for her boys. More than anything, she was tired of keeping no more than a step or two in head of the feared immigrations. Evangelina was a seventh generation illegal immigrant in the United States, living part of every year in Mexico when she was apprehended, despite all her efforts, and deported, only to return through the revolving door that served America as a border. None of her family, and no one of her immediate acquaintance, had ever become a citizen or even an authentic green card holder.

After a particularly grueling day at the motel, Evangelina sat on the Metroline bench with two other women waiting for the bus. A black boy no more than twelve walked in front of the three homeward bound domestics on the bench and began to make obscene pelvic gyrations at the work-and-life-weary women. They steadfastly refused to pay the boy any attention. He acted as if he were going to unzip his pants and expose himself. The three women turned aside their heads. He laughed hysterically and cursed them. He walked up to Evangelina and blew a piercing shrill athletic whistle in her face, causing her to jump backwards involuntarily. Then he suddenly snatched the poor woman's purse and sped away with the speed and agility of a startled rabbit. Reflexively, Evangelina leaped up and tried to run after the nimble child. Her blood pressure shot up to 210/110, her heart rate skyrocketed, her breath came in gasps as she raced to the end of the block after the audacious little thief. She collapsed fifty yards from the bus stop.

The bus driver called 911 and an EMT crew on a city fire department ambulance rushed Mrs. Juarez to the JNMH emergency room. On examination, Evangelina was found to be awake, but unable to respond to anything but painful stimuli. The emergency room physician found her to be unable to move her right side, and to have lost all speech. He checked the roster of neurology services physicians on call, found Dr. Norcroft's name beside the day's date, and called her answering service.

"What do you have, Jerry?" asked Sybil Norcroft.

She was trying to keep the exasperation out of her voice. It was her fourteenth call of the evening, the eighth to the emergency room.

"Stroke. Aphasic and right hemiplegic."

"LOC?"

"She's alert, but otherwise unresponsive to verbal stimuli. The EMTs at the scene reported that her level of consciousness was such that she was completely out and had a super high BP. She came around in the ambulance on the way in."

"Do you have a CT or an MRI?"

"No insurance. We presume she's an illegal."

"We still have to take care of her. Go ahead and get a CT with and without contrast. I'll come in and see her. Why don't you alert radiology that we might have to do a head and neck angio as an emergency?"

"I was just waiting for you to take the responsibility. The hospital will take more chunks out of my already scarred up little patootie if I order any big studies on a no-pay. They won't even grumble when you do it."

"Gimme a break, Jerry. I'm a neurosurgeon. Everybody feels free to take open season pot shots at me. Comes with the territory."

"And makes you tough. I'm just a poor sensitive hospital employee. I can't take all this confrontation."

"What a BSer you are, Jerry. You'll have me weeping. See you in forty-five minutes."

"Good-bye, Sybil. Drive in safely."

"Good-bye, Jerry."

The CT scan was normal. Sybil evaluated Evangelina. By the time of Sybil's examination, the Mexican-American woman was able to say a few words— "Hello, Doctor," "Yes," "No," and *Me duele la Cabeza*!"

Sybil thought she heard a high pitched bruit over the carotid artery on the left side.

"Jerry, I think she has a high grade stenosis in the left internal carotid. She's got a bruit. Listen."

She handed Jerry her stethoscope, and he thought he could hear the rasping sound of blood pushing through a narrowed arterial lumen also. He nodded.

"We'll have to get an arteriogram," she said.

"I agree."

"Mrs. Juarez, can you hear me?"

"Yes, Ma'am."

She had regained pretty decent speech over the past hour.

"We have to do a test to look at your arteries. Maybe you will need to have an operation. You have had a small stroke. We need to find out if we can prevent you from having another one. Okay?"

"What do you need to do?"

Mrs. Juarez's speech was thick and slurred but understandable and had more content now.

Sybil explained the procedure of the angiogram, including its hazards.

"Do you understand all that, Mrs. Juarez?"

"I think so" Evangelina said haltingly.

The ER attendants shaved Evangelina's right groin. Sybil accompanied her to the radiology procedures suite. Local anesthetic was instilled in the shaved and sterilized groin, the skin was nicked, and a large bore needle was passed into the underlying femoral artery. The angiographic catheter was carefully inserted through the needle and threaded up the artery into the arch of the aorta and into the carotid arteries. Iodine contrast material was instilled, and a series of x-rays recorded the passage of the x-ray dye along the course of the vessels. The study was normal, both in the extracranial vasculature and in the vessels of the brain. Mrs. Juarez was wheeled back to the ER and then to a hospital room.

Evangelina's husband, Jorge, was constantly at her side, fretting. He called the nurses every time Evangelina coughed, winced from the tender area in her groin, or had trouble speaking. Evangelina steadily improved until she was able to begin moving her right extremities on the second hospital day and to speak in multi-word English sentences to the nurses and in volumes to her husband.

At quarter to midnight on the third day of her hospitalization, Evangelina suddenly stopped being able to talk or to move her right arm and leg. Sybil rushed to her bed side and found the woman to be very frightened. She seemed to understand what Sybil was saying. Jorge was hysterically excited and had to be ejected from the room.

He shouted at Sybil.

"Look, big doctor lady, you aren't dealin' with no trash. I'm a person, too! What you people done to my Evangelina, eh?"

"I'll see you in a few minutes, Mr. Juarez. Take it easy. You are not helping matters."

"You just kicking me out so you can 'speriment with my Evangelina. I'm gonna sue. My Evangelina don't get better, I'm gonna sue!"

Sybil examined Evangelina. When she pinched the Mexican-American's arm, Evangelina withdrew it promptly with what appeared to be very nearly normal movements.

Sybil stepped out of Evangelina's earshot and asked the nurse, "Bring me two ccs of distilled water in a large syringe with an eighteen-gauge needle, please."

The nurse turned her head away from Evangelina and smiled broadly and knowingly.

The foreman took Gerrit van der Hoef off shift and demanded that he go see the company clinic doctors. His back was rigid with pain, and the right leg hurt like the worst toothache in his life. The doctor raised his right leg straight off the examination gurney. Pain and tingling rushed down his leg, and he cried out.

"Positive Lasegue's," the doctor said. "Let's see how you do with some bed rest. If the leg pain keeps up, we might have to send you to a specialist. I'll get Kim to give you a shot. You get yourself flat in bed for two days and call me then."

The pain got worse, not better. Every time van der Hoef had one of his cigarette coughs or strained to have a bowel movement or made the least twisting motion, he developed radiating pain down his leg. The pain seemed to grow worse by the hour and was progressively more easily elicited. On the third day at bed rest, Gerrit could not stand it any longer. He called the company physician.

"I can't stand it, Doc. You gotta do somethin'. I'm dyin'. I gotta have surgery, or somebody's gotta shoot me. Somethin'. I'm never gonna be able to work again. What am I gonna do?"

"Come back into the clinic. We'll give you another shot of Demerol and get you started on PT," the doctor told him.

Gerrit dragged himself to the clinic with the help of his harried wife—-his third—who was late for her work at the cafe as a result. The four kids had to fend for themselves that morning. Kim, the overworked clinic nurse, gave him the narcotic injection as soon as Gerrit limped in the door. In half an hour, he was feeling mellow. The pain had diminished fifty percent.

"Feeling better, Mr. van der Hoef?" the doctor asked solicitously.

"I guess so. But I'm tellin' you, Doc. That was the most terrible thing I ever felt. I gotta have a CT or some sorta test. I can't go through that again."

"The company can't cover a CT or an MRI this early, Mr. van der Hoef. I'm sorry. We have to have the mandatory three months course of conservative therapy before we can get the big expensive tests. We'll start you on PT and see if you get better."

"And what if I don't, Doc? This pain was terrible. I gotta have relief."

"Well, Mr. van der Hoef. None of us has the authority to violate the company's healthcare guidelines. We'll just have to see how you do."

"Meantime I suffer," van der Hoef said sulkily.

"I'm hoping not," said the doctor. "We have to give it a try, don't we? We wouldn't want to rush into an operation we didn't need, would we?"

Gerrit wondered which 'we' the doc was talking about. Gerrit van der Hoef was the only guy in the room who seemed like he might need an operation.

"What if I wanna see a specialist? You know, get a second opinion, like that? No offense meant, Doc."

"The company will still make you wait, Mr. van der Hoef. They've been at this a long time with a lot of different guys from the plant. They know best. Let's give it a try, what do you say?"

"What choice do I have?" The question was muttered sotto voce. "How long're you gonna give me off work?" he asked, now looking earnestly into the doctor's face.

"Probably three weeks, maybe a month."

"A month!? I don't think I'll ever be able to go back to that kind of work or any heavy work. Why don't you just give me a medical retirement? I deserve it!"

"A bit premature, don't you think? We haven't even tried conservative therapy yet. The company will not even think about you getting medical retirement until you have gone through everything they require for the treatment of bad backs."

"But what if you say, Doc? I mean, if you tell them I can't work anymore, what're they gonna be able to say? You're the doctor, right?"

"I work for the company, plain and simple, Mr. van der Hoef, same as you. The old days when the doctor made that kind of decision are gone forever. That is a company decision. I'm sure you know that."

"Yeah, I guess so."

Gerrit van der Hoef was miserable every minute of the three months on PT. The hot tubs and massages felt good for a few minutes, the painkillers cut the worst of the discomfort for a while but left him with a fuzzy head and constipation. None of the treatments gave any lasting relief. The last two weeks, Gerrit was placed on the company's mandatory work hardening program—lifting boxes, pushing trolleys, pulling on graded latex bands. He collapsed to the floor and refused to do another exercise on the twelfth day.

The physical therapist recorded in his notes, "Patient unwilling to cooperate, seems more interested in getting medical retirement benefits than in getting better. Seems to have some real pain, but hard to tell. Has a lot of overlay. Will refer back to clinic doctor for disposition."

Gerrit's wife wheeled him back into the doctor's office in a wheelchair for his appointment. The doctor thought that was overtly theatrical and made a note to that effect on his progress sheet. The man's face looked pale and drawn, the result of stress, apparently. The company was downsizing, and the doctor presumed that van der Hoef was afraid of losing his job. He could not be fired while still on the official sick list. The doctor saw cases like this all of the time.

"Well, Mr. van der Hoef. I see we're done with the PT. Ready to go back to work, are we?"

"Whadda you think?"

The patient's face was morose and angry, his voice truculent.

"We've been through the mandatory conservative treatment program, how'd we do?"

"I did lousy. You don't look too bad," complained Gerrit.

"Ha ha," the doctor laughed heartily.

Gerrit did not join in.

"Look, Doc. I don't know whether you know it or not, but I'm in a world of hurt. The only thing I got out of that treatment is that now I'm a junkie. I got more pills than Carter. I gotta have something done. Gimme a break."

"We can try and get some x-rays."

The doctor was looking more sympathetic now. He sneaked a quick glance at his watch. His next patient was waiting. He had to keep up the flow. The efficiency team monitored his patient numbers and the length of time per patient on a daily basis. He could not afford to get behind.

"Here's a request form for a set of lumbars. The administrative assistant will set up the tests for you. I'll review the films and see you in a couple of weeks."

"Can't you hurry it up some, Doc? I am in misery. I swear."

"There are others waiting for their tests. The company has a strict policy about fairness. I'm sure you'll live another two weeks, Mr. van der Hoef." He smiled broadly in an affable grin. He glanced down at his watch again.

The plain x-rays of Gerrit van der Hoef's lumbar spine were perfectly normal. When the doctor told him that, Gerrit's face fell.

"It can't be. I got so much pain in my leg I can't stand it. There's gotta be something!"

The man was clearly distraught.

The doctor did the straight leg raising test again. The shriek of agony the test elicited was convincing. There was indeed something wrong.

"Let's see you walk on your heels, Mr. van der Hoef."

The white-faced patient struggled to his feet and did as he was bidden. The right foot raised off the floor only half the distance achieved by the left. The doctor made a quick perusal of the company's guidelines for CTs and MRIs. Partial foot drop qualified.

"We'll get a CT, Mr. van der Hoef."

It was the cheaper of the two tests.

"That should help us get to the bottom of this."

"I heard the MRIs are better. The foreman told me I ought to have an MRI."

"CT is less expensive, Mr. van der Hoef. The company prefers CTs."

Van der Hoef lost his temper.

"How come they have doctors at all? They could just use a computer or a robot. Maybe just an accountant. That's all that seems to matter nowadays, *money*."

"Now, Mr. van der Hoef. Try not to be like that. After all, your medical care is free on your work comp claim."

"I'm bein' overcharged at that. I'm gonna get my lawyer to get me an MRI and a specialist. The foreman said I should oughta see that Dr. Norcroft. She's the best. This has gone on long enough now!"

He had developed a significant head of steam.

"All right, all right. Don't get upset, Mr. van der Hoef, I think I can swing getting you an MRI. The foot drop fits the profile. I think they might go for it."

The doctor backpedaled rapidly.

The company did not look with favor on doctors who got complaints from patients or their families, and the executives of the company made a doctor who got an attorney involved in a problem pay, with his job usually. There were plenty of doctors out of work. The company doctor did not want to swell the ranks. He was caught between a rock and a hard place. Ordering the MRI was only the lesser of evil for the doctor.

"'Bout time. And it's 'bout time you gave some thought about me getting a medical retirement."

"I'll do that, Mr. van der Hoef. I'll surely do that," said the doctor earnestly and sincerely.

He had no intention of doing any such thing. There were three review boards above him who could deal with that nightmare when the time came. He would stall as long as he could, but there was no use antagonizing the patient who was already being unreasonable.

The MRI was done a month later. Gerrit stayed in bed the whole month's time except to get up to the bathroom. Even going to the bathroom was a dreaded experience. He shuffled along and dragged his right leg. He could no longer bear standing long enough to urinate, so now he sat on the toilet like a woman. Even that made his back and leg ache enough to require a pill. He was in so much pain when he had an MRI that he could not lie flat on his back nor hold still long enough to get decent images.

The company physician received a terse report from the spine radiologist, "Magnetic Resonance Images unsatisfactory owing to poor patient cooperation."

"I'm sorry, Mr. van der Hoef. You did not do what the radiology techs asked, now did you? You had to hold still to get the pictures they needed, and you did not do that," the doctor said in his own defense after Gerrit exploded when he was told of the lack of results of the test.

It had been three weeks since his ordeal in the MRI chamber. He had not yet forgotten it.

"Do you think you can hold still for another test, Sir? I mean, between the two of us, is this a problem of claustrophobia?"

"No, Doctor. It hurts me to lie down. It hurts more every day. Please. Doesn't the Hypocritic Oath or whatever you call it, have something about taking pity on the patient? I'm begging you."

The man's vulpine face was knotted in pain and humiliation. He was starting to cry.

"No need for that, Mr. van der Hoef. I'll see to it that you get a shot of Demerol and Phenergan and a couple of Valium pills before you have the next MRI."

"Thanks, Doc. I really appreciate that."

He was back in control.

"Can you sign for me to be off work until after the test?"

"Sure."

He checked off the boxes on the company's printed off duty form and signed it.

"When can we get it done?"

"I'll have Kim check."

It was four and a half weeks. Gerrit had to crawl to the bathroom by the time the MRI was done. His brother and a neighbor had to carry him into the imaging center on a makeshift stretcher. He was writhing in pain. The center nurse administered the medications. When Gerrit was wheeled into the MRI scanning room an hour later, he did not care.

Two weeks later, Gerrit called the company doctor and explained that he would not be in for his appointment. His right foot did not work, and he developed too much pain to walk. The physician was sorry that the insurance did not provide for an ambulance.

"What did you see on the test, Doc?" Gerrit's voice was tired and dull.

He had taken a Percodan an hour before, and it was difficult to keep his thoughts focused.

"Oh, didn't you get the message from the clinic administrative desk?"

"Nope."

"Oh, too bad."

The doctor silently cursed the inefficiency of the system. The message girls were high school dropouts who were paid minimum wage, and the company was reimbursed 50 percent of that by the federal government because the workers would have to be let off welfare without a safety net otherwise. He groused that it was just a ruse by the socialist liberals to circumvent the welfare law passed clear back when Bill Clinton was president. But it was not his responsibility. When he went home at night, he did not have to think about it. He looked at his watch. Two more hours.

"So what'd it show, Doc?"

"Uh, yes, the MRI."

He riffled through the mounting pile of papers in van der Hoef's chart.

"Radiologist says you've got a great big herniated nucleus pulposis. Loose fragment. At L4-5 on the right side."

He paused to let the patient absorb the news.

"What does that mean...in English?"

"Ruptured disk. You have to have an operation."

Gerrit moaned. He was quiet for a moment.

"Let's get it over with. I'm ready to commit suicide. Do you do the operation?"

"Oh, no. You need to go to a specialist."

"Like who and when?"

"I'll have to get the people at the administration desk to check and see who's on the panel of surgeons. It'll take a few days."

More time? This is crazy! My foot's paralyzed already. I'm a doper and I can't get out of bed for the pain."

"Foot's paralyzed, you say? I'll check that."

Gerrit waited on the line while the physician checked the diagnosis and symptoms list.

"Good news. We don't have to wait. I can run your case before the committee on Thursday. If they approve, you can see the surgeon as soon as he or she can fit you in."

"Okay, Doc. Oh, and Doc, please call me yourself. Maybe the ones at the administration desk don't care all that much."

"I'll surely try, Mr. van der Hoef. We're pretty busy around here, but I will write myself a note."

The committee vote was a narrow one. The nurses, doctors, and therapists on the panel all voted for the surgery. The administrative staff all voted against the surgery. The vote went along party lines as was predictable. The swing vote in favor of surgery was cast by the lone chiropractor on the committee. It was her first time to vote in favor of an operation. The committee was justifiably proud of their record of saving the system's patients from the expensive hands of the surgeons. After the meeting, the chairman asked to see the chiropractor in his office.

At his request, and because she was on the approved panel, Gerrit van der Hoef was brought to Sybil Norcroft's office a week later. She was booked up for six weeks ordinarily, but the foreman from the plant called her and explained the plight of Mr. van der Hoef. She made room.

The interview, examination, and evaluation of the x-rays and MRI images took a little more than five minutes.

"You have a ruptured disk that has produced complete paralysis of your right foot, what we call a foot drop. Your only hope is to have an operation. You won't die if you don't, but you will likely have pain like this for the rest of your life if you don't have the operation. I can't promise that your foot will get better, but surgery is the only way it can. Where have you been all these months?"

Gerrit explained his struggles, his attempts to get medical retirement, to get care. Sybil went through the thorough informed consent discussion and had Gerrit watch the film on low back surgery prepared by the American Association of Neurological Surgeons. He signed the consent form for the operation with alacrity and enthusiasm. Because the schedule was so full, Sybil applied to the insurance company for permission to do the operation that evening. There was a two-hour delay while the administration desk at the company fretted over the bad precedent to be set if quick assent was given, but finally, they gave in. They had too many other matters to deal with when the end result had already been okayed by the operative permission committee.

The operation took thirty-one minutes, the half hour between nine and nine thirty that night. Gerrit woke up in the recovery room pain free but still with a partially weak foot. However, he had definite movement in his foot that had not been present before the surgery. He could raise his toes two inches. He was discharged the following morning in good condition and free of pain.

Mrs. Juarez cringed when she saw the impressive syringe and the huge needle in Dr. Sybil Norcroft's hand. Her eyes bulged in fear.

"This is going to hurt some, Mrs. Juarez. I am going to give you this anti-stroke shot. You should be much better in two hours. Nurse, will you start the timer?"

The nurse made an elaborate display of setting a medication timer for two hours hence. Sybil cleansed a large area of Evangelina's anterior right thigh and slowly inserted the large needle and then slowly instilled the placebo—distilled water. That innocuous solution was remarkably painful, and was as convincing a medication as any hysteric ever received.

When the dinger on the medication timer went off two hours later, Evangelina broke into a broad happy grin, moved her right arm and leg, and said, "Oh, thank you, Doctora, I am so much better."

Tears glistened in her eyes. Jorge Juarez let down his glowering defenses and grudgingly thanked Dr. Norcroft.

Evangelina spent the next two weeks in the stroke rehabilitation center and was discharged with a cane to receive her future treatment on an outpatient basis.

Sybil saw Gerrit in her office one month later and again two months after the operation. Gerrit expressed joy at the relief of his misery and his newly regained ability to walk without clenching his hand around a bed post and gnashing his teeth to withstand the pain. The foot drop improved to 50 percent of normal but did not progress beyond that point. On each visit, Gerrit implored Sybil to grant him full and permanent medical retirement. She refused, saying that he should be fine and able to return to work without limitations in six months, which was three more months than what she thought it would really take. Gerrit was angry, but resigned himself to his fate and returned to work with a foot brace in place.

Gerrit called Sybil two months later.

"Dr. Norcroft, I have some more back pain. Can I get off work?"

"Does it go down your leg?"

"Not really."

"Is it bad?"

"Pretty bad."

"Does it hurt all of the time?"

"Only when I work. That's why I think I should be off work. I think I should be medically retired, if you want to know the truth."

"Let's give a try at light duty for a while first. I'll sent a note to your foreman. Call me if things get worse."

He called a week later.

"The company doc put me off work. It hurts more."

"I'll get my secretary to arrange an appointment to see you as soon as I can."

"Thanks. You'll need to sign my off-work slip. It's up in three days."

Sybil gave a little sigh.

Gerrit was in her office the third day. He seemed to be in real but not severe pain. Sybil started a conservative regime and signed his off work slip.

He called back in thirteen days.

"I got leg pain, Doc. It's getting pretty bad."

Sybil groaned inwardly. Had she missed a piece of disc?

"We'll make an appointment ASAP. I think I can see you tomorrow."

The following day, Gerrit limped into Sybil's office, pain lines showing all over his taut face.

"Tell me about your pain, Mr. van der Hoef," Dr. Norcroft asked.

"Started about two weeks after I went back to work. I had to lift heavy stuff all of the time, and the foreman wouldn't let me have any time off or light duty. I think he's got it in for me because I was gone so much from before, when I had the ruptured disk."

"Where is the pain now, Mr. van der Hoef?"

"Was in my back mostly, but now that's getting some better, and it's into my left leg again—big time. It is miserable."

"Left leg?" Sybil queried.

"Yeah, same as before," Gerrit answered.

That rang a false note to Sybil. She consulted her notes.

"Uh, uh," she said. "Your other disk was on the right. You had right leg pain. How's the right leg?"

"Still part paralyzed."

"I mean, how about the pain?"

"None. I told you, the pain's on the left."

"You certainly did," she said.

She was relieved to hear that she was dealing with the opposite leg from before. This was probably a new ruptured disk. She hoped it was not at the same level. She checked his chart: L4-5 on the right.

"If you think this pain is like your other time—as severe and the same kind— we had better get an MRI done. I would say we ought to do it this week."

"I'm with you, Dr. Norcroft. The sooner the better."

It was the usual struggle with the company's insurance company. There were legions of telephone calls, e-mails, and letters over a month's period before permission was finally granted to do the MRI. The patient was ragged with pain by then. Sybil was frustrated and regarded every administrator and secretary at the insurance company with a personal animus. The millstone-like wheels of the company's administrative process finally ground to a halt, and the MRI was accomplished, again with the patient reduced to the level of a whining animal requiring heavy sedation. He had a herniated disk on the left at L5-S1, a new level and new side. It was a month before the operation was approved, and by then, Gerrit van der Hoef was bedridden. This time, he did not have any paralysis.

The operation proved to be somewhat more difficult this time. The space at that level was narrower, and it was harder to reach the smaller herniated disk and to clean out the narrowed bony canal surrounding the nerve root. Sybil finally had to take off more bone to achieve a satisfactory decompression. She did an L5 hemilaminectomy, taking off all of the roofing bone over the spinal canal on that side and at that level. The joints were left intact to insure stability.

Recovery was somewhat slower. Van der Hoef was more tired and had some more achy back pain when he returned for his one month checkup. Sybil checked his wound and it was fine. She repeated a quick neurological examination and found that he was as he had gone into the operation—neurologically intact except for a partial right foot drop.

They had their usual discussion about van der Hoef being placed on permanent medical retirement with the same response from Sybil, "Wait at least one more month."

He was better at the next month's examination. She still told him to wait a month before a final determination was made for retirement. The next month came. Van der Hoef was feeling fine.

"I want to have a medical retirement, Doctor. This is the month you promised to do it."

"Mr. van der Hoef, I think I phrased that a little differently. I said this was the month to make the decision."

"Yeah. And the decision had better be for a medical retirement. I gotta bad back. No way can I go back and do that kinda work. You gotta sign the papers, lady."

His tone was pushy, bordering on belligerent. Sybil Norcroft had never responded well to ultimatums or to men bearing down on her, particularly to do something she did not want to do.

"No."

She paused long enough for it to sink in and for the 'no' to be a simple square word, unembroidered with adjective clauses or softeners.

His face colored.

"You are doing fine," she told him. "I expect you to be perfectly well. You have had a ruptured disk, and now it's gone. I don't need to see you again unless you have more trouble. I am going to write to the company and let them know that you can come back to light duty in three more months and to full work without restrictions in six."

"I'm disabled," he said flatly, defiantly, daring her to contradict him.

"Minimally and temporarily," she replied calmly.

He looked at her as if she should be wearing a size 4 hat.

"You stupid lady," he blustered. "Anybody with half a brain can see that I can't do that kinda work. Never no more!"

He had raised his voice a couple of decibels, and his face was beet red. It was evident that the doctor's unresponsiveness to his demands ran fully counter to his experience with the women of his social circle, and he did not care for it at all.

Sybil tried to think of something to say to defuse his anger, to get him to leave, and to avoid telling him what she thought of his basic work ethic. He obviated that impulse of hers by turning around and stomping out of the examination room and down the hall towards the reception area and exit. Sybil followed him at a twenty yard distance. He stopped at the reception desk and roundly cursed the poor receptionist, a new hiree who was eighteen years old. Sybil hurried to where he was berating the girl.

"Mr. van der Hoef!" she shouted to get over his own loud bellowings. "You have no call to treat this young woman like that. If you have something to say, say it to me. There is no need to use that kind of language. We can all behave like ladies and gentlemen!"

He was snarling, his eyes snapping azure fire.

"Lot you'd know about bein' a lady, you bull dyke! You got no business doin' a man's work anyhow. I shoulda gone to a man surgeon inna first place. You can't see what's plain as the nose on your face. I gotta have disability. Your gonna hear more about this. You're just the yes-man for the company just like the rest of the docs...against the workin' man. You're gonna hear more about this!"

He stormed out the door knocking incoming patients aside with calculated rudeness. Sybil shook her head, soothed the distraught receptionist, and headed back to the examination rooms to see her next patient.

Gerrit van der Hoef missed his next appointment, one set up for him by his company. When Sybil's office people wrote a reminder letter to him, he returned it with a terse note written on the same piece of paper, "Found a new doctor." Sybil wrote him off as an unsuccessful success.

It was two months before Sybil saw Evangelina Juarez in her office in follow-up. From her office window, Sybil watched Evangelina and Jorge walk briskly into the office waiting room and take their places. When the receptionist called Mrs. Juarez's name, her husband helped her to her feet and held the feeble woman up as she hobbled miserably up to the desk to sign in. It was all the small man could do to prop his wife up. Her right side did not seem to give her any useful support.

Sybil's exam was unremarkable. Evangelina's reflexes were normal. There were no signs of motor damage, so-called 'upper motor neuron signs' suggestive of stroke damage. With noxious stimuli—a quick pinch—Evangelina was able to move her limbs briskly. She did much less well voluntarily. One oddity about the examination was that Evangelina responded only in Spanish and appeared able only to understand her native language and not a word of English. Sybil reluctantly had to resort to using one of the office girls, who was from Central America, as an interpreter.

A full year passed without Sybil or her office hearing from or about van der Hoef. The insurance paid off the bill in full and without demurrer. It was a modest one in comparison to most of those the company received from orthopedic spine surgeons with their ingrained penchants to instill costly hardware. Sybil refused to do fusions on the second operation as was the expensive routine for most of her colleagues. Van der Hoef did not respond to any of the standard follow-up letters or calls sent out at six months and a year post operatively.

Van der Hoef's name came up unexpectedly in Sybil's routine in-basket having sat there over a long holiday weekend. She paid no attention to the envelope until after she had read and reread the letter.

Dear Dr. Norcroft:

This letter will serve to inform you that you will be sued in ninety (90) days from the above date by Gerrit Evan van der Hoef for medical malpractice. The responsibility to inform your insurance company or the attorney of your choice rests solely with you. We will be in touch.

We find that our unfortunate client was obligated to sign a contract to try any disputes in a binding arbitration hearing. We hold that our client was uninformed as to his rights and about what the arbitration process versus the jury trial entailed. Therefore, we will seek to have the action transferred to the proper venue forthwith.

Yours,

Paul Bel Geddes, Esq., Attorney at Law.

Sybil then looked at the envelope. The all too familiar return address for Stewart, Bel Geddes, and Loughlin leaped out at her. She let go a guttural animal growl and crumpled the envelope into a golf ball sized sphere and hurled it across the room.

Sybil received a second friendly note from Paul Bel Geddes a little over a month later. This one informed her that she was to be sued by one Evangelina Juarez. Apparently, malpractice on Sybil's part had resulted in Evangelina's having developed permanent weakness, loss of her ability to speak English, and, as an added note of complaint from her husband, Jorge, he had suffered loss of consortium with his wife. She had become completely unable to engage in sexual relations from the time she underwent the placement of "toxic chemicals" into her arteries. When Sybil had read the letter in its entirety, she showed it to her office manager with a theatrical mock placement of her finger down her throat to stimulate retching.

CHAPTER NINE

The war of attrition launched by Paul Bel Geddes started insidiously. Sybil's deposition in the van der Hoef case was scheduled four months after she received her 90-day letter, something of a record for efficiency in a civil case. Carter Tarkington, Hyrum Willis and their client, and the court reporter showed up at the appointed hour at Bel Geddes's ornate office and waited impatiently while the customary past scheduled hour passed without the plaintiff's attorney arriving. Just as the court reporter lost her patience and was standing up to put away her machine, the conference doors opened, and one of Bel Geddes's secretaries bounced in.

She smiled sweetly—and vacantly—thought Sybil and announced, "I'm awfully sorry, but Mr. Bel Geddes is unavoidably detained. His wife is very ill, and he will have to cancel for today. He will ask for a continuance. Sorry for any inconvenience this might have caused you. Mr. Bel Geddes asked me to tell you that."

When the three of them filed out of Bel Geddes's office, Carter made his apologies for Bel Geddes's recurrent egregious behavior, mentioning in an aside that he had won another short round with a classical cheap shot.

Hyrum took the opportunity to say to Sybil, "Dr. Norcroft. I know he got us a little today, but he is way behind. It will take him two decades of playing this game to make up for the coup you dealt him in the Jason Turner affair. I have to admit that I had my doubts about you when you first snuggled up to him. I'll tell you, though, it was the best move I ever heard of, the way you pricked his balloon in the courtroom. My compliments on a master stroke or mistress stroke, whatever is proper pc."

He grinned broadly at her and gave her a two handed thumbs up. She laughed appreciatively, glad that he recognized that his cause for anger at that time had been ill placed.

Sybil's side won the contest over where the van der Hoef case would be tried. The judge wasted only one day in deciding in favor of the less formal binding arbitration format over the more expensive and time consuming jury setting.

Nothing happened in Evangelina Juarez's case for nearly two years after the 90-day letter was received and then the suit was formally filed on time. Twenty-three months after that, when Sybil had comfortably forgotten the case almost entirely, the busy neurosurgeon was noticed of a date for her deposition one month hence. The notice came directly from Paul Bel Geddes's office, circumventing the legal courtesy of dealing directly with her own attorney and arrived on a particularly frustrating day when Sybil had had to deal with the ruthless agents of two HMOs. She viewed the reception of the notice from Bel Geddes as nothing more than she should have expected from the small-minded vainglorious attack dog.

To the surprise of both Sybil and of Carter Tarkington and his firm, no notice of continuance was received before the scheduled date. Sybil gritted her teeth and trashed her office and OR schedule to allow the time for the deposition. She and Carter met in his office one day before the scheduled deposition.

The attorney met Sybil in the reception room of his firm's suite of offices as soon as the receptionist informed him that she had arrived.

"Hello, Dr. Norcroft. Come in. We'll be most comfortable in my office, there'll only be three of us—you, me, and Hyrum Willis. You remember Hyrum, don't you?"

"Of course."

Tarkington led Dr. Norcroft down the hallway to his office. Hyrum Willis was waiting there for them. He stood when Sybil entered the room.

"Hi, Dr. Norcroft. Glad to see you again."

"I would prefer different circumstances, but it is nice to see you again, Hyrum. How is your family?"

"Great. Growing like weeds. How is the horse business?"

"Booming. Not profitable, exactly, but booming. It's what passes for fun for me."

"A serious hobby," said Carter Tarkington. "Scares me."

"Me too, sometimes, but I have gotten to the point that I break even plus a little. I enjoy the diversion, and I especially like the people with whom I work."

"That's the best kind of toy," agreed Hyrum.

"I know you're busy, Dr. Norcroft. Perhaps we should get down to the business at hand—the Evangelina Juarez case."

"I suppose we must. I can't imagine what there is about the case that could take any time. This looks like a pure Paul Bel Geddes harassment case to me," complained Sybil.

"We both agree completely, but we have to defend you anyway. I'm afraid that "ridiculous" is not an accepted defense, although I think that would be completely appropriate for the present case," Carter sympathized.

Sybil smiled.

"Tell me the medical facts in this case, Dr. Norcroft. Tell me exactly what happened."

Sybil went over the history in detail, refreshing her memory from the facsimiles of the chart that the attorneys had provided. She did not editorialize or attempt to add defensive arguments.

Carter was thoughtful.

"There is something I don't understand, Doctor. How can someone lose the ability to speak English altogether and yet retain full facility with Spanish, her native language? What mechanism could be in play?"

Sybil responded.

"Occasionally, we see people, almost always older stroke victims, who have profound loss of speech, who lose the ability to use a second language. They retain something of their native language, an older and more ingrained speech usage. Virtually always these people have severe loss of speech in that native language as well as the complete or virtually complete loss of the secondarily acquired language."

"Ever see a patient who lost speech just like this claim by Mrs. Juarez?"

"Never."

"Ever hear or read of a case like this?"

"No, but then, stroke is not really my specialty."

"Of course not, that's in the purview of medical neurology, isn't that right, Doctor?"

"Much more than surgical neurology."

"I presumed as much; so, I had the office staff run a Med-Line search for English language articles in the medical literature on strokes and language retention, particularly preservation or loss of a second language. You could help us with a quick review of the synopses of the articles provided, but our experts could not find a single instance in the literature for the past five years."

"Could be further back or in another language," Sybil offered. "I'm just playing the Devil's Advocate, here."

"I'm ahead of you. I had the service extend the search back twenty years and to include the world's literature, irrespective of language. That is going to be a long project, especially if we have to get any significant number of articles translated. I'll keep you posted."

"Suffice it to say that if such cases exist, they have to be vanishingly rare," said Sybil.

"So why is Mrs. Juarez unable to speak English?"

"Seems obvious to me," asserted Sybil.

"Are you absolutely certain that the woman was able to speak English before the events of this case?"

"Absolutely."

"I presume that we won't have trouble finding people to testify to that fact?"

"You could start with her own family. Hospital personnel and my office personnel can certainly verify that she was able to speak English quite satisfactorily."

"Then the next concern relates to why this sweet, and presumably previously passionate woman, is no longer able to have sex with her husband."

"Simple," Sybil declared without hesitation. "Either she was always frigid, and nothing has changed, or she and her husband are lying. I tend to lean towards the latter explanation."

"Short of planting a TV camera in the couple's bedroom, we are going to run into some difficulty proving that she is still providing consortium as the quaint old legal phrase so euphemistically puts it," said Hyrum Willis.

"And we probably won't have to," responded Carter Tarkington. "All we have to do is establish that Evangelina Juarez is a liar. We need to come up with witnesses who will testify that they have heard her speaking English since her release from the hospital. A jury or arbitration panel can extrapolate from such a demonstration of her willingness to prevaricate in one major aspect of the case that she is lying about the whole business."

"As she most certainly is," said Sybil.

Carter looked at the junior attorney. Hyrum grinned at his superior.

"Do I detect an assignment *pour moi*?"

"One of several. Follow-up on the expanded Med-Line search as well as finding witnesses who have heard our plaintiff speaking the King's English, despite her claims to the contrary that she is unable to do so. But right now, we have to get over to Stewart, Bel Geddes, and Loughlins' for the deposition," said Carter.

Sybil knew that this was going to be a different kind of deposition from the outset of questioning. Bel Geddes stepped into his conference room on the dot of the appointed hour. He was all business and displayed none of his usual adolescent preliminaries.

"Are you familiar with the process and conduct of a deposition, Dr. Norcroft?"

"Yes."

"You understand that your testimony here is exactly the same as if you were appearing in court, and can be taken before a jury in a trial at some future time and presented as evidence?"

"Yes."

"Have you any questions about the deposition procedure, before I begin the formal questions, Doctor?"

"No."

"Good. Then state and spell your full name for the record, please."

Sybil did so.

"In the interests of time the plaintiff will stipulate to the information contained in the doctor's curriculum vitae, if that is all right with you, Counselor."

"So stipulated," said Tarkington.

"Anything to add to your CV, Dr. Norcroft?"

"Nothing."

"Why did you cause a chemical toxin to be instilled in Evangelina Juarez's arteries, Dr. Norcroft?"

"I didn't."

"Will you look at this order from the chart, Doctor?

Sybil perused her order for the performance of the head and neck angiogram. She looked up.

"Is that your handwriting?"

"Yes."

"Would you read the order, please?"

"'Head and neck angio. Stat'."

"Does that procedure not involve the instillation of iodine compounds?"

"It does."

"And is iodine not toxic?"

"It is the accepted contrast agent for angiography, has been for close to a hundred years."

"Pardon me, Doctor, but that is a *non sequitur*. I asked you if iodine is toxic or not."

"Not as a contrast agent."

"What if you put a drop in a person's eye?"

"That's not the same thing."

"Please just answer the question I put to you, Doctor. I thought you understood the deposition process. Shall I go over it again for you, Doctor?"

"Objection. You are badgering the witness, Counselor. None of that is called for."

"I apologize if I have trammeled the lady doctor's sensitivities. I'll rephrase. Dr. Norcroft, would iodine cause a burn if it were to be placed in a person's eye?"

"It might."

"Is that medically more probable than not?"

Sybil sighed. This was medical nonsense, but she could see where it was heading.

"Yes, it is more probable than not that there would be a burn to the sensitive tissues of the eye."

"How about the vagina?"

"That is not my field of expertise."

"You are a medical doctor, are you not? I believe your fine medical school education and your internship at a prestigious hospital as outlined in your CV have qualified you for a medical license in this state to practice medicine and surgery. That should not be outside your general medical education or knowledge. Would the lining of the vagina be burned by instillation of iodine?"

"I suppose it might."

"Have you ever heard of iodine contrast material having a toxic effect when placed in a patient's arterial system?"

"Do you mean an allergic response?"

Her attorney flashed her a look. She was responding like a teacher instead of a deponent. She had opened another avenue of exploration for the opposing attorney inadvertently, and she knew it. She gave herself a small mental kick in the backside.

"We'll get to that subsequently. My question relates to direct chemical toxicity, to a burn if you will, of the inside of arteries."

"There are cases of complications due to arteriography that seem to be best explained by the development of an acute toxic arteritis from iodized contrast, yes, Sir."

"Thank you, Dr. Norcroft. Now let's shift to the allergic response to iodine contrast. Does that ever happen, in your experience, or from what you have learned from your study of the medical literature?"

"Yes, that happens," answered Sybil grudgingly. "But…."

"Thank you, Doctor. You've answered my question. What kind of problems result from such allergic reactions?"

Sybil enumerated the occurrence of skin itching, tracheal swelling and difficulty breathing, and anaphylaxis.

"Could a person suffer permanent damage, even death, from such an allergic reaction?"

"Yes, that could occur, but let me…."

"Again, thank you, Doctor. Your answer is sufficient."

Sybil bristled at being peremptorily cut short. She needed to expand. When she looked at Carter, he shook his head. She could not figure out why he was not jumping in to help her. She sank back into her chair, feeling ill done by.

"Did you ever see anyone suffer permanent brain damage, permanent neurological injury from an allergic event?"

"Yes, but that was not…."

"Doctor, a simple yes or no will suffice. When your lawyer questions you, perhaps he will ask questions more to your liking. Right now, I ask the questions, and you answer the questions I ask. That's how the game is played. Have we an understanding on that fundamental?"

"I suppose I do, but there is more to be said about the subject of allergy and toxicity than your questions bring out. Certainly more to be said about the allergic reaction and toxicity that your client allegedly suffered, to be on point for this particular case."

Bel Geddes grinned at her, and Sybil knew that she had seriously misspoken. She ran her response through her mind in hot flashes of realization. She had implied that Evangelina Juarez had suffered both allergic and toxic reactions from the contrast that she had received during the angiogram, and Sybil had not intended to say or imply any such thing. She was angry at herself, felt duped. She fought to regain her composure.

"Yes, let's ask more about the toxic and allergic injuries that Mrs. Juarez suffered."

"I did not say that," Sybil protested.

Her voice had risen, and her face was red. She clenched her jaw to get hold of herself.

"I thought I heard you say that she did. Shall we have the court reporter read back my question and your response, Doctor?"

"That won't be necessary. I would like to explain my answer."

"I'm satisfied. I would like to move on to the last time you saw Mrs. Juarez."

"Objection. The doctor has every right to explain her answer."

Carter Tarkington's voice was level and quiet. Sybil thought it was about time he came up with an objection. She used the interruption to collect her wits.

"Of course," said Bel Geddes with syrupy sweet condescension.

"What I meant to say…."

Sybil went on to try and extricate herself from her verbal blunder. She knew that her explanation was sounding like an excuse. Her silly and careless outburst was going to have the ring of truth of a Freudian slip. Nothing she was saying now could erase her statement from the permanent record.

Paul Bel Geddes loved to see the haughty society doctor squirm. He, too, realized what a gift she had just given him. The words of the Rubaiyat flitted through his mind as he watched the woman he so despised twist in the wind. "The moving finger writes, and having writ, moves on. Nor all your piety nor wit can alter half a line, nor all your tears wash out a word of it." He had to suppress a mounting inner merriment.

When it came Tarkington's turn to question his client, he asked only a few questions regarding the routine character of Sybil's evaluation and treatment of Evangelina Juarez, the stress was obviously on how standard the care had been. He queried her about the nature of strokes, but stayed away from any discussion of unusual losses of speech, of possible malingering, and made no attempt to rehabilitate Sybil on the issue of allergic and toxic effects of iodized contrast media.

When Tarkington's turn was over, the hospital's defense attorney asked four or five questions about her opinion as to whether the hospital had performed up to community standards of medical care and if she had any criticisms of the hospital, of the radiology department, of the radiologist who had done the arteriogram, or of the nursing staff. Sybil answered a crisp no to each question. Bel Geddes had no further questions, and the deposition came to an end.

Sybil was furious. She waited until she and her attorneys were well away from Bel Geddes's office, then she let go.

"Carter, I am very displeased with your performance today. I'm none too happy with my own, but were you asleep in there? I mean, I expected a little help when I got into trouble."

"I thought you were doing fine, Dr. Norcroft. I did not want it to appear that you were somehow confused or were incompetent. I think that you held your own, all in all."

"That's baloney. I all but told him that Mrs. Juarez had been injured by either an allergic reaction or by toxicity from the contrast material! I needed your help. Right then! You didn't even get into that in your questions. We needed to explain that, in my humble opinion. I am angry. I don't mind telling you!"

"Dr. Norcroft. You are a fine neurosurgeon. I will defer to you every time on medical subjects. I am a very experienced medical malpractice defense attorney. I would like you to have confidence in that. There is a difference between your substantive medical defense, and my handling of the legal issues. Think about it for a minute. I did not want to share with the opposing counsel our defense. Make him produce his own work product. Doctors are used to conveying information, to teaching. We were not there to teach that lame brain. His very purpose in deposing you was to get a free peek at our defense. I went out of my way to keep him from getting that insight. You know he's wrong about the contrast: I know he is. It is very much in our favor if he does not realize that he's wrong. I would much rather he pursued an inaccurate line of reasoning and wasted his time and efforts producing a case that we can shred—at the appropriate time."

He gave her a stern avuncular look.

Sybil returned a sheepish glance.

"I stand corrected. Sorry I sounded off. Bel Geddes can get to me, even after all of this experience with him. I will have to exercise better control. Sorry, Carter. No real offense intended. I'll go home and eat a plate of crow."

"No offense taken. Let's skip the crow dinner and go out and have pheasant under glass or some other more appropriate fowl or fish at Thomasa's. It'll be a write-off for the firm."

Now that her stomach had stopped churning, Sybil realized that she was famished.

"Good idea. I always hated crow, anyway."

Carter Tarkington and his staff, noting the inordinate passage of time with no activity in the van der Hoef vs JNMH, Sybil Norcroft, M.D., PhD,

F.A.C.S., et.al. case, began to think that Paul Bel Geddes had decided to let it go. Carter called Dr. Norcroft.

"Sybil," he said as soon as she picked up the phone receiver, "I hate to be the bearer of good news, especially only tentative good news, but, here at our shop, we're beginning to think that old Bats in the Belfrey Geddes is going to punt on the van der Hoef case. He has yet to get an expert witness in your specialty as is required by law, he hasn't deposed a single witness, and he hasn't even formally defined an injury suffered by his client or a cause of injury on your part except his puny original allegation that you caused him pain and suffering by your operation."

"I would very much like this matter to be removed officially and finally, Carter. Can't we just give the man a call or write him a letter to remind him that he should let us go if he has no intention of pursuing the action?"

"I don't think that is a very wise course with a schlock like Paul. He likes to keep cases going for the annoyance value, if for nothing else. He would rather nettle you than almost anything else, I am sure. He thinks he owes you big time for the McNeely case and the Jason Turner defeat that he believes you engineered. I would rather count on Paul's general tendency towards being scatterbrained and forgetful and hope that the van der Hoef binding arbitration case will just die a lingering but deserved and sure death. If we remind him, it will more likely than not bring the case to the forefront of his consciousness and get him started all over again. I advise letting sleeping dogs lie."

"Good choice of characterizations," Sybil muttered.

Gerrit van der Hoef had not forgotten. He still had to work at the job he hated, not one of the five or six rotten excuses for doctors he had seen in the past four years had had the decency to give him his medical retirement. They were as unfeeling and cold about it as was the company. Not too surprising since they worked for the company, when you got right down to it. The big money from the company or from state comp bought their opinions. The quacks.

For the hundred and forty-second time—he kept records—van der Hoef called his do-nothing attorney, Paul Bel Geddes.

"Mr. Bel Geddes, this is Gerrit."

"How are you Mr. van der Hoef? I was just getting a letter ready to send you on the status of your case against the hospital and Dr. Norcroft." Bel Geddes had forgotten his client's name until his ever efficient secretary held the file up for him to read.

"Yeah? And what's goin' on lately?"

"I'm sending off a demand for a deposition for the doctor, Mr. van der Hoef. She's been slippery as an eel. I have had a terrible time getting her to my office to answer for what she did to you."

"Big doctors are bettern the law, can't be touched, isn't that about it, Mr. Bel Geddes?"

"They think they are, but I guarantee you, Mr. van der Hoef, that we'll get her sooner or later. I am writing to the judge this week, and I am going to write to the bar association to file a formal complaint against that attorney of hers, Tarkington. He's used every trick in the book and a few I never even heard of to keep the doc from having to appear. Don't give up. We'll get them eventually, Mr. van der Hoef."

"How about that expert witness of yours, that Dr. Dredge? You got him committed on the case?"

"It's Drenge, Dr. Drenge. And, you bet, he's the best. I use him all the time."

"But has he written up his opinion about how Norcroft butchered up my back?"

"I don't want him to do that. The defense can get at that opinion eventually. I want to save him for later, not let the defense prepare a rebuttal to his charges until the very end. Strategy. You have to be patient, trust me on this."

Bel Geddes made a mental note to have his staff hunt down Dr. Drenge. The last address Bel Geddes had was the Betty Ford Clinic in California. The man was a great plaintiff's witness, absolutely without scruples or collegial affinity. His only loyalty was to money, and Bel Geddes had provided the aging, nonpracticing, orthopedist with plenty of that over the years that they had worked as a team. Lately, the attorney had become concerned about Drenge's drinking and cocaine usage. In addition, Bel Geddes was beginning to think Drenge was suffering from a bit of judicial overexposure.

"He'll come through for us, make the case. He's great. Remind me to get the two of you together sometime, kind of get the team spirit going."

"Yeah, I'd like that. Sometime soon."

"I'll keep you posted, Mr. van der Hoef, trust me."

One of Bel Geddes's more voluptuous secretaries entered his office just as the attorney uttered his honeyed promise. She rolled her eyes and gave Bel Geddes a horsey little laugh. He made a shooing motion. She teetered out of the room on her spike heels. He wondered why he kept the woman; she couldn't type. He directed a short self-deprecating laugh at his personnel management deficiencies.

"I do, Mr. Bel Geddes. I do. "van der Hoef was saying, "Also how's the medical disability case coming? I get nothing but the run around from workman's comp."

"Slow plodding business. You know that better than anybody. The company has found every doctor it could to say that you are an Olympic class athlete, able to outdo Hercules on the job. The government is stingy, slow, and incompetent. What can I say?"

"Keep trying. Do somethin', okay?"

"You can count on me. Keep in touch, Mr. van der Hoef. I have another client coming in now. I'll get out a copy of my letter to you. Hang in there."

"As if I had any other choice. Thanks for all the work."

"Think nothing of it, Mr. van der Hoef. I'll get my reward as soon as we get that multimillion dollar jury award. Keep that in mind to keep up your spirits. Until next time, bye."

Bel Geddes had his secretary fire off a notice of a deposition to Carter Tarkington. He knew that he was going to be in trial on the date that he listed, but they did not have to know that yet. The letter would keep van der Hoef off his back for a little while longer. For good measure, he sent van der Hoef a copy of a very stern letter he composed to the state bar complaining of the "egregious judicial misconduct" on the part of Carter Tarkington. He carefully saw to it that the potentially libelous letter was never sent to either the bar or Tarkington. Van der Hoef did not have to know that either.

Sybil received her notice of taking her deposition scheduled for two months hence. The timing was abysmal. The date selected was exactly on the day that she was scheduled to speak in the American Feminist's Union Convocation held in Caesar's Palace in Las Vegas. She was the president-elect, and next to the future speech to be given by her as the outgoing president a year from now enumerating her year of triumphs against the patriarchy, this was easily the most important public address of her career.

As soon as she received the notification of the scheduled deposition, she made a frantic call to Carter Tarkington.

"Carter, this is totally unacceptable."

"What is, Dr. Norcroft?"

"Bel Geddes's latest ploy. He has purposely scheduled my deposition on the day I have to give the most important speech of my life. I can't figure out how he knows my schedule well enough to be able to torment me like this."

She felt hysterical. She hoped she did not sound as hysterical as she felt.

"Could you be just the least bit paranoid on the subject of Paul Bel Geddes?" Carter chided her gently.

"Even paranoids get persecuted sometimes, Carter. This looks like one of those times to me."

"I wouldn't put it past Paul. He is the master harrier. I'll get in touch with him. He didn't consult any of us about the timing. The date he proposes does not fit our schedule either. I think we can get a change."

"Please, Carter. I must give that speech. Bel Geddes has had years to set up this deposition. He does not have to have it on my special day You can't let him get away with this."

"I won't. Take it easy. It's my job to keep you from worrying or from being harassed until the last possible moment and to the least degree. I'll take care of it."

"Thanks Carter. You can't imagine what a load that takes off me. Let me know what happens."

Tarkington gritted his teeth in anger at his nemesis after he got off the line with Dr. Norcroft. The program of intimidation by annoyance was getting very old. Nothing he said or did fazed the insensitive legal hack, including formal complaints to the bar. Paul Bel Geddes had a Teflon outer shell when it came to complaints or criticisms. Nothing ever seemed to stick.

Carter buzzed his secretary.

"Carol, get Paul Bel Geddes on the horn for me if you can. Tell him it's urgent."

He was in luck. For once, he did not have to play telephone tag with his arch opponent.

"Hello, my friend, what can I do for you?" came Bel Geddes's annoyingly cheery voice.

"We need to talk about the Norcroft deposition."

There was a pause.

"Refresh me, Carter. What case are we deposing the eminent ball breaker for this time?"

"Van der Hoef."

"Ah, yes, poor man, poor victim. Let's see,"

Carter could hear the shuffling of pages on Bel Geddes's end.

"That's the arbitration case—depo for the 30th of November—still two months off. That should be plenty of time for you to teach the good doctor her lines."

He added a ripple of ingratiatory laughter.

Carter gritted his teeth. Half a dozen more calls to Paul Bel Geddes, and he would have his teeth worn down to the nubbins.

"Regrettably, Paul, that is not a good time. Both the defendant and I have other long ago scheduled commitments that neither of us can get out of. You'll have to come up with another date and see if it is mutually acceptable."

"Don't think that will be possible, my friend. I am in trial for several weeks before and several weeks after that date. Big cases that have been on the dockets for nearly ten years, both of them. 'Fraid I can't accommodate you, Carter, much as I would like to."

Carter half expected to hear the shedding of crocodile tears.

"There is no way the doctor can be there. She is committed to give the keynote address for the convention of the organization of which she is president on the very day that you have the deposition scheduled."

"What an unfortunate coincidence."

No one had ever sounded more sincere.

"It's more than that, Paul. She simply can't be there."

"You mean that the famous ball breaker's FemmaNazi speech is more important than the wheels of justice, Carter? Come now, where does your allegiance reside?"

"With my client, Paul, where it should. You know perfectly well you can change the date. Let's stop sparring. This stuff gets old, makes everybody's life more difficult and does nothing to further your case."

"Surely you don't think this scheduling problem is of my making? Can I help the remarkable and inconvenient coincidence of Dr. Norcroft's leap into demagoguery and the requirements of justice?"

"Paul, cut the crap. You gave yourself away when you started talking about her giving a feminist speech. Don't play the innocent with me, it ill becomes you. You set the date knowing the extreme conflict that would result for my client. Admit that you've been caught and rectify the situation."

"I will admit to no such chicanery. I'd as soon confess to the high crime of barratry, perish forbid the very possibility. In the interests of collegial fidelity, I will make every attempt to get the date changed. This is just for you, Carter, since our friendship is so long standing."

Carter Tarkington could recall only a decade-long fractious enmity between the two attorneys. *Friendship, ha*, he thought.

"Thank you, Paul. We will look forward to hearing from you at your earliest possible opportunity," he said

"You can count on me, Carter. Good-bye now."

"Thank you and good-bye, Paul."

It was six weeks before Tarkington heard from Bel Geddes again. There remained only two weeks before the deadline for the deposition and for Sybil's speech. The response from the plaintiff's attorney was a terse letter:

November 14
Dear Carter,

With regret I have to inform you that, despite all my efforts, I could not change the date for the upcoming deposition of your client, Sybil Norcroft, M.D. I will be in court and could not make the slightest change in that scheduling. Judge Devereaux reminded me of the scheduling crunch owing to the ever increasing number of cases being filed and being taken all the way to court. You defense attorneys will have to accept your fair share of the blame. Your clients commit actionable offenses, you defend them and their money against the poor victims hoping that the plaintiffs will give up in despair owing to the terrible long wait for justice, and your side of the room was responsible for the enactment of laws requiring financial sanctions against attorneys who must have continuances scheduled less than one month from trial date. Sow the wind, reap the whirlwind.
Convey my regards and my apologies for the system to your client. I remain,
Sincerely yours,
P. Bel Geddes

Carter snarled incoherently at the letter. He was sitting at his desk going through his in-basket. He rang his secretary.

"Carol. I do not want to be disturbed for the next hour except for a national emergency."

"Yes, Sir."

The attorney then quietly hissed out every cursing invective he knew or had ever heard. At a pace of clear enunciation, he was able to go a full five minutes without a single repetition. He went back over the oaths and swearings several times at ranting pitch to make sure that he had not left out anything useful. He then placed his fingertips on his temples, closed his eyes, and meditated in detail on the myriad ways of killing there were. It was very therapeutic.

Carter could not bring himself to call Sybil Norcroft directly. Instead, he mailed her a copy of Bel Geddes's letter and attached a short dictation of his own.

November 14
Dear Dr. Norcroft,

The letter from Paul Bel Geddes, Esq. speaks for itself. I regret the inconvenience that I know you will suffer as a result. I doubt that he made much of an effort to get a continuance, but it is his deposition, and there is little or nothing we can do. I look forward to a satisfactory resolution of this action. Continue to maintain your equanimity in anticipation of that future result.
I am,
Sincerely yours,
Carter Tarkington

Sybil Norcroft's command of English vernacular was adequate for most occasions, but she did not feel up to the challenge posed by Paul Bel Geddes's impertinent letter. Instead of locking herself in her office for a cathartic hour of cursing, she went to the gym and punished herself with aerobics and a body bag with her full repertoire of hand and foot attack measures. The bombastic exertions were augmented by a good private cry born more of frustration than sadness that seemed to be even more beneficial than the punching and kicking.

She dejectedly called the program director for the American Feminist's Union.

"Mazzie, this is Sybil Norcroft. I have bad news. I have to appear for a deposition at the very hour that I am slated to speak at the union's convocation in Las Vegas. I have done everything in my power to get out of it, but I can't."

"You mean you are going to dump us, Sybil? At this late date?!"

"No. I mean, I have no choice!"

"It's impossible to get a quality speaker now. Anyone worthwhile would be insulted, and anyone else would be unable to carry it off on short notice. Have you any idea what kind of bind this places us in, Sybil? I mean, really?"

"Of course I do. In my own defense, I have to tell you that this deposition was arranged by a woman hating chauvinist of an attorney who did it on purpose to get under my skin. I hate to admit how successful he has been."

"Well, sister, that being the case, we will just have to come up with a solution to beat the patriarchy one more time. I have a thought. I'll get back to you. *Illegitimi non carborundum*, girl!"

"You, too," Sybil said with no enthusiasm. "Let me know when you have a plan. My mind is no good anymore. I am a blank."

"I'll be in touch. Bye."

"Bye."

The reply followed in two days in the form of a letter:

November 16,
Dear President-Elect Norcroft,

The committee was devastated when they heard of your inability to appear in person at the convocation to present your speech. We are all profoundly disappointed. A compromise was suggested. We will arrange for a professional video photographer to tape your speech and will play it for the sisters in Las Vegas at the scheduled time for the President-Elect's address. As you no doubt realize, this will not be as stirring as your presence, and there will probably be those who regard you as one of those prima donna movie actresses who disdains the Academy Awards. That won't do you any political good in the Union, but it is the best we can come up with at such short notice. We will do all we can to convince the sisters that you are just another victim of the old-boy network trying to keep us down.

Please communicate with Agnes Cannon who is in charge of technical arrangements for the convocation. She will arrange all the details for the taping. Keep your chin up.

With sisterly regard,
Mary Margaret "Mazzie" Quinn

It took all that Sybil could do to appear confident and upbeat in her video presentation. She studiously avoided laying the blame on the attorney who had so cruelly disrupted her important plans. Instead, she concentrated her message on the great strides that women had made in the past ten years and the concrete plans the Union had formulated to cope with the specific issues facing women in the near future—most important of which was to get their soul sister, Claire Lund-Gardner, nominated as the Democrat's choice for the presidential race next year. In private, she railed at Paul Bel Geddes for destroying her own chances of being on the short list for vice-presidential candidates for Lund-Gardner to consider.

Sybil prepared assiduously for the deposition. She was determined to defeat Bel Geddes in that face-to-face match, whatever it took. She had all but memorized the chart. She and Carter and his associate, Hyrum Willis, went over every issue and nuance in the chart. Hyrum played the Devil's Advocate in a daylong grilling that exposed every conceivable flaw in the defense case. He tried to rattle Sybil with personal jibes and professional innuendoes.

Forty-eight hours before the time when she was to go head to head with Paul Bel Geddes, and she was fully primed to attack, the plaintiff's attorney sent the following letter to Carter Tarkington by courier:

November 28,
Carter Tarkington, Esquire:

I have encountered a totally unexpected and overriding scheduling conflict that grew out of the trial in which I am now participating. I have informed all parties that, due to circumstances beyond my control, I have been obliged to seek a continuance in the deposition of Sybil Norcroft, M.D. in the matter of van der Hoef vs JNMH, et. al binding arbitration. With the greatest of courtesy on the part of the court reporter and my staff, they have agreed to the setting of a new date at as yet an undetermined time. Thank you for your understanding.

I trust that the timeliness of this letter will permit you to resume your previous schedules. I am sure that the doctor will be pleased to be able to attend to the duties she had previously scheduled, after all. Give her my personal regards.
Paul Bel Geddes, Esq.
Attorney at Law

Upon receipt of this letter from opposing counsel, Carter Tarkington was unable to measure up to the demand for verbal catharsis required. He only muttered a few weak imprecations to himself and with reluctance dictated a note to Sybil Norcroft. It was too late in the day for the letter to reach Sybil, even with priority mail in the same city.

She received Carter's missive eighteen hours before she would have had to appear for the deposition, or, if her own plans had been able to be in force, from the time when she was to have given her nationally televised address to the women of the United States, and to many countries of the world.

November 28,
Sybil Norcroft, M.D., F.A.C.S.

Dear Dr. Norcroft,

Please find enclosed a facsimile of a letter from Paul Bel Geddes, the plaintiff's attorney in the van der Hoef case. The letter was delivered today by courier. I will try and get this note and the copy of Mr. Bel Geddes's letter to you by priority mail today, but I fear that it is too late in the day to accomplish that. I suppose the timing was intentional, another calculated slight by our mutual opponent. Do not let him get you down; that is his fondest wish.

Yours,

Carter Tarkington

Sybil's first thought was one of momentary elation. Now she would be able to deliver her speech in person. Then she soberly admitted that she was unprepared. She had concentrated so long and hard on the deposition and the fight with Bel Geddes that she was unprepared to make a convincing delivery of her material. She would have to stand up in front of the world-wide audience and read her talk. That would be worse than having the videotape presentation. Worse, she could not take advantage of the temporary reprieve and attend the convocation. Advance program changes had told of her "personal crisis" that prevented her from speaking in person. She would look like a nitwit if she now tried to reverse her decision. Sybil decided to take one of her horses out for a wild gallop along the tranquil byways of the countryside to purge herself of the corrosive hatred she felt roiling up from her guts.

Even that small measure of comfort could not be; Sybil developed the worst headache of her life and had to undergo the ignominy of being taken to the emergency room for an injection of Demerol, like the crocks in her practice whom she so despised.

Paul Bel Geddes dictated his last letter regarding the scheduled deposition of Sybil Norcroft, M.D. This one was to his client, Gerrit van der Hoef:

November 30,
Mr. Gerrit van der Hoef

Dear Mr. van der Hoef,

Despite my efforts, Dr. Norcroft and her attorney were able to postpone the taking of her testimony in a deposition. It had something to do with her giving a speech to a group of feminists, I understand. Although this is a setback, it is no more than we might have expected. We are up against a very clever attorney and a wealthy client who intend to fight us at every turn. I remain on your side, and together we will eventually win out against these people. Do not lose heart.

Also, I was unable to get the court to change the status of the case from a binding arbitration to a jury trial. It is a system stacked against poor plaintiffs, but we will keep on, and we will win in the end.
Sincerely,
Paul Bel Geddes, Esq.
Attorney at Law

Seven months later, Sybil found a routing message in her inbox to call Carter Tarkington. It was almost five in the afternoon when she discovered the note. She called her attorney's office.

"Hello, law offices," the receptionist greeted.

Sybil wondered why law firms always announced themselves that way instead of giving out the names of the partners.

"Hello. This is Sybil Norcroft. I am returning Mr. Tarkington's call. Is he still in the office?"

"I'll check."

Carter's voice came on the line after a brief pause.

"Hello, Dr. Norcroft. I wanted to let you know that the company will be sending you a letter to tell you about a meeting of their board that they want you and me to attend."

"What kind of meeting would the board of DPIC be having that would involve me?" Sybil asked.

"You know that Doctor's Protection Indemnity Cooperative got itself a new CEO this year, and that led to an almost complete changeover at the top levels of management and a pretty significant change in operating philosophy. Where they used to want to be known as the country's toughest malpractice protection company by fighting every case fang and claw and to attract business from more and more doctors by assuring them that the company would not sell them out by settling minor cases or very winnable cases that would then give the physician a harmful entry in his or her national malpractice registry listing, a very public piece of information. Since the changeover DPIC is more bottom line oriented. I mean, they are weighing the cost of defense much more heavily than they used to."

"And the doctor's reputation take the hindmost, isn't that about it?"

"Only to a degree. This is just a shift in the wind, not a black and white or draconian policy set in granite. Anyhow, I have been told that the purpose of the meeting is to air the salient facts about several pending cases. They want you and me to be there to discuss the Evangelina Juarez case. This is the first year they've done this, so I'm not quite sure what to expect. I've only been to a couple of these."

"I can't imagine what question there could be about the Juarez case. If ever there was a case that should have a summary judgment in the defendant's favor and be dismissed as a frivolous suit, it's that one," Sybil reacted testily.

"The last case I presented before the board concerned the question of whether or not the physician was willing to stay the whole distance and to cooperate with DPIC and the defense attorneys through the entire gamut of depositions and trial. Most likely, that's the question here. I feel the same way you do about the merits of the Juarez case."

"So what did your doctor client have to say? Did he agree to fight the good fight?"

"Interestingly, no. He wanted out of the whole thing as quickly and painlessly as possible. He was nervous and angry about being sued, felt like it was just another rotten thing that came with the territory of a medical career, like HMOs, capitation contracts, nondisclosure to patients of alternate, more expensive treatment options and the like. He didn't care if a loss got on his record. Every doctor had a rap sheet now, he said, so what? It's just the price of doing business, and he wanted to get to his business of doing cosmetic surgery. That's evidently one of the reasons the company wants to have these decision making meetings. Doctors are less inclined to fight than ever before, they seem to have lost their spirit with the plethora of suits filed, suits lost, time away from work, public humiliation of the explicit criticism of themselves. My plastic surgeon told me that he just didn't care anymore. There was no justice for physicians or for plaintiffs in general any longer. After three or four terms of ultraliberal, trial lawyer-supported presidents and congresses, the atmosphere is so poisoned that many doctors think the justice system has nothing to offer them. They would just as soon cave-in early and get the misery over with. The insurance companies are inclined to agree. It's cheaper for them to pay a moderate settlement up front than to bear the costs of defense and to have to take their chances with the caprice of juries.

"I've gone on and on, here. You asked me for the time, and I told you how to make a clock. Sorry."

Carter gave a little embarrassed laugh.

"Not me. Carter, I will fight the Evangelina Juarez case to the bitter end, no matter what. I will never quit, no matter how much crap Bel Geddes can heap on us. The company doesn't have to worry about me caving in like those weenies you just described.

"I did nothing wrong. They faked the whole business of her being unable to speak English any longer and that she is unable to make love anymore because of some completely unscientific claim about x-ray contrast. They sued the wrong person. Not only is it inappropriate to sue me—the contrast agent manufacturers would be the logical target, I would think—but also I am not going to roll over even if that is the current defense fad."

Her voice was heated. She could feel her blood pressure and pulse rate going up and her face becoming warmer and pinker. She did not dislike the feeling.

"Hold that thought, Sybil. Let's find out what the board has in mind. Maybe we're getting agitated for nothing. Who knows? We might find allies in the company and get some ideas about how to handle this stupid suit."

"I'd like to think so, Carter. I'll be there with bells on."

"All right. I'll see you then. Oh, I didn't even tell you when the meeting is going to be held, I don't think. It's next Friday."

She laughed.

"Friday the thirteenth, to be precise. Do you think that someone is trying to tell us something?"

"I hope not. Think on the bright side, Dr. Norcroft. Maybe, you and Hyrum and I can grab a bite to eat at some pricey place afterwards compliments of the DPIC board. They're supposed to foot the bill for the attorneys' and doctors' out-of-pocket expenses for the meeting. I can make myself useful by working on that. Are you up on the case well enough to proceed now, or do you need a refresher before we brave the lions in their den?"

"I'm okay. Suspicious, but okay. I'll see you on Friday, Carter. And yes, to the dinner."

"Okay, so long. Hang in there."

"Don't worry about me. Bye."

"Good-bye, Dr. Norcroft."

On Friday the thirteenth, Sybil joined Carter Tarkington and Hyrum Willis, and the three of them sat on an uncomfortable Danish Modern bench outside the DPIC boardroom. They were fifteen minutes early, and the previous meeting extended fifteen minutes late. In the half hour interim, they talked about anything but the Juarez case by unspoken agreement. Sybil told the two men about the National Soft Gait Horse Show in which her Tennessee Walking Horse, Bai Walker, had taken best in his class. She told them how much the Mexican families who worked with her to breed and care for and show her champions meant to her, and how that led to somewhat mixed feelings about Evangelina Juarez.

Carter Tarkington shyly told the other two about his secret passion, which had led to his greatest personal success of the year. He had placed fourth in the National Poker Playoffs in Las Vegas. The winnings and prizes had just about covered his losses for the five previous years of competition when he made it to the Nationals but failed to place.

Hyrum had climbed Annapurna I.

The boardroom door opened and a clutch of well-dressed men and women exited, conferring intensely and paying no attention to the three waiting supplicants. An imperious secretary followed closely at the heels of the departing group of dark-suited men and women.

"Mr. Tarkington? Dr. Norcroft?"

Carter and Sybil nodded. Hyrum was used to sitting second seat and being ignored.

"And?"

The secretary looked at Hyrum.

"Willis. Hyrum Willis."

"Oh, yes," she said as an afterthought. "Won't you please come in? We're running a bit late. I hope you don't mind if we move right along. We have some refreshments; perhaps we will be able to take time for them at a break sometime in the evening."

Sybil, Carter, and Hyrum dutifully filed in behind the severely dressed secretary and took their seats as she directed them. Sybil sat alone at the end of a table with Carter on the right side and Hyrum on the left. The three of them faced an array of about twenty people who were watching them fixedly from their seats at the sides of a long conference table, arranged at right angles to that of the three subjects of the meeting.

Directly opposite Sybil at the far end of the long cherry wood conference table sat a distinguished white-haired man with an expensive sun tan. As soon as Sybil and the two lawyers were situated, he addressed them.

"Thank you for coming. I am Max Webster, CEO of DPIC. We are here to discuss DPIC file, EJ v. SN, et. al. 5-4-13. In a moment, we would like to hear from you, Dr. Norcroft and then from your attorneys. First, in the interests of brevity, our case administrator, Beverly Clements, will give a synopsis of the case. Beverly?"

"Yes, Sir. Evangelina Juarez, through her attorney, Paul Bel Geddes… ."There was a slight collective groan from the assembled board members of DPIC,"Filed a malpractice action against our member, Sybil Norcroft, M.D., on four April, 2013. She claims that our member was negligent in providing care by ordering a head and neck arteriogram using iodine-containing contrast media. The contrast media produced a toxic or an allergic effect that resulted in a temporary stroke with paralysis, permanent loss of the ability to speak English, selectively, and her husband claims loss of consortium. The case has been assigned to the Comptrell Court, Judge Hector Dolorosa and is defended by in-house counsel."

The board members, most of them physicians, looked at each other with questioning glances and shrugs when they heard the skimpy facts of the claim and with shared concern when they heard that the case was going to be handled in the most ethnic sensitive area in the city by a judge who was a known Hispanic activist.

"Questions?" asked Max Webster.

"Why was the arteriogram ordered?"

A bespectacled small man wearing a bow tie put out the first question.

Sybil presumed he was the board's neurologist.

"Let's ask Dr. Norcroft to answer the medical questions. Let me mention that Dr. Norcroft is a neurosurgeon."

"The study was ordered as a matter of routine, a standard approach to a problem of a TIA or an early, possibly correctable stroke. More than incidentally, I heard a left carotid bruit in this woman who was demonstrating right hemiparesis and partial aphasia. I needed to know if Mrs. Juarez had a treatable carotid lesion or if she had an intracranial vascular occlusion or even a tumor. For those reasons, I felt it eminently justified to order the angiogram."

"Did you get proper informed consent? I understand this lady has considerable trouble with English."

"I made every effort to do so. Her husband was present. I asked if they had any questions, and they didn't ask any. I drew pictures of stroke victims and of the procedure. I had one of the Spanish speaking nurses translate to be on the safe side. And, as a documentable fact, she spoke English just fine at the time, thank you."

"How do you account for the post-angiogram neurological deficit, Dr. Norcroft?"

"There was very little, and it was very transitory. I think she may have had a very minor and brief period of cerebral ischemia while the contrast coursed through the arteries and arterioles that compounded her previous ischemic damage. All of that passed. In fact, at the worst period of her neurological deficit post-angio, I gave her a placebo, and she promptly returned to neurological normalcy."

"Except for being unable to speak English any longer."

The neurologist made the statement as if it were a known fact.

"And she couldn't have sex any longer," added a burly woman, the gynecologist on the panel.

She gave a small snort of derision.

"How do you account for the permanent loss of English proficiency, Dr. Norcroft?" asked the neurologist.

"And the perfect retention of Spanish, and the loss of libido? So far as I know, there is no known neurological syndrome that would account for such a presentation. Can you enlighten me, Doctor?"

"Henright. I'm a neurologist. I am not aware of any such neurological condition either. My best bet is that she's malingering, looking for a green poultice."

"That sums up the case as I see it," Sybil agreed.

"How about the legal ramifications, Mr. Tarkington?" asked the CEO.

"I'll defer to my colleague, Hyrum Willis. He's done the background work, and I think he has come up with some telling information for the defense."

Hyrum took a sip of water and cleared his throat.

"We ran a Med-Line search to investigate the question that Dr. Norcroft and Dr. Henright just discussed, namely, what does the medical literature have to say regarding selective loss of a second language? We found no instances in the last fifty years of any individual ever losing all of a second language and without loss of a primary language. There were reports of loss of all language capability, loss of more secondary language than primary, and retention of only a few fragments of a primary language with complete loss of the secondary language. Because most of the articles were written in the U.S., the primary and secondary languages most often in question were English and Spanish, respectively. I want to emphasize that complete loss of a second language was uniformly accompanied by severe loss of the primary language as well, and almost always with at least some other motor or coordination or vision loss. Usually, those losses were quite marked.

"Our next line of defense was to hire a private investigation firm to see if Mrs. Juarez demonstrated any ability to speak English when she believed she was not under scrutiny by anyone who might give her away to the defense in this case. The PIs carefully interviewed acquaintances of the plaintiff. For the most part, they were very reluctant to be communicative and were suspicious of the investigators as being police or especially as being from the immigration and customs service, despite strong reassurances.

They were able to find a witness—remarkably enough one of Mrs. Juarez's sisters, who is estranged from the plaintiff. She has stated a willingness to testify that the plaintiff speaks to family members in perfectly good English much of the time. Mrs. Juarez apparently is concerned that her children learn English at home so they won't be at a disadvantage in school.

"The most striking piece of evidence in favor of our case is a videotape of the plaintiff arguing with her butcher. He is a stolid Korean man who seems to be unable to speak a word of Spanish despite running a shop in the barrio for a decade. Mrs. Juarez is seen and heard on the tape to make her orders in Spanish, then by pointing and making hand gestures. The Korean butcher does not even make an effort to try to understand her. Finally, in frustration, the plaintiff opened up with a tirade of abuse and demands on the butcher, a display of Latin temper, pardon me for stereotyping all of you who are of Hispanic descent. The interesting thing about the recording is that Mrs. Juarez's angry speech is in perfectly understandable English. The recording is technically quite good. Her voice is easily recognizable.

"Lastly, the work of the private investigation team forces the defense to admit that one of the claims in this case is more than likely based on the truth. That is the claim by the husband regarding the loss of consortium."

Sybil and Dr. Henright both started forward, incredulous at that statement.

"Their evidence is only fragmentary, as you might presume. They have, of course, not been able to monitor what goes on inside the Juarez home."

Sybil and Dr. Henright were nonplused and shook their heads. How could the PIs support Jorge Juarez's claim of loss of consortium without seeing the intimate relationship or lack of it with his wife, Evangelina?

"The investigators have been able to obtain rather telling footage of the plaintiff engaging in a series of sexual acts with a neighborhood bachelor in his backyard. The photographers were in a fourth story apartment overlooking the backyard tryst and have produced very detailed video coverage. There is no doubt that Mrs. Juarez is capable of passion. One could deduce from the evidence that Jorge Juarez's claims that he does not get sex from his wife are likely to be quite true, but the imputed cause of his loss of consortium will necessarily have to be revised."

There was brief laughter throughout the boardroom. Sybil felt herself relaxing. The case for the defense was so convincing that she felt as if a great weight had been lifted from her shoulders. Her attorneys looked pleased. They had kept the exculpatory evidence from her to allow her to be as pleasantly surprised as the rest of the DPIC members in the boardroom. She thought, however, that Carter's pleasure and confidence seemed muted. He was not as ebullient as she thought he ought to be at this convincing evidence. She wrote her feelings off as nervousness on her part and overly strict self-control on the senior attorney's part.

"Thank you, Mr. Willis, Mr. Tarkington. The evidence you have accumulated certainly seems to counteract the plaintiff's attorney's contentions. Are there any further questions of Dr. Norcroft or of Mr. Tarkington or Mr. Willis?"

The CEO looked around the room. There were no further questions.

"Would the three of you mind retiring to the waiting room while the board deliberates?"

Sybil and the attorneys picked up small platefuls of appetizers and went out into the starkly decorated anteroom. Sybil was about to ask a question of Carter Tarkington, but he moved quickly down the hall towards the bathroom and seemed not to hear her.

"A penny for your thoughts, Hyrum," she asked.

"Seems like a slam dunk to me, Dr. Norcroft. But, you know, these malpractice cases are funny. It's like the blind men getting their impressions by feeling the elephant. You have a medical perspective. We have a legal point of view. And the board members have the purse strings to control. They have to look at the social ramifications, what's good for the membership and for the coffers of DPIC, and have to overlook the whole case to decide whether or not to risk their money. It ain't over until the fat lady sings, to quote a great poet."

"I fail to see what could move those people to want to settle, to force me to settle. Can you?" Sybil asked. "No jury could fail to find our evidence compelling, even overwhelming.

She was turned off by Hyrum's unenthusiastic facial response.

"You can never be sure about juries, especially those in high ethnic areas. In the very neighborhood where the courthouse stands, where our case will be tried, the African-Americans believe that the CIA intentionally introduced crack cocaine to destroy the black community, and the Mexican-Americans accept with minimal skepticism that there is a Chupacabra—a so-called 'Goat Sucker'—that kills animals and people and drains their blood. I've given up on speculation about what juries will do, or what directors of DPIC will do, for that matter. Let's just wait and see what the board decides."

"Do you know something I don't know, Hyrum?"

"No, Ma'am, I don't."

Sybil could not help wondering if the absent Carter Tarkington might know a little something more.

She could see her attorney down the hall speaking with one of the DPIC case representatives, presumably about another case. When the boardroom door opened, he made his way back to where Sybil and Hyrum, and now the CEO's secretary, were standing.

"Please come back in Dr. Norcroft, Mr. Tarkington, and Mr. Willis. The chairman wants to talk with you."

The three took the seats they had vacated a quarter of an hour before.

Never one to waste time on irrelevant comments or social pleasantries, Max Webster said, "Thanks for your patience. It is the policy of the board to ask the principals to depart during final discussions in order to ensure complete freedom of expression. I'm sure you understand."

The three nodded in polite, if reserved, agreement.

"The board has officially decided to agree to a settlement offer presented by the plaintiff's attorney, Mr. Bel Geddes."

Sybil felt a sudden rush of blood to her head and feared that she might faint. She gripped the arms of her chair until her hands were white. She was sure she could not have heard the man correctly. She glanced at Hyrum who looked dumbstruck. Carter wore a sickly, but not a surprised look. He did not venture to glance in Sybil's direction.

The world moved in slow motion. It seemed like several minutes went by, but, in reality, only a second passed before Sybil was convinced that she had, indeed, heard Max Webster correctly. Her composure returned, and with it, an icy anger. There was a hard impolite edge to her voice. She did not feel any particular need to maintain a facade of comity any longer.

"Would you please explain that ridiculous decision to me? I am slow, just a physician and a PhD. I will need some guidance."

If the CEO was aware of the acerbity of her comment, he did not show it. He dispassionately proceeded to give her guidance.

"We all recognize the merits of the defense case. In a just and perfect world, the case would be a defense attorney's dream. In a just and perfect world, the suit would never have been filed, for that matter. But the directors of DPIC had to deal with the world that really is, not that ideal one. In our world, we have drawn a court in the middle of an African-American section of town where the blacks and the Hispanics have been at each other's throats for decades. Only this year have the leaders of both communities been trying to mend the internecine rifts. Since the African-Americans predominate in the community, they are bending over backwards to be and to appear to be conciliatory to the sensitivities of the Hispanic minority. They have strongly supported Catholic saints' days processions, *Cinco de Mayo* parades, rallies for Hispanic causes, even Mexican Independence Day celebrations.

"This has spilled over into the courts. You must be aware that African-American juries are now acquitting 70 percent of young blacks for crimes that Caucasian juries are convicting 80 percent of young whites for. In the past twelve months, predominately African-American juries have been acquitting more than 80 percent of Hispanic youths irrespective of the evidence presented by prosecutors. And now we are asked to defend a very rich, very high profile, very educated, very privileged, very white and Anglo member of the establishment—a doctor—against the modest claims of a middle-aged poor Hispanic woman from the neighborhood. She has been victimized by the white establishment, so much so that she has lost her ability to speak English in a country that passed an English-only law. She has lost her ability to enjoy life, or for her husband to enjoy life since she no longer can have sex, probably the only pleasure vouchsafed this couple in an otherwise white dominated world. Do you really think a sympathetic African-American jury, when presented with such an inexpensive opportunity to ingratiate itself with its Hispanic cosufferers, will be swayed by such irrelevancies as evidence, especially scientific evidence? Need I remind you of the O.J. Simpson jury of some years back?"

Sybil felt thoroughly cowed and dejected. She managed only one argument.

"Can't we get a change of venue?"

"On what grounds, Doctor?"

"Prejudice, racism. You just described the bias."

"That is naive, Dr. Norcroft, if you will pardon my directness. There will be no consideration of a change of venue because there can be no possible evidence of bias. We have a Hispanic judge in charge of an African-American jury in a volatile community that, to a person, believes itself to be oppressed. Only whites can have prejudice or be racists. One has to have power to be able to be a racist, a bigot, or to discriminate. You are under the delusion that negative acts or expressions of opinion about groups alone constitute bigotry. That would be more like what we might find in that ideal world we were talking about earlier. That could not be further from the truth in this real world we have to deal with. Much as I personally might like to crusade for what I think is right and true, and make no mistake, I heartily believe that you are on the side of the angels in this one, I cannot do it. I am the CEO of a company responsible for business, for money. I cannot afford to let sentiment govern my decisions. The money decision has to be to settle, and settle we will. I'm sorry, Doctor."

"I have no intentions of settling, Mr. Webster."

Sybil had an implacable expression on her face.

"I am familiar with the bylaws and protections afforded physicians in the DPIC contract. You cannot settle the case without my permission. Isn't that a fact, Sir?"

"That is indeed a fact, Doctor."

"Then I am going to demand that you defend me in this case, whether you like it or not."

"That is your right. Now, let me tell you the rights of the company. DPIC is obligated to provide you the best possible defense. We are not obligated, however, to pay a judgment beyond a monetary level that we deem appropriate to the degree of culpability of our member and the company. This level has been well established in the courts. It is defined as the amount of money that can be agreed upon by the plaintiff with fiduciary responsibility and the defendant—the court sanctioned settlement. We are required to pay that settlement. It is not our obligation to pursue a case into court, to lose, and to pay more than that settlement. Nor is it our obligation to fund the legal costs of an appeal. For both the additional legal costs that can amount to several hundred thousand dollars, and for the above-settlement damages that can run into the millions from a hostile jury, you are on your own. As a matter of procedure, if you elect to pursue this case beyond the settlement we have negotiated, you will have to have a new set of attorneys. Mr. Tarkington, and Mr. Willis, and the members of their firm, are in our employ, and it would constitute a conflict of interest for them to defend you since they are acting in our interests, and you may well be in an adversarial position with regards our company."

Sybil looked hard at Carter Tarkington. He responded with a wan and rueful smile, acknowledging the accuracy of the CEO's statements.

"I suppose the next thing you will tell me is that this will be like car insurance. If I go on my own, and, therefore, adopt an 'adversarial position' as you call it, you can up my premiums or something?"

"I don't care for the denigrating comparison, Dr. Norcroft, but, since we have elected to take off our gloves, figuratively speaking, I will add, that, like your hypothetical car insurance company, we can take steps to remove you from membership."

That raised the ante a giant and sobering step. Sybil's mind was now working in its best logical and scientific way. She had damped down her seething anger and was working to think with a clear head. She did not want to talk herself into an inextricable and personally harmful position. There was a brief silence in the room as everyone watched her think and decide. She set her jaw in a grim line.

"And how much is the settlement offer?"

"Today, we can be removed from this action with a check for $300,000. We are prepared to send our check to Mr. Bel Geddes by courier this very night. With your signed concurrence, of course."

Sybil knew she was being extorted. She was unclear to whom she should direct her animus and disdain—Mrs. Juarez, Judge Hector Dolorosa's court, the ethnocentricity of the Comptrell community, her lawyers for failing to inform her fully of this eventuality, DPIC's policies, the CEO, Max Webster, God, or Paul Bel Geddes. Rationality prevailed, and she chose Bel Geddes.

"All right. I know when I am coerced. Let's get on with it. Get me the paper to sign, and you can go wash your hands, Mr. Webster."

It was a grim Sybil Norcroft who read the printout of the entry in the National Physicians Data Bank under her name as she sat on the stoop of her house at the horse ranch.

"Sybil Norcroft, M.D., PhD, F.A.C.S. - Out of court settlement in the amount of $300,000 to Evangelina Juarez. Improper ordering of contrast angiogram with resultant loss of speech and consortium. No appeal. For the plaintiff: Stewart, Bel Geddes, and Loughlin. For the defendant: Schmid, Principle, Tarkington, and Henley, in-house for Doctors Protection Indemnity Cooperative. Court: Comptrell Superior. Judge Hector Dolorosa, pres."

The closure of the case had been transmitted with electrical swiftness to the national data bank as soon as Judge Dolorosa had signed it, unlike the glacial pace of most other aspects of the court system. She had been absentmindedly picking at an apple. She crumpled the paper and threw it into the yard. Then she threw the half-eaten apple in the same direction, letting out a bark of rage as she did so.

"Ah, *mi Dama,*" Pancho said softly. "Can I be of help?"

His eyes caught hers and took in the fury and hurt in his benefactress's gaze.

Sybil had thought she was alone, and was embarrassed that her adolescent display of temper had been witnessed.

"You startled me, Pancho. I wish you could help, old friend, but the harm is done. I have just lost a big legal case."

"Like a suit?"

"Yes. A big settlement."

"For the malpractice? The jury gave money to the person who took you to court?"

"Not exactly."

It grated on her soul even to talk about it.

"It was a settlement—out of court. I didn't even get a chance to tell my side."

"That does not seem fair, Doctor. How does that happen?"

"My insurance company thought we could not win the case…. It involved a minority person, and the company did not think we could get a fair trial."

"A black person?"

"No, actually…." She fumbled a little. "A Mexican-American woman, an illegal, actually."

A mixture of emotions ran fleetingly across Pancho's weathered brown face. The expressions were subtle nuances of change in the placid features. They were evident to Sybil because she knew the man so well.

"I do not want to be nosy, to intrude on your privacy, Dr. Sybil, but could you please tell me something of the problem?"

His concern was genuine.

She smiled inwardly, aware of his dilemma. On the one hand, his natural sympathies leaned towards the illegal alien, whom Pancho did not know personally, presumably the victim of the monolithic system, and the important

222

doctor, who represented the power of the establishment. On the other hand, the Mexican loved his *Patrona* and knew by his own long experience that she was an eminently good and unselfish person with whom he and his family had flourished.

Sybil seldom confided in anyone except her husband. In recent years she and her husband, Charles, had tended to go in divergent directions as a result of their immersion in their demanding careers. They considered themselves to be professionals altogether capable of dealing with their own crises and, over the years, had gradually stopped sharing their professional problems, then their professional lives, and lately, even their personal lives were running ever more separately. Sybil felt a strong need to unleash some of her pent-up anger and frustration on someone, someone sympathetic. She felt the need to convince another person of the injustice she had experienced. She wanted to do that without it being a female emotional outburst. She wanted to tell her side so that the compelling truth of it would be self-evident and would produce a confidant who would feel and know the injustice of the system.

"Are you sure you want to hear, Pancho?" Sybil asked the Mexican ranch foreman.

"I am a good listener. What affects you, affects the rancho and me. I would be honored if you would think me friend enough to tell me your problem."

"All right, let's go inside."

Carlita Rodriguez was on her hands and knees scrubbing the wood floor of the spacious family room of the ranch house. She smiled broadly when her husband and the *Patrona* entered.

"*Buenas tardes,*" she greeted.

"*Hola,*" said Sybil.

Pancho nodded at his wife and smiled his greeting.

"We are going to talk," Pancho said, giving Carlita a meaningful glance.

She looked at him for confirmation. He made a gesture with his lips pointing in the direction of the doorway. Carlita stood and started for the other room.

"Carlita, I would like you to stay and hear my story," Sybil said.

Carlita looked pleased, and Pancho looked relieved.

"Thank you, Dr. Sybil," Carlita said with her soft lilting accent.

The three of them sat on the oversized leather covered couch.

"I was going to tell Pancho why I was so mad. I just had to settle a malpractice case, one that was an injustice to me. I did nothing wrong, and it makes me angry to have the justice system abuse me."

Neither Mexican spoke. They watched Sybil with undivided attention.

"Here's what happened," Sybil began.

It took the better part of half an hour to tell the whole story. Sybil had to explain how the civil justice system worked, and how her case had transpired and had been settled. She did not spare the couple the discussion about the ethnic forces that had underlain the final decision not to proceed with what logically should have been a winnable case.

Sybil concluded by showing Pancho and Carlita the formal entry in the Physicians National Data Bank with its stark descriptions. To both Mexicans, it looked like a criminal rap sheet. That was how they identified with the process. That identification evoked powerful negative emotions, memories of past brushes with U.S. law by themselves and by friends. In their minds, the system was like the one in Mexico—patently and institutionally unfair— loaded in favor of the government against powerless humble citizens. It shocked them and caused an unspoken wave of insecurity to pass over them to think that even one so important as their *Patrona* could be so poorly used by the justice system. It made them angry.

"It is not fair, Dr. Sybil," concluded Carlita in her succinct fashion.

Her dark eyes were flashing her outrage. Pancho was more thoughtful. It never occurred to him that Sybil Norcroft would lie or even shade the truth or exaggerate to make her own case. Sybil had always been completely forthright with him. He looked more hurt or ashamed than angry. Sybil was surprised and confused at his facial response.

"Please forgive us, Dr. Sybil," he said. "Not all of us Mexicans are like that Evangelina. We are more honorable."

"I didn't mean to suggest...," Sybil rejoined, embarrassed that Pancho might be feeling that she had shown disrespect for his people in general.

"Of course you did not. But I am ashamed, anyway," he interrupted, speaking earnestly.

"Evangelina shows the worst about us. She is superstitious. She wants something for nothing and is willing to tell lies to get it. She thinks it is all right so long as she can take something from the Anglos, from the big shots. It is easier and faster than working. Evangelina and her husband give to us a bad name, and I get angry with them."

Sybil nodded. She made no argument.

"Well, include that Anglo crook of an attorney, Bel Geddes, when you are angry at people. He taught Evangelina this lie. He showed her how to use the system to cheat, to use the feelings of people to get something that he and she did not deserve. I reserve most of my anger for him. He is a rat."

"I think that also. Some way it seems personal to me. Maybe because a Mexicana did it to you. I feel angry and sad for her, but the Anglo *abogado* is a bad one. I feel you should have *venganza*."

There was a chilly hardness in Pancho's clear enunciation of the word for vengeance. Sybil could not muster up enough Judeo-Christian ethic to protest that she should turn her other cheek. With Paul Bel Geddes, she could not bring herself to do that. Her own feelings ran too much in the same vein as Pancho's call for *venganza*.

"I would be willing to help if you want family with you *a vindicar*. I do not know the word in English."

"Thank you, Pancho. I think of you and Carlita and the others as family as well. I am going to work to get my feelings of *venganza* out of my mind, but if I cannot, and if I should find a way, then maybe one day I will call on you."

"I and my family will be waiting," Pancho asserted solemnly.

Carlita's serious face reflected her concurrence.

CHAPTER TEN

Once again at home, Sybil took stock of her situation. She was over-reacting to the outcome of the Evangelina Juarez case. On a purely objective plane, she had to admit that her pride had been hurt and her sense of common justice, but little else. She was out no money. DPIC had paid the entire cost of her defense. Even their costs were only moderate since they used their in-house counsel, Carter Tarkington. They were going to have to pay the $300,000 extortion to Paul Bel Geddes and his client; she was entirely free of that obligation. The item in the National Physicians Data Bank would be only one of tens of thousands, lost in the mounds of paper work, she rationalized. Even down the line when someone looked up her name, as the public was free to do, the entry would have to come across as pretty tame. Her losses were minimal. She knew that she had to resolve to forgive and to forget, knowing that the latter effort would be difficult since Bel Geddes still had the van der Hoef case with which to pummel her.

A more immediate problem loomed in her life. She was becoming increasingly cognizant of the deterioration in her relationship with Charles. He was important to her, and she knew almost instinctively that it was time, perhaps past time, to do something to patch up the fraying interconnection with her husband of seventeen years. She needed to confide in him, and it had been a mistake on her part to let their marriage sag to the point that the two of them no longer automatically sought each other out. A transitory thought crossed her subconscious. To whom was *Charles* confiding?

Absentmindedly, she made herself a Moscow Mule—vodka and ginger beer. Ever the purist, even while her mind was elsewhere, she made sure to serve herself the potent brew in a copper mug and to have a few *zakuski*—caviar and salty sardines. She thought about her drinking for a moment. Maybe she was drinking too much, letting the creep Bel Geddes get too far under her skin. She turned the bottle of Stolichinaya around in her hand glancing at the label. *Voda*, she thought, Water. *Vodka*—little water. Like the Russians, she was beginning to think of Vodka as not much more than a 'little water'. She resolved to be more careful. She would have to drink less before she found herself in a habit pattern. She downed her Moscow Mule.

Never one to ruminate for long, Sybil made a quick and firm decision.

"Donita," she called to her and Charles's cook.

Donita was the niece of Maria Innocenta Pomposo-Alvarez, who was now part of the partnership at the Caballos Suave Ranchero.

"We are going to make a dinner fit for *El Emperador*!"

Donita looked at her *Patrona* with amusement. Anglos were strange, and they said that Hispanics were impetuous.

Charles came home at seven. He was a man of careful habits. He lunched at noon and had dinner at home at seven-thirty without fail whenever he was not traveling. One of the niggling little suspicions Sybil had come when Charles missed coming home for dinner once and sometimes twice a week for the past several months. It was unlike him. She had never questioned him.

"Hello, Charles," she said brightly and helped him out of his suit coat. He gave her a raised eyebrow look.

"Just glad to see you. We don't get enough time together. I wanted this to be quality time," she laughed, his look of bemusement was not lost on her.

Donita served them icy lemon vodka in crystal glasses. The chilling was just right, vodka slush was beginning to congeal around the margins of the pale yellow liquid. Then she brought them Sybil's personal contribution: *mezedhes*—little delicacies—from their travels to Greece and Cyprus, including twenty diminutive cold and hot dishes to sample, among them cream of fish roe, pickled octopus, *kalamari* with *halloumi* cheese, *Moussaka*, and grilled lamb kebab.

"Quality time," he hummphed. "I'd settle for time, just time."

It came out abruptly and more seriously than the moment dictated.

"Sorry, Sybil. I didn't mean to spoil the mood. I've had a long day."

He sipped his drink with obvious appreciation. He liked the special attention all of this implied and did not want to interrupt the pleasant flow with questions that might suggest his natural niggling suspicions.

"You're right, Charles. Too right. I'm going to work on being here for you more often and longer. Starting tonight."

She paused to catch the affect on her husband. He looked genuinely pleased.

"Good," she said. "Donita and I have whipped up a little something. All you need to do is sit at the head of the dining room table and be served."

"Do I get the chair with arms?" he queried facetiously.

They both laughed. It had been a while since they had shared little verbal intimacies. It felt good.

"Could we go as far as exchanging my brogans for my fleecy slippers?"

"Don't push your luck," Sybil rejoined light-heartedly.

The table was splendid, one place setting at each end of the long dining room table that was covered with an heirloom Cypriot Lefkara linen table-cloth and decorated in the center with a simple sterling silver and cut glass Victorian epergne holding four slender ivory tapers. The dinner was splendid: Portabello mushroom salad, Lobster Vera Cruz, spinach with ponzu sauce, baby peas, slivered almonds, and pearl onions with lemon pepper, rose-lime pasta, fluted glasses of Dom Perignon, Kahlúa Crème Brûlée for dessert, and a demitasse of dark frothy espresso.

Donita had set out the nearly translucent gold rimmed Lenox Ivory china dinnerware and the Rosepoint silverware. She had insisted on the delicate ivory candles, and Sybil had to admit that the effect was not overdone as she had feared, but as perfect as Donita, with all her romantic soul, had foreseen. He sat at one end of the magnificently spread table, and Sybil sat at the other like an emperor and empress. Donita had such a joyous time serving them that Sybil and Charles said little except to laugh together at the *Hispañola's* exaggerated airs.

"Can you sit with me in the family room, maybe rot your brain with a bit of tube watching?" Charles asked when they had finished.

"Love to. I'll even watch a sitcom, if you insist," she said. "I do draw the line at reality shows."

That was the ultimate offering for her. She hated the mind numbing inanities of the popular thirty-minute comedy programs. He enjoyed them because they relaxed him and usually put him to sleep.

"My, my, to what do I owe this unexpected personal sacrifice," he smiled.

"We always sit on the couch and watch four hours of antenna TV, what are you talking about?" she bantered.

"Come on, Sybil. Name two sitcoms. Any two."

She squirmed. She shook her head sheepishly.

"Name one."

"Can't," she had to admit.

"You'd do great on "Jeopardy" or "Trivial Pursuit"," he joked as they settled onto the expansive leather couch.

He laughed out loud when he saw the perplexity on Sybil's face. She obviously had not heard of the two question-and-answer game shows.

Donita brought each of them a small glass of Williams Liqueur. They both enjoyed the scent of pears that wafted from the sweet drink. They were quiet for a long time, sitting relaxed with his arm around her. He broke the stillness.

"So Sybil, what's up? I mean, this is a little different from our usual evening at home—me home and you at the hospital, more usually. Have you wrecked the car? You jockeying around to get a fur coat?"

"No, Charles. I have had a little time to think. I had a rotten time of it with the Juarez case and was finding myself immersed in the ugliness of my profession whenever we come up against lawyers. I was losing perspective, and I thought I ought to get back to the things that are really important to me before I hate neurosurgery as much as I hate that bloody plaintiff's attorney that keeps plaguing me. In all candor, I have started to have concerns about you and me. You have always been my rock. Lately, you seem more distant, less involved with me."

"I think I would not be far from the mark if I made the same observation, Sybil. It's a two-way street."

"I know that. It worries me. I have been neglectful. Each of us values our career greatly. We have made real sacrifices and compromises—the decision to have no children, your acceptance of my absences at your social affairs, my traveling alone to the neurosurgery conventions—the whole bit. But I think we have become too sophisticated, too separate. We're developing an open marriage. I don't like it. I want you to myself. I want more time with you. I want us to draw closer instead of the divergence I am seeing of late."

Her declaration was one of affection and love. Her expression, however, did not convey that sentiment alone. Her suspicions were intermingled with her warmth. She had an expressionate face and was no good at hiding her feelings and intentions from her husband. Charles had learned to read her face with a high degree of precision.

"There's something on your mind, Sybil, something that underlies all of these other feelings, something more that prompted the beautiful dinner and evening."

"I don't want to talk about it. I don't want to detract from the aura we have tonight. Let's just watch something vapid on the TV and talk. Maybe you'll get lucky tonight."

It was an odd trigger. Sybil prided herself on her enlightened feminism and never joked about old attitudes about coyness or other Victorian silliness. She started to cry. It was completely irrational and surprising, as much to her as to him.

"What is it, Sybil? C'mon, out with it. It has to be important, more important than that Bel Bees guy, or whatever his name is, more important than your work. You never mix emotion and your profession. Tell me...please."

She had sworn that she would not bring it up. She was probably being silly and paranoid anyway. But here she was crying, being overtly, mindlessly foolish, like a jealous school girl. She swore at herself.

"Charles, I don't want to go into this. I'm afraid that I am losing you, driving you away, by my obsession with Paul Bel Geddes and his series of malpractice suits. I...I'm afraid you have someone else."

When he started to speak, she put her hand up to prevent him.

"Even if you do have someone else, I don't want to know about it. I only ask that you give me assurances. Not platitudes or excuses or, heaven forbid for our marriage, lies. I want you. I want exclusivity. And I want to be made to feel secure in that. I am going to work at being home and doing better."

She was crying silently but freely now, cathartically.

Charles raced his options through his mind at computer speed. He could lie outright, protest his innocence, but her woman's intuition, for all her professional and scientific objectivity, was as acute and accurate as any wife's. She knew. Even without real evidence, he knew that she knew. He could bring his stupid sordid affair with the purchaser from his competitor's office out into the full light of day, spare no details, throw himself on her mercy, beg and plead if he had to. He did not want to lose her. The beauty and vivacity of the temptress with whom he was ensnared was not worth it, and Sybil meant everything to him. He decided to rely on her eminently good breeding and personal poise. His only desire was to convince her in such a way that she would be able to cease from her fears once and for all.

"Sybil," he murmured softly. "I care for you more than for anything or anyone else. I am deeply sorry that I have caused you grief, or even concern. Rest assured that you will have no more reason to worry. I think we will fare better if we don't open this Pandora's box. Accept my assurances. Let's work at the future rather than cursing the darkness of the past, all right?"

She heard what he was saying and what he was not saying. It was enough.

"All right, Charles. That is good for me. I need you, all of you. I think we need each other. I won't speak of it again."

"There will be no reason to, Sybil."

They sat together in the gathering darkness without speaking further. Sybil recognized a peculiar dichotomy of understanding in her thoughts about what had just transpired between her and her husband. She had heard him all but admit infidelity. She accepted his communication and felt reassured. She did not feel any particular need to forgive Charles, and it would not be especially difficult for her to forget her distress at his transitory drift from the course of their union. She was happy to accept her husband's charm, his steadiness in his support for her, his genuine caring. She could, without any sense of illogicality, relegate his supposed secret to the outer darkness of their lives, secure in the conviction that it was an ephemeral dusky episode that would not resurface again in the light. She was content to accept the temporary chiaroscuro of Charles's complex life as well as she could accept her limitations and failures counterpoised against her own intellectual and physical talents now that she was content with his assurances.

The obverse side of the coinage of her feelings was an element of her own irrationality. She harbored an antagonism towards Paul Bel Geddes, the plaintiffs' lawyer and her self-appointed nemesis, as the ultimate source of her marital problems. All of the rage that she might have held for her husband or for the deterioration of their marriage, or for herself and her own part in the growing estrangement, she directed at Bel Geddes. He had caused her to rivet her mind and attentions on the unproductive malpractice suit, that gross miscarriage of justice and fairness. He had caused her to learn to hate, and that had driven out her capacity to love temporarily. She could not forgive him for that. All of her forgiveness had been used up for her husband and for herself. Paul Bel Geddes would have to wait until another day to receive his absolution. Until then, there were scores to settle. Not only did the man have to account for his stalking, grinding attacks on her professional well-being, but he would have to do penance to the last farthing for her perception of his arrantly egregious influence on her marriage.

Some years ago, Dr. Sybil Norcroft might have been able to look at her own situation more objectively, but after nearly a decade of dealing with the dogged attorney, she no longer gave great credence to or emotionally cared about objectivity when it came to her feelings about being sued for malpractice. She had in her breast a small white-hot flame of antithesis against Paul

Bel Geddes, Esq., hypocritical self-styled attorney to the downtrodden, that no end of rational argument could assuage. And she could not let it go.

Carter Tarkington called Dr. Norcroft two months later, mid Monday morning.

"I hesitate even to mention this, Dr. Norcroft," he announced apologetically as soon as she had said hello. "I know it's the last thing you want to hear."

She was pretty sure what her attorney's message was, but she was in a good enough of a mood to banter with him a bit.

"The stock market crashed," she said in a matter-of-fact but appropriately depressed tone.

"Worse," he said.

"The Pope died, and they elected a Dutch cardinal as the new Holy Father."

"You're getting warmer," Tarkington said, entering the low level levity despite himself.

"I would be crushed if you were to tell me that one of your esteemed colleagues had suffered some wee accident, say fell astraddle a set of gears, for example."

"You mean you are concerned over a particular colleague, whose name shall go unspoken but whose initials are Paul Bel Geddes?"

"That would touch me deeply."

"Your Christian attitude well behooves you, my daughter, but no, I am not the bearer of such bad news."

She sighed into her end of the phone.

"But you are all but prescient in being able to focus on just the person involved in my communication. I will grant you that."

"As the magical fish said to the fisherman regarding his persistent wife, 'What will that bane of my life have now?'"

"Dr. Norcroft, as I think I said when you first answered, I hesitate even to mention this."

"Plow straight ahead. You've wrecked my day by your mere reference to that name, a curse on his house."

She could hear him swallow.

"Bel Geddes has scheduled another deposition in the van der Hoef case... forty-five days from yesterday."

"Think this one will be for real, Carter?"

It was no longer a bantering matter. The connection of the two ideas, 'Bel Geddes' and 'deposition', could not be part of any sustained set of civilities, let alone bonhomie, for Sybil.

"We're talking about Paul Bel Geddes, Dr. Norcroft, what can I say?"

"You've said it all."

They firmed up arrangements to meet and refresh each other on the van der Hoef suit and to go over predeposition strategy and put down their receivers, each with a decidedly darker outlook on the day than they had before the call.

Paul Bel Geddes, himself, met Sybil Norcroft, Hyrum Willis, and Carter Tarkington in the foyer of his office complex on the day of the van der Hoef case deposition. Sybil noted that the gilt lettering on the door to the suite of offices now read, Law Offices of Bel Geddes and Loughlin. Of Counsel: Horace Pilgrim Stewart. She presumed that Bel Geddes's venerable old warhorse of a partner had been eased out or blatantly defeated in some internecine office struggle. Bel Geddes appeared to be in top form, so Sybil concluded that he had not been much scathed in the battle.

"Well, greetings, learned colleagues, gentlemen, scholars...and Dr. Norcroft."

She winced at his deprecatory humor.

"I can't tell you how much pleasure it gives me to greet you once again for an exchange of opinion and wisdom on our mutually favorite subject, civil justice."

He was so full of himself, of *it*, that it was a wonder that he did not pop instead of just verbally leaking it, Sybil muttered behind her teeth.

Bel Geddes escorted the two attorneys and Dr. Norcroft into his handsome wood paneled board and conference room. The most remarkable thing about the entire experience up to that point was that the plaintiff's attorney was actually on time, unheard of for him. They had all arrived before the court reporter and were in their seats when she was shown in by Bel Geddes's pneumatic secretary.

"Ready, gentlemen? Dr. Norcroft?" Bel Geddes inquired with exaggerated and uncharacteristic comity. "Ready, Ms Hutchins?" he asked the court reporter.

Everyone nodded that they were set to proceed.

"For the record, I am Paul Bel Geddes of the law firm of Bel Geddes and Loughlin, and we are about to begin the deposition of Sybil Norcroft, the defendant, in the case of van der Hoef versus Norcroft. Also present in the room are attorneys for the defendant, Mr. Carter Tarkington and Mr. Hyrum Willis, of the firm of Schmid, Principle, Tarkington, and Henley. The court reporter is Miriam Hutchins.

"Dr. Norcroft, do you have any questions before being sworn?"

"No."

She was sworn in for the record.

"State and spell your full name, please, Dr. Norcroft."

She complied crisply.

"State your occupation."

As if he did not know it. She cautioned herself not even to feel sarcastic. She answered his question.

"Please give us a brief summary of your curriculum vitae and qualifications as an expert."

"My undergraduate…"

Sybil was interrupted by a sudden loud opening of the conference room door. All eyes turned towards Bel Geddes's secretary who strode directly and purposefully to her employer.

"Mr. Bel Geddes," she said in a loud whisper. "You are needed in your office… an emergency!"

Bel Geddes's look changed from one of annoyance to one of alarm.

"Excuse me, ladies and gentlemen. I'm sure this will be brief. I can't imagine what could constitute an emergency in the law profession."

He arose quickly from his chair and followed his secretary from the room and closed the door behind him, leaving his case papers, briefcase, even his wallet and keys on the table in front of where he had been sitting.

Sybil, the lawyers, and Ms Hutchins looked around at each other in surprise and bemusement.

Sybil leaned over to whisper to Carter Tarkington, "I hate to sound paranoid, but this smells of a Bel Geddes performance to me."

"Probably," he had to agree. "Let's wait and see what develops."

He was working to keep an expression of anger from his face. It would be just like Paul Bel Geddes to do something like this for annoyance's sake. Hyrum Willis frankly rolled his eyes to express his disbelief.

"I don't care what this is about. He is not going to get away with stiffing me for my time," the usually quiet and retiring Ms. Hutchins said with ill-concealed peevishness.

She had been in Paul Bel Geddes's office before when stranger things than this had taken place.

After twenty minutes, Carter said, "Feel free to get up and walk around. I see no need to be particularly formal. I never seem to be able to maintain any feeling of high decorum when I come to this office for some reason."

"My buns are aching. I'll get myself a drink of water," Hyrum announced. He left the conference room.

"Might as well powder my nose," Ms. Hutchins said. "Not much else to do. Who knows what the rest of the day will bring?"

Sybil stood up and paced around the room.

"You want to go with Ms. Hutchins, Dr. Norcroft? No telling how long this commercial break is going to take. I think I'll join my colleague, for lack of anything more useful to do."

After speaking, Carter slowly got up and started for the rear door.

Sybil shook her head, peeved at the disruption and at the idea that her nemesis, Bel Geddes, was going to get away with some piece of nastiness again without anyone being able to call him on it. She walked around his side of the table to get to the rear door and to follow Carter out.

As she passed Bel Geddes's cluttered space, she looked down to see if she could read anything useful on his notes. All's fair in a war, she reasoned. Without making the effort obvious, she could not decipher anything from the yellow foolscap legal notes Bel Geddes favored. Her quick and observant eyes saw his wallet and keys. Impulsively, and for no thought out reason, she swept up the set of keys that lay so prominently on top of the briefcase and dropped them into her purse. Even as she did it, she asked herself what she had in mind. It was adolescent and silly. She was totally unrepentant, however, and had no intention of returning them. As she walked towards the ladies' restroom, it seemed altogether fitting that she be the cause of considerable inconvenience to Mr. Bel Geddes. She remembered times when she had lost keys and what a time-consuming nuisance it had been. The more she thought about it, the more she liked the idea of what she was doing. She intended to drop them into the trash bin in the ladies room.

The defendant and her attorney and the court reporter all reassembled in the conference room thirty minutes after Mr. Bel Geddes had been called away. His secretary was waiting with coffee and bagels.

"Please, have some. They're very fresh. I just got them from Einstein's," she said.

"What's the message?" Carter asked brusquely, ignoring her offer.

"I am personally sorry, and Mr. Bel Geddes is truly sorry to inconvenience you. He asked me to tell all of you how sorry he is."

"*Bel Geddian overkill,*" Sybil said to herself.

She patted her purse and got a small feeling of pleasure from the heavy bulge of Bel Geddes's keys. She might have been imagining the heft and feel of the keys, but the idea was a positive one, rather like putting one over on her parents as a child. She had held off on throwing them into the trash.

"What is he sorry about, young lady?"

Carter's politeness was strained.

"Of course... Oh, forgive me, I didn't tell you, did I? Mr. Bel Geddes was called away from the office for the day."

"What?!" all the remaining parties to the deposition exclaimed together in incredulity.

"Yes, didn't he tell you? He had an emergency at home. He canceled all of his day's appointments."

Sybil, the two lawyers, and the court recorder sat in stunned disbelief for several seconds. Carter Tarkington broke the silence.

"I suppose there is nothing to do but to leave. I will report this to the court. I will demand a written explanation, but from past experience, I don't expect to get one, at least not a satisfactory one."

"But, but, Mr...uh...I told you...," the secretary stammered.

"Bel Geddes has turned in another sorry performance. Yes, you told us. The explanation is inadequate and unacceptable. I expect a communication as to the excuse for this incredible breach of ethics. You can tell your employer that it had better be a good one, or we will be filing a formal complaint with the bar. While I'm at it, my firm will submit a bill for expenses, and I expect you'll be hearing from the court reporter in short order, as well."

"No. I won't be leaving the office without a check, Ms..." Miriam Hutchins said as caustically as she could.

"Garnucci, I'm not in charge of checks. I can't help you."

Ms. Garnucci looked flustered.

"Someone will. And neither I nor any of the associates in my group will be returning for future depositions. We've had enough. You can tell Mr. Bel Geddes that. Now, *Ms. Garnucci* where is your manager's office?"

"I...I...I'm not sure I can...."

"You can. Specifically, you can get out of my way. I'll find it myself."

Miriam Hutchins gathered up her equipment and began marching purposefully for the conference room door. Her eyes were glowing with indignation, and her fists were clenched. It did not look like a good idea to get in her way.

"Please...Ms...Ms...Court Recorder...Reporter...I'll take you. Please."

Ms. Garnucci hurried awkwardly to gain the lead on the angry court reporter.

Hyrum Willis asked Carter, "Do you want me to send a letter off to Judge Hicken demanding an explanation or a doctor's note, or something from Bel Geddes?"

Carter looked at Sybil before he answered. He shook his head.

"It is pointless. The only reason to do so would be to appease Dr. Norcroft, to make a show of our outrage and feistiness. I think we are far enough into our relationship with her to dispense with futile demonstrations. The judge won't even consider such a request. We'll look petty and mean-spirited. Paul will have a ready excuse, probably write the doctor's note about his dying aunt himself. It would be a waste of time."

He looked angry and discouraged at being subjected to yet another Bel Geddes shenanigan.

Hyrum shrugged his understanding and compliance.

"There *is* a reason to send the letter of request," Sybil put in. "I would like you to do it, Carter, just for the record."

"I'm not sure I follow," he said.

"This is outside the good-old-boy network of lawyers. I am being abused and should not have to take this, not lying down, at least. Maybe your unspoken code requires it, but not mine. I want some kind of formal record of Bel Geddes's misbehaviors, accent on the plural here, to be kept with the court. Even if nothing comes of this particular egregious episode, maybe in aggregate the pattern will emerge even for the densest and most partisan of judges. In fact, I want you to send off a carefully detailed list of all of the abuses perpetrated by this jerk, for the record. This was not the first one, and I am pretty sure it won't be the last. You can list me as being mean-spirited. I'll bear that burden gladly where it applies to Paul Bel Geddes."

"Sure," Carter responded. "If you feel that way...and maybe you're right. Maybe the accumulation will finally catch up with this guy. He acts like antics of this sort are all in jest, it is all such a big joke, a frivolous game. Maybe, if we call him on it, someone in a position to matter will come down on him eventually. Don't hold your breath that it will be this time."

"I have lost any naiveté I once had regarding Paul. I'm done with phony politeness. I consider that the gloves came off years ago, and it is a bare-knuckle brawl all the way now. I want you with me in this, Carter. Paul gives your whole profession a bad name. He's the kind of guy that makes people dubious about attorneys. Attack him and help your image. While you're at it, why not send a letter to the bar as well. Might as well let the evidence accumulate there as well as with Judge Hicken."

Sybil had an adamant, uncompromising look on her face. Carter knew that a line had been crossed that day.

"I'll do it. There's no love lost between me and Paul Bel Geddes either. I have had to put up with him for years. It's not likely that I will have to sit next to him for dinner in the future. I'll send you a copy of both letters."

He wondered if this latest caper, presumed caper, to give the eccentric trial attorney some slight benefit of the doubt, had not simply awakened the sleeping tigress. Carter had mixed feelings about what might transpire in the episodes that were sure to follow.

"Thanks. Let's go home," Sybil said.

They walked out of the conference room, still expressing their anger and not caring who heard them.

Paul Bel Geddes watched the trio's exit from his vantage point in his partner's office with an expression of fulfilled amusement on his puckish face

In the parking lot, Sybil reached for her keys. She immediately encountered the bulk of Paul Bel Geddes's keys that she had surreptitiously dropped into her purse earlier and had temporarily forgotten. Her emotions ran from vindictive—she would just drop the keys in the nearest waste bin—to sheepish—she would march right back up to Bel Geddes's office and return them. Her long training in dealing with crises took over, and she stopped to think. In a moment, she saw a clear potential advantage for herself, and in a few moments more, she envisioned a plan that would allow her to take the initiative and to get away from always being the patsy in her ongoing acrimonious feud with Paul. Her envisioned plan made her feel momentarily guilty. She even looked around furtively, but she also felt as if a weight had been lifted from her. Her feminist convictions ardently rejected playing the role of a victim. She wasted no further time concerning herself about the morality of her assertive plan.

Sybil looked over her shoulder, trying to recall. It was there, a kiosk near the entrance to the building's parking lot that duplicated keys. She wasted no time and walked briskly to the small building. The operator was a blind man, an African-American with a totally unruly and out-of-style graying Afro hairdo. He wore opaque dark glasses and clenched a thick, unlit cigar between tobacco stained, carious teeth.

"Hello, Ma'am, how kin Ah hep youse?" the operator asked as soon as Sybil walked into the kiosk and before she had a chance to speak.

She was certain that she had not made a sound when she entered.

"Hello. How'd you know I was a woman?"

"Easy as pah. Smelt ya'all. Nice."

He smiled avuncularly.

"Thanks. How about making two copies of each of these keys."

She handed the man the keys she presumed were to Paul Bel Geddes's car and office."

"Cain't see, little lady. Any o' these here not suppos' to be duplicate?"

"No. They're all okay. I'm just getting my boss a second set. He's always losing his."

"He work in the buildin'?"

"Yes."

"Old Stewart?"

"That's right," Sybil lied. "Good guess."

"Heard he quit."

"He did."

Sybil had to think fast.

"I take care of a few secretarial needs for him while he ties up some loose ends from his years of practice."

"Lots of those Ah reckon. Let's have a look at those keys."

He "looked" with expert fingers.

"No problem. Take jist a minute."

He was done in five. Sybil paid him four dollars and left. He asked her name, but she pretended not to hear.

As she walked back towards her car, she considered how to get the original keys back to Bel Geddes, ideally without him knowing that they had been missing or, certainly, without knowing that they had been in her possession, however briefly. She looked around for a person whom she might pay to drop the keys off at the office or in front of the door to Bel Geddes's suite of offices. She saw several but demurred from contacting any of them because she thought better of the idea. She figured that there was as much of a chance that a spur of the moment courier would lose the keys, take them to the wrong office, or put them in front of the wrong door, or would steal them as there was that the return would be accurate and anonymous. She elected to do it herself, hoping that stealth would see her through.

She reentered the building. No one gave her a second glance. There were too many people entering and exiting all of the time. She rode up to the eighth floor in an elevator that was packed with people intent on their own business, and no one seemed to pay her any mind. She got off and looked around. She was alone in the hallway. She was able to look all the way into the suite of offices of Bel Geddes and Loughlin. From her position in front of the bank of elevators, Sybil could not be entirely certain that there was nobody sitting at the receptionist's desk, but it did not seem that there was. She mistrusted, even disbelieved such uncharacteristic luck, at least as it might benefit her.

"He who hesitates is lost," she murmured and advanced towards the open door.

She held her purse up to her face as if looking for something as she came to the door. There was no one there. Sybil took one quick look around then walked swiftly in. She considered dropping the keys on the completely empty desk, but that would invite too much question. She looked around and assessed the situation in a fraction of a second then bent over and quietly set the keys on the rug by the door supports of the entryway into the offices proper, counting on the presumption that Paul and his staff would make that the keys had been dropped there by him. She turned and quickly walked out, taking a brief second to turn and see if she had been witnessed. There was still no one around. Her luck was holding.

She took giant steps, just short of running, back to the elevator and pressed the down button. The elevator took forever. In a sidelong glance, Sybil saw Bel Geddes's buxom receptionist return to her place in the outer office. She was talking over her shoulder to another employee, a man in shirt sleeves. Sybil faced away from them and willed the elevator to hurry. It finally came, the door opened, and five Japanese men stepped out bowing vigorously and speaking loudly to one another. Sybil knew that the receptionist's attention would be drawn to the outlandish commotion in the hall. She braved a quick look. The woman was now at her desk looking into her compact mirror and applying makeup as if she were about to be discovered by an MGM talent scout, and her coiffure and facial presentation were the be-all and end-all of existence right then. Sybil edged around the Japanese business men and into the elevator while still more occupants disembarked. They gave her a look. She smiled sweetly and stepped to the anonymity of the back of the elevator. Only then did she realize that she had not been breathing.

Sybil fought back an urge to flee the building. She had an irrational fear that there would be some sort of metal detector that would expose the newly made set of keys she was so guiltily clutching. She forced herself to act natural, to walk normally out of the building and down its three steps to the city sidewalk. She avoided the temptation to look back over her shoulder. She started to calm down only after she pulled her car out of the parking lot and onto the arterial thoroughfare.

"I am just not up to this sort of thing," she sighed and shook her head at her reflection in the rearview mirror. "I can't see how crooks do it. I would go all to pieces before I got done with a crime, let alone if someone should consider me a suspect. I can just see myself confessing abjectly to some cop and him looking completely surprised since it had never crossed his mind to think that I, the great doctor, could be the guilty one."

She drove out to the ranch since she knew that Charles was out of town. She needed to take it easy, to calm down among friends. Scheduling time for the deposition had completely vacated her work day, the deposition itself had been aborted, and she now had time on her hands. Sybil parked in the driveway and opened the heavy plank and iron bolt doors of the ranchero hacienda. They were not locked. On her way to her study, the spacious room she had designed for her own and no one else's taste, she got a Diet Coke out of the refrigerator and shook her head what-the-heck and picked up a bag of greasy potato chips as well. She settled into the heavy leather overstuffed chair, kicked off her high heels, and lifted her aching feet to the nirvana of the Ottoman.

The room was restful, and for Sybil, at least, full of warm earth tones and comfortable Spanish and Southwestern gentility. The walls were hung with Navajo tapestries between which hung the Southwest's matron saint, Georgia O'Keeffe's, print of *From a Day with Juan*. The floor covering was a wool Madras, India kilim that had a Southwestern look. Sybil had bought a wonderful deadhead accent table—old growth wood log that had been soaked under water for years—topped by half-inch thick edge beveled glass. Wall niches held brilliant indigo, magenta, and sand-toned Talavera pottery from Puebla, Mexico. In one corner stood an imposing 19th century New Mexican *trastero* hand painted with Pueblo Indian geometric motifs. In another corner a table held an ornate polished antique Pavoni Ideale expresso machine. Sybil's desk, a heavy oaken heirloom Spanish *escritorio*, was a gift from the grateful Mexicans who shared her ranch. The wall opposite the *escritorio* contained a granite boulder and sandstone fireplace large enough to accommodate four-foot logs on its heavy iron grates. On the wrought iron and weathered plank coffee table in front of the fireplace stood an aged copper Mexican *olla* filled to overflowing with brightly colored ripe fruits.

Sybil heard Pancho and Carlita laughing in the adjoining room. It was a gentle and affable sound passing between comfortable long time friends and marriage partners. They approached her study, animatedly talking with him intermittently emitting a basso belly laugh and her counterpoising with a melodic soprano ripple of unfeigned gaiety.

Sybil called to them, "Hey, Pancho and Carlita, what's so funny?"

They had not known Sybil was there and were momentarily startled. They peeked around the corner and saw her, saw that she was not annoyed by their noise, and began laughing again as they strode arm in arm into her study.

"The kids brought home their English *lecciones*, *Doña*," Carlita smiled. "See what they learn thees days."

She handed Sybil a printed page.

Sybil glanced at it quickly—tongue twisters.

"Okay, let's hear you…," she requested.

They blushed.

"C'mon - Peter Piper…."

"Peeked a peck of peekled peckers," Pancho said.

His wife looked at him, then at Sybil and blushed scarlet in embarrassment.

"Such talk," Sybil chided Pancho amusedly.

She started to laugh. Peels and rolls of cathartic laughter.

"Hokay, esmartie," Pancho countered. "Let's hear you say fast, "The sixth Sheik's sixth sheep's seek."

"I'll try," Sybil laughed. "The sixth sheep's sixth's sheep's sick."

Pancho and Carlita laughed.

"Not quite. Close. Not quite."

"The sixth Sheik's sixth sheep's sick. The sixth Sheik's sixth sheep's sick. The sixth Sheik's sixth sheep's sick."

Sybil sat back in triumph. Pancho and Maria applauded.

"Let's hear you and Carlita do, 'Bloody black bugs'."

They tried, but most of their efforts were a mixture of 'Bladdy blek blugs', 'Bloody back brugs', and 'Bruddy black budge'.

The couple had to call an intermission because of laughter.

Sybil laughed with Pancho and Carlita until Carlita said it was Sybil's turn.

"Jou try, *Tres tristes tigres comen trigo en un trigal!*"

Sybil tried three times before succeeding.

"Hokay, now jou try, *El cuero del cuerpo del puerco.*"

It took four times to get it right.

"Okay, *Doña*, "Sapito sapon - ponte calzon. No puedo papito porque soy pipon."

Sybil did not have a clue what the words meant, but she struggled until she got the words and their pronunciation perfect and smiled in mini-triumph.

Carlita feigned anger and put on a determined look.

"All right. Here is thee real test. Leesten careful."

The Spanish then came out like a machine gun on full automatic, "*El amor es una locura, qui ni el cura lo cura y si el cura lo cura es una locura del cura.*"

It was Carlita's turn to smile in triumph.

Sybil shook her head in surrender. Carlita then repeated the impossible phrases three more times in rapid succession, more staccato and at a greater velocity than the first time.

Sybil did not even try.

She simply clapped her hands and said, "Bravo. You win. Write that down, so I can practice, all right?"

Carlita stood and did a little curtsy, gracious in her victory. Her Chiapas amber earrings rustled and caught the natural ocher light from the hallway.

Sybil laughed and said, "We might as well make it a party. Why not call the others? Charles is out of town, so we might as well have some fun. I'm too weak to do any work or anything else."

It turned out to be a great impromptu celebration of nothing more than life, the best party since they won the all-around championship at the Dallas International with the prize four year old Paso Fino gelding. The company and the joy of being with her friends almost caused Sybil to forget all about her smoldering hatred for Paul Bel Geddes.

The only time that a thought of that demon crossed her mind was when she felt the two copies of his keys in her purse and decided to give one of them to Pancho for safe keeping with a cryptic admonition to be sure not to misplace them, "They will be important one day. I'll ask for a favor that involves them."

"Anything, *Patrona*. You have only to ask," Pancho replied.

CHAPTER ELEVEN

Things were going too well, it seemed to her. Dr. Norcroft was now established officially as the region's certified skull base and neurovascular surgeon-in-chief. Only four other neurosurgeons in the state were allowed on the panel. It was ironic because Sybil had been one of the most outspoken opponents of the system of regionalization when it had first been proposed by the American Association of Neurological Surgeons seven years previously. Finally, the members of the AANS had had to admit, however grudgingly, that there were far too many neurosurgeons for the population of the United States. Sybil, herself, had come to recognize that the patient pool, especially for the uncommon skull base tumors and aneurysms, was being so diluted that most neurosurgeons did no more than one case of either kind a year or even in two years. As a result, she and her colleagues were unable to keep their skills honed to the sharpness that the patients deserved. It had been a compromise. Sybil had had to give up back surgery, her bread and butter operations, in exchange. Now, she was busy enough with the more delicate and challenging operations that she did not miss the income from the back operations, nor did she miss the aggravation of caring for the people with their chronic pain, narcotics needs, and workman's compensation hassles.

Sybil Norcroft was the current secretary of the AANS, and in line to become the association's president three years down the line. With that position came the prestige of the organization and invaluable connections in the neurosurgery world; she was now part of the "old-boy" network, a fact that gave her and her feminist sisters a sweet source of amusement. The previous month, Dr. Norcroft was elected president of the medical staff at JNMH for the second time, indicative of approbation from her local colleagues as well as on a national level. She had not had a new malpractice suit or even the threat of one in the past year, a fact that made her almost unique among neurosurgeons across the country.

Sybil felt that she had matured into her professional success at this point in her career. This was in positive contradistinction to the mistakes that she had made in overemphasizing that segment of her life earlier on, the mistakes that had caused a weakening of her bonds with her husband, Charles Daniels, and had led to his brief flirtation with a stray relationship. She had developed the wisdom to make certain that she gave him a full measure of her time and attention, and he was responding with a spirit of renewal that bordered on being a prolonged second honeymoon.

The ranch was almost on automatic pilot so far as the need for her to be involved in its day-to-day management. Pancho, Jose, and Marcos ran the place smoothly and had matured into sophisticated businessmen and horse showmen. They were now earning a profit that was better each year than the one preceding. No longer was the ranch business an effort or burden or even a hobby. It was a deeply satisfying avocation that permitted Sybil to participate with love and pride in the nurturing and development of prize Tennessee Walkers, Paso Finos, and Missouri Foxtrotters without any stress being attached.

Although the ranch had been a gift from Charles Daniels, Sybil had taken great pride in paying him back with a twenty percent return on his investment. The two of them had used the occasion of her presenting the final check to have a major celebration. They had included the Rodriguez, Alvarez, and Hernandez families and all of the ranch hands in a blow-out fiesta.

It was on the morning following that great party when Sybil, feeling a trifle hungover, conducted a brief review of her life to date and her current standing and found herself nagged by the recurrent thought that things were going too well. Perhaps it was prescience or just serendipitous anticipation that made her flinch when her secretary brought in the day's stack of mail. She flipped quickly through the pile of envelopes looking for bad news. As if in self-fulfilling prophecy, the bad news leaped off the print on the second to the last envelope she touched. The return address was Bel Geddes and Loughlin, Attorneys at Law. The last envelope bore the return address of her own attorneys.

The text of the letter from Paul Bel Geddes was:

September 20
Re: van der Hoef vs Sybil Norcroft and
Joseph Noble Memorial Hospital
My Dear Sybil,

How the time flies! Here it is deposition time again. The date is November 22, a full two months from the date of this mailing, plenty of time to prepare. See you then.

And, incidentally, I was sorry not to hear from you regarding the family illness that caused the cancellation of the last scheduled deposition. I am sure it was just an oversight. Until the 22nd of next month, I remain,
Truly yours,
P. Bel Geddes, Esq.

Carter Tarkington's letter bore the following day's date:

Dear Dr. Norcroft:

I regret that you have received or very shortly will receive a communication directly from Paul Bel Geddes in clear violation of the long standing rule that attorneys communicate directly with opposing attorneys and never with clients. Rest assured that I will add this breach to the growing list of complaints against Mr. Bel Geddes, as you have requested.

Without the usual courtesies among attorneys and clients, Mr. Bel Geddes has gone ahead and scheduled another date for a deposition in the van der Hoef vs Norcroft suit. As it turns out, that date is entirely acceptable to Hyrum Willis and me. You most certainly have the right to refuse that date, even to convey the unspoken message to the plaintiff's attorney that you refuse to be manipulated. I have no good idea whether or not this date is serious or whether we will be exposed to more of Bel Geddes's capers.

In responding to this announcement, please communicate only with me, and I will convey your message to the plaintiff's attorney and will do all of the necessary negotiating and scheduling so as to suit your schedule.
Sincerely,
Carter Tarkington

The taunting quality of Paul Bel Geddes's letter infuriated Sybil. She gave Carter's suggestion of refusing the date for spite several minutes of consideration. However, the fact was that November 22nd was one of the few free days she would have before the end of the year. She had originally planned for that to be her Christmas shopping day, but she had already done most of her shopping, and her secretary could attend to the rest. November 22nd was as good a day as any. She dictated a letter back to Carter:

September 21
Dear Mr. Tarkington,

I received your letter and also the communication from Paul Bel Geddes regarding the proposed date of November 22 for the next scheduling of my deposition in the van der Hoef case. Although I, like you, take exception both to the fact of his writing directly to me and the unprofessional manner of over familiarity that he adopted in his communication, the date is not the worst he could have picked. I accept the date, but will have to ask that the formal deposition begin promptly at eight o'clock in the morning on that day. I have several very important appointments that day. I will reschedule them for the afternoon.

On your advice, I am making a strong effort to avoid allowing Mr. Bel Geddes and his antics to provoke me. I believe that I have been successful, so do not concern yourself over much about the state of my psyche. Until the 22nd,
Sincerely,
Sybil Norcroft, M.D., PhD, F.A.C.S.

Sybil felt calm about her decision to cooperate with Paul Bel Geddes. She did not feel any inclination to curse him, or to play games of scheduling and continuing the proceedings to still another day seemingly endlessly. She planned to allow Bel Geddes free rein in that game. She had another plan

On the 15th of November, Sybil drove out to her ranch and met with Pancho, Jose, and Marcos in the ranch's kitchen after first arranging with them by telephone. They were in the kitchen where Carlita and Maria Innocenta were cooking. Carlita was making jalapeño fritatas, frying the hot chilies with Muenster cheese with never a thought for fat or cholesterol, the ingredients that gave the delicacy its unique flavor. Maria Innocenta was making her specialty, Mexican chocolate soup. When Sybil entered the kitchen, Maria was filling the soup pot with the vegetables she had chopped—onions, carrots, celery, zucchini, green peppers, and jalapeños.

"Greetings, *Patrona*," said Jose. "I am most pleased to see you. It has been a while, I think."

"You're right, Jose. And it has been too long. My excuse is that I have been too busy. "

Carlita passed a platter of fritatas, still sizzling in the frying pan. Maria Innocenta added tequila and cinnamon to her soup and sniffed it professionally.

"You had something of importance to discuss with us, *Patrona*?" asked Marcos, who was uncomfortable with his country's exasperating preliminaries to every serious discussion.

He was like Sybil. He liked to get down to business and to have the social amenities afterwards. He did pause to take his share of the fritatas.

"I do. I know you men are busy, so I won't keep you long. I think you all remember that I told you about the attorney, the *abogado*, who has been making my life difficult, no?"

"The one who was attorney for the Mexican woman...Juarez, I think," Pancho said.

"That is the one, Pancho."

Maria Innocenta caught Sybil's eye.

"Taste this, *Patrona*, you theenk eet needs *mas sal o pimienta*?"

She ladled in the final ingredients, cilantro and cocoa.

Sybil tried a spoonful and sighed. She was hungry, and the smells of the specialties of the house were intoxicating.

"Perfect. Just let it simmer a few minutes," she said.

Maria smiled broadly.

"And I take it that that same *mal hombre* is still doing bad things to you," Jose pushed on in the conversation, not so much as a question as a verification of what they all presumed.

"It is true. All too true."

"I once told you that I would be happy to assist you in the matter of thees *serpiente*. I believe I speak for Jose and Marcos when I make the offer again. Is there anything you would have us do?"

Pancho spoke, and all three Mexican men nodded their affirmation.

"I thank you for asking. The time has come when you could do me a service. It would involve doing something illegal. No one has to do this, but it would be important for me."

"It would be important for us as well, *Patrona*," Pancho said in all earnestness.

The other two men nodded in accord.

"Thank you, *amigos*. I will not forget," Sybil responded.

She then laid out her plan including the reasons and expected results.

The men were all smiles when she finished. They all then sat down at the round hacienda kitchen table and shared the chocolate soup and the business of the ranch without again discussing Sybil's plans.

The deposition was to be on the 22nd at eight in the morning. The night of the 21st-22nd was densely black, and visibility was further reduced by a drizzling rain. There were only scattered travelers on the main arterial thoroughfares at two in the morning on the 22nd, and no traffic at all on the quiet streets near the law offices of Bel Geddes and Loughlin. There was no one about to see three men in dark ponchos open the front door of the building with its flamboyant facade. Even if someone had noticed, the interest would have been only cursory since the door was obviously being opened with a proper key.

Pancho, Jose, and Marcos stood on the rug in the large entry foyer until they were no longer dripping on the floor.

"Eighth floor, says the *Patrona*," whispered Pancho.

"*Si*," answered Jose who was running his gloved fingers down the list of offices posted in the lobby. "Let's get eet done."

The men took the elevator to the eighth floor and stepped quietly into the well-lit hallway leading to the suite of offices occupied by Paul Bel Geddes and his partner Martin Loughlin. They stood stock still listening for sounds of cleaning women or security guards. When they were sure they were completely alone, they walked briskly to the ornately inscribed front doors, used the key Dr. Norcroft had provided them, and stepped inside. They moved into the main office corridor where the light was more subdued. Pancho pointed down the hall, and the three men crept silently along the plush carpet to the office marked, *Paul Bel Geddes, Attorney at Law, Director*.

They paused briefly one more time to detect any noise, checked the doors for any visible alarm system, then used their key and slipped into the darkened office. They turned on their flashlights and scanned the room. The outer office, obviously Bel Geddes's personal receptionist and secretary's, was scrupulously neat, ready for the action of the upcoming day. Pancho motioned the two other men to follow him. They walked through the door marked, *Private*, and hurriedly looked around. As Dr. Norcroft had suggested, a large leather briefcase stood on the top of the huge desktop that was covered with papers in a welter of disarray.

"Get the files out of the case, Marcos, I'll get the other file from the cabinet. Jose, watch the door and leesten for guards."

Pancho turned towards the filing cabinet, adjusting the fit of his rubber gloves. He looked at his compatriots to see if they had remembered to wear latex as well. They had.

"Thee notes, too, Pancho?"

"Everything, Marcos."

Marcos removed the contents of the case and laid them on the desktop. Pancho found a file at random, under F, and removed it. He brought it to the desk, switched the papers in it for the papers in the file from the briefcase, and placed the mismarked files into wrong places. The file labeled *Ferranzo vs. Webster Corp.*, but containing the documents for the van der Hoef case, he placed at random in the filing cabinet, this time in the C's. The file labeled *van der Hoef vs JNMH & Norcroft* but containing the documents for the *Ferranzo* case, he placed back in the briefcase. He took pains to be sure that the meticulously handwritten notes on yellow legal paper that contained the attorney's questioning sequence for the deposition were switched as well. He had memorized the exact position of the briefcase on the desktop and replaced it with care. He and the others scanned the room for any telltale evidence that they had been there, and finding none, slipped quickly out of the offices, down the elevator, across the lobby, and through the main doors and into the dark wet street. They were back home at the ranch by three-thirty in the morning.

"*Déjà vu*," muttered Hyrum Willis as he, Carter Tarkington, and Sybil Norcroft stood waiting for the elevator in Bel Geddes's building shortly before the eight am starting time.

"Act III, scene iii," replied Sybil. "Doesn't it fill you with wonder to contemplate what Paul will come up with today?"

"I'll lay you seven to three that we have another continuance."

"No takers," said Carter. "The continuance is a given. I am just waiting to see what ingenious excuse he comes up with today."

"So you can send in another complaint to the court and to the bar?" Sybil said to Carter, giving him a little verbal jab since they both knew how much effect the last complaint had produced.

"Makes my day," sighed Carter.

The elevator opened, and they stepped in.

"Eight, please," Carter asked a balding man in a three-piece suit who was standing nearest the row of floor indicator buttons.

The trio announced themselves to the receptionist and were escorted into the now all too familiar conference room. Ten minutes later, the court reporter appeared. They waited thirty-five minutes for the plaintiff's attorney to appear.

"Hi, all," came Bel Geddes's jaunty greeting as he burst into the room in a typical grand entrance.

"Paul," Carter nodded.

Evidently, he spoke for them all because no one else responded to the cheery salutation from Bel Geddes. The plaintiff's trial attorney did not appear to notice or chose not to consider the lack of response as a snub. When he extended his hand to the attorneys and to the court reporter, they responded with insipid clasps. Sybil sat on her hands when Paul stood in front of her with his arm outstretched. After a brief incommodious moment, he shrugged and took his seat directly across from her.

"Everyone here?" he asked unnecessarily.

"So far as I know," answered Carter. "Unless you have someone else coming."

"No, I'm all here," laughed Bel Geddes.

The opposing attorneys politely responded with wan smiles. Sybil remained expressionless.

"I have a treat today...warm bagels...whipped garlic cream cheese...capers...lox."

He looked as expectantly as a cat presenting a mouse to its master with the mention of each new delectable. His audience was lukewarm. Paul laughed out loud for some inexplicable reason. He was in an indestructibly good mood that day, probably because of the destruction he had planned for the arrogant doctor and her overconfident attorneys.

"Fine, Paul. I hope we won't have to wait. We are busy, as we know you are. We want to get on with the deposition. There have been several continuances already, and it is time to get this done and to get on to other steps in the discovery phase."

Carter's voice was brusque.

"No delays today, Carter, old friend. I intend to decimate your client fully today and to talk settlement before the close of business. I think you will be amenable to my suggestions after you've seen what I have in store for her."

He looked pointedly and malevolently at Sybil. She returned his gaze with a calm, almost disinterested look. Paul knew better than to try and stare the famous feminist down. She was a soulless expert. He returned his attention to Carter.

"But first, the amenities."

He pressed a buzzer near his place at the conference table.

A secretary marched through the doors almost immediately. She had to have been waiting right outside. She carried in a huge platter of steaming bagels with all of the trimmings. Sybil noted that this woman was new, just as buxom and underdressed as the earlier model, but new. She had a bubbly voice that did not bespeak great typing ability. She looked darkly exotic, foreign, but Sybil could not place her origins.

"Here we are, Paul. Hot off the griddle."

Giggle.

"Thank you, dear. I'll give you a buzz if I want anything else."

Giggle.

Paul pushed a paper plate loaded with assorted flavors of bagels and generous dollops of cream cheese, capers, and lox to everyone in the room. Sybil moved hers to the middle of the table without sampling a bite. There was a pause while Paul finished off three of the more exotically composed confections followed by a small satisfied burp.

"Excu-uuse me!" he apologized, dabbing his lips with a shiny monogrammed linen handkerchief.

The defendant's attorneys and the court reporter each took a small courteous bite of one of the bagels sitting before them, sharing glances that said they were not about to get seduced into being Paul Bel Geddes's dupe again, no matter what he had planned.

"All right, now. Let's begin," Paul announced, his hunger temporarily sated.

He took Sybil through the now familiar introductions, explained in annoying detail the process of the deposition, asked about her curriculum vitae, even asked her current occupation, as if he had never seen her before, and explained her rights. He was elaborately polite, sometimes courtly, and Sybil, in kind, maintained civility throughout the preliminaries.

"Now, that behind us, we can get down to the nitty gritty, if you'll pardon my informality," Paul announced airily, but with a hint of menace.

He opened his large leather briefcase and extracted the file folder marked *van der Hoef vs. JNMH & Norcroft*. The letters were bold enough for Sybil to be able to read them upside down.

"I am sure other attorneys like to do this off the cuff, so's to speak, but I am a stickler for details and order. I have to rely on my notes, so we get just the right questions in just the right order."

He gave a quick, insincere apologetic smile. Once again, Sybil had the distinct impression that the attorney was toying with her, displaying small hints of the personal vendetta that existed between the two of them over and above the professional adversarial relationship that was the core purpose of their present dialogue. Paul took a moment to put on half glasses, then he began to thumb through the yellow legal sheets. A cloud passed over his face. He took out the bound copies of medical chart history. A few glances at the documentary materials caused him to abandon the facade of hale-fellow-well-met. He murmured a curse under his breath.

"Excuse me," he said. "A small problem."

He pushed the secretary button. In a second, he pushed it again. In a third second, he pushed down on the button and kept his finger there. The new secretary rushed into the room, wiping something from her mouth.

"Yes, Paul?" she asked.

"Mr. Bel Geddes. And would you come here? I need to say something to you in private."

She walked over to him, bent her ear down, so he could whisper. The others could hear the rustle of sound coming from Bel Geddes, something like hearing the ocean from a conch shell. The secretary blanched and stepped back, as if he had hit her. She did an agile about face and hurried out of the room.

She was gone five minutes. No one spoke. It seemed the usual Bel Geddes scenario—the initial trappings of a standard deposition with all participants settling into a familiar process and preparing for the thrust and parry of the anticipated questions and answers, then the outlandish shenanigan. She was gone ten minutes, then ten minutes more. Bel Geddes's face was at first bland, then taciturn, then began to grow pinker. He was struggling to keep emotion out of his expression, but as the time passed by at a glacial pace, he demonstrated, by degrees, a morose, then wrathful, then ill-concealed rage in his countenance. His face grew dark, his eyes narrowed, and his lips thinned into a flat hard line.

The intercom carried the voice of the secretary.

"Please come to your office, Mr. Bel Geddes. We have a situation you will need to deal with."

Bel Geddes arose and left without excusing himself. Carter Tarkington, Hyrum Willis, Sybil Norcroft, and the court reporter were left without explanation in their places. They shared questioning looks.

"Now, what?" growled Hyrum. "What's your best guess about what the excuse will be this time?"

Carter shook his head. His face was set in what looked like a permanent frown. Sybil looked as if she had seen it all before and was not all that surprised. The only indication of her displeasure was a slight clenching of her jaws.

The court reporter spoke after a few minutes.

"I was warned about this. I am going to wait five more minutes then I am going to march right out there and demand my money, and I am going to file a protest with the bar."

Her face was flushed. She was young and inexperienced and had obviously drawn the short straw when the day's work was being divvied out by the members of her group. Sybil noted with slight amusement that she never saw the same court reporter twice in Paul Bel Geddes's depositions.

The threatened five minutes passed. The court reporter made an elaborate display of checking and rechecking her watch. She looked from one of the remaining people in the room to the other for some sort of signal. Finally, with a flourish, she gathered up her machine and materials and marched defiantly for the door.

"Does this seem vaguely familiar?" asked Hyrum, more rhetorically than for any concrete purpose.

On her way out of the conference room doors, the court reporter encountered Bel Geddes on his way back in.

"Mr. Bel Geddes, I'm leaving. I will thank you to have your staff prepare a check. Our minimum is $300 for cancellations with inadequate warning. I have waited more than the maximum time required."

Bel Geddes surprised everyone with the benignity of his reply.

"No problem, dear. You're right. We find that we must cancel. You will have your check by mail this afternoon."

"I'm sorry, Sir, that won't do. I need to take a check with me now."

"No trust for an eminent officer of the court? Don't think I'm good for it, dear?"

"I am no one's dear. My name is Ingrid Housfeld. You may make the check out to me or to the Court Reporter's Bureau, whichever you wish."

"I will send a check to your office this very morning by courier. Will that satisfy you? You can see that I have to deal with other matters for the moment."

"I'll wait."

Sybil silently gave a hearty "bravo" for the plucky girl. She was standing her ground, and that brightened Sybil's day.

"Then, for heaven's sake, take a seat in the waiting room. I'll have my secretary...my new secretary, deal with you when I've finished here."

He and the court reporter had a short staring down contest that he won. She trotted out to the waiting room, still determined not to relent.

"I have a terrible confession to make," said Paul to the defendant and her attorneys.

He was forcing an unconcerned smile.

"What is it this time, Paul?" Carter Tarkington asked snappishly.

"Ah, Carter, try for some of that Christian charity for which you are so renowned," Paul replied.

Carter emitted a small groan.

"My imbecile of a secretary has completely destroyed my filing system. Nobody can locate the van der Hoef file or my notes. I can't go on without them."

"What was that file I saw come out of your briefcase? If I am not mistaken, it was entitled *van der Hoef vs. JNMH & Norcroft*, was it not?"

"Yes...mistakenly. Somehow, my newest attempt to assist the unemployment among the ethnics has proved to be my undoing. She seems to have managed to misfile several key cases. I can't find anything pertinent to this case."

"How about running off your records from your computer?"

"I could do that, but it would take two or three hours before I could sort it all out. My notes are another thing altogether. They are my work product in my handwriting and are irreplaceable and there are no computer copies available."

"I am not going to sit around here on my dime while this man plays another of his endless games with us, Carter," said Sybil with calm aridity.

It was the first time she had spoken since Bel Geddes had left off his preliminary questioning of her.

Carter gave her a resigned nod. He made one more unenthusiastic effort.

"You are perfectly welcome to use our copy of the medical chart. Surely you can get your questions asked and answered by referring to that copy as well as to yours. They are identical."

"I must have my own work product to be able to go on. This is a case of great subtleties, and I have prepared to counter any evasiveness on the defendant's part with adroit and well prepared queries. You would require no less. I am unable to go on. Write another of your famous letters to the court and to the bar for all the good it will do you. This deposition is at an end. Good day. Until next time..."

He gave a dismissive back hand wave and walked out.

Hyrum rolled his eyes back in his head.

He said, "Doesn't it bug you that this state lets this sort of crap go on year in and year out? This guy and half a dozen like him give the whole profession a bad name. We mitch and bone about doctors for not policing their own, isn't that the height of hypocrisy?"

He was not expecting an answer, just ventilating.

"Sorry, Dr. Norcroft...again," Carter said, his voice heavy and angry.

"Is there anything you can do to prevent this happening another time?" Sybil asked. "I mean, something that matters, something with teeth. This is ridiculous. It is a calculated insult to every one of us. To say nothing of his total disregard for the system, for all of those formal rules that we are supposed to abide by that govern how we deal with disputes in our supposed civil society."

Her face looked angry. She felt quite calm and unruffled, however. She did not think it would do to allow Carter and Hyrum to see her momentary inner placidity in that angry situation. She had no desire to invite questions.

"As a matter of fact, I think there is something I can do. I want you to write a formal protest. Hyrum and I will do the same. I think I can easily convince a court reporter or two, or three, to join the campaign as well. Then, I will make a formal request that the arbitration hearing judge be present at the next deposition, so we can terminate the nonsense and get onto the substance of the deposition. Maybe, eventually, we can get beyond this step and on to other depositions and inquiries."

"Umm- hmm," mused Sybil doubtfully.

"Don't become entirely cynical about the process, Dr. Norcroft. It is still the best one in the world, despite the Paul Bel Geddeses in it. I am confident that I can get the judge to attend. He gets a fee, after all. I will do everything in my power to see to it that Bel Geddes pays for that fee. That ought to frost his nubbins a little."

CHAPTER TWELVE

There were seven continuances, in all, for the van der Hoef case, stretching over nearly as many years, before the day finally arrived that it suited the plaintiff's attorney to schedule one that he intended to take place. Volumes of pretrial motions, affidavits, interoffice letters, and complaints to the judge and to the bar association mounted up in anticipation of the deposition. Sybil was the first deponent on Bel Geddes's list for the van der Hoef vs. Norcroft and Joseph Noble Memorial Hospital case even after the extended period since the filing of the suit.

In the interim seven years since the date of receiving her ninety-day notice that she was to be sued by van der Hoef, she had been free of any further malpractice suits. The main reason was that the state passed a California-type law that made the simple requirement that malpractice cases have merit as evidenced by the fact that an expert, one in the same specialty as the defendant doctor, be willing to act for the plaintiff, and that expert must produce a list of professional complaints upon which the accusation of malpractice was to be based throughout the course of the suit, from filing, through the evidentiary—fishing—phase, during depositions, and in trial or in binding arbitration hearings.

Sybil's state went beyond the California model. Part of the malpractice suit act made former testimony of medical witnesses admissible in the present action's early phases. If the professional witness's current testimony was found during the evidentiary phase to be contradictory to his previous sworn testimony, then that witness had to be summarily disqualified by the sitting judge. The result was that the number of flagrant medical whores, advocating, nonobjective physicians, who peddled their M.D.'s into courtrooms and pandered to the requirements of each succeeding attorney and client irrespective of medical evidence, dropped precipitously. As a consequence, the number of malpractice suits had leveled off to the point that the malpractice defense firms were now advocating settlement much more commonly because they believed that the principal cause of filing malpractice suits in the past two or three years was, in fact, malpractice.

Defense attorneys and their clients, the doctors, and their insurance companies, were now openly advocating a no-fault insurance plan to reimburse and to help medically injured individuals irrespective of fault by a medical provider, even to the point of recommending a provision for sensible punitive damages. The plaintiff's attorneys' organizations, one of which was headed by Paul Bel Geddes, were mounting an implacable opposition against the discontinuation of the golden cash cow that the previous system represented. The other, more personal result, was that Sybil Norcroft had all but forgotten about the problem of malpractice in her own work and had begun to go about her practice with more zeal and compassion and less paranoia.

It was a reality check to have the van der Hoef case brought back into the sharp focus of reality again. Bel Geddes had filed the suit before the change in the state law and was not bound by the common sense rules of the Medical Malpractice Act. Despite the fact that he had not yet been able to find a medical prostitute expert to use in the case, he was obviously going to continue on his course of attacking her, the lack of an expert witness being considered not to be a crucial factor in achieving that aim.

As soon as Sybil received the eighth notice of the scheduling of her deposition, she called Carter Tarkington.

"Carter, am I expected to drop everything for this year's deposition or can you get it canceled without going through the usual rigmarole with Bel Geddes?"

"It's his show, Dr. Norcroft. He called the office a week ago. He sounded serious. I think he's beginning to feel the pinch from the approach of the statute of limitations. I think he may be getting static from his client, the other abused victim in all of this."

"Since when has the statute of limitations ever affected a plaintiff? I didn't think any legal protections extended to civil defendants, especially doctors, and especially for a statute of limitations to be beneficial to me. Come now, Carter, you know as well as I do that Bel Geddes will get an extension just for the asking if he lets it go right up to the wire."

"I know it seems that way, Dr. Norcroft, but there finally comes a point when every judge's patience wears out. Judge Hicken has agreed to be present to ensure against the silliness factor. I had a serious talk with the judge about the abuses of the continuation privilege in this case. Bel Geddes was invited but failed to show at the meeting at the last minute. Judge Hicken was miffed and had us go ahead with our complaints anyway. The judge definitely means business, as near as I can determine."

"What about the Medical Malpractice Act and the need for a qualified expert witness against me, and a list of supposed wrongdoings to be consistently presented and defended, and all that?"

She knew the answer. She was just ventilating.

"Can't go retroactive, Dr. Norcroft. You know this case was filed well before the new law. No way around it. Bel Geddes can proceed his merry, irrational, emotional way. That has made him a rich man, and it doesn't look like he's going to get religion at this late date. He wants to use the old rules to every advantage he possibly can before he has to bend to the new law, kicking and screaming all the way."

"I know that. It just bothers me that it is all so illogical and prejudicial towards me and any other person or company thought to have deep pockets by those vultures."

"We call them learned colleagues," Tarkington laughed.

"Reptiles and vultures...present company excepted."

"Thanks for that vote of confidence. At any rate, I think it would be good for us to prepare for the scheduled date. Feel ready?"

"Not the least bit. I'll have to go over the entire case again from Able to Zots. And, by the way, that means that you and I will have to put in another session."

"I anticipated that. I have blanked out two days in advance of the deposition for us to go over the case and your testimony. Can you rearrange your schedule and come to the office?"

"Why not? I didn't have anything important to do—just half a dozen major operations. I'll do it again, but you know that that jerk will just get another continuance."

"We'll have to see. One thing that occurred to me is that you might like to have sort of a mock deposition with a video. That way we can critique your answers and tweak them until they are the best we can produce."

"I don't feel up to that. I think I might clutch up on the video, or at least, I won't behave naturally or think spontaneously. I would rather take my chances with a review and another verbal joust with the Emissary of Darkness himself."

"Whatever you like best. I'll look forward to seeing you again on the 21st of February. That will give us three days before the actual deposition date, enough time to work on the case, to give you a day off to rest, and have the material fresh in mind on the 24th when we are once again braced by the lion in his own den. That's two months away. Let me do the worrying in the meantime."

"I can hardly wait, and I will worry despite your platitudes, but maybe there's hope that this will bring this absurd case nearer to a close."

Sybil took note of the fact that she could not even discuss this case or anything to do with attorney Paul Bel Geddes without losing her temper—to her own detriment. She would have to do something about that.

"See you then. Bye."

Sybil eased back into her desk chair and willed herself to calm down. She was successful; although she did not achieve outright placidity, she did avoid developing the fierce competitive edge that Paul Bel Geddes always brought out. She wanted to be able to think clearly, rationally, ruthlessly, and with a mind to the smallest details. Sybil had ruminated on a plan for nearly seven years. At first, she had approached her idea with an inflammatory passion. As the years passed, and she knew that the day of the deposition would have to come despite all her hopes to the contrary, she became less impassioned and more calculating. She had eventually written down a matured plan complete in every detail of its execution of how to deal with her nemesis, Paul Bel Geddes, if or when he elected to open the old sore again. She kept the handwritten plan in her personal safe.

There were times when she felt that her plan was beneath her dignity and that she should just forget it and go along with the standard judicial program. There were times when she felt an outright sense of guilt, and she had not yet put into motion a single step of her plan of action and payback. With the announcement of the newest date for her deposition and the expressed feeling on her part and on that of her attorney that this one was for real, Sybil shed her illusions, her trepidations, and the conventional mores of her thinking as a civilized woman—interpreted victim—in her mind. She sought out her Mexican friends to set her plan in motion.

It was a week before she could get free enough of her work schedule to meet with Pancho, Jose, and Marcos. This was one talk that had to be in person, no phones or memos. She had long since destroyed her own incriminating notes.

Sybil pulled up to the circle drive parking area in front of the ranch house at seven in the evening. She was half an hour late. The Mexicans were always late in their meetings with her, but it bothered her that she could do no better, she was always late, too. The three couples who ran the ranch were seated at supper when Sybil entered. The kitchen was warm with inviting aromas.

"*Sientate, Patrona,*" invited Maria-Innocenta.

The smiling woman pointed to a vacant chair with a ready table setting. She got up to fetch warm food.

"*Gracias,*" said Sybil.

She was glad to sit down after a long day of standing at the operating table. It was a relief not to have to cook. Charles Daniels was in Mexico City attending an agri-business convention sponsored by United Nations Development Organization. Sybil had purposefully waited until his departure before having this meeting. She did not want to neglect him on one of the sparse occasions when she was home of late, and she was determined to keep him completely away from the plan germinating in her angry fertile mind.

Maria-Innocenta offered a platter.

"*Bocaditos, botanas, and antitojitos, Patrona.*"

These little bites, appetite stoppers, and little whims were Maria-Innocenta's claim to fame. The appetizers were interesting, and the *antitojitos* were a nice hint of the larger versions to come. A pumpkin-seed sauce, *pián verde,* in a small earthen pot complimented the small dishes.

There was little talking and nothing serious until the *mariscos,* black bean and rice salad, and fresh tortillas and butter were finished and the seven of them could savor their sweet potato flan. The seafood dishes were Carlita's specialties and were never better. Viviana contributed the flan.

Sybil helped the women clean up and enjoyed the amiable chatting. They all had a gossipy laugh over a package of penne pasta that Carlita had used in one of her seafood dishes. Viviana told about her husband being asked by a store clerk if he had a penny he would like to give her to take care of the tax. Sybil knew that the *penne* was the male organ of reproduction and that Hispanics thought it hilarious that Anglos used the term so frequently in public.

"It is almost time for my plan to begin, *amigos,*" Sybil said when the time for serious talk came. "The whole thing must be completed before February

24th. I have written out the plan. Please read it now, then we will burn it. We don't want papers around."

The coconspirators all nodded their heads in agreement.

The Mexicans took their time to read and to digest the very detailed plan presented to them by Dr. Norcroft. It was not a matter of acquiescence, they had all agreed to execute her plan when the time came. It was now only a matter of understanding and memorizing details. The Mexicans had no more qualms or waverings of conscience than did the author of the plan. They read in silence. When all had finished, they looked at Sybil in an invitation to proceed.

"First thing is to get the place ready," Sybil said.

Paul Bel Geddes was jubilant as he walked from the courthouse to his Mercedes. In the past month and a half, he had won three straight court cases that would result in his firm garnering two and a half million dollars in contingency fees. The latest and the largest judgment had been handed down twenty minutes previously in favor of his client, Michael Drummond, an unfortunate who had been bicycling along the city's scenic aqueduct bike and jogging path when his front bicycle tire struck a pebble on the asphalt. It may well have been the only uneven fragment in the entire fifty miles of pathway. His wheel had swerved, and he had toppled face first into the shallow waterway, breaking his neck. A passerby had pulled him out of the water and undoubtedly saved him from drowning. Ever after the fall, Michael Drummond had been quadriplegic. Through the good offices of the firm of Bel Geddes and Loughlin, Mr. Drummond had sued the city corporation as being 90 percent responsible and the Good Samaritan for being 10 percent responsible. It just so happened that the Good Samaritan was well-to-do, and the city and the state's Good Samaritan laws applied only to highway situations. Those responsible for the lifelong paralysis of the plaintiff were found liable in the amount of $1,750,000 and to provide lifelong medical care. Bel Geddes was going to use this case in his TV ad.

He planned to treat himself to a picante dinner—crab cakes stuffed with a sauce of sour cream and fruity Caribbean hot sauce and deviled eggs with an Asian sriracha—to compliment the main treat—the picante new secretary in his office who had been overjoyed to have dinner at his penthouse with him.

The thought of the vivacious girl was the last one he had before strong arms encircled his neck and forced a chemical with a strong smell, something like a sweet smelling fabric stain remover, to his face.

"This chloroform is good estuff, no, Marcos?" observed Jose as the two men hoisted the unconscious attorney into the backseat of his own long silver and black vintage 600 class Mercedes.

"Roses are red, violets are blue, does this rag smell like chloroform to you?" laughed Pancho, remembering a little ditty his mother, an itinerant nurse anesthetist, used to quote.

Pancho had been standing watch, innocuously sweeping the curb and gutter near Bel Geddes's large black car.

"Nobody seen a thing, *compadres*," he said.

What little activity there was in the large parking lot was nearer the front entrance to the court building. Bel Geddes liked to park well away from the crowds to prevent dings on the gleaming paint job of his classic car.

"Les go," Pancho said as he slipped into the backseat beside Bel Geddes's inert body.

As they approached the exit, Pancho pushed the attorney into a sitting position. Marcos was driving. He showed the attendant the plastic card key that had been conveniently set in the car's immaculate ashtray. No one took notice of the attorney and his Latino driver and his body guards as the Mercedes pulled out onto the busy thoroughfare. It was a sign of the times.

The men drove past the city building and Joseph Noble Memorial Hospital and out onto the interstate. It took them an hour to reach the small cabin in the foothills beyond the city. Pancho had to apply the chloroform soaked gauze pad briefly one more time during the trip.

The cabin was in the perfect location, its nearest neighbor was thirty miles to the west, and the small private road with its locked gate was obscure and uninviting. The cabin belonged to Henri DuChamps Moncrief, a citizen of the village of Altos de Chavón in the Dominican Republic. The unfortunate man had a glioblastoma multiforme and had undergone a major resection of his malignant brain tumor by Dr. Sybil Norcroft. He had lived in the cabin during the early postoperative convalescence with a nurse from the home health care pool. When Moncrief was able to care for himself and to resume his passion for reading and to do a little business, he returned to Hispañola Island to enjoy his last few months of life.

Henri Moncrief had rejected Dr. Norcroft's suggestion that he undergo radiation therapy and a course of chemotherapy. He preferred to avoid the attendant miseries of the treatments and to fade away in the city of his birth and that, for all of his worldly urbanity, he still loved. He wanted nothing more to do with hospitals, doctors, needles, and operations. He planned to finish out his days among the 16th Century red-tiled European architecture, the stone arches, and cobbled streets. At a small farewell gathering at the cabin, he told Dr. Norcroft that he would leave the cabin and property to his heirs rather than selling it and would let his executors handle all of the details. Sybil kept up with him by post cards and knew that Henri was still alive, and, in fact, still lucid and able to be up and about. She knew that the cabin would be undisturbed for as long as she might like to make use of it.

The three Mexican men carried the unconscious Bel Geddes into the cabin. Pancho turned on the light to the basement, then they carefully lugged the heavy corpulence of the attorney down the narrow stairs and over to an old army cot. Jose and Marcos shackled Bel Geddes to the cot with bindings on all four extremities. They took care to pad the shackle sites well to protect against causing any visible marks. They covered his eyes with duct tape. Pancho busied himself upstairs in the kitchen laying in supplies for a two week stay.

Sybil remained in the city carrying out her part of the plan. She called on Karen Mollison, one of her oldest friends from her years at her boarding school, the Cate School, on the California coast.

"It's been way too long, Sybil. I was so glad to hear your voice again. The invitation to lunch couldn't have come at a better time. I have been having a serious case of the blahs lately," Karen said after the two women embraced in the entryway of Karen's house in the exclusive suburb of Glen-to-Glen Heights.

"I never even see you and Stan at the Country Club any more," Sybil said solicitously.

"Probably that's because you're never there. Annette di Contini told me how hard she tried to get you to work on the Autumn decorating committee last year. I even remember what you said when she chided you with the old saw, 'All work and no play makes Jack a dull boy.'"

"And what am I supposed to have said?"

"'All work and no play makes Jill.'"

She looked at Sybil with mock severity as if daring the famous doctor to contradict her.

"I didn't," Sybil said, laughing. "You made that up."

"You *did*."

"You're right to get after me. My vain ambitions have been getting the best of me for the past couple of years. I am turning over a new leaf, however, you may be glad to hear. Today's little tête-à-tête is the first step in my rehabilitation."

"It's about time. Welcome back. I propose a rule for today: no business talk."

"Deal," smiled Sybil.

The two old friends decided to lunch at The House of Mezedhes, a Cypriot cafe, on the walking street. They were seated at the front window with a view of the street, a great place to watch the parade of strange urbanites passing by.

"Can I bring you something to drink?" asked the Mediterranean looking middle-aged man who stepped softly up to their table.

"Perrier, please," requested Karen.

"Diet Coke for me," asked Sybil.

"I presume that's the owner," said Karen. "I'm curious about the name of the place."

"Your drinks, ladies," the waiter said. "Can I tell you about our specialties?"

"Why not surprise us? You choose for us. We don't know anything about Cypriot food. Are you the owner?" Karen asked in a staccato stream.

Sybil was very familiar with Cyprus, its customs, and its food, but she did not interrupt the dialogue between Karen and the restaurant owner.

"This humble place is mine. The name means Little Delicacies. It is a Cypriot word. In my country we usually serve twenty or more little dishes."

"I'll start with that," Karen grinned. "I'm famished."

"The best way to come here. Would you like for me to treat you to my best?"

"Pamper us," said Sybil.

The Cypriot gave them a courtly bow and an infectious grin.

He and two assistants returned with great platters of food. Karen and Sybil could only laugh, they had no one but themselves to blame.

"Now, ladies, I tell you that this Cypriot food I bring is a nice mixture of Italian, Turkish, Lebanese, Syrian, Armenian, French, and British influences. Enjoy!"

The owner and waiter spread cold plates with bread, Greek salad, hard crackers and dips—one made of yogurt, cucumber, and mint and one made of sesame and pureed chick peas. There were little dishes of creamed fish roe, cracked olives with coriander seeds, cold potatoes in oil, thinly sliced ham, snails in tomato sauce, and pickled squid and octopus.

Sybil and Karen felt like they would need to gasp for air by the time they had sampled the cold fare, and then the trio of servers brought on the hot food—Greek moussaka, tavas, pork in red wine, kebabs of grilled lamb. Before either woman could protest the servers returned with sugar drenched pastry filled with fresh curds. Sybil was afraid she would be unable to talk, and that was the purpose of her get together with Karen.

They were sipping lightly minted espresso that was strong enough to hold a spoon upright.

Sybil said, "I heard you are going to go off gallivanting again."

"Yep. Stan and I are off to the Canaries for Carnaval."

"Some people get all the luck."

"I hear it's great fun there. Maggie Best told me about one of their traditions. They have a thing called "Burial of the Sardine". They have parades that are a mock funeral for a big stone, wood, and cardboard fish. Maggie said the whole thing's full of eroticized sight gags. They believe in whatever that sardine is supposed to represent so it's an exotic mingling of the sacred and the profane. Mick and I plan to get involved in all the hiding the sardine we can."

Karen laughed wickedly.

"You're naughty, Karen. I don't know if I would feel comfortable in all of that," Sybil said, looking ingenuous.

She was having vivid recollections of her trip to those islands off the coast of Western Sahara. She remembered the sardine tradition with particular fondness although she did not admit to Karen that she had ever been there.

"You need to loosen up a bit. All of a sudden you and Charles will be old, and all of the fun stuff will have passed you by, and you will wonder what happened to that business of living while you were so engrossed in making a name for yourself."

Sybil said, "I know you're right. Hopefully, next year. Oh, your mentioning fun reminded me. I'd like you to do me a little favor while you're over there."

"Sure. Tell me about the fun part."

"I want to play a little joke on a guy I know."

"I'm into jokes. What do I have to do?"

"Just mail these cards from the Canaries. Put a date on them and mail one of them every three days or so. They're numbered."

Sybil handed a neat package of assorted tourist post cards, all prominently emblazoned with the name of the Canary Islands. She had picked them up the previous year when she and Charles had attended a tax write-off international meeting in the Spanish Islands.

"Completely spontaneous, I see," Karen laughed with a dubious look on her face.

Each of the cards she held was addressed to the office of Bel Geddes and Loughlin and had a typed message on the order of "Wish you were here,"

"Having a great time roasting myself. It's tough work, but somebody has to do it," "Don't work too hard. I'll be back in a week or so if I sober up. Go ahead without me if I don't show." Each card was signed "PBG" in ink. Sybil had seen his signature initials enough times to be able to copy them well enough to fool anyone but a seasoned handwriting expert. Bel Geddes had made it easy for her by always using his initials, an affectation he had picked up from one of his senior professors in law school.

"I'm getting back at this guy. He and I have little tit for tats—all in jest. He is one up on me, and it's my turn. He's off to a very serious set of meetings, and I want him to have to explain to his partner and the office staff about this evidence that he has been kicking back during Carnaval in the Canary Islands instead. Will you do it for me?"

"Sure, anything for you. Anything else?"

"A small thing."

Karen lifted her eyebrows.

"I have gone so far as to buy a round trip plane ticket in this Bel Geddes guy's name. Why don't you take that nice brother-in-law of yours along with you, the traveler, and he can use the ticket? I'm serious enough about this practical joke to be able to enjoy treating that handsome hunk."

Karen shook her head and laughed.

"You're something else, Sybil. And here I thought you were a stick-in-the-mud old doctor working yourself to death. It restores my faith in you to see that you still have some sparkle. Is that about it for this little prank?"

"That's about it.... Oh, Charles doesn't know anything about any of this, doesn't need to know, okay?"

"Ooh, a little mystery. You having a little playtime on the side, Sybil dear? You used to tell me everything. Out with it."

Sybil groaned inwardly. It was all she would need to have get back to Charles, a rumor about her having an affair. It would probably blow her real activities vis-à-vis Paul Bel Geddes.

"You know me better than that, Karen. Don't get the rumor mill started."

"Ooh, touchy. Sorry, no offense meant."

Karen was smiling an appeal. She was relieved to see Sybil's responding smile.

"No, I just want to do this myself. Charles will know when it hits the fan for old PBG. Everyone in the club will know. I don't want to release the pussy from the container too soon, so's to speak."

"My lip's zipped. You can count on me to carry out the mission and to keep mum. This will put me in good with Mick's family forever. His brother Alex is a travel bum and never has any money. They're tired of footing the bill and will be grateful for a little help."

Somehow, the look on Sybil's face suggested that she already knew that.

Karen added, "Okay if I take credit?"

Sybil nodded.

"Now...how's about some shopping?" Karen suggested, getting to the serious work of the afternoon.

Paul Bel Geddes began to wake up and to retch. He felt like a spherical hangover. His tongue was furry; his head ached; and he was having trouble moving. It was pitch dark. It occurred to him that he might have drunk some methyl alcohol or something that had blinded him. He began to panic. As the fog cleared in his head, he became aware of the restraints on his wrists and ankles. He moved his eyelids and felt the sticky constricting pressure of the duct tape and could tell that his eyes were taped shut. It was completely silent in the room...wherever the room was. He began to yell.

"Our hesteemed guest waked up," Jose said grinning.

He, Pancho, and Marcos were finishing up their lunches.

"I'll go and see if he's okay," said Marcos.

"Remember, Marcos, not a word. Don't say nothing to that one," reminded Pancho.

"The *Patrona* told us fifty times. You think I'm a *viajito* that I can't remember anything?" asked Marcos, taking mock offense.

"Just remember. We got a long time to go. We got to keep alert, not make any slips."

Pancho wanted the last word.

Marcos shrugged and left for the basement. He walked on rubber soled shoes, so he was able to step right beside the prisoner without being heard. He could have ridden a motorcycle and not been heard over the stream of shouted imprecations, threats, and curses that came from the bound man. Marcos wanted to tell him that he could make all the noise he wanted, no one would be able to hear him, but he remembered the plan to say nothing for the full time they kept the man in the basement. He knew the plan was for self protection, but the noise was getting on his nerves. He reached out and tapped Bel Geddes on the shoulder.

Paul started in fright. He had been terrified that he had been shackled and blindfolded and left to starve. Now he was terrified that the monster who had done this thing to him was standing right beside him like a specter.

"Who are you? What's this all about? What do you want?"

The disembodied hand no longer touched him, and there was no reply to his questions.

"I gotta go," he shouted, for fear the specter had gone or was deaf or something. "I'm dying of thirst."

Still no sound.

Then he heard water running from a faucet into a sink. A hand lay firmly on his forehead and the rim of a cup touched his lips. His first thought was poison. He started to shake his head. Then his thirst bothered him more than his thought; so, he opened his lips enough to allow a little of the liquid in. It was water, but it tasted faintly of metal. He touched the cup with his tongue. Probably pewter. Still, it might be some sort of metallic poison. He clamped his lips and turned his head away.

"Look," he said. "Enough is enough. Now let me out of here, and I promise that I won't press charges. I'll leave the cops out of it. You've gotten yourself into trouble, but I'm not really hurt, so I'm willing to drop the whole thing," Paul said.

In a pig's eye, he thought.

"Hey, you listening?"

There was not a sound. During Paul's last speech, Marcos had ascended the stairs and returned to a cup of coffee.

"Hey, you moron!" shouted Paul.

He stopped to listen.

"You simpleton!" he screamed.

He was a man who had a serious temper but had spent a professional career controlling it and channeling it into more vindictive and less self-destructive avenues. Now he allowed himself to lose his temper completely. He scrolled down his entire list of profane and obscene expressions, imprecations and invectives, oaths and curses until he was tired. Also he had had no further contact with the hand, and that convinced him that no one was listening. He felt a little silly. And he was thirsty. He did not know how long he could hold out without having something to drink.

The celebration in the offices of Bel Geddes and Loughlin started at noon that same day. Paul Bel Geddes, the author of the current avalanche of money into the firm's coffers, was late, which was not unusual.

"Where's Paul?" Martin Loughlin asked of Bel Geddes's secretary. "It's not like him to be late to accept kudos."

"Oh, yes, it is," said Petra Sloan, Martin's secretary of seventeen years, sweetly. "You, of all people, should know that Mr. Bel Geddes operates on BGST?"

"That some sort of new computereze?" asked Horace Pilgrim Stewart, who had taken a break from his golfing retirement to attend the firm's success.

He was puffing on a contraband Cuban Cohiba.

Petra laughed.

"Just Bel Geddes Standard Time," she said. "And he'll show up sometime, no doubt with a good excuse."

"Check his collar for lipstick," said Loughlin.

They all laughed and went back to their partying.

Sybil alighted from her cab and entered the Rent-a-Wreck office on 12th and A Street in the middle of the city. She did not get into the heart of the city often and was always surprised at how much more the center city deteriorated each time she did. Or, at least, it seemed to get worse, maybe it was only that her capacity to tolerate the dirt and squalor diminished over time.

"Yes'm, kin I help ye?" the young man with an acne studded face inquired.

He had a tattoo of Jesus hanging on a cross in the middle of his forehead.

Sybil watched his eyes as he appraised her. She imagined the wheels in his mind trying to decide if she might be a looker if she wore decent clothes, put on some makeup, and shed the old scarf. She suppressed a smile.

"I'd like to rent a car for a couple of weeks, something cheap. I understand you have that sort of thing."

"Ye've come to the right place. We got wrecks and old wrecks. You'cn take yer pick."

He gave her a vacuous gap-toothed grin.

Sybil wondered if her difficulty in understanding the young man's speech came from the unfortunate crookedness of his teeth.

"It has to run—start when I turn on the key and stop when I put on the brakes. I don't much care about looks except I don't want it to be gaudy."

"What's Goddy?" he asked.

Sybil figured that he must think she was some sort of anti-religion intellectual.

"Too bright or showy."

"I gotcha," he said, the light bulb coming on over his head.

"Do you have that sort of thing?"

"What?"

His dull face looked at her expectantly.

This was getting difficult. She wondered if sign language or a simple drawing would help.

"A decent used car with blah colors, nothing fancy."

"Yup."

"Could I look at it?"

"Yup."

The two of them walked down a row of nondescript automobiles of various makes and types.

"How about this one?" Sybil asked.

It was a faded grey Ford with a dented front bumper that was otherwise serviceable looking.

"Okay," he said. "I'll get'ye the keys."

He started the engine, and it sounded fine. The seats were none too clean, but she could put a blanket over them. For her limited purposes, it would do.

"Sure it will work for two weeks?" she asked.

"Yup. Garrunteed," he said, stressing the 'gar' in garrunteed.

As it turned out, there was an actual guarantee—in writing. Sybil drove the vehicle away from the lot with confidence. She had written illegibly on the forms but paid cash in advance which assuaged any trepidations the young man might have had. Most of the information she had tendered had been false, but her conscience was relatively clear. The last thing in the world she intended was to steal the car.

She drove to Henri Moncrief's cabin in the beat-up Ford. She was assiduous about avoidance of association of her own car with the roads leading to the cabin. She was equally careful to dress in bulky drab clothing that would subdue any display of her statuesque figure and to cover her well coifed hair with a plain scarf.

"Do you have him?" she asked Pancho as soon as she walked into the kitchen in the cabin.

He was taking his shift as the guard of the prisoner. The other two men had returned to the ranch to do the day's chores. Pancho nodded and pointed with his thumb at the basement door.

"Is he okay?"

She was a little worried that he might have been roughed up in the kidnapping or made ill by the chloroform she had provided.

"Fine. Except he won't eat or drink. Keeps saying we're going to poison him."

"No problem. I have the solution for that. I planned to feed him IV anyway. This makes it all the more necessary. I don't want him to be able to connect any kind of food or utensil or anything to this place or to any of us. I hope nobody has talked to him."

"No, *Patrona*. We have been very careful. Just like you said."

"Good. I'll get the stuff to put in the feeding line."

"I have to warn you, he stinks. We didn't let him up, and he finally did it in his clothes. Both kinds."

"Good," she said blandly.

It gave her a perverse pleasure to think of Paul Bel Geddes, in all his sartorial splendor, undergoing the humiliation of soiling himself.

In the basement, Paul seemed to be asleep. Sybil and Pancho padded silently up to him. She moistened a pad with chloroform. He started when he smelled the pungent aromatic anesthetic but responded to its powerful effects in seconds after the pad was applied to his face. Sybil worked swiftly to insert the long IV cannula into his antecubital vein and to thread it up his arm and over into his heart. At least she estimated that it was in his heart. She maintained strict sterile technique. When the tube was securely taped in place, she attached a total parenteral feeding mixture to the intravenous tubing and started it dripping.

She made several large needle holes in the line of the large vein in the bend of Paul's anterior forearm that did not penetrate the vein. Pancho, who was looking on with fascination, raised his eyebrows in a silent question. Sybil pointed upwards, indicating the kitchen and later. Pancho nodded his understanding.

Sybil had Pancho help her strip the once elegant clothing from Paul, taking care not to damage them. The smell was thoroughly rank. They dumped the $1800 suit, Sea Island cotton shirt, Jacquard silk tie, and Bruno Magli shoes unceremoniously into a corner of the basement.

Once again in the kitchen, Sybil said, "The extra holes in his arm?"

"Yes?"

"They'll look like needle tracks like you see on all of the dopers."

Pancho smiled in understanding and agreement with this little extra touch.

"Give him two bottles of that mixture every day. They are to run in at the rate of one and a half drops a second. Give him one bottle of this as well, every day at ten o'clock am sharp."

She showed Pancho a 500cc glass IV bottle of USP Ethyl Alcohol.

"I have a box in my car trunk. I have the IV food, too."

Together they brought in the load of medical supplies and the food stores for the watchers that she had purchased at several different supermarkets. When the instructions were repeated and appeared to be fully understood, Sybil bade her old friend farewell and returned to the ranch where she had just enough time to change and get to the hospital in time for her eleven o'clock case.

Paul was disoriented again. He felt nauseated and had a headache, but had no memory of what had happened to him. It took an hour for him to feel that his mind was clear, but, even then, he was unable to string together and hold thoughts with his usual sharpness. He had lost all sense of the passage of time. He had no idea how long he had been in this place. His only sensations were of being almost naked, of being covered with his own filth, of being blindfolded, and of being shackled. There was a new sensation: his left arm was bound down on some sort of splint. He was virtually unable to move it. He ran his tongue around in his mouth and over his lips. He could not recall having had anything to drink, but he did not feel thirsty. He could not recall going to sleep, but he felt rested. It was all very confusing.

Then, a new, odd thing happened. He had heard nothing, but suddenly his bed began to move. He was being wheeled somewhere. A creaky door opened, and by the feel of it, he was being pushed up a ramp. It was quite warm, given the time of the year. He could feel the sun on his bare skin, could hear birds, insects, and the gentle rustle of wind through leaves, could smell grass and dirt, country smells. He made a mental note of the few things he could learn about his environment. Maybe it would be useful to the police when he got free. If he got free.

"Who's there? What's going on?" he demanded with his authoritarian voice.

He did not want to have his captors think he was cowed by them.

No one replied.

It was most disconcerting. He felt rattled.

"C'mon, what do you guys want? We can negotiate."

Nobody negotiated.

After what seemed like about ten minutes, his shackles were undone, one at a time, and he was forced to turn over onto his abdomen. His backside was exposed to the strong rays of the sun for about ten minutes, then he was again roughly turned onto his back again and wheeled back into the building. He laid plans to break free the next time his shackles were loosed for whatever reason. He heard a slight clink of glass against metal, a completely unfamiliar sound.

"Hey, you guys. What's going on now?"

No reply.

"I gotta go...You know. I don't want to do it on your nice bed!"

It was the worst bed he had ever been in, but somehow, it did not seem to be the time or the place to lodge a petty complaint. His voice was becoming shrill. He tried to control the quality of his voice that suggested that he might be begging, but knew that he was only partially successful. There was no more activity, no more sound from anyone or anything but himself. It was strange, but he felt quite drunk, not really drugged, but drunk. It was a giddy, escapist feeling. He soiled himself again.

"There," he said aloud, not knowing if there was anyone in the room with him or not. "See how you like that."

That stank. He, for one, did not like that.

Carter Tarkington called Sybil Norcroft at her office.

"Hello, Carter," she said after her administrative assistant told her who was on the line.

"Hello, Dr. Norcroft. Everything all right?"

"Pretty much. How about with you?"

"Can't complain. I think we are about as ready for the deposition as we are ever going to be. I just called to confirm a date for us to meet and go over your testimony."

"You said that you wanted me to be available for the two days before the depo. I've cleared my schedule for the tenth time to accommodate our nice Mr. Bel Geddes. Still think it's a go this time?"

"So far, so good. I put in a call to Paul's office. They said that they had not heard of any scheduling conflicts and expected that the deposition would go as scheduled. I told them that Judge Hicken planned to be in attendance and reminded the secretary that their office was going to pay for the judge's time.

The secretary sounded like the idea had sobered her, but it did not change her conviction that the depo would go on as planned."

"Did you talk to Bel Geddes himself?" Sybil asked ingenuously.

"No, I didn't. In keeping with his usual zany life-style, he seems to have taken a sudden fancy to go to the Canary Islands for Carnaval, of all things. The office read me a post card he wrote from there indicating that he would be back two days or maybe only one day before the depo. He told them not to worry, he was completely prepared."

"Well, good for him," said Sybil crossly.

"And good for us. Don't forget the positive side, Dr. Norcroft."

"Um-hmm," she hummed reflectively. "We'll see. Frankly, I doubt that we've seen the last antic on the part of Paul Bel Geddes."

"One day at a time. I don't have anything else to report. I'll see you in the office on the 19th. Call if you have any problems or concerns."

"Will do. See you then, Carter. Thanks for the call."

Alex Butterfield, the nineteen year old brother-in-law of Karen Mollison, enjoyed his good fortune without questioning why anyone would be nice enough to give him a round trip ticket to the Canary Islands during Carnaval. Karen told him only that a rich friend was playing a little prank, and that he was not to ask questions. She assigned him the task of seeing to it that the numbered post cards were sent back to the states in the order of their numbers. Otherwise, she gave him no directions about how to spend his time, and did not ask for any accounting. She asked him no questions, and he told her no lies. She and his brother—her husband, LaVell—put him up in the Hotel Mencey and told him they were on their second honeymoon and not to bother them. They would see him on departure day.

The Carnaval of Santa Cruz de Tennerife, held from February 7 to February 16, was the best Carnaval Alex had ever seen. He had been to Mardi Gras in Mobile, Alabama, the oldest in the United States, with all its parties, coronations, and mystic societies and exhausted himself watching 22 parades. He had survived the ubiquitous masked balls at the Winter Carnival in Quebec City and participated in the silly canoe race across the icy St. Lawrence River, and to Carnevale in Venice that dated back to the 15th century. The big public bash in the Piazza San Marco with its Brazilian music had been great.

The Carnaval in Rio de Janeiro, billed as the "world's biggest party," had been big but seemed overly commercialized. His favorite to date had been the Carnival in Port of Spain, Trinidad—steel bands, calypso dancing parties in costume, willing girls. The total package in the Canaries was the best, perhaps because it was this year's party, and Alex had a short memory. Gorgeous, gregarious, uninhibited, skimpily clad girls everywhere. Noise, booze, food, and music all day and all night. He must be getting old. It was almost too much. He strolled around the crowded streets half drunk, half exhausted, and with near sensory burn out. *Murgas*—street bands with their Latin flavored music, and *rondollas*—impromptu choral groups—roamed the streets and alleys day and night. It was heaven, or close enough for Alex.

The mailbox stood immediately outside La Gabarro, his favorite restaurant. It made the mailing of the practical joke post cards convenient and jogged his memory, which needed some jogging what with the lack of sleep and largely liquid diet. Alex was in the restaurant twice a week anyway to sample from the large seafood menu; so, it was simple for him to remember his one little task. He could eat *papas arrugadas*, the island specialty of unpeeled potatoes boiled in heavy salt and *chipirones en mojo*—grilled squid in a garlic and cilantro sauce—watch the world go by, and contemplate the profundities of life, like how good it was for him at that moment and how difficult it must be for other people, like his benefactor back home, who had to work.

After a week of absence, Paul Bel Geddes's secretary, Amber Winters, was quietly furious at her boss. It was all well and good to live the life of the carefree *bon vivant*, but there was such a thing as responsibility, especially for an attorney. The call-back messages were piling up. The DPIC in-house defense firm was calling daily and insistently about the depo with the doctor from Joseph Noble Memorial. She—the doctor—had been put off Lord knows how many times in the course of this case, and the bar was not going to wink at any more phony continuances. The judge had even agreed to be in attendance at the deposition to ensure that her boss behaved himself. It was humiliating to Amber even if it didn't seem to bother Bel Geddes that much. Somebody had to be responsible around here. The Canary Islands, indeed!

Amber could do little but fend off the most persistent of Bel Geddes's callers. He had made no provision for this absence, the callers were becoming angrier by the day, and all Amber could do in reality was to lie. It came with the turf in that office, she grudgingly had to admit. Amber made sure that everything was set up for the deposition because Bel Geddes had told her in the first stupid postcard, one with a bare chested native girl on it, that he would be back no sooner than two days, and maybe even only one day, before what she had been led to believe was one of his key depos. The conference room was scheduled, the famous depo and trial briefcase was stuffed with the chart, the pertinent letters from opposing counsel and the court, and his yellow legal pad work product, without which he was lost. The computer files were completely up to date, checked and rechecked.

Amber had called the court reporter service herself and had been insulted to have to send a facsimile of the check that they were to receive before they would agree to come. The service secretary had been outright curt, insisting that the check be handed over at the time the deposition was to begin, not after, and whether or not it actually took place. The woman from the court reporter service office would not take no or maybe for an answer.

Everything was ready. Now all the firm needed was for the Great Man himself to make his entrance.

After one week in total darkness (except for twice daily sunbathing sessions), without eating a bite of food, and in near total silence, Paul Bel Geddes was thoroughly disoriented. He did not know the time, not even whether it was night or day. He could not estimate with the least assurance how much time had elapsed since he had materialized in this dreadful place. It could have been two days or ten or even a month. It seemed like a month. He had not been abused, exactly, unless you counted neglect. He smelled to high heaven. His greatest longing was for a shower, probably with a fire hose. He had the strange sensation of becoming drunk at about the same time every day. He knew that the feeling followed a visit by one of the phantoms who came by him and did small things but who never spoke. He thought he might be able to count days by the number of times he felt drunk, but the problem was that he could not make his mind work that well. One of the worst things about the entire ordeal was not knowing what it was about. The other worst thing was that he was finding himself looking forward to the drunkenness and was developing a craving at about the same time each day like one of Pavlov's dogs. It seemed to him that he was getting a little more drunk each day and that it was lasting a little longer as each day passed. It was hard to bring himself to care over much about that or any other problem.

In the interim periods when his mind fog cleared somewhat, he tried to concentrate on his pending cases. He was going to have to depose that snotty FemmaNazi, Dr. Norcroft. If he did not show at that depo, his butt was going to be grass. Judge Hicken had told him that he had had his last continuance. No depo this time and he would have to show cause why a summary judgment should not be rendered for the doctor.

He had put off his preparation for the depo that, for personal and philosophical reasons, was of critical importance to him. Norcroft was one enemy he had to best. He could taste sweet victory and wanted to see defeat on her face and on that of her pseudo-patrician attorney, Carter Tarkington. He would have to do his homework in order to accomplish that laudable goal, and here he was frittering away his time, the victim of some lunatic. He tried to bring up the pictures of the case files and the medical chart into his consciousness and to go over the devastating questions he was going to hurl at the ivory tower doctor, but he was only partially successful.

At times he almost wished the lunatic or lunatics would come in and start the torture sessions. It would be a break in the routine, at least. He was a physical coward, he knew that, and admitted it to himself; so he did not take his momentary wishes for change that seriously. His mind wandered, and he was afraid that he would go nuts.

Sybil checked at the cabin daily, always driving her Rent-a-Wreck, always remembering to wear her country matron babushka outfit and varying the times of arrival. The day of her meeting with Carter Tarkington and Hyrum Willis to go over her testimony in the van der Hoef case was no exception although she had had to leave early.

"Any problems, Jose?" she asked.

He was the only one in the house that time of day, other than Bel Geddes in the basement.

"*Nada*. All routine. Looks like he's losing a little weight. I think he looks better."

"Let's take a look."

"Be warned, *Patrona*, it smells like an outhouse down there."

"Nice work, Jose," Sybil commented deadpan.

He laughed and shook his head. She was the coolest.

The two kidnappers padded silently to where Bel Geddes lay. He still had the duct tape over his eyes. It was going to be miserable when that finally came off. He seemed to sense their presence and began to shout obscenities at the darkness. They smiled at one another and otherwise ignored him. Sybil did an inspection of her patient. Aside from being filthy—encrusted filthy—and smelling like a concentrate from ten outhouses, he looked quite good, none the worse for wear. He had developed a great all over tan with the Mexicans taking him outside to slow roast every day on a graduated schedule determined in advance by Dr. Norcroft.

When she and Jose were back upstairs and out of Bel Geddes's earshot, Sybil asked Jose to, "give him a bottle and a half of the alcohol starting today. Get him up and make him exercise hard twice a day, run him around the yard and make him do pushups, sit-ups, and the like until he is tired. He will protest tomorrow but make him keep doing it.

"And make sure his car is in running order. Put these in the backseat."

She handed him a small stack of Carnaval posters, ads, Tenerife menus, and travel brochures relating to Santa Cruz de Tenerife and its splendid Carnaval.

"Oh, I almost forgot, hang on a minute."

She trotted out to her Rent-a-Wreck and picked a suitcase out of the trunk. She brought it to Jose.

"Put this in the trunk of his car, okay?"

"Sure."

The suitcase had several stickers from the Canaries. She opened it. Inside were assorted garish articles of beach attire. They were large sized, appropriate to the needs of Bel Geddes. The suitcase also contained a few dozen flagrantly pornographic photos including some perilously close to child porn. A copy of the round trip plane ticket and three hotel receipts rounded off the vacation collection. Jose closed it up, and after she left, did as she had asked, and had dropped the case into the trunk of Bel Geddes's sleek silver and grey Mercedes.

Amber Winters checked through the incoming mail. She spied another of the now famous postcards and set aside everything else to read it.

Dear Everybody,

   All good things must come to an end. I'll be back at the salt mines on the 22nd ready for bear. I had a great time and will come back carrying gifts for all. That will soften the renewed slave driver that I will become. Amber, will you be sure to set out all my materials for the depo on van der Hoef vs Norcroft on my desk? I'll need it all at my fingertips because I have been a naughty boy and left everything to the last minute. It will be like law school. I'll get in late, cram like crazy all night, and be brilliant the next day in the depo. My best to all.
PBG

Amber shook her head and laughed. This was PBG to the max. He probably would be brilliant just like he said. More than once she had seen the mercurial character leave everything to the eleventh hour and then study furiously for the few hours before he had to perform. Most of the time he was able to pull it off. She hoped this was going to be one of those times. Amber gave a sigh of relief and dialed the law offices of Schmid, Principle, Tarkington, and Henley and asked for Hyrum Willis.

"Mr. Willis, this is Amber Winters, secretary to Paul Bel Geddes. I'm calling about the van der Hoef vs Norcroft case."

"Let me guess... his majesty has been called to advise the pope and won't be able to attend our lowly deposition. He regrets the need for a continuation, but knows that we will be interested in the greater good of humanity and will sacrifice."

"No, Mr. Willis...."

"So who's sick this time?"

"If you'll give me a chance to tell you...."

"Go ahead, I'm all ears."

"He will be there for the Norcroft depo. He sent a card assuring me. No continuation this time. We trust your principals are ready."

"Yes, as always, and so is our client, Dr. Norcroft. Please be sure to remind Mr. Bel Geddes to bring his principals. That should not be a particularly heavy burden."

His voice dripped with irony.

She ignored the jibe.

"Thank you, Mr. Willis. We will see you in the office in two day's time."

Amber detested that firm. They were forever sending complaints to the state bar about Mr. Bel Geddes like kids tattling in a school yard. She sighed and resigned herself that not all attorneys could be the complete professional her boss was.

She had already put together all of the files and had filled Mr. Bel Geddes's briefcase with every conceivably pertinent paper relating to the van der Hoef case. She rechecked to be sure nothing was left in the file cabinet. The two file boxes of motions and legal maneuvers plus an extra copy of the medical chart and van der Hoef's statements were neatly stacked along side his desk. She made a second copy of his depo notes and proposed questions and put that into the file boxes as a back up for good measure. She made sure the computer files were up to date and orderly. She left a small instruction note to help her boss get into the van der Hoef file immediately if he needed to. The firm of Bel Geddes and Loughlin were as ready as they could be to take on the devil's advocates from Schmid, Principle, Tarkington, and Henley. As an afterthought, she put the stack of postcards from the Canary Islands on the desktop beside his case.

At first, Paul had welcomed the significant change in routine. He had transitorily thought that his captors might be about to let him go when they unshackled his ankles and wrists from the bed. But they promptly bound his wrists together and applied a second set of shackles on his ankles, this set had a longer chain between the cuffs. Despite his great disappointment that he was evidently not to be released, Paul was thrilled at the prospects of being able to walk, even to exercise. It seemed like an eon since he had been able to get in touch with his body in a set of exercises. At first his legs were wobbly and unsure. He worried that he would fall. He vowed to get back into some sort of healthy routine when he got out of this. He had let himself get soft. A man should keep in trim, he reminded himself. One never knew what might come up. The first day he had been taken outside to exercise twice, dressed only in his briefs.

He had hoped his kidnappers would let him have a shower after he worked up a sweat, but nothing had changed in that department. No one spoke to him, and he stayed dirty. The afternoon exercise session had been more difficult, more forced, since he was tired and achy from the first session and was now drunk, drunker than usual. He was in misery the following morning when his captors came in to force him to do their exercises. His muscles were sore everywhere, stiff and unresponsive. He groaned at every exertion and attempt at effort. They were torturing him, mercilessly pushing him to continue to work his screaming muscles. He walked like a halting old arthritic.

There was nothing left for her to do, so Amber left the office early. Mr. Loughlin took the afternoon off for a golfing rainmaking date. The associate attorneys, paralegals, secretaries, and file and mail room clerks all took their cue and vacated the office suite before five o'clock.

Pancho and Jose entered the building at half past two a.m. the next morning, the day of the deposition, using the key Sybil had provided them. Use of the door key prevented the tripping of any alarm, and they had taken the usual precaution of wearing rubber gloves. They swiftly walked to the bank of elevators, pushed the up button, and in less than two minutes they were standing in front of the office suites of Bel Geddes and Loughlin on the eighth floor. The two men looked around swiftly and furtively, then Pancho used the office key and let the two of them in. He looked for a key punch alarm and saw none. They looked at one another for confirmation then moved into the lighted hallway and walked with the assurance of familiarity to Bel Geddes's office. Pancho fumbled with the keys for a moment, found the right one, and they were inside. Bel Geddes's inner office door was ajar. Pancho and Jose halted for a moment and eased it open all the way.

The room was dark and no one was inside. They moved to the desk, easily found the briefcase, and removed its contents, which they put in the shredder. Jose took the shreds of paper down the hall and put it in three separate waste bins. Pancho took several file folders at random from the steel filing cabinet and placed them in the trial briefcase until it was as full as before. He saw the two file boxes on the floor, read the caption on them, and knew that they related to his *Patrona's* case.

Jose returned.

Pancho whispered.

"We take these. You find two more just like these and bring them to me."

Jose looked at him a moment.

"Please," Pancho added.

Jose grinned, his large white teeth gleaming in the ambient light.

While Jose was gone, Pancho found the note left by Amber Winters to Mr. Bel Geddes. It told about where in the computer to find the van der Hoef vs Norcroft file and how to do it most quickly. Pancho was adept with computers, this one was IBM compatible like the ones he used to keep the ranch records. He did a few key punches as directed by Amber's note and shortly was looking at the complete file relating to Sybil Norcroft. He thought for a moment then highlighted the entire file, and pressed delete. The printing disappeared. In its place came up another file, another case against a physician. For spite, Pancho deleted that one as well. Jose returned and watched as his *compadre* scrolled through a dozen files and got rid of them.

"So *amigo*, what did you come up with?" asked Pancho after shutting down the computer.

"A couple of empty boxes, like thee ones we are taking."

"Ah," Pancho murmured. "*Bueno*. We'll put some junk in them and leave those boxes sitting here as a little surprise."

"In a series of surprises," laughed Jose.

He was getting to enjoy this spy stuff. He could envision how the tormentor of his *Patrona* was going to react, and it gave him pleasure. The evil *abogado* deserved everything he was going to suffer.

"*Si,*" said Pancho. "Now let's get to work before some cleaning lady or night watchman pops in here."

They swiftly transferred files at random from the steel filing cabinet and into the new grey file boxes. They were careful not to take too many from any one file drawer to lessen the likelihood of immediate detection of their handiwork.

Pancho rummaged around in the desk drawers until he found a Magic Marker. He carefully wrote *van der Hoef, plaintiff vs Joseph Noble Memorial Hospital and Sybil Norcroft, defendants* as exactly as he could to correspond to the captioning on the older boxes. The entire process took ten minutes from the time Jose had entered the room with the new boxes. They made a quick inspection of the room to assure themselves that they were leaving nothing incriminating, then each man picked up a file box, Pancho hefted the briefcase, and they slipped out of the office, down the elevator, and exited the building.

The night security guard arrived in his company's car ten minutes later. He covered four buildings for a cooperative of owners who had united to save some of the escalating costs of security. He methodically checked every office door in the building over the next hour and a half. Finding them all secure, he called it a night and reported back to central that all was quiet, as usual. It was one of those deadening jobs where nothing ever happened.

CHAPTER THIRTEEN

S ybil was nervous and cranky the morning of the deposition. She ran her preparations over and over again through her mind. The beat up old car had been returned to Rent-a-Wreck yesterday, her men knew to leave the Moncrief cabin free of any hint that they had ever been there when they vacated the place. They knew what they had to do with their kidnapee and had gone over the timing *ad nauseum*. She could not think of a single thing that she had failed to go over with her Mexicans. Nothing had been left to chance. She had spent the last two days in intense review with her two lawyers. Hyrum Willis had just made partner and was ebullient. That had produced a very upbeat atmosphere in the meetings at Schmid, Principle, Tarkington, and Henley. Sybil had come away with a positive sense of how things could be expected to go in the deposition over and above the little insurance she had arranged. Besides, at every step she had established an unshakable alibi.

She dressed and changed three times to be sure that she would have exactly the right image. The judge was going to be there in person. She wanted his impression of her to be flawless—intelligent, competent, professional, but caring, and above all else, not arrogant or showy. She decided finally on a tailored mauve Azzedine Aláia business suit with silver and black pumps and a cream colored silk blouse offset by a single strand of grey Venezuelan pearls. The outfit was conservative but not penitent, tasteful and fashionable without being boastful.

She drove her BMW convertible to the offices of Bel Geddes and Loughlin, leaving in plenty of time even if she encountered unexpected traffic. She would be glad of a wait in order to be able to calm down.

At nine in the morning the same day, Paul Bel Geddes was dreaming a kaleidoscopic montage of faces, voices, foods, and disjointed thoughts while Pancho, Jose, and Marcos gave him his last dose of IV Ethanol. His dreams faded into nothingness, and he evacuated his bowels and bladder peacefully onto his bed. He was no longer troubled by that departure from civilization. Suddenly he was being aroused, awaked from a benumbed torpor by rough hands. They were forcing his clothes on. Something was happening. Something big. They probably wouldn't go to all the bother of dressing him just to kill him; so, maybe this was not only a big new event, but possibly even a good one. Maybe someone had paid a ransom for him. It was hard to think. It never occurred to him to resist. They were not brutal, and there seemed to be nothing to gain by fighting them. They seemed to be strong and determined. It would be blind man's buff with him being the blind man.

They were wearing latex gloves, he could tell from the sensation on his skin. On went his cotton briefs, then his shirt. He was sure they buttoned it out of order by one button. It did not feel right, but he was not about to protest and spoil whatever was intended. He hardly dared to hope that they might be about to free him. Maybe they had gotten a ransom. He groaned inwardly that he would probably have to pay back the ransom. He didn't have any kind of insurance. He didn't even know if there was any kind of insurance for that sort of thing. His mind was wandering.

Finally, he was dressed, even to his tie.

"Hey, that kind of chokes," he said as the unseen helper cinched the knot around his neck.

The knot was loosened—too much, he presumed. He would have to attend to that later. He was going to look altogether too casual for work. He would fix his tie later. If he could remember. The handcuffs and leg shackles went back on. Maybe he should have struggled, shown some spirit, when the bindings were off long enough for his captors to get his clothes on. With the last ratchet of the leg shackle he knew that idea was too little, too late. His thinking was slow, and he could not formulate a plan, could not keep a string of ideas together. He walked with complete docility between the two—or was it three?—men up the stairs and through a room, maybe two, and out a door into the morning sunlight. Walking was sheer torture with his muscles knotted up from the unaccustomed exercise of the past two days.

Sybil was shown into the Bel Geddes and Loughlin conference room where she joined Carter Tarkington, Hyrum Willis, and a third man whom she had not met.

"Dr. Norcroft, may I present Judge Hicken?" Carter said.

The judge extended his hand diffidently, and Sybil shook it politely.

"I'm pleased to meet you, Doctor. Please take a seat. We have a few more minutes before the court reporter and Mr. Bel Geddes are due to arrive," Judge Hicken offered in a courtly old world fashion.

He was in his seventies with frost white hair trimmed short. He was wearing a severe black pinstripe suit and vest and an unpatterned deep magenta bow tie.

Sybil sat between her two attorneys near the middle of the long table with the judge at the far end. The arrangement prevented even the suggestion that there might be communication between the defendant's side and the judge. While they waited in silence, Sybil looked around the spacious ornate room that had been redecorated since her last visit to the inquisition chamber. The rug was snowy white, thick, soft, and presumably ghastly expensive. It was hard on the eyes and must have been the latest rage among the gay decorators. The walls were overly busy with an original Andy Warhol still life, Federico Pallavacini paintings and prints, poster sized framed black and white blowup photos of Ansel Adams's Yosemite series and a life size image of the imperially slim Coco Chanel, Lucien Freud doodles, Gruau sketches from old issues of the long since defunct *Flair* magazine, and a Picassoesque distortion of a more or less human figure of nonspecific gender.

At the far end of the room hung the law school diplomas of the firm's attorney partners. Sybil got up to look more closely. By Paul Bel Geddes's diploma was a second framed document. It was entitled simply, MENSA. The certificate read, *This is to certify that Paul Bel Geddes, Esq. took up the Mensa Challenge and has been awarded this certificate of merit as a result.* Sybil shook her head at the crass self aggrandizement of the flamboyant attorney. Counterpoised against his partner's extra document was one that read, *To Marty Loughlin, the best grandpa in the world.* The certificate was signed in block print, "FRED". It was written in Crayon in a childish scrawl and framed as ornately as the one of Bel Geddes's.

The court reporter was ushered in and introduced around. She took her place across from Sybil, being careful not to sit in the high backed chair presumably reserved for Bel Geddes. Sybil noted that the reporter slipped a check into her purse. The attorneys and the court reporter shared a few jejune pleasantries; otherwise, little was said in the room. They were marking time. Bel Geddes was five minutes late.

At the Moncrief house, Paul shambled over to the car supported by the strong hands of his captors, unsure of himself because of the blindfold, and his legs resisting activity owing to the pain that any movement produced. Pancho checked his watch frequently and pushed on the slow moving kidnapee to help him to hurry. Paul's mind was thick and suffering from inertia. He wondered what was the hurry. Even that idea was suffering from dystocia, simple as it was. He didn't feel any great rush. Jose and Marcos pushed Paul into the backseat of the newly washed Mercedes. Pancho drove. He was afraid to exceed the speed limit, but it could not be too soon to get away from the foul smelling man. It was twenty minutes to ten when the four men pulled into the parking lot of Paul's distinctive art deco building and found a spot in the shade of a tree.

In the backseat Jose opened the bottle of chloroform. Bel Geddes recoiled from the vapors, but did not actually resist as Jose placed a guaze pad soaked in the general anesthetic briefly over the attorney's face. He slumped against Marcos. Marcos worked the duct tape slowly off Bel Geddes's eyes, making sure that he did not take any skin with the tape. The underlying skin was edematous, giving his eyes a rheumy look. Tags of tape adhesive clung tenaciously to the skin. Jose and Marcos assiduously removed every trace with acetone.

Pancho turned his head to the backseat and urged, "Hurry it up. Somebody's going to come, see us."

"We're going as fast as we can, *compadre. Te pacientia,*" Marcos croaked in a hoarse whisper.

The chloroform had irritated his throat, causing an accumulation of phlegm. The two men in the backseat looked over their handiwork and pronounced it adequate.

"Here," said Pancho, producing a bottle of Old Turkey. "Pour a little of this in his crotch."

Marcos laughed and choked a little. It was a good last touch.

Jose did the honors, just enough to soak the fly and surrounding area of Paul's pant front. He and Marcos took hearty swigs from the unfinished bottle as a reward for their labors. The three men did a 360 degree inspection of the parking lot before getting out. Jose placed the whiskey bottle in Paul's lax grip, making sure that the attorney's finger prints were all over it. Then, the three Mexicans slipped quietly out of the car and closed the doors. They removed their rubber gloves and walked to a rental car they had left in the lot the previous night. It was fifteen to ten. The three Mexican men paid the exorbitant exit fee and drove directly back to the smooth gaited horse ranch to the sense of security and home that came from being among the prize Tennessee Walkers, Paso Finos, and Missouri Foxtrotters, whom they preferred to the company of most people.

Willis and Tarkington began stealing looks at one an other when the opposing attorney was fifteen minutes late. Willis could hardly wait to see it hit the fan when the judge finally decided that he had had enough of being stood up. Hyrum was as sure as he could be that Bel Geddes was not going to show. He avoided looking at Sybil in order not to give her false hope. You could never tell with Paul Bel Geddes. This time it would have to be something good. The court reporter was less reticent. She theatrically looked at her watch at two minute intervals and rolled her eyes in undisguised exasperation. Sybil kept her eyes on the facsimile of the medical chart on the conference table in front of her. Her face was a serene uncommunicative mask. No one looked at Judge Hicken.

Petra Sloan and Amber Winters salvaged the moment by bringing in a small plate of hors d'oeuvres—Devonshire clotted cream, crumpets and marmalade, tea and coffee. The women left the platter on the table and quietly left. The people in the room ate in an awkward silence. Sybil cast a quick sidelong glance at the judge in time to see him take a brief look at his watch.

At five minutes past ten, Paul began to rouse. He promptly threw up a bilious mixture on his shirt front. He was aware of a vile odor in the room. He dropped something. In a few minutes he realized that it had been a whiskey bottle. He was in a car, in the backseat. Of his car! He remembered vaguely leaving the courthouse after winning a case. Could that have been today? Yesterday? Must have been today, else why was he drunk. He really must have been on a celebrating toot. He was aware that he stank.

At ten thirty, Judge Hicken stood up and strode out of the room.

"So what do you think he's going to do?" Hyrum asked Carter.

Sybil and the court reporter turned to look at the senior partner as if he had the clairvoyant answer.

"Give Paul the benefit of the doubt. Our interests are best served by keeping mum. It looks like Paul is going to be his own worst enemy. We won't need to add a thing," Carter said.

His face was losing its usual professional taciturnity, however.

The court reporter had not put her recorder roll into her machine, and it did not look like she was going to have to. She was very pleased with herself that she had insisted on getting the check from the office manager up front. This was turning into another Paul Bel Geddes weirdo depo.

At fifteen past ten, Paul forced his phlegmatic body to get out of the car. His muscles screamed as if it was the second day of football season. Every contraction of his leg muscles hurt, and he limped stiff-leggedly. The pain and the fog in his brain made him stagger some. He looked around and recognized that he was in the parking lot of his building and considered himself to have made a real mental milestone with that deep thought. His briefcase was beside him, must be some reason for that, so he took it along as he wove his way across the asphalt to the main entrance to the building. To him it seemed as momentous a trip as the original search for the source of the Nile. Heads turned as he entered the foyer. It smelled like a flying pigpen wherever he propelled his languid body. He was vaguely aware that the odoriferous emanation came from him. He became progressively aware, but could not overcome his internal inertia to the point of caring. He pushed the elevator button. The elevator door opened and the people exiting gave him a wide berth. He stepped inside with several other riders. They pushed the hold open buttons and allowed him to ride up alone. Fortunately for Bel Geddes, the eighth floor button had already been pushed. It was twenty-five past ten.

Paul walked into the reception room of his office suite and into the main hallway. He turned right by habit to go towards his office. A man was coming down the hall from the direction of the conference room. That sent him a signal, but he could not hold the thought that seeing the man evoked.

Amber Winters—he recognized her—dashed up to him and roughly grasped his arm. Who did she think she was handling him like that?

"Mr. Bel Geddes, what in heaven's name is going on with you?" she was saying.

It came from a distance.

"M'okay," he said.

It was nice to hear another person's voice. She sounded upset with him, though. "You certainly don't look 'okay'."

She hustled him into the nearest room; it was the transcription pool room with five small cubicles. It hurt to move fast.

"You smell awful. You look awful. Whatever happened to you?"

"Wash kidnap," he slurred.

His voice sounded very funny. He began to giggle.

"Stop that! This instant!" the angry woman ordered. "This is serious. Jeez...I think you're drunk. One of the smells is whiskey, I think. Do you know that this is the day for the Norcroft depo? Am I getting through to you?"

He knew what it was that he had been trying unsuccessfully to think about that morning. Depo. Norcroft depo. FemmaNazi. He remembered something about that. It was hardwork this remembering. Something important. Norcroft. A bit of the mental haze cleared away for a moment. He still felt very drunk and languorous.

"Look, Mr. Bel Geddes, we have to get you into that room, pronto. The judge came out and is asking for you. He did not want to hear about some other attorney coming in, and you know that we don't have anyone who knows this case. This has always been your personal baby as you like to call it. Snap out of this!"

She was almost in tears.

Judge Hicken was talking to the office manager. His legendary calm and patience were beginning to fragment.

"I have been far more than patient, Mrs. Tucker. This is not the first incident in this case, but I assure you it will be the last."

"I believe he has entered the office and is here somewhere, Judge. Try and be patient with him for a little while longer. He's been having some problems."

The judge snorted.

"I will give Mr. Bel Geddes the benefit of the doubt only because I do not want to prejudice the case for his client. I don't think Mr. van der Hoef deserves that. But the court's patience is not unlimited. Understand that. Either the man himself will be in that conference room in fifteen minutes, or a substitute. We will go ahead with the deposition with or without the lead counsel, fair enough?"

"More than fair, Judge," Mrs. Tucker said ruefully.

She was heaping a stream of mental curses on the head of her boss.

"All right, I am going to go back into that room and sit calmly for fifteen minutes."

He checked his watch.

"Ten to the hour. The deponent will be sworn in at that minute precisely, or we will all go home. And...Mrs. Tucker, if we do, we won't be coming back."

"Thank you, Judge. I will see to it. We'll bring some coffee and Danishes to help you pass that short period of time."

Judge Hicken turned on his heel and walked purposefully back down the hall to the conference room. It was ten thirty-four.

Amber propped Bel Geddes up against the wall, cleared the transcription office of its occupants, and hurried out to find Mrs. Tucker. The two harried women almost collided in the hall.

"Where is he, Amber? What is going on? The judge is fit to be tied."

"We don't have time to talk. He is drunk as the proverbial skunk. He stinks to high heaven. Thank goodness he has his briefcase. He's in the typing room."

They rushed in to the room. Paul was sitting on the floor, more than half asleep, with a silly grin on his face. He was completely disheveled, his shirt buttons were misaligned, and his expensive silk tie looked like he had tried to tie it in a square knot.

"What is that dreadful smell? He must have slept in a pig pen for a month without a shower. We have to get him out of these terrible clothes. His suit's ruined," said Mrs. Tucker.

She paused to allow Amber to start removing the awful clothes.

Amber faltered.

"I...I just can't do it. I have to have gloves. I think I'm going to be sick."

Almost immediately, she vomited all over herself and Mr. Bel Geddes, adding freshness to the already scintillating stench of putrefaction. It was more than Mrs. Tucker could handle. She, too, vomited, although in keeping with her station, she plastered the wall and the rug and avoided further besmirching any people.

The women took a breather. Mrs. Tucker was seated on the floor in a place that did not seem to have received any offal. Her watch showed ten forty-five.

"We need a plan," she said. "This is not going to work. You watch him. I will go out and grab the first attorney I can lay hands on and get him to go in there and stall. Where is that briefcase?"

"Over there," Amber gestured feebly.

She did not feel able to get up yet.

"Over there, over there," Paul began to sing softly.

He giggled again.

Amber shook her head with total disdain.

Mrs. Tucker rushed out into the hall toting Bel Geddes's trial briefcase, feeling lightheaded but fighting the waves of nausea and syncope, and poked her head into each office down the line to find an attorney, any attorney, to go into the conference room and save the day. The third door was Angie Richards's, the probate specialist.

"Angie! We have an emergency. The firm has to have your help. Right now!"

"Take it easy and tell me what all of this is about."

Mrs. Tucker gave Angie the short version but omitted nothing of critical truth. She told the elderly spinster lawyer that she did not have time to explain why, but there could be no continuance. It was now or never for one of the firm's biggest cases.

"And you expect me to go into a deposition for a medical malpractice action completely unprepared. To go up against one of the top brains in the United States? The world!?"

"That's it in a nutshell. Here's the briefcase. His questions are on his legal pad. Fake it. Stall for a little while until you get your bearings. We'll work on him and get him to you if it is humanly possible. Now go!"

There was never a condemned felon walked across the infamous Bridge of Sighs in Venice who felt lower or closer to panic than Angie Richards as she walked the long hallway to the conference room lugging the heavy briefcase.

When Judge Hicken returned to the room, he remained standing to address the company.

"There has been some sort of problem. The nature of the problem is unclear, and I am not even sure that I want to know. However, I have made a ruling in this case. The deposition will start in fifteen minutes, at exactly ten fifty, with or without Paul Bel Geddes, lead attorney for the plaintiff, or we will pack up and go home."

Carter Tarkington stood to reply.

"If the court pleases...."

"You don't have to be so formal, counsel. We are not in session."

"Yes, your honor. But we of the defense cannot simply let this go. This is a lamentable pattern. We are being abused. I have tendered several formal complaints...."

"You needn't tell me, Mr. Tarkington. I will not allow a travesty against the dignity of this court. If we do not proceed today, this case will never proceed, and I will inform the plaintiff, himself, of his rights to redress. I trust that I do not need to say more."

"No, your honor, that will suffice, thank you."

The group sat in silence while the minutes slowly ticked away. Sybil's face was as stiff as a Grecian statue. She communicated no more by speech or mannerism than the others could have gotten from an oyster cracker.

The front office girls—Bel Geddes always referred to them as his FROGS—rounded up a decent white shirt, and a pair of Mr. Loughlin's golfing pants that were a little too small, but were reasonably clean. The main drawback was that they were an almost iridescent chartreuse in color and were bell bottomed. They had been sitting in the partner's closet since the last pass from favor of the perennially recurring bell bottom style. Mrs. Tucker had to rip out the rear seam to get them around Bel Geddes's waist and hips. The front office girls rounded up enough safety pins to keep the edges closed, and they were able to get the trousers waist around him. He was sobering up a little and was able to help, but he was spiritless. Nothing was helping the smell.

Caroline Bagely, the pool secretary for the junior associates, took that matter in hand. She entered the empty attorney's offices and returned with several bottles of men's cologne. They doused him with the mixture of scents. It was debatable whether the Eau d' Manure alone or the heady aroma of mingled Aqua Velva, Mennen's Skin Bracer, Farenheit, English Leather, and Eau d' Manure was worse. It seemed a lost cause. Bel Geddes giggled when the women soaked him in the new scents, and he giggled harder when he saw himself in the mirror one of them provided.

Angie Richards took a long deep breath as she stood gathering her courage outside the conference room door.

"*Has to be a first time for everything,*" she said to herself.

She meant that this would be the first deposition she had ever conducted. She expected it to be emblazoned on her memory forever.

"*Morituri te salutamus*—We who are about to die salute you," she whispered inaudibly

She stepped into the room at the stroke of ten fifty.

"Hello, ladies and gentlemen. I hope you haven't been too inconvenienced. I am an associate of Mr. Bel Geddes. I will start the deposition. We expect Mr. Bel Geddes to be with us shortly."

She looked completely at ease and in charge. Ms. Richards took her seat and looked across the room at Hyrum Willis.

"Dr. Norcroft, I presume." She smiled. "We haven't met. I'm Angie Richards of the firm of Bel Geddes and Loughlin."

"I'm Hyrum Willis, attorney for the defense," returned Hyrum with a deadpan voice and facial expression.

The court reporter had to turn her unruly face aside to avoid looking at anyone in the room.

"Oh," said Angie.

Nice start.

She would not make that mistake again.

"May I ask if you are Dr. Norcroft, Sir?"

Now she was looking at Carter Tarkington.

"No, Ma'am. I am Carter Tarkington, attorney for the defense."

By a process of elimination, that left the handsome icy woman across from her and to her left. She was pretty sure that the woman beside her inserting paper into her machine had to be the court reporter. She knew that the sour faced elderly gentleman at the far end of the table was the judge. She had seen his face in the newspaper. She took a sustaining breath and looked Sybil Norcroft in the eye. Then she stood up and extended her hand to the doctor with a false but broad smile.

"Dr. Norcroft, I presume," she said, looking to the woman for a small measure of woman-to-woman compassion in this horrendously discomforting situation.

Sybil Norcroft remained frozen in her chair, her hands firmly folded in her lap and said nothing. She did not move so much as an eyelid. She refused to make eye contact with the straining woman attorney. The pregnant silence ground on. Angie flushed and self-consciously withdrew her hand and sat down with as much dignity as the circumstances would allow.

"Yes, well, then. We should begin. I think we should swear in the witness. Isn't that the thing to do?"

It seemed like the thing to do.

No one in the room made the slightest sound or movement to be of help. So much for collegial solidarity. This was going to be a no-quarter-asked-and-none-given, eat-your-own-dead, kind of war. So be it.

"Raise your right hand, defendant," she snapped.

"We will insist on the deponent being treated with civility. Her name is Dr. Norcroft," objected Hyrum Willis coldly.

"So noted."

Chastened.

"Doctor, please raise your right hand."

Sybil put her arm to the square.

"Do you swear to tell the truth, the whole truth, and nothing but the truth, so help you God in this court of law?"

"This is a deposition in a binding arbitration hearing, counselor. But, I presume you know that," said Carter with a caustic meanness in his smooth modulated voice. "And it is customary for the court reporter to do the swearing-in."

"There are some things about which I am a little rusty having come in late. I would appreciate it if you would cut me a little slack procedurally speaking, *Counselor*," she said.

She seemed to be pleading, but her voice had an uninviting edge.

Carter responded in kind.

"Speaking officially for the defense, we would rather stick to the strict formalities. I will be quick to assist in keeping the proceedings proper. Judge Hicken is here and can render such assistance as he wishes in that regard as well."

Angie was afraid she was going to cry. It was a most unseeming situation. At least she was following the instruction of Mrs. Tucker to stall the deposition. That provided very small consolation.

"We'll go on, then."

She shuffled through the papers in Bel Geddes's trial and deposition briefcase.

"For the record. I am Angela Bardwell Richards, representing the plaintiff. This is the deposition of the defendant, Dr. Norcroft. Please state your full name and spell each name for the reporter, please."

Sybil did so.

"Do you swear that the testimony in the matter before this deposition will be the truth, the whole truth, and nothing but the truth?"

"I so swear."

The court reporter shook her head.

Angie felt that she was getting the hang of it. Now, all she had to do was to follow the course of Paul Bel Geddes's written out questions, and it should be smooth sailing. She extracted the legal pad from the briefcase as unobtrusively as she could. Her heart was beginning to slow down, and her brain was beginning to shift into gear. All did not look so hopeless now. She glanced down and saw a set of handwritten questions neatly set out. Even the handwriting was legible, would miracles never cease.

She read the first question, "Ms. Norcroft..."

"We prefer the courtesy of referring to our client as doctor," Carter interjected.

"*Dr.* Norcroft. On the evening of 26 June, were you driving on state highway 72 at or about nine fifteen in the evening?"

Sybil paused, a little bewildered.

"Not that I recall."

Angie's face became slightly malevolent. She departed from the prepared questions.

"Come now, Doctor, are you going to deny that you were involved in a major traffic accident at that time and place? Maybe you would have us believe that someone stole your car and was subsequently involved in the accident I described."

"No."

That was an unresponsive answer, and a confusing one, Angie had to admit to herself. This was getting strange.

"Let me refresh you. Our records...the police records indicate that you were driving under the influence of alcohol on the evening of June 26 last. While in that condition—later established by police lab tests of your breath and your blood—you drove your car into one Pedro Dominguez, an interior decorator. As a result of severe neck injuries, Mr. Dominguez is now unable to work, unable to participate in sports—and I might add that he had received professional opportunities—and his wife has lost conjugal happiness, to put it delicately."

She stared revelatory daggers at Sybil.

"No."

The defendant's response seemed like a glaring non sequitur. This was becoming stranger by the minute. Angie could not follow Paul's outline of questions because she could not get off square one. How could this ice queen sit there and deny that it had ever happened? She took a breath and scanned the police report again to see if she could find a clue to trip up the defendant and get this interrogatory back on track. Her finger traced down the simple police report in its straightforward Dick-and-Jane language.

"Do you own a 2014 Buick Skylark, Powder Blue in color, license number AG 429839, Madam?"

"No."

"Frankly, none of us has the foggiest idea what you're talking about, Ms Richards. This sounds like a cut and dried ambulance chaser motor vehicle accident to me. If you would not think me too bold, I might suggest that you are reading from the wrong file. At least, I have to tell you that you are reading from a different page of the script than me," said Carter Tarkington.

A hint of sympathy had slipped into his voice, since he was virtually certain that his supposition was correct. Angie looked at the senior attorney long and hard to see if he was trying to confuse her or to denigrate her inexperience. His face was bland and unrevealing, but she did not think that he was playing a role in some sort of bizarre plot to discredit her deposition effort. She blushed a rich scarlet as she began to suspect that what he had said might be true. She gulped.

"Why don't you check the rest of the briefcase? Maybe someone slipped a wrong folder in by mistake. Then we can get on with this, Ms. Richards."

Sybil sat impassively. She glanced at the judge. He shook his head slightly, but was otherwise not reacting to the odd and embarrassing little legal drama unfolding before the assembled group.

Angie read the caption of the folder from which she had been working. PEDRO DOMINGUEZ vs QUENTIN BARTHOLEMEW. She was dismayed. She took out a second folder. DANIEL RANDCLIFFE vs CITY OF PETERSBOROUGH. She felt a wave of nauseating desperation sweep over her. She dumped out all of the contents of the briefcase on the table in front of her, heedless of any lack of professional decorum she might be demonstrating. There were five files in all, none of them even mentioning the name of Sybil Norcroft. There were no other sets of notes, no medical charts, no summaries of privileged expert opinion suggesting anything to do with a malpractice action. She had been sandbagged. It was time to cut her losses.

"Excuse me lady and gentlemen, Judge Hickman."

The judge did not flinch at the mispronunciation of his name.

"I seem to have picked up the wrong briefcase. How foolish of me. I will just be a moment. Please excuse me."

She abruptly stood up and practically ran from the room clutching the briefcase and its file folders disarrayed in her arms. The other occupants of the conference room looked at each other in smiling bemusement. Even the judge had to stifle a smile. Only Sybil maintained her icy demeanor. No one spoke for fear of appearing insensitive or that he or she could be accused of attempting to benefit from the unfortunate circumstances.

Outside the conference room, Angie Richards allowed herself to cry. Actually, she had no control over the surprising and totally spontaneous outpouring. She could not recall having shed a tear since she was sixteen and had been turned down by a pimply faced boy whom she had asked to take her to the Junior Prom. She was furious at being humiliated as well as feeling injured. She marched to the room where the office staff was working on Paul Bel Geddes. She entered the room without knocking and was shocked by what she saw. Bel Geddes looked slimmer than she had remembered him and tanned, was dressed in a garish pair of old fashioned pants that did not, in any way, go with his expensive mirror finish black wing tip dress shoes. He wore a facial expression of befuddlement. There was a freakish smell in the room, like someone had died and had not been embalmed, but the mourners had tried to cover the odor with flowers.

"What happened?" Mrs. Tucker asked her in dismay at seeing Angie out of the conference room.

Angie gave the assembled company a quick and accurate and impassioned account of what had happened and of her humiliation.

"I don't deserve that, Mrs. Tucker. There won't be any further participation in this charade by me. I am going to submit my request for partnership this afternoon. It will either be accepted, or you can have my resignation. I have done more than the call of duty, and I will not be here another day unless that is suitably acknowledged."

She cast an angry look in Bel Geddes's direction.

"Let him clean up his own mess."

With that she did a smart about face and marched out on her sensible shoes to the security of her probate files.

"I'm ready to face the lions in their den, Mrs. Tucker. I...I'm still a little under the weather, but I can handle it if I go slow. Take me to the conference room. Lead on, MacDuff!"

Paul giggled a little.

"You're in no condition," protested Amber Winters.

"And we have no choice," countered Mrs. Tucker. "I have no idea how that junk got into that briefcase—that will have to be a subject for another day's discussion. Right now, you get the back up files, and I will lead our fearless leader into the conference room. We are going to salvage this day, or my name is not Agatha Tucker."

Her face was set in rigid determination.

Amber ran to her office and looked at the boxes of trial documents on the floor by Mr. Bel Geddes's desk. They looked different somehow, but she was so rattled that nothing seemed right that day. To facilitate and simplify matters, she went into the computer, intent on printing out the pages that were the most important to the case. She key punched in the code. The screen was a bright, blank, blue. There was no typing on the screen and no heading indicative of the file she was seeking. She tried again, taking care to avoid any mistakes in punching in the numbers. Once again, she came up with a blank screen. It was maddeningly frustrating, but she did not have time to figure out what ridiculous problem the computer was having at this particularly inopportune moment. She hated computers at the best of times. Now, she had murder in her heart. She was grateful to the guardian angel of the firm of Bel Geddes and Loughlin that she had made back up copies and had put them in the file boxes. She had even copied his question sheets, thank the lucky stars. She scooped the heavy boxes up, one under each arm and sped down the hall to the conference room. By now, all useful work in the office had ceased, and the staff was watching with fascinated awe to see the rest of the soap opera evolve.

Mrs. Tucker herded the weaving, limping Paul Bel Geddes into the conference room. He was oblivious to the expressions of consternation on the faces of the people in the room. He was unaware or uncaring of the picture he presented—the well-tanned beach bum in shiny chartreuse bell bottom pants and open collared white shirt of questionable fit with the gait of a recently overexercised aging jock. He weaved his way to his chair and sat down awkwardly.

"I'm a little late," he slurred.

It was twenty past noon.

Carter leaned over to Sybil and whispered conspiratorially, "At last and at least our *miles gloriosus* has arrived."

Sybil nearly cracked a smile at the reference to a vain-glorious soldier parading his way to center stage.

"Are you prepared to go on without further delay or interruption, Mr. Bel Geddes?" Judge Hicken spoke for the first time.

All eyes studied his face.

"You betcha, your honor. Ready as rain," Bel Geddes responded.

The judge shook his head.

"By all means, proceed," he ordered.

"Need my files," said Bel Geddes. "One of my lovelies will bring it forthwith."

He flourished an arm in the direction of the door and grinned broadly at his clever wit.

"Your honor…" Hyrum Willis appealed. "Haven't…."

The door opened and a puffing young woman struggled in carrying a pair of obviously heavy folder boxes. Mrs. Tucker was close behind her.

"Thank you, Amber," said Mrs. Tucker. "We'll deal with them now. You may go."

Amber was all too glad to be quit of the place.

Mrs. Tucker set the boxes on the floor beside Paul.

"Now, where were we?" he asked vacuously and smiled a knowing smile.

"We were beginning," snapped Carter Tarkington impatiently.

Sybil was a veritable portrait of serenity. She sat with her well manicured hands comfortably folded in her lap. She looked about only occasionally, but without any marked interest in the proceedings. Her attorneys marveled at the level of her composure in the midst of all of this chaos.

Mrs. Tucker opened the first file box and began to rifle through the contents. Obviously not finding what she was after, she went to the second box. Failing again, she turned the lids of the boxes over and inspected the labels, *van der Hoef vs Joseph Noble Memorial Hospital and Sybil Norcroft, M.D.* Unfortunately for her cause, the titles belied the contents. When she turned her face to Paul Bel Geddes, she was pale and sweating.

"Not here, Paul. We have nothing on the case. Some sort of screw-up."

She downcast her eyes, taking full responsibility for the disaster.

Paul sobered up a measure upon hearing that news.

"Get Amber," he ordered peremptorily.

Mrs. Tucker rushed out of the hall and returned in two minutes with Amber Winters.

"Get files from computer," Bel Geddes demanded, raising his voice insultingly as if talking to an illiterate field hand.

"I'm sorry, Mr. Bel Geddes. They're not there. The files are gone. I can't find them."

Paul sobered even more.

"Whadda you mean, you stupid nincompoop?!"

Amber started to cry.

"They aren't there," she moaned.

Bel Geddes stood up, his face a contorted mask.

"You're fired...the both of you!" he shrieked.

The rest of the people in the room were stunned. Even by Paul Bel Geddes's standards, this was horrendous. The two women stood up bravely and walked out with more dignity than their situation might have dictated.

Mrs. Tucker looked back and said, "I, for one, quit. You won't have the pleasure of firing me. Now, *you* try and make heads or tails out of the workings of this place."

With that, she and Amber stalked out of the room. In thirty minutes, they left the building as well, having the meager satisfaction of knowing that they had completely undone the computer files for the firm as their parting gesture.

Paul sat down.

"I have to have a continuance, your honor," he said to the judge in a completely matter-of-fact tone as if it were a foregone conclusion apparent to all beholders.

The judge's face was rigid.

"No continuance. Proceed."

Paul looked as if he were about to protest, but thought better of it.

"Let's see, where were we?" he asked rhetorically.

"We were beginning," said Carter Tarkington with exaggerated courtesy.

He wore a thin smile.

Paul's adrenaline rush had subsided and with it the brief and partial lucidity. The mental fog rolled in again.

"I, uh, I know what we should do. We oughta ask that sweet girl over there some good old questions."

He glared at Sybil as if he had posed some profundity for her to wrestle with.

She looked calmly back at him and ventured nothing.

There was an awkward pause.

"Well!?" he demanded.

He could not remember his question.

She said nothing, gave away nothing with her face or eyes.

"Would you like me to have the reporter read back the question, girlie?" Paul demanded cuttingly.

He had had stonewallers before. He knew how to handle them.

"We protest, your honor. Counsel has the obligation to address our client with civility at least, if he cannot manage professional courtesy. 'Girlie' won't do," said Hyrum brusquely.

He looked directly at the judge expecting action.

Judge Hicken betrayed no loss of patience.

"Mr. Bel Geddes. I expect you to call the defendant by her name—Dr. Norcroft—and I don't want to hear 'girlie' or anything akin to that sort of an insult again. Is that understood?"

His tone was completely bland.

"Yes, Sir," Paul said and gave a poorly executed salute in keeping with his *miles gloriosus* posturing.

He giggled a little as well.

The court reporter snickered behind her hand. Bel Geddes cast her a flaying look.

"We'll go on. Where were we?" Paul asked again, the confusion apparent on his face.

He looked around the room but found no help in the taciturn faces before him.

"Why did you commit malpractice on my poor client?" he asked.

Now he was getting to the heart of the matter. He liked questions that surprised the witnesses, cut them to the quick.

"My care of Mr. van der Hoef was completely within the standards of practice for the community."

Van der Hoef. The name jogged Paul's befogged memory.

"Then what about his back?"

"What about it?" replied Sybil.

"What about it?" Bel Geddes shot back.

"I'm afraid my client does not understand the question, Counselor. Perhaps you should rephrase it," Carter said.

"Well, now," he said. "We'll go on then. Where were we?"

Judge Hicken stood up.

"Enough," he said. "It is abundantly clear that this is an abject exercise in futility. Although I am no physician, you are clearly drunk. And you are a disgrace to your profession. I have reviewed this case thus far and have seen a pattern of abuse of professional practice unprecedented in my career thus far. Much as I hate to cause your client, Mr. van der Hoef, to suffer an injustice, I cannot, in good conscience, allow this travesty to continue. I will leave here and return to my office where I will render a summary judgment in favor of the defendant. I will forward a copy to you, Sir, and one to your client. In addition, I am going to take the liberty of informing your client of his rights to seek the services of an attorney to press charges of legal malpractice against you. Good day, Sir."

Judge Hicken arose, placed a note paper in his attaché case, and peremptorily left.

"You can't do that. I don't care who you think you are!" shouted Bel Geddes at the closing conference room door. "You guys saw what he did. Old tyrant. I'll have his judgeship. You are all witnesses!"

He was on his feet and ranting.

Carter replaced his papers in his trial briefcase, stood calmly, and said quietly, "It's over, Paul. You have no one but yourself to blame. My office will be sending a full description of this sorry affair to the bar. Now, I suggest, as one colleague to another, that you go somewhere and sleep it off."

He looked at Sybil and Hyrum.

"I suggest we adjourn to more convivial surroundings."

Sybil, Carter, and Hyrum sat in a booth in Isaac Newton's Pub at the Sheraton.

"What a day!" sighed Hyrum.

"I thought I had seen everything. Paul Bel Geddes is eccentric by anyone's most conservative definition, outright strange by mine. But this performance today was tantamount to self-destruction. I cannot, for the life of me, fathom what possessed the man."

"Try supreme arrogance, total hedonism, and a perfectly sociopathic personality for starters," supplied Hyrum.

He shook his head in wonderment.

"I wouldn't have taken him for a skid-row level alcoholic, though."

"Certainly didn't do our side any harm, eh, Dr. Norcroft?" asked Carter.

"Seems that way. I'll believe it all when I see the summary judgment."

"Don't be too cynical or pessimistic. I know it seems like the civil defendant, even the uncivil defendant, if you will, always gets the short end of the stick in judicial decisions. This was too flagrant to ignore. Too many witnesses. We'll get our judgment," Carter said authoritatively. "Rest assured."

"Boy, I'd like to know the rest of the story—to coin a phrase—though, wouldn't you?" asked Hyrum.

"Think we ever will?" asked Carter.

He looked at Sybil Norcroft's pacific face. Her very placidity in the face of the upheavals of the day vaguely bothered him.

"You wouldn't know anything more about this, would you, Dr. Norcroft?" It was a shot in the dark.

"Me? How could I know anything about the goings on of the likes of Paul Bel Geddes and his lunatic asylum of an office?"

Hyrum said, "I'd like to be a fly on the wall at the bar hearings. It would make my day to watch Paul squirm around under the hot lights."

"I don't think we'll be able to spit on Paul Bel Geddes's grave anytime soon," mused Sybil.

"He's resilient and as nonstick as the proverbial Teflon, I'll give him that," said Hyrum.

"Pardon me for saying, but the system is corrupt and hypocritical. Attorneys, especially those in the American Trial Lawyers Association, are great hovering harpies about the perfidy of physicians when it comes to policing themselves. If that isn't the pot calling the kettle black, nothing is. I'll lay you odds that Bel Geddes comes out of the Bandini sprouting sellable mushrooms," said Sybil with arch emphasis.

"Amanita phalloides, no doubt," put in Hyrum.

Sybil raised an eyebrow in a question mark.

"Death caps."

She nodded her recognition and appreciation of the aptness of his choice.

Carter looked at his client thoughtfully. She was an enigma to him. But then, what could she know beyond what they had all seen?

"Nevertheless, given even the most cautious reading on this little vignette of history, we would have to declare that the Christians carried the day, and that it will be sometime before Bel Geddes and Company is able to play the Phoenix," he said.

"I'll believe in truth, justice, and the American way if that proves to be true," asserted Sybil.

It took six months for the documentation of the summary judgment to arrive at Sybil's office. She used it as an occasion to have a congratulatory dinner for herself, her husband, and her copartners on the ranch and in the cooperative stock and bond investment company they had formed.

Before Charles Daniels arrived at the ranch, Sybil walked outside with Pancho, Jose, Marcos, and their respective wives. The gardens of vegetables were flourishing, the horses were gamboling about their paddocks, and the flower beds around the windows of the house were in resplendent bloom with penstemons, Astilbe, and summer icicle in a patternless array suggesting a vivid patch of wild flowers.

Little Quina, Jose and Maria's baby, set up a protesting howl as the adults started to meander through the yard.

To the tune of "Frere Jacque" Maria sang softly,

"La Lechuza, La Lechuza,
Hace chuz, hace chuz
Todos calladitos, como La Lachuza
Que hace chuz"

The baby quieted immediately upon hearing the lilt of her mother's mellow voice.

"Here's a little thanks for all your work on the lawyer," she said and handed each of them a $75 cigar—a 175th Anniversary Special Edition Partagas and a mother of pearl inlaid cigar cutter from Herrod's.

The men smiled their appreciation. There was no need for money to pass between them; they were well beyond any employer-employee relationship. They were flattered that she recognized that the men who had hardly been out of peonage when they met Sybil had come to appreciate the finer things—the best cigars and wines, the smoothest gaited horses, good cars, and friends that can be trusted.

At dinner—pomegranate glazed squab, white asparagus spears with a delicate mango port sauce, lamb tartare basted in truffle oil, pumpkin gnocchi, wild white strawberries and a fruit Brûlée—they toasted each other with Roederer Cristal Moet champagne and Matanzas Creek Merlot until they were mellow.

Charles asked Sybil and the assembled company, "So do you think it's all over, and we can just get on with our lives in peace?"

"I think so" said Sybil. "It's time posthumous, but I think we've heard the last of Paul Bel Geddes."

"Let's drink to that," said Pancho.

"Amen," echoed the rest, and they lifted their flutes in a silent and heartfelt toast.

On the seventh of December, a letter came to Sybil's office. Her secretary discarded the envelope, so Sybil had no foreshadowing of what the contents might be until she read it while sitting at her desk late in the evening. It read:

Dear Dr. Norcroft:

This letter will serve as the formal announcement that a suit for medical malpractice will be filed against you in ninety (90) days. Action is being taken against you by the family of Mortimer Elbe, a patient at Joseph Noble Memorial Hospital, who was treated in the neurosurgical intensive care unit under your supervision. The family seeks redress for gross negligence, medical care below the community standard, and for a brain operation that resulted in the wrongful death of Mr. Elbe.

You are advised to communicate with your attorney and with your medical malpractice insurance company if you have coverage.

Respectfully submitted,

Paul Bel Geddes, Esq. Attorney at Law

For the plaintiff

Sybil clenched her fists and blinked away her first response which was consternation. There was a postscript written in cursive using a pencil:

P.S.

You will be pleased to know that the matter that led to the untimely termination of our recent action together is well on its way to being satisfied in my favor. The state bar recognized extenuating circumstances and has recommended a probationary period of monitoring under the recognizance of Martin Loughlin, Esq, an attorney of note, in our city. I look forward to resuming our interesting and cordial relationship.

PBG

-END

And by and by,
They'll all deny,
...and protest,
'Twas all in jest.'
Old English Madrigal

AUTHOR CARL DOUGLASS, Former Neurosurgeon turned Author, writes with gripping realism. He grew up in a medical family; and in the

 course of his rich and varied life in medicine has seen the best and the worst of doctors and lawyers and knows full well the challenge imposed by a malpractice suit. He developed his ability to cope by a refiner's fire experience in a major university, in the Navy as a general surgeon and later as a neurosurgeon, in the competitive crucible of a big city trauma center residency, in medical academia, as a scholar and researcher, and in a busy diverse private practice of neurosurgery. He has retired to a life of world travel, international big game hunting, teaching martial arts, writing—he has seven novels and two nonfiction books to his credit--and a satisfying family life. He and his wife own a French hunting lodge house in the Rocky Mountains, and life is currently good.